Play On!

Play On!

JUDY DEARLOVE

RCWMS | DURHAM, NORTH CAROLINA | 2019

PLAY ON!
A Novel
© 2019 Judy Dearlove

Designed by Bonnie Campbell

Printed in the United States of America
ISBN: 978-0-9960826-7-9
Library of Congress Control Number: 2019945378

Copies of this book may be ordered from:
RCWMS
1202 Watts Street
Durham, NC 27701
www.rcwms.org
info@rcwms.org

For Mom and Dad, who encouraged me to
dream my own improbable dreams,
and to Joan who enabled me to pursue them.

CONTENTS

ONE

OPENING BID

1

TWO

DOUBLED AND REDOUBLED: THE INTERVIEW

59

THREE

FINESSE: THE OPPOSITION

127

FOUR

GRAND SLAM: THE PRESENTATION

175

FIVE

PLAY ON!

249

ACKNOWLEDGMENTS

321

PART ONE

OPENING BID

1

SHE SMACKED TOM'S side of the bed with her pillow.

It had been ten years, and Maxine was still angry. They'd been married half a century. Then one night he died—in his sleep. Not just any night, but this very night ten years ago. His heart simply stopped. No warning. No suffering—at least not for him. It was precisely the way everyone here at the Foothills Retirement Community wanted to go. It was the way she wanted to go. But she was still furious with him for going and not telling her, for going without a sign or a sound.

She threw off the blankets and swung her feet over the edge of the bed. No point in lying on her half of a double bed. Far better to watch the sun rise over the mountains that surrounded Tucson than to watch that blasted clock. Even without her glasses she could read the extra-large numbers: 4:00 AM.

She rocked herself to a standing position. Her knees cracked with arthritis, but they held. She waited a moment for her hips and back to realign themselves before pulling on Tom's navy blue bathrobe. She patted the bedside table for her glasses. Instead, her fingers closed around the silver frame of Tom's photo. Clutching the photo to her chest, she marched through her condo to the sliding glass patio door, tugged it open, and stepped outside.

Neither the moon nor the stars were out. Even the mountains that guarded Tucson's northeastern perimeter were barely perceptible, black shadows against a black backdrop. The darkness was broken only by the spotlight Fred Grosskopf insisted on using to illuminate his hundred-year-old saguaro. Thankfully, her own condo was separated from Fred's by an arroyo, and his light was partially obscured by the tangled branches of two palo verde trees and by the potted plants that she kept on the top of her chest-high patio wall. Tonight the light bobbed and flitted about like an oversized hummingbird.

But Fred's light should be stationary and more to the right.

She moved to the wall. Another bobbing light appeared. Beneath the silence of the desert, she imagined human voices. Angry voices.

She needed a better view. Setting Tom's photo aside, she placed her foot on a large rock and her hands on the wall between two flowerpots. She sucked in her breath, counted to three, and pushed herself up. In the process, she bumped her newest flowerpot. She watched in frozen admiration as the pot danced across the top of the wall, pirouetted over the edge, and crashed to the ground.

The light disappeared. Maxine held her breath and waited.

The light did not return. She lowered herself to the ground.

She could call Security, but what would she say—*My husband died ten years ago, and I saw a light that isn't there*—?

She hugged Tom's robe tighter and reached for his photo. Darkness obscured the details, but she knew the picture by heart. She'd taken it on their first hike up Pusch Peak: Tom's tanned face against a cloudless sky, thick hair tousled by the wind, blue eyes sparkling with mischief, his smile an invitation that warmed her still.

For a moment the patio swirled and all she could hear was the blood pounding in her ears. She grabbed the table.

A second later, her breathing returned to normal and her vision cleared.

She raised her head.

The skies were beginning to lighten. The mountains had emerged in silhouette, their dark ridges sharp against the first thin slashes of orange and purple.

Straightening her shoulders, Maxine crossed to an old-fashioned glider and sat down to wait for the sunrise. Without Tom she might be a meaningless speck inexorably drawn toward the dark abyss, but she would *not* be absorbed by that abyss. Not yet.

AT THE BREAKFAST BUFFET, Maxine paused. Residents clustered in groups of two or three, quietly eating. None seemed disturbed by the previous night's bobbing light. In fact, the dining room was filled with its customary and comforting low hum. Silverware clinked softly on china. People spoke in hushed tones. Tension drained from Maxine's shoulders. It was a good thing she hadn't called Security.

Clutching her breakfast tray in both hands, she threaded her way to a table by the window where two of her bridge buddies huddled over their breakfasts. An incongruous pair, Rosemarie Dukakis was tall and thin with a penchant for dark knits, while June Silverman was short, round, and frosted blonde with a passion for pastel. Where Rosemarie was quiet and retiring, June was funny and effervescent. Where Rosemarie loved details and order, June was endearingly scattered and over-extended. June and her husband, Harry, participated in all of the Foothills' classes, clubs, and outings. Rosemarie joined none.

Rosemarie looked up first. "We were worried," she said.

Maxine chose a chair with her back to the room. "I couldn't sleep," she said. With practiced ease, she slid her tray onto the table without spilling her tea. "I finally dozed off about the time I usually wake up."

"June couldn't sleep either." Rosemarie inclined her head toward June.

Under normal circumstances, June would be perfectly attired, but today dark shadows underlined her eyes and her hair poked out sideways as if the wind had caught its frosted waves. She wore mismatched earrings and a rumpled top.

"What happened?" Maxine asked.

"Daisy woke us," June said without looking up from her coffee. "We thought she had to go out, but when we took her, she just wagged her tail."

Maxine jerked to attention. "What time was that? I saw a strange light bobbing around by Fred's condo about four o'clock."

"I saw it too!" another voice announced. Louise McMaster wheeled up to the table with Seabiscuit, the walker/oxygen cart that she was tethered to by arthritis and emphysema. "But I thought the light was coming from the guest condo."

"What were you doing up at that hour?" Rosemarie said as she helped transfer Louise's breakfast tray to the table. "Was I the only one asleep in my bed last night?"

Maxine couldn't resist. "We don't know. Do you have any proof that you *were* asleep? Or that you were the *only* person in your bed?" She added a couple of suggestive eyebrow lifts.

"You look like Groucho Marx when you do that."

"Did you say four o'clock?" June yawned and poured herself another cup of coffee from the pot she'd pilfered from the buffet bar. "That's when we were out. I thought I heard a crash."

"That was me," Maxine said.

They all looked at her. No one seemed surprised, just expectant and resigned, as if they were accustomed to her being caught in the middle of things, which was a bit unfair. She couldn't help it if someone wanted to dodge about with strange lights in the middle of the night when she was minding her own business on her own patio patiently waiting for a sunrise.

"You?" Louise said.

"I was trying to get a better look at the bobbing light and knocked my Bird of Paradise off the patio wall," Maxine said. "The pot shattered, but I think the plant is salvageable. I put it in an empty mixing bowl for the time being."

June lowered her coffee cup. "Not that hand-painted pot you bought in Nogales?"

June had helped Maxine select the pot and negotiate the price. They'd probably paid twice what the pot was worth, but they'd enjoyed haggling with the shopkeeper, who introduced them to his entire family and two of his neighbors before the deal was finally struck.

Maxine shrugged.

Behind them a door banged. The hum of the room stopped. The

silence was almost electric, then the hum resumed at a higher pitch. Coffee cups clattered onto tabletops. Voices grew louder. Staccato footsteps tapped across the terrazzo floor.

Rosemarie hunched her shoulders and ducked her head. "Don't look now," she whispered. "Here comes Carlotta."

Maxine reflexively turned toward the disturbance.

Carlotta Helmsley gloated her way toward them, brandishing an empty cigarette holder and fluttering her eyelids as if she were caught in a dust devil. She no longer smoked, but she still wielded her ebony and silver holder like a weapon.

Maxine suppressed a shiver. Carlotta got on her nerves like ice cream on a loose filling.

Today she wore a flowing black pants suit that Maxine might have worn to a cocktail party.

Carlotta twitched her cigarette holder in an artificial wave, and her jacket opened to reveal a top made out of something that looked like gold confetti.

Maxine corrected herself: she would never wear that outfit anywhere.

Carlotta's eyes glittered like her outfit. "You don't mind if I move Old Paint, do you?" she said and shoved Louise's oxygen cart into a corner where Louise couldn't possibly reach it. "These things are so dangerous, you know."

Maxine set her cup down so hard the tea sloshed. For two years Carlotta had been trying to change their bylaws to ban walkers, wheelchairs, and walking canes. The Foothills Retirement Community was an independent living facility. If you couldn't navigate unassisted, Carlotta wanted you out. Fortunately, most of the residents were more sympathetic, and Carlotta's attempts to ban walkers had repeatedly failed.

Maxine pushed herself out of her chair, retrieved Louise's cart, and returned it to its place at the head of the table. Hands on hips, she glared at Carlotta.

Carlotta hissed through clenched teeth.

"Actually, it's Seabiscuit," Louise said.

Carlotta blinked and looked blank.

Maxine snorted and sat.

Louise reached for a toasted English muffin. "Originally, I named it Rocinante after the nag in *Don Quixote*. But it kept breaking down, so I changed it to Man of War."

"Changed what?" Carlotta draped herself across the chair next to Maxine.

Maxine inched her own chair away.

The hum in the dining room modulated into an everyday buzz.

Louise spread a thin layer of orange marmalade across her muffin. "The name of my cart. But then it became unruly, so I changed its name again—this time to Seabiscuit after the 1938 Horse of the Year. *You* probably remember him." She saluted Carlotta with her perfectly spread muffin.

Carlotta's nostrils flared.

Louise prattled on as if she were unaware of Carlotta's sensitivity to any suggestions that she might be as old as the rest of them. "Knobby-kneed and undersized, Seabiscuit—the horse, that is—came back against improbable odds to win time and again."

Carlotta waved her cigarette holder as if casting a spell. "Never mind all that. What do you think of the news?"

"What news?" June asked and poured herself a third cup of coffee.

Carlotta turned toward June for the first time. "You're not supposed to bring the coffee pot to your table."

"It was an emergency. Someone was about to expire."

"Who?" Carlotta asked.

Maxine and Louise exchanged glances. For months, they'd debated whether Carlotta was (as Louise argued) someone who took everything literally, or whether she was (as Maxine asserted) someone with absolutely no sense of humor.

June took a long pull on her cup. "Whoever got between me and my coffee."

Carlotta pointedly turned her back on June. "We need a new assistant director. Sandra's quit! She's going back to Los Angeles."

"Why did she quit?" June asked.

Carlotta tilted her chin and tossed her platinum blond hair. "Because she and Rupert were having an affair. He, of course, wouldn't marry her. Last night they had a fight, and she quit."

"How do you know?" Maxine asked.

For years Carlotta had attempted to ingratiate herself with the good-looking but rather ineffectual, thirty-something director of the Foothills. For his part, Rupert Brookstone had learned how to avoid Carlotta and her wiles. It was unlikely that he'd confide anything to her.

Carlotta's chin dropped and her face turned red. "Um . . . Fred overheard them. They were staying in the guest condo right next door to his place."

"But Fred is so hard of hearing," Louise said. "I wouldn't think he could hear them."

Maxine nudged Louise's foot under the table. Carlotta and Fred had been romantically involved for months. They thought the relationship was a secret, but everyone at the Foothills knew about it.

Carlotta swept her cigarette holder under Louise's nose.

Louise smiled angelically.

"Maybe Fred fell asleep with his hearing aids on," Carlotta said. "At any rate, Rupert and Sandra were quite loud. And they were on the patio with flashlights.

"Was it around four?" June asked.

Carlotta waved her holder at June as if trying to make her disappear. "Who cares? The point is: Rupert is hiring a new assistant director."

Maxine looked at the others and then back to Carlotta. Surely there was more to the story. Rupert was a poor excuse for a director, but even he would realize that he'd need a new assistant if Sandra left. Not that Sandra had been much of an assistant director to start with. In theory, she was responsible for the budget and the social life of the Foothills, including all activities involving the residents, their committees, and even their rules and bylaws. In reality, Sandra had arranged a limited and boring repertoire of tiresome events that Maxine avoided whenever possible.

Carlotta shook her head. "You won't believe the idiotic application he created for the job," she said. "I sometimes wonder if anyone is home behind those beautiful blue eyes of his."

Surprised by the criticism from Carlotta, who normally oozed affection for Rupert and all of his ideas, no matter how inane, Maxine dropped her guard and asked the obvious question. "Do you have a copy of the application?"

Carlotta puffed out her chest. "It's on the Foothills' website. *I* found it this morning. But of course you don't *do* computers, do you?"

Maxine flinched. It was true. She didn't have a computer, didn't want a computer, and couldn't imagine anything that needed to be checked on a computer *ever*, much less before breakfast. Even the thought of using a computer made her palms sweat and her heart race.

Carlotta lifted her cigarette holder in victory and inhaled as if sucking power out of the very air itself. Slowly, she stood until she loomed over them. Then, even more slowly, she lowered her cigarette holder until it pointed directly at Maxine's heart. "Don't worry, dear. *I'll* take care of everything." With that, she spun on her heel and glided away.

Maxine rubbed her chest and stared at Carlotta's retreating back. The gauntlet had been tossed. The game was on. If only Maxine knew what game they were playing.

Louise touched Maxine's arm. "Don't worry about her. I don't 'do' computers either."

"That would be a great title for a dirty movie," June said, awake at last. "*Carlotta Does Computers.*"

Rosemarie, who'd owned her own accounting firm and actually did use computers, snorted with disdain. "Carlotta doesn't *do* computers," she said. "She knows how to surf the internet and access email. That's all."

To Maxine that sounded like a lot.

Rosemarie checked her watch. "Speaking of computers, I need to go. I'm discussing tax laws and spreadsheet software with the high school accounting club."

June rocked to her feet. "I've got to go, too. It's time for Water Aerobics. The class is hell on the hair, but I think it's helping my arthritis."

"See you at dinner," Louise called after them.

Maxine waved absently.

"Maxine, you have that look again," Louise said.

"What look?"

"That 'damn the torpedoes: full speed ahead' look. I can always tell. It's something about the way you furrow your brow and tap your index finger."

Maxine furrowed her brow and tapped her index finger. "That woman is up to something, and we're going to find out what. Come on."

2

MAXINE HURRIED LOUISE out of the dining room, past the formal living room, and into the library. With its well-stocked bookshelves and overstuffed chairs, the library was one of Maxine's favorite retreats—or rather, it had been a favorite until the computer arrived.

The electronic monster overwhelmed the handsome table on which it sat. Lashed to it by a tangle of black cable was an astonishing array of printers and speakers and modems and microphones. The whole thing sprawled across the mahogany, obscuring the craftsmanship of an earlier era.

Maxine scowled at the computer. The screen didn't acknowledge her, not even with a pale reflection of some little old lady. It gave back nothing. She stared at the monster and tried to fathom why Katie, her own daughter, practically lived in cyberspace, or how Peter, her godson, could be a computer genius. Months ago, Peter had even set her up with an email account and a page of simple instructions, but she'd never attempted to use them. If she ever tried and failed, they'd think her old and incompetent, and *that* would break her heart.

She pointed at the monster. "How do you make it work?"

Louise's mouth fell open. "You're asking me?"

"You don't get to be a black belt in bridge without being brilliant."

"Life master, not black belt," Louise said. "And it only means that I've played bridge ever since Moses brought down the tablets and a deck of cards."

"*And* that you have a good memory," Maxine said. "You were up here last week when Rosemarie was teaching June how to find the Foothills' house page."

"Home page."

"So, what do you remember?" Maxine dragged two ergonomic chairs away from the table. In their place, she arranged a matched set of intricately carved Chippendales. She perched on the front of one chair. Louise reluctantly followed suit on the other.

"Well?" Maxine said.

"You push the round button on that big box on the floor and wait. When the screen wakes up, you shove the hand thingee around until the arrow is over the *E* with a satellite around it and click."

"Click what?"

"I don't know. That's just what Rosemarie told June to do." Louise looked at the computer skeptically. "Should we wait for them to get back?"

"I'm eighty-two; I'm too old to wait for anything." Maxine spoke with more determination than she felt. She stretched a finger toward the large button and hoped that Louise couldn't see the tremor in her hand. The button felt cold and unyielding. She took a deep breath and pushed.

"Nothing happened," Maxine said.

"Let me see." Louise bent down to examine the box. "I don't think that's the button. I think that's the logo. Try pushing the smaller button above it."

Maxine glared at the box. It had tricked her already, and it wasn't even running. She mashed the smaller button. The computer clicked and whirred. She jerked her hand back. Lights flashed, images raced across the screen, and music bleated out of the speakers. Then everything stopped, the screen turned a deep blue, and tiny pictures popped up everywhere.

Maxine pumped her fist. "Yes!"

"Now what?" Louise said.

"Now what, what?" Maxine said, still basking in their success.

"How is this going to help us figure out what Carlotta is up to?"

Maxine's bubble burst. "I'm not sure. I thought we might get an idea if we looked at that application Rupert put on the web."

Louise rolled her eyes.

"What? It's a plan—sort of." It was more of a wing and a prayer, but it was all she had.

Louise wisely said nothing.

Maxine stared at the computer in the hope of discovering a better plan, but none came. Faint sounds of June's water aerobics class filtered through the window. Maxine watched the bobbing heads. Behind her, the wall clock urged her to action with its unremitting electric tick.

She straightened. "So-ooo?" She drew out the question in the hope of teasing out an answer.

"So, what?" Louise said.

"So, how do we get to Rupert's application?"

Louise rolled her eyes again, but their twinkle betrayed her. "Try typing the address on that top line after all the w's and push the key that says *Enter*."

Emboldened by her earlier luck, Maxine typed her address—The Foothills Retirement Community, 1314 N. Buena Vista Drive, Tucson, Arizona—and pushed the Enter button. A small box containing a message appeared. She leaned closer to get a better look.

"It says I no longer exist or may have moved." Maxine turned to Louise. "I find that rather presumptuous, don't you?"

"Let me see." Louise adjusted her glasses. "Not that address. The Foothills' *website* address. Try again. The address is right here." She pointed to a label taped to the computer.

Maxine narrowed her eyes at Louise but resumed typing.

After several false starts and much extraneous clicking, they managed to find the Foothills' homepage with Rupert's application. They bent to study the form. In unison, they sat up, looked at each other, then bent to study the form again.

Louise finally broke the silence. "Carlotta's right. The form is idiotic. Rupert only asks four questions and two of those are name and address."

Maxine's blood pressure mounted. "It's not only idiotic, it's insulting. June asked better questions when she was looking for someone to walk Daisy."

"It's as if we don't matter," Louise said with a small catch in her voice.

"How dare he?" Maxine jabbed an accusatory finger at the computer. "He doesn't ask anything meaningful. He doesn't even ask for references. Anybody could apply."

Her words hung in the air. Anybody could apply. Anybody.

"Well." Maxine straightened.

Louise leaned back in her chair.

Maxine raised a questioning eyebrow.

Louise smoothed her skirt.

"Well?" Maxine raised both eyebrows.

"Well, it would serve him right," Louise said.

"It would be a form of protest." Maxine drummed her fingers on the table. "A rebellion against age discrimination."

"Should we?" Louise said. It was more invitation than question. That's why Maxine loved Louise. She could be depended upon.

"Let's!" Maxine said.

She bent to the task and read from the offending form: "Name?" She typed: Maxine O. Olson.

Louise grabbed the keyboard. "No, no, no. You can't use your own name. I'll type; you think."

"Good idea," Maxine said. "Instead of Maxine O. Olson, use M. Octavia Olson."

Louise spun back toward Maxine. "Octavia? Your middle name is Octavia?" Louise's voice went up an octave with each question. "We've been best friends since Shakespeare was an infant, and you never told me your middle name was Octavia?"

Maxine studied the underside of the mouse.

"Didn't you tell me that you didn't have a middle name?" Louise practically levitated off her seat. "No name, you said, just an initial."

"Well, I never actually use that name." Maxine fidgeted with an imaginary scratch on the table. "So it's practically the same as having only an initial."

Louise glared.

Maxine pulled herself up to her full height. Although she had shrunk over the years, at five feet five she still towered over Louise, who need- ed to stand on the Tucson telephone book to reach a full five feet. "You tell," she said, "and I'm putting helium in your oxygen tank."

Louise harrumphed and returned her gaze to the application. "Mailing Address?" She stopped. "Rupert's not the brightest bulb in the chandelier, but surely he'll recognize the Foothills' address."

"Use Peter's address: 4468B Calle Ocotillo."

Maxine adored her self-appointed godson. When his family had first moved to Tucson—his father to be an engineering professor at the university and his mother the head of IT support—Peter had been the irrepressibly curious, impossibly energetic neighborhood terror. Maxine smiled at the memory.

She'd come home one day to find Tom immersed in his newspaper and a ten-year-old Peter, dressed in basketball shorts and a Hampton University t-shirt, studiously taking her stereo apart. In the sunlight, his arms and legs glowed a rich, warm brown, like the color of a concert violin. She watched him in silence. His hands moved with swift preci- sion, removing parts and arranging them into an elaborate pattern. He reminded her of Katie at that age. Beneath the obvious differences lay the same intensity, the same absorption in the creation of order out of chaos. In this case, the chaos of stereo parts. Without a word, Maxine sat down to help. When they finished dismantling the stereo, she told him he had an hour to put it back together again. He did, and they became fast friends.

With his parents' blessing, she'd bought him his first car—a battered Chevrolet he restored and named Old Betsy. In return, he kept her Buick in perfect condition. She taught him about the desert and hiking, and he acted as an intermediary between her and whatever portions of the electronic revolution she couldn't avoid.

"Earth to Maxine," Louise said.

Maxine blinked.

Louise pointed at the computer. "What should I enter for your email address?"

"Oh." Maxine refocused. "ToTheMax."

"Honestly, Maxine. Your email sounds obscene. How do you expect to get a responsible job as an assistant director?"

"Peter created it for me, and I don't know how to change it."

"We could change the capitalization," Louise said and typed. "You're now ToThemAx."

Thirty-five years of college teaching rose up in rigid protest. "But that's not grammatical," Maxine said.

"Do you think Rupert will know the difference?"

"I will."

"Well, Octavia doesn't care."

Maxine huffed, but the discussion was over.

Louise acknowledged Maxine's capitulation with a barely perceptible nod and returned to the form. "Degrees and/or Experience?" Louise looked at Maxine. "Do you really think that Sandra had any degrees? I doubt she graduated from high school. Her only qualification was that she was sleeping with Rupert."

"Well, I don't intend to do that. Not even for better bridge clubs." Maxine pulled the keyboard to herself and started entering her own degrees.

Louise jerked the keyboard back. "What are you doing? They'll never hire you if you put down a Ph.D. They'd have to pay you too much. Let's go with experience instead. Do you have any?"

"Yes," Maxine batted her eyes.

Louise waited.

"Put down seven years as Director of Community Outreach for St. Matthew's."

"What?"

"Well, I didn't exactly have that title, but I did run a volunteer tutoring program for them. Rupert will never check the details. He's afraid of ministers."

"OK. Last question: 'What kinds of activities do you consider appropriate for the elderly residents of a retirement community?'"

"Appropriate?" Maxine bristled. *"Elderly?"* She heard blood rushing in her ears. She pushed out of her chair and began to pace and gesticulate wildly. "Put down bungee jumping, safe sex, and counter-terrorism."

"No, really." Louise grabbed Maxine's arm. "Sit down. What would we like our assistant director to plan?"

"Trips to the Arizona Wildcats' basketball games," Maxine said. Tickets were impossible to get, but Louise hadn't asked for practical suggestions.

"Perfect. What else?"

Surprised by Louise's willingness to accept the impossible, Maxine began to warm to the task. "Put down gambling at the Indian casino."

"Oh, I like that," Louise said. "How about dinner and a play at the Wild West Theatre? I love it when they do melodramas."

"You just like booing and throwing popcorn." Maxine flopped back into her chair.

"At least I didn't hit the villain in the eye."

"Can I help it if I have a good arm?" Maxine flexed her bicep.

Louise gave a melodramatic sigh and returned to the form. "What else?"

"How about a hot air balloon ride over the mountains?" Maxine said. "And a trip to the opera at Santa Fe? And to the Shakespeare festival in Oregon? And snowboarding on Mt. Lemon?" She rattled off suggestions faster than Louise could type.

"Yes to the hot air balloon, to Santa Fe, and to Shakespeare," Louise said. "No to snowboarding; it's too hard on the hips."

They cranked out a long list, but when they sat back to admire their handiwork, Louise's smile faded.

Maxine shook her head. "Rupert won't like this list. He doesn't want anything that might cost money, cause controversy, or lead to a lawsuit."

"And we haven't even gotten to my trip to the Giant Redwoods yet." Louise sounded wistful.

"I didn't know that you wanted to go to the Redwoods."

Louise stared into the distance. "Chuck and I were always going to go as an anniversary present to ourselves." Her voice became almost inaudible. "But he died before we made it."

Maxine inhaled. She felt Louise's sorrow as if it were her own. They'd raised their kids together. Their husbands had golfed together. They'd shared tuna casseroles and Girl Scout cookies, gone on cruises and tramped over New Zealand together. Maxine placed a hand on her friend's shoulder. Louise reached up and squeezed it. Neither spoke.

"When old Saint Pete asks me if I regret having smoked," Louise gestured toward Seabiscuit, "I'm going to say, 'Not nearly as much as I regret having stopped.'"

Maxine smiled at the old joke and pretended not to notice the tears welling up in Louise's eyes.

"The only thing I really regret," Louise said, "is not having seen the Redwoods."

Maxine's heart constricted. It wasn't a heart attack—not in the medical sense. It was more of a sympathetic contraction of grief. She exhaled slowly and waited for the pain to pass, aware that time and opportunity no longer lay before them in abundant supply.

Louise sniffed once. "So what do we do now?" she asked, all business once more.

Maxine reviewed their list. "We've done the wrong list. We should put down all the dumb things we don't want to do. The kind of things Sandra was forever suggesting, like monthly trips to the Breakfast Bar for their 'Famous Five Star Breakfast'—at our own expense."

Louise nodded and typed. "Or movie nights watching Charlton Heston as Ben-Hur, Charlton Heston as Moses, Charlton Heston as El Cid, Charlton Heston as Michelangelo, Charlton Heston as an ape."

"I don't think he was an ape," Maxine said. "I think he got to be a human in that one. Roddy McDowall was an ape."

Louise finished typing and sat back. "What do you think?"

Maxine adjusted her glasses and studied their work. The humdrum application they'd built for Octavia was perfect. It showed experience that was adequate; qualifications that were sufficient. They'd claimed nothing exceptional, nothing that challenged Rupert's ego or threatened his budget. "Our new list is dull and paltry," she said. "Rupert will love it. Let's send it."

Louise nodded and maneuvered the mouse until the arrow was over the box labeled *Submit*. She turned to Maxine. "Would you care to do the honors?"

Maxine stretched out her right index finger and let it hover dramatically above the unsuspecting mouse. Then, before they could change their minds, she struck. Her finger plunged. The mouse clicked. The application disappeared, and a reassuring message emerged: "Application successfully sent."

"We did it!" Louise said. "We made the computer work and nothing exploded and no one died."

Maxine made a show of dusting off her hands, then rose. "Let's go, kemosabe. Our work here is done."

3

MAXINE WALKED LOUISE home, then cut across the shuffleboard courts to her own condo. The air was dry and fresh: no hint of rain. The weatherman was going to be wrong again today with his daily predictions of scattered thunderstorms. A few cotton-puff clouds drifted lazily across the sky, but they were too scattered and high to turn into showers. It was, in fact, a glorious day. She raised her arms in a wide-V salute of appreciation.

Tom would have liked it here. The Foothills had opened two years after his death, and she'd moved in immediately. Here southwestern architecture blended with the desert landscape. The buildings were painted a color lighter than taupe, softer than yellow, deeper than white. They were crisp and clean without being obtrusive. Here she could still smell the desert air and feel the mountain breezes.

She and Tom had visited other retirement communities but hadn't cared for any of them. Mountain Estates had been the best of the bunch, but it was too intrusive. Everything was far bigger, brighter, and more angular than it needed to be, like a spoiled child shouting, "Notice me." The worst was The Amphora, where the builders had obliterated acres of cactus and wildflowers in favor of ornamental cedars and imported palms. Streambeds and hilltops had been bulldozed to make room for cement-lined water features and faux-marble fountains. Everything rang false. Even their logo looked more like a funeral urn than an amphora.

Maxine surveyed her surroundings as she fished out her keys.

Yes, Tom would have liked it here. She could imagine him on the patio right now, sipping his coffee and working the crossword puzzle in ink.

She raised her arms in a second salute, then unlocked her condo.

Inside, she picked up the newspaper, settled into her grandmother's bentwood rocker, and kicked off her shoes.

Before she could open the paper, there was a loud bang, her front door crashed open, and a large figure burst in.

Maxine yelped. Her eyes blurred.

The intruder brandished a club.

Maxine froze.

The intruder swayed.

Maxine exhaled and her eyes refocused.

A large, chestnut-colored woman in a red and gold kaftan leaned against the doorframe, gasping. A feather duster dangled from her upraised arm.

"Goodness!" The woman lowered her arm. She placed a hand on her ample chest. "You nearly scared me to death!"

"*I* frightened *you*?"

"*You* need to be more careful. You could hurt someone that way."

Maxine was speechless.

The woman examined her through narrowed eyes. "But it was probably an accident." With that, she tugged a cart into the condo and dragged it toward Maxine's bedroom.

Maxine struggled out of the rocker and, despite her bare feet, followed the stranger. "Excuse me."

"No need to apologize," the woman called over her shoulder. "No harm done. You just go right on with your reading, and I'll take care of everything."

Maxine pushed past the intruder and folded her arms. "Just exactly what do you take care of?"

The woman stared over the tops of her glasses. "Didn't you read your newsletter?"

Maxine shrugged.

"I'm the new housekeeper."

"Oh." Maxine recollected her manners and stretched out her hand. "I'm Maxine. Maxine Olson."

When the woman shook the proffered hand, half a dozen bracelets danced along her arm, exposing a small tattoo of a cherub. Before Maxine got a good look at it, the woman whirled away and attacked the bathroom. She Windexed almost as fast as she talked.

"I hope you don't mind if I work while we chat. I don't want to get behind my first day. I used to be the bouncer at Benny's Bar and Grill. I really liked the people there, but I needed my nights free on account of . . ."

The woman stopped and took a breath.

"You keep a really clean house," she said. "Clean and neat: that tells a lot about a person. My name's Celine. Celine Dianne Jackson."

"Like the famous singer?"

"Almost. Some coincidence, isn't it? Some people think we look a lot alike." Celine twirled her full figure in a tight circle as if she were a child showing off a new dress. "And we're both singers, but I'm a lot sturdier. She's got a pretty face though. I can see how people might confuse us."

Maxine was fairly certain she would not confuse the pale, delicate features of the popular singer with the robust face before her.

Celine lifted a vacuum cleaner off of her cart and stomped on the power switch. "You go on back to your paper. I'll be finished in no time, and I'll be so quiet you won't even know I'm here."

Maxine doubted that, but she returned to her rocker and pretended to read. Much to her surprise, Celine actually was quiet except for her soft singing—gospel with some complex improvisations. Maxine closed her eyes and tapped out a soft accompaniment on the arm of the rocker. Her daughter had loved music as a child, all kinds of music. If Maxine took her to a symphony, Katie conducted the musicians from her seat. If she took her to a pops concert, Katie danced in the aisles. If she took her to a jazz quartet, Katie fingered the chords on an imaginary keyboard. "Amazing Grace" had been Katie's first piano recital piece. She'd looked so tiny in her white organdy dress. She'd only been eight—couldn't even reach the pedals.

Maxine's fingers stilled.

Celine's voice drifted down the hall from the master bedroom. "I once was lost, but now am found . . ."

Maxine wiped her eyes and checked her watch. Even without the time zone changes, it was too early to telephone her daughter in New York: Katie would still be at work. Not that Katie would expect a call. In fact, she'd probably wonder what was wrong. When Katie had left for college, Tom had called every Sunday to wish her well on the upcoming week. Somewhere along the way, the Sunday call had turned into a ritual and then a rule. If Maxine called on a weekday, she felt like an intruder.

In the bedrooms, Celine's voice moved seamlessly from one song to the next, from "Amazing Grace" to "Simple Gifts."

Maxine sighed. Simplicity *would* be a gift.

She checked her watch again, then dialed New York despite the time.

Katie picked up on the second ring. "Katherine Olson speaking."

"Katie! This is Mom. How are you, love?" Maxine blurted it all out before she could stop herself. Her daughter preferred to be called *Katherine*; she referred to Maxine as *Mother*; and she hated to be called *love*.

In the half-beat of silence from the other end, Maxine corrected herself. "Katherine, how did your presentation go last week?"

"It was typical. I did all the work and wrote up the report; Jerry Fulsome did a few meaningless charts and took all the credit. I don't know how he gets away with it. If I knew, I'd do it too."

"No, you wouldn't," Maxine said. "That's how he does it." In the background, Maxine heard the burping sounds of Katie's call-waiting system.

"Just a minute, Mother. I've got another call coming in."

To Maxine, call-waiting remained an unfathomable annoyance. Why would anyone sign up for a service whose sole purpose was to interrupt conversation?

"'Tis me, O Lord."

Judging by the music, Celine was now in the guest bedroom.

"Mother?" Katie was back. "I've got to go. There's a crisis in Dallas. Jerry Fulsome sent his biggest client the wrong contract. Are you all right?"

"I'm fine," Maxine said breezily to mask her disappointment. "I was just calling to chat."

"OK then. I'll call you Sunday." Katie disconnected.

Maxine stared at the receiver. In the background, the singing ended.

"IS THERE ANYTHING you need before I go?"

Maxine dropped her unread newspaper. Celine and her cleaning cart were lined up at the front door.

"You remind me of my daughter," Maxine said without thinking.

"Say what?"

"Not that you look alike," Maxine added, as if that were an explanation.

Celine narrowed her eyes.

"She's older than you, but you're both musicians."

Celine's eyes lit up. "Does she sing or play?"

Maxine stared into the past. "She used to play the piano: mostly jazz."

"*Used* to play? Why did she stop?"

"I don't know." Maxine had thought her daughter's life would be filled with music, but Katie had quit playing when she started her MBA.

Celine stroked the small tattoo on her wrist. "I can't imagine life without music."

Maxine shook her head. "Nor can I."

Celine shifted. "Tell you what." She stopped as if uncertain what to say. "Next time, I'll get behind the appliances for you."

Maxine smiled and shook her head. "That would be foolhardy. No one has ventured back there in years. I absolutely refuse to let you endanger yourself."

For the first time since she'd arrived, Celine smiled. "You're OK, Maxine."

"You too, Celine Dianne Jackson."

Maxine walked Celine to the door and watched as she pulled her cleaning cart toward Fred Grosskopf's condo.

A flurry of movement to the right caught Maxine's attention.

Carlotta bore down on Fred's condo like a rampaging elephant.

Well, to be honest, Carlotta was far too thin to be an elephant. She was more of a weasel. No matter what the comparison, in her right hand, she clutched a fistful of fuchsia and orange papers: the distinctive colors of Rupert's authorization forms. Whatever Carlotta had been up to at breakfast, she'd gotten permission to proceed.

Despite the sun, a chill swept over Maxine. She rubbed her arms and retreated into her empty condo.

4

AT BREAKFAST THE NEXT DAY, Maxine selected oatmeal, a small carton of lactose-free milk, and tea, then crossed the room to sit with Paul and Peggy Stone. After five and a half decades of living together, Paul and Peggy unconsciously dressed alike. Today they wore khaki slacks and pink tops: hers a hot pink scoop neck and his a pale pink polo.

"Are you ready for bingo tonight?" Maxine said and passed Peggy the milk.

Peggy rolled her eyes, but Paul's face remained noncommittal. Maxine resolved never to gamble with him. As a retired minister, he was far too experienced in maintaining a poker face.

Peggy poured a miniscule amount of Lactaid on her Raisin Bran and slid the carton back toward Maxine. "Bingo will be delayed an hour to allow for an emergency meeting of the Foothills' residents."

"What's the emergency? Is someone smoking in the laundry room again?" Maxine reached for the milk.

"Oh, no. This is far more important." Peggy sounded grave.

Maxine's hand hung suspended over the forgotten carton. "Carlotta's not trying to change the bylaws again, is she? If she tries to ban walkers one more time, I'm going to get Seabiscuit and trample her. Honestly, I think she's afraid she'll catch an infirmity if she sees a walker."

"Oh, no. It's not the bylaws," Peggy said. "It's far more serious."

Maxine lowered her arm and looked to Paul.

"Sandra is leaving," he said.

His tone was somber, but the laugh lines deepened around his eyes. Maybe Maxine would play a little Blackjack with him after all.

"And?" Maxine said.

"And we need to organize, socialize, theorize, and proselytize before a new assistant director is appointed." Paul made no attempt to keep the humor out of his voice.

"You can't be serious. Who called for the meeting?"

Peggy waved an imaginary cigarette holder and batted her eyelashes.

"Carlotta!" Maxine backhanded the milk carton across the table where it skidded to a stop next to Paul's pancakes.

"What about Carlotta?" Louise and June said as they joined the breakfast group.

"She's called for one of those horrible residents' meetings," Maxine said.

June lifted her head from her coffee. "Whatever for?"

"To flatter her sense of self-importance." Maxine stabbed a spoon into her congealed oatmeal.

True to his profession, Paul gave a somewhat more charitable explanation of Carlotta's meeting and nudged the milk closer to Maxine.

She snatched the carton and dumped half the contents into her bowl. The milk puddled on the hardened surface of her oatmeal. The day had not started well.

THE DAY HAD NOT improved by the time Maxine and Louise trudged to the elevator that would take them up to the recreation room for Carlotta's meeting and Peggy's bingo.

Maxine jabbed the elevator button. "I hate these after-dinner meetings. They're just a bunch of old people complaining. Nothing is ever accomplished. I always end up with a migraine." She mashed out the opening of Beethoven's Fifth on the elevator button.

Louise pulled Maxine's hand away from the button. "You said it yourself: Carlotta is plotting something. We can't afford to skip this meeting."

"Carlotta is always plotting something. I'm going home. I'd rather clean my storage shed, and I haven't done that in the eight years I've lived here."

The elevator binged and the door opened to reveal Carlotta and Fred poring over an open file folder.

"Good evening." Maxine greeted them with her most polite tone— the one she might use if she were attending a state dinner for the visiting dignitaries of countries known for their human rights abuses.

Carlotta slapped the folder shut and handed it to Fred, who hugged it to his chest with both arms as if he thought one of them might try to wrestle it away.

"Aren't you going the wrong way?" Louise asked.

"Always interfering," Fred said. Spittle formed in the down-turned corners of his mouth. "Too bad you don't have a husband to keep you in line."

Louise inhaled so sharply that Seabiscuit wheezed.

Maxine stepped between Louise and Fred. "Isn't your meeting upstairs in five minutes?"

Fred tucked the folder under his arm like a football. "Don't know what you're talking about," he said and shoved past them.

Maxine turned to Carlotta. "You really ought to follow him. I think the poor dear is losing his memory. After all, it is *his* meeting."

"It's not his meeting. I did all the . . ." Carlotta stopped short and narrowed her eyes at them. With a toss of her head, she hurried after Fred.

When they were out of sight, Maxine hitched up an imaginary gun belt in a poor parody of John Wayne. "Think you can make it, pilgrim? We're going to a shootout at the O.K. Corral."

"I think you've mixed up your cowboys and gunfights," Louise said. "You should either be Burt Lancaster or shoot Liberty Valance."

"Liberty Valance is not the person I'd most like to shoot right now." Maxine stabbed the elevator button so hard she broke a nail.

"D.A.M.N." Maxine had long argued that the English language was too rich to settle for profanity, but at especially aggravating moments, she sometimes resorted to spelling. This evening threatened to turn into a spelling marathon.

MOST ACTIVITIES AT the Foothills were held in the recreation room because it could be transformed from an empty hall to a staged auditorium to anything in between in a matter of minutes. The formal living room downstairs was reserved for occasions that required real furniture, cut flowers, Oriental rugs, or a grand piano. For Carlotta's meeting, folding chairs were arranged in soldier-straight rows, each chair directly behind the one in front and touching the chairs on either side.

"I see Fred has arranged the furniture for maximum discomfort and minimum visibility," Maxine said and pulled several chairs into a more comfortable arrangement. She selected a seat against the wall so that she could observe everything.

Rosemarie, June, and Harry joined them. They all held something to entertain themselves during the meeting. Rosemarie carried a hardback from the *New York Times* bestseller list; Harry, a paperback of Sudoku challenges; and June, a bag of knitting. She was making scarves for her grandsons in the colors of their favorite teams: the Giants' red, white, and blue for the oldest grandson and the Jets' green and white for the younger. Or maybe it was the other way around.

"What's the matter with Carlotta and Fred?" June asked. "We rode up in the elevator with them, and, as my youngest grandson is overly fond of saying, Fred had his 'knickers in a knot.' He was fuming—something about memory loss and impertinence."

Carlotta and Fred burst into the room. While Fred raced to the front row to claim a chair, Carlotta stormed the podium. Once she'd captured the microphone, she shot them a look and produced a gavel.

"She must have gotten that from Mrs. Babcock," Louise said. "That's where they were going: to borrow the illusion of authority."

Mrs. Babcock had been sent to the Foothills by corporate headquarters. Ostensibly, she was Rupert's secretary, but everyone suspected she'd been sent as a spy. She'd been a sergeant in the Army, or maybe it was the Marines. At any rate, she'd never gotten over it. Built like a bunker, Mrs. Babcock was an old battle-ax who wanted to know—and control—everything. She never met a rule she didn't love, and she seemed determined to report any and every infraction up the chain of command. Predisposed to bend rules, Maxine tried to avoid both Mrs. Babcock and her signs of authority.

"Quiet please!" Carlotta tapped on the lectern and glared at their group. "The special meeting of the residents of the Foothills Retirement Community will now come to order."

Maxine and her group were quiet, but the rest of the room continued to talk. Carlotta hammered her gavel until she had beaten the group into silence.

"My dear friends," Carlotta began. Someone to Maxine's left snickered.

"As many of you know, Sandra has resigned her position as assistant director. We believe that it is imperative that residents of the Foothills be involved in the search for her replacement."

"Hear, hear," Ralph Jordan cheered, to Maxine's surprise.

Ralph was soft-spoken and genial. A widower of fifteen years, he was considered by many to be the Foothills' most eligible bachelor. He still had his own teeth and a full head of wavy silver hair. More importantly, he was a tasteful dresser who knew how to cook and iron. However, Ralph seldom spoke at the residents' meetings, and when he did, it was with a barely audible whisper. Tonight he must have extended his cocktail hour a bit longer than usual.

Carlotta waggled her gavel at the audience. "We propose a Residents' Advisory Committee be formed to assist Rupert in his selection."

"So moved," Fred said.

"Second," Ralph joined in.

"All in favor signify by saying 'Aye.'"

A half dozen folks, those who sat at Carlotta's dinner table, shouted "Aye."

"Opposed?"

The residents' committee seemed like a good idea, so Maxine did not try to stop Carlotta's railroad.

"I nominate Carlotta and Fred to be on the committee," Gladys Black shouted.

"Second," Ralph sang out.

Maxine began to suspect where Ralph had gotten his extra cheer.

"All in favor?"

"Excuse me," Maxine said as pleasantly as she could. "I think we should discuss what kind of assistant director we want before we decide who should represent us."

Carlotta hoisted her gavel over her head like a tomahawk and glared at Maxine. In the ensuing pandemonium, it became clear that Carlotta and Fred had planned the meeting to promote their not so hidden agenda of selecting an assistant director themselves.

"Order. Order." Carlotta banged her gavel until the room fell silent. "We"—she looked at Fred, who nodded obediently—"intend to select an assistant director who will provide activities that are appropriate."

Maxine jumped to her feet. Fortunately, Paul Stone spoke before she could vent her fury.

"What do you mean by appropriate?" he asked.

Maxine sat down.

Carlotta placed the gavel on the podium and pulled out her cigarette holder. "We want someone who understands the dignity and seemliness with which residents should be treated."

Maxine gagged.

Rosemarie raised her hand. "I'm not sure I know what you mean. Could you give us some specific examples?"

Carlotta and Fred exchanged confused looks. They didn't know what they meant, but once the dice had been cast, Carlotta would not back down. Maxine tried to remember the Latin for "The die is cast." Julius Caesar had said it when he crossed the Rubicon on his way to capture Rome.

"Iacta alea est!"

Everyone looked at Maxine. She smiled politely and wished she hadn't spoken the Latin out loud.

"As I was saying," Carlotta said, "now is the time to act. No more Sandras! We want an assistant director to plan coffee klatches, not book clubs. She should arrange for speakers from the Chamber of Commerce, not bake sales for the victims of natural disasters. We want Halloween parties for our grandchildren, not giveaways for the poor."

The last comment was a jab at Maxine and Louise, who had gone Reverse Trick-or-Treating the previous year. They'd dressed as Robin Hood and Friar Tuck and given away candy at one of the more disadvantaged grade schools. Carlotta's comment proved to be a tactical error, however, as many of the residents had asked Maxine to include them on the next Halloween giveaway.

The meeting quickly split into partisan factions. Carlotta wanted an assistant director who would be under her control. Maxine and her friends wanted someone who would enrich their lives with innovative programs. An undecided group, led by Norman Tisdale and Gretchen Rothberg, wanted the argument to end before anyone's feelings were hurt. The longer the discussion went on, the more militant Carlotta and her faction became. In return, her opponents threatened to walk out and end the quorum.

"Madam Chair." Paul Stone rose like a minister intent upon shepherding his flock. "I suggest we appoint a five-person committee comprised of Carlotta and Fred—"

Carlotta's group interrupted with cheers.

Paul continued undeterred. "A five-person committee comprised of Carlotta and Fred, as well as Norman Tisdale and Gretchen Rothberg."

The independent faction nodded their agreement.

"That leaves one more slot for us to fill." Paul smiled at his congregation.

After a half beat of silence, Ralph Jordon jumped to his feet. "So moved."

Someone in the back seconded the motion, and the room erupted.

"Good idea."

"No way. The committee is stacked."

"Take the deal."

"Let's get out of here."

Carlotta banged the meeting into submission, and the motion passed.

"Nominations are now open for the fifth and final slot," Carlotta said, her face flush from battle.

Maxine shot her hand up. Carlotta looked the other way.

Everyone else sat as if frozen.

Finally, Paul Stone raised his hand.

"Yes, Paul?"

"Thank you, madam chair," he said in his best Sunday-sermon voice. "I yield the floor to Maxine."

Carlotta reached for her gavel.

Maxine spoke before Carlotta could start banging again. "I nominate Rosemarie. She'd be perfect. She ran her own business, so she's used to interviewing people. She knows how to get things done. She's honest, and everyone likes her."

"I second the nomination," June shouted.

Rosemarie tried to jump up to object, but Louise grabbed her arm and Maxine stepped on the hem of her long skirt, pinning her to her seat.

"People. People." Carlotta banged her gavel and glared. "All in favor of adding Rosemarie to the proposed five-person committee signify by saying 'Aye.'"

The residents shouted their assent in obvious relief to be done.

Unwilling to relinquish control, Carlotta banged her gavel. "The next order of business is—"

"Bingo," Ralph Jordan shouted, and everyone adjourned.

While Peggy supervised the reconfiguration of chairs and tables for bingo, Paul came over to congratulate Rosemarie on her election. "I'm so glad that someone with sense is going to be part of our new Residents' Advisory Committee."

Rosemarie thanked him and shot Maxine a dirty look.

"What?" Maxine asked.

"You know what," Rosemarie said.

"You can handle the Queen of Mean and her grumpy consort," Maxine said.

As if on cue, Carlotta skulked up to their group. Maxine stepped closer to Rosemarie.

"I suppose congratulations are in order," Carlotta said, unable to keep her lip from curling.

Rosemarie nodded noncommittally.

"As chair of the committee"—Carlotta announced her self-appointment with a wave of her cigarette holder—"I've already set up a meeting with Rupert for tomorrow morning at nine o'clock. If you have a conflict, I'm sure we can manage without you."

"I wouldn't dream of missing the first meeting," Rosemarie said with a level gaze.

Maxine's chest swelled with pride.

"Fine," Carlotta said. "Our first order of business is to inform Rupert that we want to improve the application form."

Maxine's knees buckled. She grabbed Rosemarie's arm to steady herself.

"Are you all right?" Rosemarie asked. "You're as white as a sheet."

"Yes. No. I'm fine." Maxine wiped her damp forehead. "It's just a post-menopausal hot flash."

Everyone stared, open-mouthed.

Maxine blinked. She was quite certain that she'd never uttered those words in mixed company before. She waved vaguely toward the room. "Why don't you get us some seats for bingo," she said, grabbing Seabiscuit. "We'll be right back."

"We will?" Louise said.

"Yes. I need to talk to you about that thing."

"What thing?"

Maxine tugged Louise down the crowded hall, into the half-full elevator, around the corner, and into the empty library. She sat at the computer and began to click furiously.

"What are you doing?" Louise asked.

"I'm looking for my application." Maxine heard a hint of hysteria creep into her voice.

Louise sat down with a plop. "Oh, dear."

"We need to get it off of here before anyone sees it."

"But Maxine, it's not there. We sent it. We can't get it back."

"But that was before Carlotta had her silly meeting," Maxine said. "Before I nominated Rosemarie to be on the Residents' Advisory Committee. She's going to kill me."

Louise's eyes reflected the same mounting panic that was making Maxine's palms sweat. "She'll kill us both."

They looked at each other, their chests heaving.

The click of the electric wall clock filled the room.

Their breathing slowed.

"Well," Louise said tentatively. "If we don't tell, Rosemarie won't necessarily know it was you. After all, I didn't know your middle name was Octavia, and I've known you since the Redwoods were saplings."

"That's right." Maxine chewed on her lower lip. "And Rosemarie has more sense than to select someone who wants to plan the dumb events we listed."

Louise began to chew on her own lip. "It's true that Rosemarie won't choose you, but . . ." She took a deep breath. "But Carlotta will think you're perfect!"

Maxine jerked as if bitten by a snake.

The two old friends stared at each other, their eyes wide.

The clock ticked inexorably.

The corners of Maxine's mouth twitched.

A snort of laughter escaped from Louise.

"You're right!" Maxine felt giddy. "Carlotta would love Octavia!"

Louise's whole body shook from trying to keep silent.

The harder they tried to repress their laughter, the funnier it became. Finally, they gave up, and their laughter bubbled up and danced off the library walls. They laughed until tears streamed down their cheeks.

Louise was the first to recover. "Can't you just see Carlotta's face."

Maxine pulled off her glasses and wiped her eyes. "And we can't get the application back anyway."

"It would be fun," Louise said.

"What could go wrong?" Maxine asked.

Louise gave Maxine one of her "You've got to be kidding" looks.

"Let's do it anyway," Maxine said. "Iacta alea est!"

5

THE MORNING AFTER Carlotta's meeting, Maxine was out of sorts. Even her clothes felt wrong; they bound and bagged in places where they'd never bound or bagged before. She needed to get out.

Balancing a mug of tea, a plate of biscotti, her journal, and the morning newspaper, she stormed out to her patio, plopped onto the glider, and snapped open the newspaper.

Two minutes later, she tossed the paper onto the table in disgust. Were all politicians defective? Members of the current gaggle were obsequious toadies. Or was that tautological? She made a mental note to look up the words, then sighed and reached for her spiral-bound notebook to make a written note instead.

Louise had tried to talk her into buying an expensive journal with gilt edges and luscious Italian leather, but Maxine had refused. She didn't want a journal whose cover was more valuable than its contents. She wanted to be free to write drivel—grocery lists and doodles if she felt like it. Italian leather demanded something more elegant—complete sentences at a minimum. Maxine's only rule for journaling was that she actually had to put pen to paper, not just drift off in a stream of consciousness, as if she were a character in a novel—perhaps *To the Lighthouse*.

Maxine tapped her pen on the table and stared at the page. Like her mind, it remained blank.

She pushed herself out of the chair and shoved open her patio gate.

MINUTES LATER, MAXINE PEERED into June and Harry's patio. Harry was reading, with his Golden Retriever asleep at his feet.

Maxine rattled their gate. "Come save me from myself."

Daisy jumped up and wagged while Harry waved.

Maxine let herself in. "Let's go for a walk."

"Daisy and I would love to," Harry said. "June is at the—you know—place for food."

"Grocery store?" Maxine bent to ruffle Daisy's ears. Daisy leaned against Maxine's leg and closed her eyes. Maxine was Daisy's official sitter when June and Harry went to New York to visit their children and grandchildren. Daisy was the perfect guest: she never complained about the food, and she could entertain herself for hours.

Harry clipped a worn leather leash onto Daisy's collar and opened the gate with a flourish. "Ladies first."

Daisy led the way.

"What were you reading?" Maxine asked.

Pleasure flooded Harry's face. "A book on the history of the circle."

"The circle?"

"Actually it's about the circle and the sphere. They've had an enormous impact on everything: art, architecture, philosophy, life!" Harry swung his arms in gigantic circles to illustrate his point.

Maxine took the leash from his hand so that he could elaborate without choking Daisy. Daisy wagged her thanks and moved closer to Maxine.

"Take Pythagoras's theory about the harmony of the spheres," Harry said, warming to his subject. "The Earth is at the center of a series of concentric spheres bearing the sun and the stars. Each sphere moves in a circular pattern that produces a precise tone. The whole thing vibrates with perfect harmony."

Maxine already knew about the harmony of the spheres. In literature, human beings were forever disrupting that harmony through impulsive acts. But she enjoyed Harry's lectures, so she nodded encouragement.

"That theory influenced people's conception of the universe for two thousand years." He swept his arm in an expansive arc that would have boxed her ear if she hadn't ducked. "Even the Foothills follows Pythagoras's theory."

Maxine paused to visualize their retirement center.

Daisy took advantage of the moment to mark a rock.

Harry's eyes sparkled. "The main building is the physical center of the Foothills, but it's also our social center." His gestures expanded as his excitement mounted. "It includes the places where we interact: the dining rooms, recreation room, offices, et cetera. Moving out from there, we have alternating circles of private space—like our apartments and condominiums—and common space–like the pool and shuffleboard courts."

He spun in a circle of his own. "All of it is encircled by this very trail we are on."

Maxine waited. She knew Harry. More was coming.

Daisy looked at them both, sat down, and yawned.

Harry swung his arm in another enormous arc, "Beyond this trail are circles made by the desert and the mountains and even the horizon. We're connected to it all. The harmony of our spheres radiates out from our main building and the business of our daily lives to the grandeur of the desert and the mountains beyond."

A frisson of pleasure ran down Maxine's spine. "Harry, that's beautiful! It's comforting to think that we have a place in the grand scheme of things. It gives us . . . significance."

Harry resumed walking.

Daisy gave herself a good shake and followed, pulling Maxine gently along.

Harry rubbed his bald head with both hands, a sure sign of complications.

"There is one tiny glitch," he admitted.

Maxine raised a questioning eyebrow.

"At the very center of it all, in the middle of the main building is . . . what?" Harry asked.

Maxine considered the first floor of the main building. "The fireplace in the formal living room?"

"Close. That's the perceived center, but the mathematical center is twenty-seven yards to the southeast."

Maxine knew better than to quibble with Harry. He was a retired accountant. He'd probably measured the distance himself. She closed her eyes and refocused. What was twenty-seven yards southeast of the fireplace?

"The kitchen?" she asked.

"The kitchen sink," Harry said.

"That's rather uninspiring." Maxine couldn't keep the disappointment out of her voice. "It ought to be something like our chapel—even if it is nondenominational."

Harry nodded his agreement. "The kitchen sink flushes my analogy down the drain."

Maxine disliked most puns, but she smiled at Harry's. His delivery was so deadpan that his friends engaged in heated arguments about whether his verbal games were intentional or accidental. Personally, Maxine gave him credit for all of his jokes—even the bad ones—and extra credit for his restrained delivery.

They walked on in silence, enjoying the day and each other's company.

Back at her patio gate, Harry favored Maxine with an old-fashioned bow. "You, my dear, are home, but I must circle ever onward."

"Don't forget Daisy."

"Who?"

Maxine waved the leash at him.

"Oh, right." Harry blushed and reclaimed Daisy's leash. "We make a complete metaphor, Maxine: you're the professor, and I'm absent-minded."

Maxine watched Harry and Daisy continue down the path. Despite the kitchen sink problem, she liked Harry's analogy. It linked them to something beyond taxes and death.

She stooped to fill her watering can.

But if there was a grand scheme of things, what was her place in it?

She splashed water generously into each of the pots and onto her garden.

She used to know the answer to that question. She'd been a teacher, a wife, and a mother. Now she was the absence of those things; she was retired, widowed, and only as much of a mother as Katie would allow. She used to have an active role. Now she felt as if she were just marking time. She used to be productive; now she was merely predictable.

She upended the watering can and emptied the last of the water onto the broad, blue-gray leaves of a century plant.

That was the problem. Her life *had* become predictable and repetitive. She needed to *do* something. Something more than water plants and walk in metaphoric circles.

She left the watering can on the patio wall and marched inside to her desk. She pulled out the old recipe box she used for storing other people's business cards and flicked through them.

She remembered perfectly the one she sought. It was the card of a consultant she'd met at a conference in Michigan. Carol. Carol something. Instead of being white, the card was an extraordinary deep blue, and the information she wanted was on its back.

She sorted through the box twice before she found the card and flipped it over. "Assuming you live to age 80, you have exactly 29,220 days on this planet."

Maxine stared at the card. She'd met Carol Anderson ten years earlier. Maxine had been seventy-two then, and the number of days on this planet had seemed pathetically small. But Maxine was now eighty-two. She had already outlived the card by 730 days. It was time to get going.

She began to pace. Something niggled at the back of her mind. Then it hit her.

She'd already applied for a job—to be assistant director. She'd applied on a lark, but . . .

Absently, she fingered the fossilized sand dollar she kept on her desk. She'd given it to Tom because—like him—it was beautiful. She traced the petal-like pattern on its curved surface. Next to the sand dollar was the wooden carving of Don Quixote that Tom had given her in honor of her tendency to tilt at windmills. She looked from one to the other. Then to Tom's photo. It smiled back at her.

"The thing is, I really could do it," she said. "Louise and June and Rosemarie could help me. We could plan all those activities Louise and I had on our first list. We could even go to the Redwoods."

Tom's eyes twinkled in the light.

Maxine shrugged and smiled sheepishly.

"It was an absurd application form," she said. "*Really* it was. And I wanted to see if I could make the computer work. And then we couldn't get the application back anyway. And things just kept snowballing."

The word momentarily transported her back to their yard in Glen Ellyn: Tom and Katie waging a massive snowball fight. Katie couldn't have been much more than two. She was too young to understand snowballs. She'd grab a handful of snow and fling it into the air. Invariably the flakes fell back on her face, sticking to her eyelashes and sliding down her neck. It didn't matter: Tom had pretended to be overpowered by her assault, and they quickly turned into a giant snowball themselves as they giggled, rolled down the hill, and randomly tossed fistfuls of snow into the air.

The telephone rang and her memory melted.

Maxine snatched up the receiver. "Hello."

"What are you doing?" Louise asked.

"I've decided to become our assistant director."

"Yes," Louise said. "I know. I was there."

"No. I mean I really *want* to become our assistant director." Maxine bowed her head. "I think I could be good at it."

"Well, of course you would be!" Louise sounded a bit impatient. "The real question is why aren't you over here?"

"Over where?"

"The recreation room," Louise said. "Today is the monthly bridge club meeting. Don't tell me you've forgotten."

"Of course not," Maxine lied and crossed her fingers. "I'm on my way right now."

6

MAXINE WAS THE LAST TO ARRIVE. The monthly card game was open to anyone from the Foothills, and the quality of both the bridge and the conversation suffered as a result.

Unlike Louise, who was gracious even in the face of the most extraordinary stupidity, Maxine suffered fools poorly. She sometimes thought of these monthly sessions as part of her charitable contribution for the year, except that she wasn't particularly charitable about them. At least she wasn't as bad as Rosemarie, who considered the violation of a bridge convention roughly equivalent to murder.

Maxine walked in and Louise waved her over. Despite her petite frame and omnipresent walker, Louise managed to look powerful. Today she also looked positively chic in black slacks and a vermillion silk top she'd bought at the art museum's silent auction.

"I have bad news for you," Louise said.

"What?"

"You have to partner with Fred."

"What!"

"Actually, you have a choice. Carlotta or Fred? I'd do it, but I promised to teach Gladys Black and her table how to play."

"How many times have you taught Gladys how to play?"

"I lost count when it hit double digits," Louise said without even a hint of exasperation. "Rosemarie will take whichever one you don't."

"What happened to June?"

"She's taking Harry to the doctor."

"What's wrong? I just saw Harry, and he seemed fine."

"Don't know. June's message said he needed some tests." She handed Maxine a glass of unsweetened sun tea and gave her a let's-discuss-this-later look.

"I'll take Fred. Carlotta might hex me with her cigarette holder."

Maxine made her way across the room to the last bridge table, where Fred and Carlotta whispered at each other while Rosemarie busied herself picking cashews out of the nut dish.

Rosemarie had dressed for the occasion. With her high cheekbones, olive complexion, and straight hair, Rosemarie was sometimes mistaken for a Native American. In reality, her family was from Boston and her heritage was Greek, but Fred and Carlotta were convinced that Rosemarie was a full-blooded Navajo. For her part, Rosemarie did nothing to disabuse them of that notion. Today she wore stunning Navajo jewelry that she'd purchased long before it was in vogue: half a dozen silver bracelets, a large turquoise ring, a silver and turquoise squash blossom necklace, and long silver earrings. Although Maxine didn't wear much jewelry herself, she admired Rosemarie's ability to wear a fortune's worth of museum pieces and make them look natural, even essential. With her dark pewter hair pulled into a loose twist, Rosemarie was positively handsome and totally imposing.

As Maxine approached, Rosemarie looked up, tilted her head toward Fred and Carlotta, and rolled her eyes. Maxine responded with a conspiratorial eye roll of her own before switching to her best Miss America smile, the one that involved only her lips.

She sat down across from Fred with Rosemarie to her left and Carlotta to her right.

"Fred, dahling, I understand we are to be partnered," Maxine said in a bad imitation of a Southern drawl.

Fred glared.

Carlotta looked pointedly at her watch. "How good of you to join us." She nodded across the table to Rosemarie. "Your deal, partner."

So much for pleasantries.

While Rosemarie dealt, Maxine tried to decide whether Carlotta's bra was supposed to show through her white silk jumpsuit, or whether she'd forgotten some essential layer. A chemise, or perhaps a teddy? It was a shame June wasn't here. June would know the answer; she knew all the latest fashion trends even though she had more sense than to adopt the tacky ones for herself.

Rosemarie opened the bidding with one heart. Fred jumped to four hearts. Maxine tried to approach the situation with the generosity of spirit that Louise would show. "Excuse me," she said in a polite, Louise-like tone, "but I think Rosemarie bid one heart." She refrained from adding that only a fool would bid his opponent's suit.

Fred scowled. "Pay attention. She said *one* heart and I said *four*."

"But you are *my* partner, *not* Rosemarie's," Maxine said.

"Yes, but I can see that if I want to win this hand, I'll have to do it by myself."

Maxine flashed him a polite smile. "You've got that right." She turned sweetly to Carlotta, "Your turn, dear."

"One club."

Maxine's jaw dropped. She was trapped in bridge hell. Before she could say anything, Rosemarie intervened with her own version of diplomacy: "Fred bid FOUR hearts. You need to bid at least FIVE clubs."

Carlotta simpered. "Oh, yes. Whatever was I thinking?"

Maxine suspected Carlotta had been thinking of ways to turn them all to stone. Or maybe she'd been thinking about her missing chemise.

Carlotta raised her fingers to her cheek where she tapped out her points as she recalculated them. An observant opponent always knew how many points Carlotta held. Right now she was holding an impressive twenty-one points.

"Let's see," Carlotta said. "I think I'll just pass this round."

"Pass," Maxine said. The quicker they got this hand out of the way, the better. Clearly the hearts were divided between Fred and Rosemarie, and Carlotta was holding a fistful of face cards. Fred would be lucky to win any tricks.

"Too bad we don't play for a penny a point," Fred said, fingering his cards. "I'd teach you ladies a lesson."

"What?" Rosemarie's fingers twitched as if she were getting ready to scalp Fred's bald head with her bare hands.

The tops of Fred's ears turned red and his jowls trembled.

Maxine stepped on Rosemarie's foot to keep her from kicking Fred.

Carlotta led off with a low club. By the end of the hand, Fred had captured only three of the tricks he needed, and the air between him and Rosemarie crackled with hostility.

To distract them all, Maxine asked Carlotta how the Residents' Advisory Committee was going. Carlotta's eyes lit up. Too late, Maxine realized that Carlotta was dying to talk about her committee.

"Well, as *you* may not know," Carlotta said, "*we* met with Rupert this morning, and he agreed to our demands."

"What demands?" Maxine asked as she arranged her cards for the next hand. She couldn't remember the committee being asked to make any demands.

"Well," Carlotta said, "I don't like to toot my own horn."

Maxine glanced up in time to see that even Fred had rolled his eyes on that one. She bit her lip to keep from laughing and forced herself to look at Carlotta instead.

Once again, Carlotta tapped her fingers and added her points. Twenty-seven!

Maxine closed her eyes. There was no justice in the bridge world. Carlotta, who could hardly tell a club from a spade, held a bountiful harvest of points while Maxine had a single, paltry point with which to do battle. She'd never seen such lousy cards.

"One spade." Fred planted his elbows on the table, as if daring them to bid his suit.

"After much debate and complex negotiation." Carlotta paused as if she had completed her sentence.

While they waited for Carlotta to get on with it, Maxine shot Rosemarie a questioning look. Rosemarie gave a barely perceptible shake of her head. As Maxine suspected, there'd been no lengthy debate or intricate negotiations.

"Rupert agreed to my suggestion." Carlotta waited until they had all looked up from their cards. "My suggestion," she said with a self-satisfied smile, "that he modify the application."

Maxine nearly knocked over her sun tea. "What?"

Fred, Carlotta, and Rosemarie all stared at her.

"I mean . . ." Maxine steadied the glass and tried to sound casual. "Haven't people already applied?"

Carlotta slammed her cards on the table. "How did *you* know?"

Her voice carried across the room like a clarion call. All the other players looked over to see what the commotion was about.

Louise shot Maxine an accusatory look. Maxine shrugged with wide-eyed innocence. Rosemarie seconded Maxine with a shrug of her own and a shake of her head. Louise cocked an eyebrow at them. The rest of the room returned to their cards.

"I mean," Carlotta sputtered, "I think *some* people may have applied. Rupert said so. Didn't he?" She turned for confirmation to Fred, who was busy picking the remaining cashews out of the mixed nuts before Rosemarie could get them. "Didn't he?"

Fred, who seemed to have no idea what Carlotta was talking about, nodded.

"But how can he modify the application after people have applied?" Maxine said. "Is that even legal?"

Rosemarie gave her a look of incredulity, but Maxine pretended not to notice.

"That's not an issue," Carlotta said. "Three no-trump."

Maxine nearly dropped her cards. "Excuse me?"

"I bid THREE no-trump." Carlotta gloated as if she had done something to earn all the points in her hand. "This afternoon Rupert's going to send emails to the early applicants and ask them for the additional information."

"What information?"

"Just an essay," Rosemarie said as she fished the last cashew out of the bowl.

"Essay?" A bead of sweat rolled down between Maxine's breasts. "What kind of essay?"

"The candidate's philosophical approach to retirement communities." Carlotta sounded as if she were reciting lines from a bad script. "*All* the *best* schools require their students to develop a statement of philosophy before graduation. My granddaughter did one in graduate school and received the only A++ ever awarded." She spoke with the absolute authority of a snake-oil salesman.

Maxine turned to Rosemarie in a mute appeal for a return to sanity.

Rosemarie shrugged. "It's a way of finding out how the applicants view the job. You know, do they see themselves as babysitters, prison guards, events coordinators. After all, that initial application was just plain silly. Anyone could have applied."

"Don't I know it," Maxine muttered.

"What?" Fred said. "I bid one spade, and Carlotta said three no-trump. What did you say?"

"Pass." Maxine folded her cards. "I pass for now."

7

MAXINE SLIPPED INTO THE LIBRARY with her copy of the day's newspaper tucked under her arm. Thankfully, the room was empty. She could check her email without an audience. If Carlotta had been right, there would be a note from Rupert waiting for her.

Maxine hesitated. The computer loomed, as daunting as ever. She placed her newspaper next to the keyboard and perched on the edge of the nearest Chippendale. She couldn't remember how to start the monster. She hung her head. There, neatly folded in her lap, were the prim and prayerful hands of a little old lady.

Maxine catapulted herself out of the chair. She would *not* become a stereotype.

She grabbed the Chippendale and dragged it to the far corner of the room. In its place, she rolled over one of the ugly ergonomic chairs and cased herself into it, uncertain whether the mesh seat would hold.

She fiddled with adjustments, riding the chair up and down like a carnival ride. She played with the height, the tilt, and the tension. Like Goldilocks, she was in pursuit of the perfect fit.

Comfortable at last, she sat back in triumph and eyed the computer with impudence. "Take that!" she said and powered on the beast.

To her chagrin, operating a computer was not like riding a bicycle. Nothing came back automatically. Even the cursor had grown unbridled. No matter how gently she jiggled the mouse, the cursor leapt wildly across the screen. She might as well be trying to control the mouse with her left hand. Well, why not? It was time her left hand learned to do something more than wear a watch and a wedding band.

She shifted the mouse to the left side of the computer and practiced until she could force the cursor to go where she wanted it to—more or less.

She rolled her shoulder to loosen the tension.

A door slammed somewhere down the hall.

Startled, Maxine spun her chair around to check for intruders.

The room was empty. She checked over both shoulders once more, then slid her fingers between the folds of her newspaper and extracted a single sheet of paper. On it were the instructions Peter had given her for opening email. If anyone could help her get into her email, it was Peter. But that was a big "if."

She did as directed and magically a note from Rupert appeared.

She felt light-headed and slightly sick to her stomach. She was only one click away.

She swallowed and clicked on the note.

"D.A.M.N."

As Carlotta had predicted, Rupert wanted an essay. The last time Maxine had written an application essay, America had been a British colony.

She reread Rupert's note. What was a "statement of philosophy" anyway? Rupert's request sounded exactly like the kind of assignment that led students to write drivel—mindless pages filled with meaningless abstractions, words heaped upon words in the vague hope of stumbling upon a solution to a problem not fully comprehended.

Well, the English professor in her wasn't going to be a party to any such nonsense. She was going to be crisp and precise, no matter how long it took.

She labored through draft after draft, refining her language and honing her essay until she had a half-page statement that crystallized her philosophy. More than anything, she wanted her friends to have an assistant director who would encourage them to stay active and productive. She wanted someone who'd help them live their dreams, not sleep their lives away. And if that someone had to be her, then so be it. Her essay might not be what Rupert wanted to hear, but it captured the essence of what she wanted to say. Besides, knowing Rupert, he wasn't going to read the essay anyway.

Drumming her fingers lightly on the keyboard, she was trying to decide how to sign her essay when she heard voices outside the door. She barely had time to close her email before Carlotta barged into the room, towing Fred in her wake.

The temperature in the room dropped twenty degrees.

Carlotta and Fred glared and nodded wordlessly.

Maxine returned the nod and the silence.

Fred picked up a newspaper and laid claim to the couch on the far side of the room. Carlotta shuffled through the magazines, selected *Sunset*, and enthroned herself in the overstuffed armchair next to the couch.

Maxine turned back to the computer. A search box had appeared where her email had been, so she entered "Giant Redwoods."

"SEQUOIA SEMPERVIRENS?" Louise's voice made Maxine jump. "You're reading about the Giant Redwoods?"

"Don't sneak up on me," Maxine said.

"Sneak? Seabiscuit and I aren't exactly known for our stealth."

Maxine inspected the room. Carlotta and Fred were gone, and long shadows stretched across the fake Oriental carpet.

"What are you doing?" Louise asked.

"I was writing an essay for Rupert when Fred and Carlotta came in. I didn't want them to see what I was doing, so I started to ski the internet."

"Surf, Maxine. You were *surfing* the internet. Honestly, sometimes it's hard to believe you're Peter's godmother. You'd think some of his computer genius would rub off on you."

"I know. He's such a leek."

"*Geek*! And I think you are deliberately pretending to know less than you do."

Maxine was sure she looked guilty. "I feel so inept around this, this . . ." She pointed at the computer. "This thing."

"It's like training a dog," Louise said. "You just have to show it who's boss."

Maxine rolled up her newspaper and whacked the screen.

"Don't you be abusin' that machine," a deep voice said.

Maxine swiveled her chair around. Celine stood in the doorway, majestically draped in a burnt orange and blue kaftan.

"I must be going deaf," Maxine said. "Everybody sneaks up on me."

Celine beamed. "Why thank you. I went to school with a girl we called Everybody on account of every time she went into the room she'd look around and ask if 'Everybody' was there. I always thought she was looking for the popular girls—you know, the cheerleaders." Using her duster as a pompom, Celine mimed a cheer. "Who knew that all that time she was looking for me?"

"I wouldn't use that name around Carlotta," Louise said. "The woman is always making up rules for Everybody. Last week she wanted to put a requirement in the bylaws that forced Everybody to use black ink on sign-up sheets."

"What happens if you use another color?" Celine asked. "Personally, I like blue or red or purple."

"If you use blue, you're all through." Maxine chanted in the singsong voice she'd used as a child jumping rope. "If it's red, then you're dead. If it's purple . . ." She stopped. "What rhymes with purple?"

They looked at each other and shrugged.

Maxine turned back to the computer. "Anyway, I'm almost done with my application essay. Tell me what you think."

"I will," Celine said, "just as soon as you tell me what you're applying for."

Maxine's hands froze over the keyboard. "Um." She looked at Louise for help, but Louise stood rigid with guilt, her mouth open and her eyes darting about in search of an escape route.

"Uh-huh." Celine rubbed her hands together. "I can tell this is going to be good."

"Well," Maxine said. "You never know when you might need one?"

"Uh-huh," Celine said again. "And pigs have silk purses."

Maxine squirmed in her ergonomic chair.

Celine waited.

And waited.

After a moment, Celine's face hardened. "That's OK. You got secrets; you don't need to be telling me. Everybody's got secrets from Celine. Mrs. Helmsley can't make a phone call if Celine's there cleaning. Mr. Grosskopf won't use his computer if Celine's in the room. No wonder Mrs. Babcock's been trying to enlist me as a spy."

Louise cocked her head. "She has? What did you tell her?"

"Told her I'd keep my eyes open. Didn't tell her I'd also keep my mouth shut." Celine stared at Maxine. "I can keep a secret even if some folks don't think so." She turned to leave.

"Wait!" Maxine grabbed Celine's sleeve. "I've applied to be the new assistant director for the Foothills, but I'm afraid my application won't be taken seriously if anyone knows it's mine."

"Are you serious?"

Maxine nodded. She folded her arms across her chest and waited for objections.

Celine whooped, spun Maxine's chair around, and high-fived Louise. "You go, girl!"

"You don't think we're silly?" Louise asked.

"Lord have mercy, no. You'd be great." Celine mimed another cheer. "Show me your essay."

"OK," Maxine said. "But don't laugh." She turned to the computer and clicked. Then clicked and clicked again. "I can't find it," she said, her voice rising.

"Where did you have it?" Louise asked.

"Right here!" Maxine pointed at the computer. "It was right here."

"No. I mean, don't you have to put them in files and folders and things?" Louise said.

"I didn't put it anywhere. I just clicked on that big *X* in the corner and it disappeared."

"Uh-oh," Celine said. "That's not good. You need to save things before you click the *X*."

Maxine and Louise looked at Celine. "How do you know?"

"Hey." Celine ruffled her metaphorical feathers. "Just because I'm beautiful, that doesn't mean I'm not brilliant. I did all the computer stuff for Benny's Bar and Grill—even Photoshopped the menus and ads."

"Benny's has menus?" Louise sounded more than a little surprised.

"Does that mean I have to start all over?" Maxine asked. Traces of a temper tantrum crept into her voice.

Celine and Louise exchanged glances.

"I think I better go clean Rupert's office," Celine said and backed out the door.

"Coward," Louise called after her.

"D.A.M.N." Maxine thwacked the screen with her newspaper. "I'll never get this."

"Yes you will. It's just because you were in a hurry."

Maxine glared at the computer. Virginia Woolf had been right. A woman needed 500 pounds a year and a computer of her own, one that didn't have to be shut off whenever Fred or Carlotta circled past.

"I can *almost* see why Peter and Katie surround themselves with these bloody machines at work and at home." Maxine gestured toward the computer. "At least they can work without interruption."

"Come on." Louise patted the top of the computer. "We can finish the essay right now."

"Oh what's the point?" Maxine pushed back from the computer and started to stand.

"No, no, no." Louise shoved her back into the chair. "You want this job, don't you?"

Maxine started to protest, but she looked into Louise's blue eyes and saw six decades of unconditional support smiling back. Their friendship was companionable silences. It was acceptance. It was knowing she could call Louise in the middle of the night, and Louise would come without question or complaint. It was having entire conversations through a lifted eyebrow or an almost imperceptible nod across a room filled with others. It was Maxine knowing that Louise needed to change her oxygen canister before Seabiscuit started to snort, and it was Louise knowing that Maxine needed help on her essay.

Louise raised her eyebrow.

"Yes, I do want this job," Maxine said. "I want to prove that we can do it."

Louise pumped her fist. "That's the spirit. We can do this. We need to do this. We will do this."

Maxine gave an exaggerated sigh and returned her attention to the computer, which had gone blank. She stared at the empty screen. Behind her, the electric wall clock grew louder with each unrelenting click.

She heaved herself out of her chair and stomped across the room. She grabbed the clock with one hand and an empty wastebasket with the other. She banged the basket onto an end table and raised the clock high over her head in preparation for a slam-dunk.

"Stop!" Louise said.

Maxine snorted and glared. With excessive care, she lowered the clock into the basket and covered it with throw pillows until the clicking was muffled. "There," she said, dusting her hands. *"You* can put it back when we leave."

Louise rolled her eyes but didn't object.

Maxine returned to the computer and began once more to type the essay.

PART TWO

DOUBLED AND REDOUBLED:

THE INTERVIEW

8

IN THE DIM LIGHT of Gladys Black's storage shed, Rupert checked his watch. If he left in the next ten minutes, he'd beat the Friday evening rush hour. He could get in an extra hour of cycling and still get his registration to the post office before the deadline. His entry form and check had been in an envelope in the center drawer of his desk, ready to go, for weeks.

He rubbed his jaw. Funny how much quicker he'd been to register for the Arizona Ironman. He'd done it ages ago, and that race was still months off. But that race would take place over a hundred miles away in Tempe. The Tour de Tucson wasn't a full triathlon, only a half, but it was right here—where anyone might see him. And it was only two weeks away.

He checked his watch again. He needed to get going.

He banged some cookie tins together to simulate the sounds of a serious search, then stepped out of the storage shed. Every time Gladys forgot to shut the door, she was certain that some creature had gotten in. Last month she was sure there was a mountain lion gnawing on her Christmas decorations. She'd made Rupert move a million cookie tins and a billion boxes of colored lights, musical Santas, and stuffed reindeer before she was satisfied. Today she thought she'd heard a coyote rustling through her collection of *National Geographics* from 1949 to 2009.

"Everything's fine, Gladys," he said, locking the door. "The coyote didn't disturb anything. You must have frightened it away."

"You're sure?" Gladys asked from the safety of her living room, where she'd hidden under a purple and pink afghan. "I don't want him howling in there in the middle of the night."

"He's gone," Rupert said, dusting off his sage-green designer slacks. "You'll be fine."

Gladys dropped the afghan and came to the door. "Then won't you come in and have some milk and cookies? I made sugar cookies this morning."

Rupert backed toward the patio gate. "Thanks, but I've got to check the laundry room. The smoke detector went off again." It wasn't true, but he was *not* having cookies and milk with Gladys, especially not sugar cookies. She always coated them with a pink icing that looked like Pepto Bismol.

"Maybe a raccoon got into the dryer," Gladys said.

"I'll check it out," he said, edging out the gate.

He headed back to his office taking long, loping strides, flexing his biceps as he moved. In school he'd been the clumsy, near-sighted kid who was chosen last for every team. His father, who'd lettered in every sport known to real men, had been embarrassed to have such a wimp for a son and told him so at every opportunity. It was as if his father had wanted Rupert to fail. Like that football game in high school.

His team had been up by three, but their opponents had the ball with seconds left. They gave it to Bart Rice, the biggest damn running back in the state. Bart broke his tackles and was hell bent for glory with only Rupert between him and the goal line. Of course, Rupert wasn't supposed to be there. He'd missed his assignment, run the wrong way, and ended up shit-out-of-luck in the big bastard's path. Rupert tried to backpedal to safety, but he stumbled and fell. Next thing he knew, Bart tripped over him and crashed out of bounds. The clock expired; the stadium erupted; and Rupert was a hero. The fans yelled for him; the cheerleaders waved their pompoms at him; his teammates bumped chests with him. He'd run off the field straight for his dad, but his father had turned away. The tackle had been an accident, and his dad knew it.

Rupert rubbed and waggled his jaw. Must have been clenching again.

If he wasn't careful, his dentist would want him to wear that damn night guard twenty-four hours a day.

Thank God for cycling. He'd discovered it in college. It required neither a team nor eye-hand coordination. He didn't have to catch or throw or hit anything. And he was good at it. His father, of course, sneered. It wasn't a real sport if you wore spandex shorts with a padded butt.

Last year he'd discovered running and swimming. He was good at them too. All he had to do was ignore the pain and keep going. And if there was one thing his father had taught him, it was how to ignore the pain and keep going. Now Rupert was training for an Ironman competition. Even his father couldn't deny *that* was a real man's sport.

Except Rupert wasn't going to tell his father about the race. Or anyone else, for that matter. Not that anyone cared. But just in case.

So he trained in secret. He came early, left late, and took long lunches to run or bike up the mountains. He swam laps when the residents were at dinner. Things had been going fine until corporate sent Mrs. Babcock—aka the General. She was a royal pain in the tush. She always wanted to know what he was doing and where he was. She manufactured busywork for him to do and tracked his lunch hours. And she saved and filed everything. He'd fire her if he could, but the General was somebody's sister or aunt or something. The best he could do was avoid her and hope that a job would open up in corporate finance. He could deal with numbers. He understood numbers. Numbers were unambiguous. Their feelings didn't get hurt, and they never heard coyotes in their storage sheds or monitored someone else's lunch hours.

He ducked into the main building through a side door. Like a Navy Seal, he slipped down the hall toward his office. It would be just like Mrs. Babcock to pounce out of her own office for no good reason right now. Soundlessly, he opened his door and slid in.

"Crap!"

His desk was buried under piles of paper. On his chair Mrs. Babcock had taped her orders. "Here are the applications for the assistant director position. It would be expeditious to familiarize yourself with any objectionable candidates before your Monday breakfast meeting with

Carlotta Helmsley and the Residents' Advisory Committee. No doubt, they will want to review the applications themselves."

The Residents' Advisory Committee: what an effing nightmare that was going to be, especially with Carlotta leading the charge. Hours of his training time would be wasted.

He fingered Mrs. Babcock's note.

He had to admit the old biddy was right. If he could steer Carlotta's committee away from the objectionable applicants, this whole interview process would go a lot smoother. In fact, why not go one better? If he worked fast enough—and stalled the committee long enough—he might be able to interview and appoint an assistant director before they knew what was happening.

He sat down and began to sort through the mountain of files. He should have asked more questions on his application form, but it had taken forever to figure out the online system, and he'd wanted to post the job before breakfast to show Sandra who was boss. That was then. This was now. And now he was paying the price for the short form—and for Sandra too.

He checked his watch. If he got out of here in the next hour, he could still get in a decent training ride and make it to the post office before closing. He just needed to set up criteria that would quickly downsize the pile of papers.

First, no one from out of state. That would save time and cut expenses. In fact, no one from out of town.

He flipped through the files and eliminated half of them.

Second, no men. He would have to work with the assistant director, and he didn't want to get one of those bossy guys who always had to do it his own way. Rupert was better at avoidance than he was at confrontation.

Third, no women who identified themselves as *Mrs.* something. He intended to avoid the seriously married and their potentially intrusive families.

He checked his watch. In just fifteen minutes he had built an impressive stack of rejections. He transferred the stack from his desk to his credenza. Mrs. Babcock could deal with it on Monday.

Next, he eliminated anyone who would need to be paid more, like Roberta Ramirez with her fifteen years of experience, or Evangeline Helmsley Hill with her master's degree, or Gwen Todd, who'd actually been a director herself. And he definitely didn't want to read any supplemental materials. Like this article from Michelle Lafayette. He was not about to waste his time reading stuff like "Reversing Aging in a Retirement Community by Increasing Variety in Planned Activities." Anyone who couldn't fill out a simple form without complicating his life was toast.

He shoved the files of the over-qualified aside. In less than thirty minutes, he'd reduced the unmanageable stack of applicants to seven thin folders.

He hadn't asked for a photo or birth date, so he couldn't pick out a potential replacement for Sandra's extracurricular contributions to his life. Just as well. It had been a scare when she'd started pretending she had morning sickness.

He scanned the surviving folders and selected three applicants he was willing to consider. In an effort to preempt Carlotta's committee, he sent each applicant a brief email congratulating them on making it through the initial screening process and inviting them to participate in an interview the following week.

He sent the last invitation and checked his watch. He had time.

He grabbed the last stack of rejections—the applications of the over-qualified—and dumped them on his credenza next to the others. Then he squared the already perfectly aligned items on his desk: an executive phone with a dozen impressive but functionless buttons, a gold pen and pencil set that he never used, and a six-inch sculpture of a bicyclist made out of nuts and bolts and springs. He'd made the sculpture himself. The bike wheels actually turned.

He ran his fingertips over the now immaculate surfaces of his mahogany desk and adjoining printer stand. When the desk and printer stand were pushed together, even he had trouble seeing the seam between them. Together, they looked like one enormous desk—a desk far more imposing than any his dad had ever owned.

Rupert rose.

Halfway out the door, he realized the flaw in his plan. Even though he'd already invited candidates for interviews, Carlotta's committee still might want to review the applications themselves, and those annoying applications of the overqualified were precisely the ones they would find most appealing. Life would be much simpler if those files disappeared altogether.

He crossed the room in two quick steps and jerked open his closet. He dragged out the cardboard box that held his supply of office paper and yanked off its lid.

Perfect. There was only one ream left.

He tossed the ream onto his credenza and shoveled the applications of the overqualified into the empty box. He jammed the lid on and kicked the box into the back corner of his closet.

That should do it.

As Rupert left, he felt the tension drain from his jaw.

A second later, he returned. He opened the center drawer of his desk and fished out the envelope. It was time.

9

MONDAY MORNING MAXINE was at her desk watching the birds at her feeder when the phone rang. "Hello?"

"Maxine, can you hear me?" Louise shouted into the phone.

"Don't use that blasted speakerphone," Maxine shouted back. She'd taken Louise to one of the big-box stores to buy a speakerphone like June's, but they'd never gotten the thing to work properly. They'd be able to hear each other better if they went outside and shouted across the shuffleboard courts.

"Darn." There was a loud clatter as Louise fumbled with her handset. Then her voice returned to a normal volume. "This phone isn't worth the plastic it's made of. Maybe we should return it. At any rate, what did you want?"

"You called me," Maxine said.

"I did?" Louise seemed befuddled. "Whatever for?"

"I don't know. I just saw you at breakfast."

"That's it." Louise sounded relieved. "After you left, Rosemarie came in and told us that Carlotta's committee had just finished a breakfast meeting with Rupert."

"Whatever for?" The skin at the back of Maxine's neck began to prickle.

"They want to review the applications and help select candidates for interviews. But that's not the important part."

"It's not?" Maxine tried to be hopeful despite an insistent pounding just behind her eyes. She removed her glasses and massaged her temples.

67

"No. The important part is that last Friday, Rupert sent emails inviting three people for interviews this week."

"What!" Maxine rocketed out of her seat. "Without waiting for the committee? How dare he!" She began pacing as far as the telephone cord would allow. "What's the committee going to do?" She envisioned protest marches and sit-ins, placards and bra-burnings. Well, maybe not bra-burnings.

"They're going to review all the applications themselves. Mrs. Babcock is making copies."

Maxine slowed her pacing. "What a mess. I'm glad I'm not on that committee."

"But you *are* an applicant."

Maxine stopped pacing altogether. The pounding behind her eyes quickened into a tango. "Oh, right."

"Right! So let's go."

"Go? Go where?" Maxine was having trouble keeping up. Maybe she should get a speakerphone so she'd have her hands free to take notes.

"To check your email." Louise sounded exasperated. "To see if Rupert invited you for an interview."

Maxine's brain went blank. "Uhhh."

"I'll meet you in the library as soon as I feed Seabiscuit."

Alarms went off in Maxine's rattled brain. "Wait! I thought you just changed your oxygen tank. Are you all right?"

"I'm fine," Louise said with a bit of a wheeze. "You go ahead. I'll be right over." She disconnected before Maxine could probe or protest further.

"Damn," Maxine said, too distracted to spell.

MAXINE CIRCLED IN FRONT of the library door until Louise cantered up on Seabiscuit.

"Why didn't you go in?" Louise asked.

Maxine pointed to Fred snoring on the couch, the day's newspaper spread across his lap.

"What's *he* doing in there?" Louise asked.

"Shh. Don't wake him. He'll harangue us about all of the editorials and most of the sports stories. We'll never get rid of him. Frankly, I'm tempted to give him his own subscription to the paper so he stops lurking about in the library."

"Make it an anonymous gift, or he'll think you're trying to seduce him."

Maxine shuddered at the thought of Fred naked. "So how do we get rid of him?"

Louise flashed an innocent smile. "Tell you what," she said in an offhand way that made Maxine wary. "I'll bet you a box of Mrs. See's chocolates that I can get him out of there in less than sixty seconds."

"How are you going to do that? Fred doesn't do anything in less than a minute."

"Is it a bet?"

Although Maxine was loath to take advantage of her best friend, Louise was asking for it. "You're on," she said, motioning Louise into the library.

Louise positioned Seabiscuit next to Fred. "Ready?"

Maxine waited until the second hand on her watch was precisely at twelve. "Go!"

"Fred," Louise called loudly and shook his shoulder.

Fred stirred and slowly opened one eye.

Maxine checked her watch. Ten seconds.

"Fred, wake up!" Louise called again.

Fred opened his other eye.

Twenty seconds.

"Fred, get up!"

Fred closed both eyes.

Thirty seconds.

"Fred, Carlotta is looking for you."

Both eyes opened.

"You're supposed to be playing canasta in the recreation room right now."

"Shit!" Fred leveraged himself to his feet and stumbled out of the room, trailing clouds of newspapers.

"No fair!" Maxine signaled a technical foul. "How did you know that Carlotta wanted him?"

"I passed her on my way over." Louise smirked and tapped her watch. "How did I do?"

Maxine scowled. "Fifty-two seconds."

Louise raised her arms in a victory salute and blew kisses to an imaginary crowd of fans.

Maxine glared at her over the tops of her glasses.

"Tell you what," Louise said when the imaginary cheering finally died down. "Double or nothing. I bet it takes you over two minutes to log on and find your email."

"No thanks." Maxine plopped into the closest ergonomic chair. "I don't gamble with professionals."

"Sore loser." Louise perched on the chair next to Maxine and looked at her watch.

Maxine took a deep breath and began mashing buttons and manipulating the mouse. Without once consulting Peter's crib notes, she managed to log on and find her email.

Louise consulted her watch. "You should have taken the bet. You did it in a minute, twenty-five."

Maxine gloated. "Elementary, my dear Watson." With dramatic nonchalance, she clicked the mouse and opened her email. Her gloat morphed into a gulp. She had one message, and it was from Rupert.

"Well open it." Louise leaned closer.

Maxine pushed her chair back. "I'm not sure I want to."

A voice boomed behind them. "Well then, move over and let me see."

Maxine and Louise spun around. Celine loomed over them, larger than life in a royal blue dashiki accented with golden lions and silver giraffes.

"Where did you come from?"

"What are you doing here?"

Celine put her hands on her hips. "Well, excuse me!"

"We just meant, that is, we didn't know you were here."

Celine sniffed. "For your information, I work here."

"Oh, don't get your knickers in a knot." Maxine slapped a hand over her mouth. She couldn't have been more stunned if she'd spoken in tongues. "I'm so sorry. June's grandson says that all the time, and it just popped out."

Celine stared at her the way a kindergarten teacher might stare down an unruly child.

Louise shook her head, then pointed at the computer. "We were checking Maxine's email about—you know—the job." She looked around the room as if checking for spies. "We have to be careful. You know how rumors spread, especially when they're true."

"Well, why didn't you say so?" Celine said. "I'll turn on the vacuum cleaner. No one ever comes in here when I'm vacuuming on account of this here cheap cleaner makes more noise than a locomotive. You open it and I'll stand guard." With that she flipped on the Hoover and gave it several one-handed shoves and tugs.

Maxine tapped the desktop.

"So, open it."

Maxine's fingers refused to move. "What if Fred comes back?"

"Don't make me hurt you." Celine brandished her feather duster like a rapier. "How many times a day do you think I can pretend to vacuum this room?"

Maxine tried to speak, but this time no words came out.

Louise poked Maxine in the ribs, then pointed at the mouse.

Outnumbered, Maxine clicked on the email from Rupert.

Dear Miss Octavia Olson:

I read with interest your application to be Assistant Director at the Foothills Retirement Community. I would like to discuss the position further with you. Would you be available for an interview this Friday at 11:00?

Thank you for your interest,

Rupert Brookstone

"All right! You go, girl!" Celine swung the Hoover around in a dance move that pulled the plug out of the socket.

Maxine and Louise high-fived each other and cheered.

The three women laughed until tears came to their eyes. Victory was theirs.

Then, one by one, they fell silent until the only sound was the clicking of the infernal wall clock.

Maxine finally broke the silence. "This Friday?"

Louise pursed her lips and squinted into space the way she did when she was about to make a grand slam. A smile played at the corners of her mouth. "I bet he's thinking that if he hurries, he can preempt Carlotta's committee."

Disappointed, Maxine bent her head and massaged her temples. "So?"

"So, that's not such a bad idea. You should go ahead and accept the interview before Carlotta can interfere."

Maxine raised her head and lowered her hands. Louise was right. "But Friday? I need more time to prepare—about fifty years more."

"Girlfriend, you've got another problem." Celine plugged the noisy Hoover back into the outlet and propped it in the doorway. "I know Rupert's not the sharpest knife in the drawer, but don't you think he'll notice that you're Maxine, a resident, and not Octavia, a potential bunny squeeze?"

Maxine melted in a full-body slump. "Celine's right. If Rupert knows it's me, he won't hire me. I'm too old to do the bunny hop with him."

"But that's age discrimination." Louise banged her fists on the table. "You have the right to do the bunny hop with him!"

Maxine looked at her friend for several moments. "I think you may have lost the point. I don't *want* to do the bunny hop with him: I want to *be* the assistant director."

"Oh, right." Louise sagged into her chair.

Celine drew herself up to her full and imposing height. "Don't you two be giving up on me, now. You gotta go for this job precisely *because* Rupert would turn you down on account of your age."

Maxine and Louise shrank into their chairs.

Celine narrowed her eyes, "But, of course, if you want Mrs. Helmsley to select someone else to be your new assistant director, that's no business of mine."

Louise snapped to attention. "Good heavens. No! There's no telling who she'd come up with."

"But an interview?" Maxine said.

"What you need is a holograph projector," Celine said. "Something that makes it *look* like you're there, when you're *not*."

Louise readjusted her oxygen. "What we really need is something that makes it look like she's *not* there, when she *is*."

"Yeah," Celine agreed. "Like an invisibility cloak, or like that computer game Alternate Universe. My nephew says it has totally taken over the computer lab at his middle school."

Maxine looked up. "What did you say?"

"Alternate Universe? It's this really cool game with dungeons and dragons and transformers and transporters and—"

"A *computer* game?" Maxine said.

"Girl, that's what I'm saying."

"That's it." Maxine shoved herself out of her chair. "You're a genius. You're both geniuses. I'll drive." She looked at Celine. "Right after work."

"Where are we going?" Louise asked.

"To talk to Peter. He can make a computer do anything."

"Who's Peter?" Celine said.

Maxine beamed. "My godson. You might have noticed his photo in my condo."

"And on my mantel," Louise said. "He's the good-looking young man standing between us."

Celine frowned. "You mean the tall guy?"

Louise nodded like a bobble-head doll. "Yes, that's him!"

Celine raised her eyebrows. "He's black."

Louise froze.

Maxine's eyes turned to steel. "Is *that* a problem?"

"Seriously?" Celine stared at them over her glasses. "*That's* a recommendation."

10

MAXINE PULLED INTO Peter's driveway just as he stepped out of his silver Prius. He grinned and waved and in two strides was opening her door.

"Are we too early?" Maxine asked, getting out of her car.

"Never!" Peter gave her a bear hug that lifted her off the ground. Then he gave Louise an equally large, but more careful hug—one that did not crush or crimp her air hose.

Turning to Celine, Peter held out his hand. "Hi. I'm Peter."

Celine took half a step back, as if worried Peter might start swinging her around too. "I am Celine Dianne Jackson." She extended her hand, but she looked and sounded stiff.

"Celine Dianne Jackson!" Peter's eyes sparkled. "That's perfect! You look just like that other Celine. Well, not just like her, but she has your smile. Do you sing too?"

Celine nodded almost bashfully.

Maxine smiled. Peter's enthusiasm was infectious.

"What kind of music?" Peter asked and began herding them toward his door.

"Jesus, Mary Mother of God, and Joseph of Nazareth! Look at that!" Celine pointed into Peter's garage.

"That's Old Betsy," Peter said. "My first car. Maxine gave her to me. Want to take a look?"

"I've done died and gone to heaven." Celine moved as if in a trance to the old convertible. She reached out a hand but paused inches from the car's vinyl pinpoint top in a gesture reminiscent of the ceiling of the Sistine Chapel—the part where Adam's hand receives life from God. "This here's a '56 Chevrolet Bel Air in Sherwood Green and India Ivory."

Peter jammed his hands in his pockets and rocked up and down on his toes. "Isn't she a beauty?"

Celine stroked the hood. "This was my husband's dream car. We had a calendar picture of it over our bed."

Maxine gaped, Louise gasped, and Seabiscuit snorted.

"What husband?"

Celine moved on without hearing. "Look! It even has the optional wire wheel hubcaps."

Peter opened the door and motioned her into the driver's seat. "Get in. I've taken the battery out, so we can't take her for a ride, but you can still get a sense of her."

Celine caressed the dashboard with her fingertips and started humming "Amazing Grace."

"What husband?" Maxine and Louise asked each other.

Peter clambered into the passenger side and started pointing out dials and gauges.

Maxine and Louise peered in the driver's window.

"What husband?" they said.

"The one I used to have," Celine said and rolled up the car window.

PETER'S CONDO WAS furnished with a surprising collection of restored Modernist furniture in primary colors. Unable to afford other people's artwork, he'd decorated the walls with his own photographs. Maxine's favorites were the magnified close-ups: a drop of rain suspended in a spider web; the needles of a teddy bear cholla turned to gold by a shaft of sunlight; the bark of a mesquite tree after a rare dusting of snow.

"I have a new photo you'll like." Peter handed Maxine a glass of unsweetened sun tea. He gestured across the room. "Over my desk."

Maxine turned and inhaled sharply. Even from this distance, the photo was stunning. Peter had caught a cactus wren peering from a hole in the top of a saguaro. "Oh my!"

Peter beamed. "Wait until you get closer. I was playing with a new telephoto lens and didn't realize what I'd caught until I printed it."

While Louise and Celine settled next to the cheese and crackers, Maxine and Peter crossed the room to inspect the photo. Reflected in the wren's eye was a miniature desert landscape in minute detail. Maxine could identify individual plants and even count the spikes on the closest ocotillo. And the mountain ridge in the background was unmistakably Pusch Peak, Tom's favorite hike.

"Peter, it's fabulous. How did you do it?"

"No idea."

Maxine moved closer to the picture. "I love how the circles draw us in, from the hole in the cactus, to the wren's head, to her eye, to its pupil."

Peter nodded. "And then the surprise. In the smallest circle of all, a perfect reflection of a circle beyond the photo's frame."

"The harmony of the spheres caught by a digital lens." Maxine spoke more to herself than to Peter. She looked out the window to the riverbed and cottonwoods where she and Peter hiked on each other's birthdays. Despite the difference in age, they hiked well together. Each loved to walk in silence and listen to the desert. Each preferred savoring small details—an unusual insect or brightly colored stone—to clocking miles or conquering peaks. The photo captured that spirit.

She turned back to the wren's eye. "Everything is simultaneously much simpler and more complex than we ever imagine."

Peter rocked on his toes. "I knew you'd understand."

They studied the photo in silence for several minutes. Behind them, Maxine could hear Celine and Louise debating the relative merits of speakerphones and cell phones. Maxine turned.

Louise gave her an almost imperceptible nod.

Maxine steered Peter back to the couches, then cleared her throat. "Speaking of things that aren't as simple as they seem, we need your advice. I have a job interview this Friday. I can't go to the interview, but I want the job."

Peter nodded as if that were an everyday request. "If you can't go to the interview, can it come to you? We could use my computer's camera and microphone to do an interview. It would be almost as good as face-to-face."

Louise shook her head. "There's the rub. Rupert can't know it's her."

"Rupert?" Peter turned to Maxine. "Your Rupert?"

Maxine shrugged. "Well, he's not mine, but yes, Rupert. I want to be the assistant director at the Foothills, but Rupert would never consider me."

Peter's eyes darted back and forth as if he were sorting options.

"OK," he said, leaning forward. "Tell Rupert you'll be out of town, but you'll be happy to arrange a webcam interview. He'll think he's going to see you and talk with you, but we'll manufacture some technical difficulties so that all he gets is a blurred picture and no audio. The two of you will type your questions and answers like a live chat."

A chill raced down Maxine's spine. She wasn't out of the game yet. She lifted an eyebrow at Louise who raised her own eyebrows in reply. Maxine pumped her fist. It was a plan.

Celine cleared her throat and set her glass of sun tea on the coffee table with a *click*. "I hate to be a party pooper, but if Rupert's more interested in finding his next bunny squeeze than in hiring an assistant director, won't he insist on seeing a photo or something?"

Peter's eyes did some more darting. "Not necessarily." His fingers twitched on an invisible keyboard. "If the servers were crossed, Rupert might receive an image of someone and erroneously assume it was you. The mistake would be his, especially if you told him that your camera was not working."

Celine waved her hand like an eager student. "I've got it. I've got it. I've got the perfect someone, if you can cross the computer thingies."

"Who?" Louise asked.

"How?" Maxine said.

"Just leave it to us." Peter winked at Celine.

"All right!" Celine rubbed her hands together. "Meet me at Benny's Bar and Grill tonight at nine o'clock sharp. This is going to be fun."

Everyone turned expectantly toward Maxine.

She studied her motley, generous band of co-conspirators. Damn the torpedoes: if anyone could pull off this cockamamie scheme, they could. She hoisted her sun tea. "Game on."

"Game on," they chorused.

While her friends congratulated each other, Maxine looked across the room to Peter's photo. The unblinking eye of the cactus wren stared back. Worlds within worlds, indeed.

11

MAXINE PAUSED TO take inventory: purse, keys, granola bar, water bottle, and a mini flashlight on her keychain. Some kind of flashlight was standard equipment at the Foothills. No one wanted to trip over an errant rock and break a hip. In reality, about the only time she ever used her flashlight was to read menus in dimly lit restaurants.

Her gear in order, she shifted into drive.

Louise waited outside her apartment dressed in black: black slacks, black top, and a black pashmina that looked more like a blanket than a scarf.

Maxine got out of the car and studied Louise over the top of her glasses.

"What?" Louise said.

Maxine raised one eyebrow.

"I borrowed it from Rosemarie," Louise said. "I wanted to look the part."

"And what part is that?" Maxine asked, opening the passenger door.

"Well, I couldn't quite decide whether I should be a vamp or a spy," Louise said as she arranged herself and her oxygen canister in the car.

"Go for the vamp. I think it's the real you." Maxine closed the door, stabled Seabiscuit in the trunk, and slid behind the steering wheel once more.

Louise flipped down the visor mirror and studied her reflection. "I'm not sure I have the right shade of lipstick for vamp. Do you think this Dragon's Blood Red will do?"

Maxine looked at the new lipstick. "No one will recognize you, that's for sure."

Louise stared at Maxine. "Surely we won't see anyone we know!"

"What if we saw Rupert there? Or Fred?"

"Or Fred *with* Carlotta!"

"Wouldn't they die?" Maxine edged her car out of the parking lot and onto the divided road.

"I can't believe they still think no one knows they're dating."

"The thing is," Maxine said, flicking on her turn signal to change lanes even though there were no other cars in sight, "I don't think anyone cares, do you?"

"No. They're consenting adults. She's a widow, and he's a widower."

"Besides, they make the perfect couple: who else would have either of them?"

Maxine lapsed into silence and concentrated on the drive. Although cataract surgery had helped, the glare from streetlights and headlights still made it hard to see at night. She gripped the steering wheel with both hands and leaned forward slightly. Next to her, she knew Louise was also leaning into the dark, watching the traffic, helping her navigate through the night.

Thirty minutes later, Maxine pulled into a parking space in front of Benny's. They remained in the car. She pushed the door lock button and left the engine running. Benny's was not in the best section of town. Not that Maxine had ever actually been to this section of town, but the street reminded her of an Alfred Hitchcock movie set: it was narrow, dark, and deserted. At the corner, an ineffectual shaft of light leaked from a solitary streetlamp and puddled onto the pavement without illuminating anything.

Benny's itself was a dingy adobe affair with two plate glass windows so dark they revealed only shadowy figures and a small blob of pool-hall green light. Over the door, a surprisingly discreet neon sign announced in blue letters that this was *Benny's Bar and Grill*. Maxine gave Benny credit for including the apostrophe and avoiding the ampersand in his sign. Grammatical precision probably cost extra in neon.

She fidgeted and checked the rear-view mirror. She half expected to spot Hitchcock's signature silhouette disappearing down an alley, but nothing stirred: no cars, no people, not even a scrap of newspaper blowing down the empty street. The only sound was the soft "tap, tap, tap" of Louise patting her pockets.

"What on earth are you hunting for?" Maxine asked. "I hope you're not going to pull out a gun."

"No, just this," Louise pulled out a can of pepper spray.

Maxine jerked back and shielded her head with her hands. "Do you even know how to use that?"

"The instructions said to hold the lever, pull the pin, and toss." Louise mimed the action.

"That's for a grenade, not pepper spray."

"Oh right," Louise said a tad too innocently. "I had trouble deciding which to buy. The man at the Army-Navy Surplus Store recommended the spray and night-vision goggles."

A figure emerged from the dark and pounded on Maxine's window.

Louise screamed.

Maxine jumped and hit the horn.

"Come on, girlfriends," Celine called through the closed window. "It's time to boogie. And don't be making so much noise out here. People in Benny's are trying to drink."

Celine was dressed in a skin-tight red dress that sparkled when the light caught it. "How do you like it?" She slowly rotated in front of them. "Thought I might as well dig out one of my old bouncer costumes. It doesn't hurt to be prepared."

INSIDE, BENNY'S WAS LOUD, crowded, and dark. In front of them, a spotlight revealed a small stage, empty except for a microphone and a battered piano. To the right, a mirrored bar glittered its welcome. Behind the counter, a bleached blonde of indeterminate age glided about making drinks, making change, making small talk with patrons hunched on their stools or propped on the bar.

As her eyes adjusted to the light, Maxine saw that most of the tables were occupied. Everyone had a drink and a stack of cardboard coasters emblazoned with beer logos. That was it. No frills. No neon martini glasses or pink flamingos. No candles. Nothing that could be turned into a weapon or hurled across the room. Nonetheless, the hairs on the back of her neck began to tingle as if she were being watched.

"Celine!" A commanding voice rang out from across the room.

The bar fell silent. Everyone turned toward the speaker.

A tall redhead dressed in a slinky emerald green cocktail dress and white feather boa rushed over and pecked the air on either side of Celine's cheeks.

Celine pecked back and beamed.

"Ladies, this here is Fermez La Bouche, the best drag queen this side of the Mississippi. By night, a beautiful, if grossly underpaid bouncer at Benny's, and by day, a mild-mannered massage therapist at Shady Acres Hospice Home."

"Shady Acres?" Shady Acres had helped several of Maxine's friends exit this world for the next. Too many friends, really. But when her own time came, Maxine wanted to go there. Well, actually, she wanted to go the way Tom had—at home, asleep in his bed, under his own sheets and blankets. But if she couldn't go like that, she wanted to go via Shady Acres.

Fermez extended a gloved and bejeweled hand. "Bon soir. Welcome to zee Ben-neez."

Maxine shook the regal hand. There was something about Fermez that seemed familiar. When she turned to greet Louise, the light fell across her aristocratic nose and dimpled chin, and Maxine gave a start of recognition. "Alan?"

"Shh!" Fermez glanced furtively around the room. "Not tonight I'm not."

"Oh, yes. Of course," Maxine said. "It's just that you were, or rather, he was such a comfort to one of our dear friends, Anika Nordstrom. She had bone cancer throughout her whole body. Couldn't get out of bed. Alan read poetry to her. I never thanked you, or rather him, for . . ." Maxine faltered, overcome by sudden tears.

Fermez's beautifully lashed eyes turned soft. "In the end, Anika went quite peacefully, you know. She simply smiled and slipped away."

Maxine bit her lip and nodded.

Louise clasped Fermez's hand in both of hers. "Thank you for . . . for all that you did for . . ." She broke off and fished a packet of tissues from her purse. She handed one to Maxine and used another to blot her eyes.

Fermez began to blink back tears of her own.

"Oh no you don't!" Celine snatched Louise's packet of tissues and shoved it at Fermez. "Don't you get started. You'll ruin your makeup, and we'll be here all night waiting for you to fix it."

Fermez delicately dabbed her eyes. "You know me so well, mon ami." Her voice returned to its faux French accent. "So, what brings vous to zee Ben-neez? I hope you don't want zee old job back. I'm quite attached to zee income."

"No way, girlfriend. The wardrobe is too expensive. Give me the cleaning life." Despite her avowed disinterest, Celine scanned Benny's as if she owned it. "We're here to see Mimi. Can you let her know?"

"Mais oui." Fermez leaned closer and lowered her voice. "Her set is about to start. She has to be her own accompanist tonight, JJ's got the flu. Take the staff table and I'll let her know you're here."

With a toss of her boa, Fermez swished her way across the room. Celine guided Maxine and Louise to a small round table at the back. "We save this table for ourselves. It's got a good view of the room, easy access, and even easier egress." She pointed to a door just behind them.

Maxine perched on the edge of her chair, ready to take flight at the slightest provocation. She ran her hand over the tabletop. Although their table bore the gouges and stains of the centuries, someone had recently coated the top with half an inch of polyurethane, which glowed a comforting yellow-gold. Maxine absently traced her finger over a carving of a coyote howling at a heart-shaped moon. She tried to think of a polite way to suggest they get the heck out of Benny's. "You know, Celine, I'm beginning to think that coming here was not such a good idea."

Celine's smile vanished and her chin jutted ever so slightly. "What's the matter? Don't you like Benny's?"

"No, no. That's not it," Maxine said. "Benny's is . . ."

"Interesting?" Louise said.

"No . . ." Maxine saw Celine's lower lip begin to pout. "Yes. I mean Benny's is lovely."

Celine snorted.

"All right, Benny's isn't exactly *lovely*, but it's better than *interesting*— that word covers a multitude of sins."

Louise nodded as if that were precisely what she had meant in the first place.

Celine narrowed her eyes at Louise.

"What I mean," Maxine said, "is that I don't feel right asking a stranger to help us."

"Mimi's not a stranger to me," Celine said.

"Yes, but—"

Maxine was interrupted by a loud burst of static.

"Sorry, dahlings!" Fermez cooed into the microphone. "I didn't mean to get you all . . ." She paused, winked, and swayed her torso along the microphone stand before continuing in a throaty voice, "I didn't mean to get you all . . . excited." She breathed the last word into the microphone and a man at a table to the far right let out a whoop.

"Goodness," Louise said, patting her hair. "I never knew a microphone could be so, so . . ." She looked at Maxine for help.

"Vibrant?" Maxine said.

Celine nodded. "Oh, yes. Fermez's good. When she starts doing her Marilyn Monroe imitation, the men sit up and notice. If you know what I mean."

Maxine tried not to think about what Celine might mean.

"And when she does her Mae West, they get flat out . . . alert. But don't worry. She won't get to Mae West for a couple of hours. Right now, she's going to introduce Mimi."

"Ladies and gentlemen and anybody else," Fermez's voice purred through the sound system. "For your listening pleasure, straight from the Windy City, the Fever herself, Miss Mimi La Fievre."

Mimi's soft, sun-blonde hair and delicate features projected a curious aura of innocence and sensuality. She wore a strapless black evening gown and a single strand of pearls. Where Fermez went for raw sensuality, Mimi went for classic simplicity. She floated to the piano, sat down, and smiled at her audience—a smile that said *You know me better than anyone in the world.* Then she began to sing "There Will Never Be Another You."

Celine leaned forward. "I can sing some pretty hot torch songs myself, but no one can get them to smolder the way Mimi can."

A waitress with hip-hugger jeans and an exposed midriff slunk over to take their orders. Celine ordered a tonic and Tanqueray without the Tanqueray. "I'm here on business," she said.

Maxine went for a screwdriver, but asked the wait to hold the vodka. "I'm the designated driver."

Louise looked at them with disgust. "I thought this was going to be a Ladies' Night Out." She turned to the wait. "I'll take a double Scotch—Glenmorangie, on the rocks."

When the wait explained that Benny's only carried bargain-brand scotch, Louise changed her order to decaf tea with lemon.

MIMI'S VOICE WAS low and sultry, perfect for her selection of songs from the '40s and '50s.

Maxine closed her eyes and listened as Mimi sang "Love Is Here to Stay."

It reminded her of her courting days. Tom on her parents' front stoop, shuffling from one foot to another, a bouquet of handpicked flowers clutched in his fist. Tom in a gray pinstriped suit, holding her on the dance floor, humming along with the band, slightly off-key.

Mimi improvised a musical bridge to "Unforgettable."

Maxine inhaled sharply.

Tom. Always and forever, Tom. Maxine squeezed her eyes against the tears. Beside her, Louise gave a ragged sigh. Mimi could sing the songs—sing them beautifully—but Maxine and Louise had lived them.

WHEN HER SET ENDED, Mimi joined them. Although Mimi had appeared to be in her mid-thirties on the stage, in person Maxine could see that she was closer to her mid-twenties.

"Celine! How are you?" Mimi embraced Celine.

Celine returned the hug, then cocked an eyebrow at Maxine.

Maxine shook her head an emphatic No.

Celine cut to the chase before Maxine could object. "My friends and I need a little acting job, and we think you'd be perfect in the role. What do you say?"

Mimi's eyes grew wide with astonishment. "Acting? Me?"

"Of course not, dear." Maxine rose to leave. "You must be terribly busy. It was thoughtless of us to ask. We just let our imaginations carry us away. I'm so sorry."

Celine grabbed Maxine's hand and pulled her back down. "This would be for a couple of hours during lunch this Friday. Maxine wants a job where she lives, but the director won't hire her unless he thinks he can get her to dance the hoochie koochie with him on the side, and she doesn't want to, and frankly I don't blame her, not that Rupert isn't good looking, but the man's got the personality of overcooked pasta."

Mimi looked a trifle confused, so Maxine tried to clarify. "We were hoping you would pretend to be me for a webcam interview with cross-stitched wires."

"Criss-crossed servers," Louise said.

"Right," Celine said. "Something goes kerblooey with the computer. Rupert ends up with your picture and Maxine's answers to his lame questions."

They all stopped talking and looked at Mimi, who continued to look a trifle confused.

Fermez, who had been lurking within earshot, undulated over. "Allow me to translate, if I may." She paused.

Celine shrugged.

Fermez struck a pose worthy of a *Vogue* cover. "Rupert sees Mimi looking young and lovely and perfectly professional. He falls in lust, and Maxine gets the job."

"Girl, that's what I'm saying," Celine said.

Fermez swished her hips, flapped her boa, and flashed a coy smile.

Celine crossed her arms. "Nuh-uh."

Fermez batted her eyelashes and smiled provocatively.

"No way," Celine said.

Fermez airily waved an arm. "I'll do it."

Maxine and Louise exchanged glances.

"What?" Fermez asked.

Maxine cleared her throat. "The thing is, Rupert's a bit of a . . . well I don't know what he is. But I think he could be easily intimidated."

"I can fix that." Fermez winked.

"I mean, he'd be smitten with you," Maxine said. "But you're way out of his league."

Louise tried to help. "If he saw you in that gown, for instance, he'd pass out."

Fermez flicked her boa. "You mean he'd be horny as a bull, but too chicken to leave the coop."

Maxine and Louise exchanged glances again, each hoping the other would speak up. Finally, Maxine nodded. "Well, yes. I guess you could put it that way."

Fermez drew herself up into a persecuted Marlene Dietrich pose, or perhaps it was a Lauren Bacall moment.

Mimi placed a placating hand on Fermez's arm. "I don't know Rupert, but I can see how Fermez might be too . . . too much of a good thing for him to process all at once. Rupert probably needs someone less dazzling, more bureaucratic, more . . . mundane."

Fermez drew back in distaste.

Mimi pressed her advantage. "You simply aren't mundane, Fermez. I have more practice at it. Think about it. By day, I work as an events coordinator in the State Office of Tourism. What could be less glamorous?"

Fermez shuddered.

"Let me take the first crack at Rupert," Mimi said. "If that doesn't work, we'll call on you for the knock-out punch."

Fermez pondered the proposition, then stepped aside. "You may have Rupert; I'll take glamour." With that, she sailed away.

Celine turned to Mimi. "You have any idea what movie that last scene was from?"

Mimi shook her head. "No, but she was very convincing."

Maxine fanned herself with a beer coaster. "Goodness, that was close. Fermez might have been a tad . . . excessive."

Mimi's eyes filled with laughter. "Fermez's only excessive on her down days. The rest of the time she's over-the-top outrageous."

"You've got that right," Celine said. "If Fermez had done the interview, there's no telling what Rupert would have wanted to hire you to do. Thank goodness we've got Mimi instead."

"I'll do my best," Mimi said.

Maxine pressed her palms on the table as if to restore order. "Thank you for saving me from Fermez, but I don't want you to feel obligated to participate in our charade. I suspect we haven't even explained it very well."

Mimi laughed a deep, throaty laugh. "I have no idea what you're up to, but count me in anyway. Celine got me this job, so I owe her one."

Celine busied herself rearranging the already neatly stacked beer coasters on their table. "Girl, you don't owe me anything. People tipped better when you sang. That's all."

Mimi put her hand over Celine's.

Celine pretended not to notice, but she stopped stacking the coasters.

The microphone spat out another burst of static. Fermez was back onstage.

Mimi rose. "I need to go back to work. Can you stay another set?"

"With pleasure." Maxine smiled.

AFTER HER SECOND SET, Mimi rejoined the table, and Maxine explained more fully both her plight and their plan.

"As you can tell," Maxine said with a crooked smile, "it's really a long shot, but—"

Mimi waved her hands. "No 'buts' about it," she said. "I'd be honored to help, and Rupert will be lucky if you decide to accept his job."

Louise applauded and Celine ordered another round of drinks to seal the deal. Fermez reappeared with the drinks and began an impassioned discussion with Louise and Celine on the accessory value of fishnet stockings and elbow-length gloves.

Maxine turned to Mimi. "I don't know how to thank you. You're very kind."

Mimi blushed and dipped her head. "It's my pleasure. Really."

She looked as embarrassed as Maxine felt. To spare them both, Maxine changed the subject. "So, are you a native of Tucson?"

"No. I'm from a suburb of Chicago."

"Me too," Maxine said. "Which one?"

"Wheaton."

"I'm from Glen Ellyn! We're neighbors."

Mimi's eyes sparkled. "I loved to ice skate on Lake Ellyn."

"My daughter, Katie, practically lived at the lake. She skated on it in winter, fished in it in summer, and ran cross country around it in high school." Maxine smiled at the memories. "I loved Glen Ellyn. Never wanted to leave."

"What brought you to Tucson?" Mimi asked.

"Winter," Maxine said. "We retired from work and decided to retire from snow shovels at the same time." She absently sorted beer coasters by color. "What brought you to Tucson?"

"Graduate school, but once I was here, I fell in love with the mountains. After graduation, there were no job openings in my field, so I took a job with the state."

Maxine leaned closer. She was having trouble hearing over the din of the bar. "Do you ever miss your field?"

The corners of Mimi's mouth turned up in a crooked grin. "Oh, I'm still looking for jobs. The right one will come along one day."

"What kind of job do you want?"

The microphone squawked again. "Sorry, dahlings," Fermez purred into the mike.

Mimi shook her head. "I think Fermez deliberately over-amps the microphone to quiet the crowd."

Fermez flashed a surprisingly seductive smile. "Are you glad to see me?" She paused and winked. "Or is that a pistol in—"

"Oh, dear." Mimi jumped up. "She's onto Mae West already. I've got to go, but I'll see you Friday."

12

MAXINE STRAIGHTENED HER already neat stack of index cards. All week long, Louise, Celine, Peter, and even Mimi had been giving her potential questions to practice before tomorrow's interview. But frankly, she was bored.

She leaned her elbows on the desk and watched a cactus wren work on its nest in the saguaro outside her window. She'd already invested a fair amount of time observing a rabbit as it sorted through her plants, rejecting the orange marigolds in favor of the red geraniums.

The ringing of the phone jolted her back to reality. She stretched a hand toward it, but stopped inches from the receiver.

It was probably Louise calling to nag her about the practice questions.

The phone continued to ring.

Then again, it might be Peter calling to say he couldn't get the servers crossed.

She grabbed the receiver. "Hello. Peter?"

"Mother? This is Katherine."

"Katie!" Maxine snapped to attention. "What a lovely surprise."

"You act as if I never call you."

"No." Maxine readjusted the phone. "I just meant it's the middle of the workday for you, isn't it?"

"Actually, I'm between meetings. In fact, I'm calling about business, in a way."

"Really?" Maxine couldn't imagine that. She understood neither Katie's work nor her world in which cyber-chat passed for communication and electronic gizmos substituted for companionship.

"I'm in Phoenix with a new client. I was supposed to take the red-eye back to New York for a meeting on Friday, but the meeting's been postponed. Jerry Fulsome's blown another project, and they're all off doing damage control." Katie hesitated. "And I thought—if you're not busy—perhaps I could catch an early flight to Tucson tomorrow morning, spend the day, and fly back to New York first thing Saturday morning."

Maxine nearly dropped the receiver. Katie never came to Tucson. Maxine had to fly to New York. Not that Maxine minded. Katie's apartment, with its fashionable Central Park West address, epitomized understated elegance. Being there was like living in a modern painting: a crisp white-on-white canvas with startling accents of turquoise and vermillion. Along one wall, an enormous aquarium gurgled and glowed, its soft light shimmering on iridescent corals and exotic fish that a designer had selected to match the splashes of color in the room. Katie's housekeeper fed and maintained the fish. Maxine had no idea what one did to maintain fish. She suspected that the housekeeper simply bought replacement fish in matching colors whenever an original died.

"Mother?"

Maxine shook herself and refocused. "That would be wonderful! Can you stay the weekend?" She knew she shouldn't ask, but she couldn't stop herself.

The reply was automatic. "No, I need to get back to work."

In the background, Maxine could hear people asking Katie about rates and rollouts. "Mother, hold on a minute. I'll be right back." There was a click and the line rolled over to canned music.

Maxine clutched the phone to her ear and tried to imagine what was behind Katie's visit.

At forty-four, Katie was the youngest person—and the only woman—to make managing director at Littlehouse, Ferris, and Jones, one of New

York's premier investment banking firms. But to Maxine, Katie's life seemed devoid of happiness.

The canned music began to repeat itself. Maxine moved the phone to her other ear.

"I'm back," Katie said. "I can't stay the weekend. I need to work. In fact, I will need to do a conference call mid-morning, but I thought we might have dinner at that restaurant Dad used to love off River Road. Is it still there?"

"It is, and the prime rib still melts in your mouth."

"Good. I'll rent a car and be there in time for your second cup of tea."

Maxine would have picked Katie up anytime, anywhere, but she knew better than to offer. The rental car was Katie's security blanket. It left her free to flee anytime anyone came too close.

In the background, the din of voices calling for Katie began to swell again.

"I'll be right there," Katie said to the voices. Then she was back on the phone. "I've got to go, Mother. See you tomorrow for tea."

"Love you," Maxine said into the dead line. It didn't matter. Katie was coming.

Maxine wiped her eyes with the back of one hand while attempting to hang up the phone with the other. In the process, she knocked over the stack of interview questions. Index cards spread across her desk like a paper tidal wave.

"D.A.M.N."

The interview! She couldn't let Katie find out about the damn interview. She'd never approve. As a child, Katie had resented Maxine's teaching. She'd wanted a stay-at-home mom like all the other kids.

Maxine's hands trembled as she tried to sweep the index cards into a stack.

She'd have been a terrible stay-at-home mother. The days would have been too long and empty. She'd have ended up lonely, angry, stupid, and neurotic. Nonetheless . . .

Maxine's eyes misted, and she gave up trying to straighten the index cards.

If Katie had resented Maxine's teaching as a child, as an adult she'd think Maxine foolish for even considering a job. Katie would feel embarrassed, responsible, and resentful.

Maxine needed help.

"We have a problem," Maxine said.

"What? I can't hear you," Louise shouted. Evidently, she was trying the speakerphone again.

In the background, something clattered. Maxine heard Celine tell Louise to turn up the volume.

"How?" Louise asked, still shouting.

Maxine heard a shuffling noise and then a clicking sound.

"Try it now," Celine said. "Maxine, say something."

"Whan that Aprille with his shoures soote . . ." Maxine intoned.

"Something in English," Celine said.

"That was Middle English."

"Much better." Louise spoke in a normal volume. "Celine fixed the phone. Now if I could just fix the caller."

"Very funny, but I do need fixing. Katie is coming tomorrow morning and staying until Saturday."

"How wonderful!"

In the background, Maxine could hear Celine moving something—dishes perhaps—and singing "Too Darn Hot."

"Yes, but what am I going to do with her?" Maxine said.

"Go out to lunch. Go shopping. Go to the Desert Museum." Louise started to list possibilities.

"The interview. What about the interview? She mustn't know about that."

There was a mysterious thump, and Celine stopped singing.

Louise cleared her throat. "Well . . ."

Maxine shifted the phone to her other ear and began to pace as far as the cord would allow. "Well?"

"Give me a moment."

Maxine wiped her hands on her slacks and tried to remember how to do yoga breaths.

"I know," Louise said. "Tell her you have a bridge tournament and can't find a substitute. Then arrange something else for her to do."

"Like what?"

"Like a massage," Celine said in a voice so clear she must have been standing next to the phone. "Everybody loves a massage. Fermez can give her one. Fermez gives the best massages in Tucson."

"Do you think she would?" Maxine asked.

"I know she would. Her nose has been out of joint ever since we asked for Mimi's help and not hers."

Maxine stopped pacing and sank onto her desk chair. "That might just work."

"Good," Louise spoke in her take-control voice—the voice that usually signaled trouble. "Now that we've settled that, how's it going?"

Maxine poised for flight or fight. "How's what going?"

"The interview questions. Aren't you practicing interview questions?"

Maxine tapped a rapid tattoo on the phone's disconnect button. "What? Can't hear you," she shouted. "Must be that speakerphone." She hung up.

In front of her, the unanswered interview questions lay in disarray.

Outside, the cactus wren sunned herself on the top of the saguaro. Evidently *her* chores were done for the day. Lucky her.

13

OVER THE TOP of her mug, Maxine studied her daughter. Katie had been right. The early flight from Phoenix had gotten her to Tucson in time for a second mug of tea on Maxine's patio.

Katie was a beautiful woman: tall and elegant, with a pianist's perfect posture, even sitting as she was now with one leg curled under her. Yet something of the child showed in the wistful way she looked at the mountains and toyed with her mug. The woman was beautiful, but the child was troubled. It was time to find out what her unexpected visit was all about, but Maxine didn't know how to start.

Katie blew on her tea. "Remember when we hiked the Ape's Head?"

The question startled Maxine. The Ape's Head was the name Katie had given to the top of Table Mountain, where dark green vegetation splashed across the stark white rock in sharp contrast to the muted blue-gray-browns of the surrounding range. With a little imagination, the peak looked like a recumbent ape.

"From the first moment your father and I moved to Tucson, I wanted to climb that mountain," Maxine said. "I tried to climb it a million times with my hiking buddies, but we never made it."

"It was a bitch of a climb," Katie said.

Maxine nodded. "It was the hardest climb I've ever done. Once was enough."

"Those shin daggers were horrible. Like slogging through miles of razor wire."

"Miles and miles and miles," Maxine said. Her daughter hated it when Maxine exaggerated for the sake of a story. She enjoyed catching Katie doing it herself.

Katie's eyes sparkled. "I swear I had the points of every one of those bloody plants in my legs by the time we got to the top."

"You were a good sport to go with me."

"It was a birthday present, wasn't it?" Katie said. "How old were you?"

"Sixty-eight. And it was the best present ever. You even brought Champagne and cupcakes and a candle. Remember?"

"I thought we should do it right, if we were going to bushwhack our way up there."

"I'm glad you did. I've still got that cork."

"You're kidding!"

"No. It's my trophy. I keep it in my jewelry box."

"Well then," Katie puffed out her chest. "I still have the jeans I tore on those cacti. They're my trophy."

"Seriously?"

A crooked grin tugged at the corners of Katie's mouth. "They were my favorite jeans. They're so worn now that you can see through them, but I can't bring myself to throw them out." Her grin dissolved into a self-dismissive smile. "It's like I'm keeping my options open."

"But it's good to keep your options open."

Katie stared into her mug. The steam rose around her hazel eyes, masking the lines and making her look younger. "I'm thinking about my options now."

Maxine willed herself to remain still.

"I'm fairly certain I could demand a promotion to partner and LF&J would have to give it to me. I control an extraordinary percentage of their revenue. Or, I could take my clients and start my own company." Katie ticked off her options with analytical precision. "Or, I guess I could retire early."

"I don't think you could retire; you'd be lost."

Katie slammed her mug on the table and stood up so fast that she startled the cactus wren off its saguaro. She glared at her mother much the way she had as an adolescent.

Maxine flicked an imaginary crumb off her slacks. "That wasn't a criticism," she said. "Your passion is solving problems, creating order from chaos, and harmony from discord. You shouldn't stop doing that. But you could change careers: create a different kind of harmony, another type of order."

As quickly as it had flashed, Katie's anger morphed into thoughtful silence. "I wasn't really serious about retirement." She sat down. "But I've never thought about changing careers. Just venues."

The cactus wren resettled on its nest.

Maxine blew on her tea with studied indifference. "It's another option. If you're getting ready to make a change anyway, you might want to consider all your options. That's all."

"You're right."

Maxine placed her mug on the table to keep from dropping it. "So tell me about it."

Katie stared into the distance. "I'm not sure where to start. LF&J has been wildly successful, but they take unnecessary risks. I sometimes feel I'm the lone voice of reason, the only one asking the questions the others skip over in their rush to close the deal and log the next bonus."

"They must like your questions," Maxine said. "They keep plying you with work."

Katie backhanded the air as if shooing away an annoying insect or unhappy memory. "They played me like a baby grand."

Uncertain which of a million possible questions to ask, Maxine simply raised an eyebrow and let Katie take the conversation where it needed to go.

"On Monday, we had a status meeting with the senior partners." Katie spoke in clipped tones as if she were giving a formal report. "Jerry Fulsome was up last. Everyone knew that his latest project was rupturing money and someone was going to get tagged to repair the damage— probably me."

Maxine clenched her fists. As far as she was concerned, LF&J was criminally abusive. It had appropriated Katie's life and squeezed it dry. Even the fish in Katie's aquarium seemed to swim in regimented order.

Maxine exhaled and forced herself to remain calm. She opened her hands. Her fingernails had left deep grooves in her palms. Fortunately, Katie seemed lost in thought and hadn't noticed.

"When Mr. Littlehouse brought up a PowerPoint of the out-of-control project, with its missed dates and overrun budgets, the senior partners began to flay Jerry with questions he couldn't answer. He'd brought nothing to the meeting: no files that he could be asked to consult for research he had failed to do, no smartphone to contact and assuage irate clients. The meeting stalled. Even the PowerPoint timed out."

Katie held her mug in both hands as if seeking its warmth. "In his haste to restore the PowerPoint, Littlehouse hit the wrong button and brought up an entirely different presentation." Katie shook her head as if to clear it. "The partners never release any data that compares our performances, but there, on the front wall, was a bar chart depicting precisely that. Revenues and market share by individuals."

The color drained from Katie's face, giving her a quizzical look. "I knew I was doing more than the others, but I had no idea how much more."

Maxine longed to hold her child. Instead, she picked up her tea and pretended to drink.

"My bar was more than twice the height of anyone else's."

Katie's voice had become so low that Maxine had trouble hearing it, much less reading its undertones. If she were Katie, she'd be outraged by the chart and its evidence of the company's abuse, but she'd also feel vindicated. The chart was proof of Katie's extraordinary success.

Maxine lifted her chin in pride, then saw the pain in Katie's eyes.

"I'm so sorry," Maxine said.

Katie leaned forward, her eyes locked on Maxine's. "The thing is, without meaning to, LF&J has given me real power, but I don't know why. I mean, why don't they just take some of my clients and give them to someone else?"

Maxine resisted the urge to shake her head. Her brilliant daughter could be surprisingly dense.

"Because you're the only one who knows their businesses right now," Maxine said. "Your bosses don't want to risk losing your clients, so they're content to overwork you instead. If they had anyone else as talented as you, they'd steal your clients in a heartbeat. In fact, they probably will steal them very soon."

"What? Why soon?"

"Everyone in that room—even Jerry Fulsome—understood the significance of that chart."

"Ah." Katie leaned back.

She traced her finger around the top of her mug. It was a habit she'd had since grade school. It meant her mind was racing through the possibilities, reconsidering data, structuring solutions.

Maxine ran her finger around the top of her own mug. She hadn't been asked for an opinion, but Katie needed to look beyond corporate paradigms.

"Katie," Maxine said and braced herself. "*Katherine* has already been extraordinarily successful. I'm confident that she can be equally successful as a partner at Littlehouse, Ferris, and Jones, or as the CEO of her own company."

Katie narrowed her eyes. "But?"

"But I wonder if *Katie* might like an opportunity to wear her tattered hiking jeans more often."

Katie rolled her eyes. But she did not stand up, or slam her mug down.

Maxine exhaled softly. She'd planted the seed. That was enough. *All she could manage: more than she could.* Someone had said something like that once. She sipped her tea and wondered who.

The conversation lapsed into silence. High overhead, an airplane flew past. Behind them, some creature, probably a bird, rustled through Maxine's garden.

Katie stretched and closed her eyes. "This feels great."

Uncertain what was meant, Maxine turned her face to the sun and let it drain some of the tension from her shoulders.

The merest hint of a breeze ruffled the dry yucca blooms. Somewhere a sprinkler system cut on.

Katie cleared her throat.

Maxine opened her eyes; Katie's remained closed.

"After Littlehouse adjourned the meeting, everyone fled. I had the room to myself. I tried to visualize my options, but the image that floated up was of me as an eight-year-old, playing the piano. Do you remember?"

Maxine remembered perfectly. Katie had loved to play, loved to practice, loved everything about the piano—the feel of the ivory, the action of the pedals, even the hardness of the bench. For her birthday, she'd wanted curtains and a bedspread that looked like piano keys. Maxine had bartered with a neighbor who was a good seamstress but a lousy cook. The neighbor made the spread and curtains, and Maxine made double dinners for a week. Tom had painted red and blue musical notes across Katie's sunshine yellow walls. The effect had been magical to their eight-year-old.

Katie studied Maxine. "It was my first piano recital. I was dressed in stiff lace and starched cotton, waiting to go onstage. You were holding my hand. Do you know what you said?"

Maxine didn't trust herself to speak.

"You said, 'Play because you love it. Don't worry about the audience. Just enjoy the music. Play for the love of the music.'"

Maxine took a yoga breath. If only life worked that way.

Laugh lines softened Katie's eyes. "Then you misquoted Shakespeare: 'If this be life, play on.'"

"Really?" Maxine frowned. "The original line would have been more appropriate. 'If music be the stuff of life . . .'"

Katie shook her head. "No. Your version was perfect." She sat back and closed her eyes. "Anyway, that's why I'm here."

"I don't understand."

Katie shrugged and shook her head. "Me either."

They fell into a companionable silence.

After several moments, Katie checked her watch. She unfolded her long legs and rose. "I'd love to have another cup of tea, but I have a conference call to make, and you have a bridge tournament to play."

Maxine's stomach lurched. "I'm not going to a bridge tournament," she said. "I'm going to . . ."

Katie turned expectantly. In the morning sunlight, she looked young and vulnerable.

Maxine's heart skipped a beat. Her daughter had enough problems of her own. It wasn't fair to burden her with Maxine's self-inflicted ones.

"Yes?" Katie said. "You're going to . . .?"

"I'm going to . . . to . . . to be in something less well-defined. More like a contest than a tournament." Maxine knew she was babbling. "Are you sure you'll be all right?"

"I'll be fine," Katie said with a bemused smile.

Maxine nodded and clutched for straws. "Don't forget your massage at Shady Acres. Turn left out of the drive. It's three miles down the road, on your right, just past the new hospital."

"Got it." Katie's crooked grin returned. "Isn't Shady Acres a hospice facility? I know I could use more exercise, but are you trying to tell me something?"

Maxine straightened so quickly she startled the cactus wren. "I never thought of that. I mean, my friend works at Shady Acres, but she does private massages on her lunch hour. Just ask for Fermez." Maxine stopped, aware for the first time of the ambiguity of her plan. "Actually, you might not get Fermez. You might get Alan."

"You don't know?"

"It's a long story, but they're both wonderful. Do you mind if your massage therapist is a man? We can always cancel."

Katie laughed. "It's OK. I'm from New York, remember? We have male massage therapists, and female massage therapists, and everything in between."

"I hope so," Maxine said.

"Sorry?"

"Nothing, dear. Are you sure you'll be all right?"

"I'll be fine. Go get ready."

14

MAXINE GAVE HERSELF a cursory once-over in the mirror. Her wavy snow-white hair had a mind of its own. No point wasting time on it. But she had dressed in one of her best pants suits: black slacks with a smart black-and-white Art Deco jacket and a white silk blouse. She got compliments whenever she wore the outfit; it made her look younger. Although she wouldn't be visible on camera, she wouldn't feel right interviewing for a job if she weren't appropriately dressed. She reached up and fluffed her hair. It immediately fell back into its usual position.

In the living room, Katie was already on her conference call and deep into the line charts, bar graphs, and balance sheets she'd spread across the coffee table.

Maxine bit her lip.

If Tom were here, he'd know whether she should confess. To do, or not to do? Now that was a real question. She hesitated a moment, then slipped silently out the door.

MAXINE PARKED UNDER the acacia in front of Peter's condo. The tree wouldn't provide much shade; nonetheless, some was better than none. She reached forward to switch off the ignition, but her hands trembled so badly that she had trouble turning the key.

Without thinking, she turned the car back on, as if to leave. A light touch on her arm stopped her before she could shift into gear.

"You'll do fine," Louise said.

Maxine swallowed.

"In fact," Louise said, "you'll knock Rupert's socks off."

"Do you think he's wearing dress socks, or white socks and running shoes?"

"Definitely the running shoes," Louise said. "And he'll need them to keep up with you." She gave Maxine's arm a gentle squeeze. "I'm proud of you."

Maxine ducked her head. "Me too," she said, studying the stitching on her purse. "I mean, I'm proud of you."

"Well then." Louise opened the car door. "Damn the torpedoes: full speed ahead."

Maxine saluted. She'd come too far to turn back. Damn those torpedoes, anyway.

Mimi greeted them at the door dressed in a cream-colored designer suit with a navy blue silk shell. An expensive gold necklace and matching earrings completed the outfit. Her hair was swept up into a soft French twist. She looked stunning: sophisticated and sexy, divine and a bit devilish all at once.

"Gracious sakes!" Maxine pointed at Mimi. "I had no idea that I could look so good. We won't need to bother with the interview. Just focus the camera on Mimi and the job is hers—ours—mine—whatever."

Mimi hugged Maxine. "Look at you. You look terrific. Don't worry. You'll be great."

"Max!" Peter grabbed her in his patented bear hug. "You rock!" Then he picked up Louise in a mini bear hug. "You both rock!"

He set Louise down and pointed to masking tape that ran across the hardwood floor in a fan shape. "I've marked out the video area. During the first few seconds of the interview, anything inside the lines will be picked up by the camera, so don't jump in and upstage Mimi."

Mimi took a seat and smiled at the webcam. The effect was perfect: professional yet drop-dead gorgeous, competent with a hint of vulnerability. Rupert was going to think he'd died and gone to manager heaven.

"Your computer is over here." Peter guided Maxine around the coffee table to his desk under the photo of the cactus wren. "You can see

Mimi, but the camera cannot see you. And over there is the computer that I'll use to control everything."

Maxine tightened her grip on Peter's arm.

"Don't worry," he said. "You'll be able to see Rupert, even though he can't see us. You won't be able to hear him, and he won't be able to hear us." He took both her hands. "Any questions?"

Maxine surveyed the room. "Just one: what on earth are we doing?"

Peter pulled out her chair. "We're on a mission of mercy. We're saving the residents of the Foothills from death by boredom."

Maxine sat down and went blank. A few seconds later, Louise's hand stilled hers. She'd evidently been tapping the keyboard, not hard enough to actually type, but loud enough to generate a frenetic flamenco.

Then everything happened at once. Peter held up a cue card. Mimi smiled at the webcam and mouthed something. She pointed to her computer, shrugged her shoulders, looked apologetic, and typed a message. Maxine knew it told Rupert that she was having trouble with her equipment, that the video kept picking up someone else's image, and that the audio was not working at all. The message suggested they simply type the interview.

Maxine held her breath. There were a million things that might go wrong. Rupert might see through the scam. He might know Mimi. Why hadn't they thought of that? Had they even told Mimi what job she was interviewing for?

Then something did go wrong. Mrs. Babcock's image appeared in the screen. Maxine flinched and Louise ducked. Mrs. Babcock stared into Rupert's webcam and fiddled with the computer. Maxine felt as if the old battle-ax was looking into her soul and stripping it bare. She longed for someplace to hide. Beside her, Louise pulled a bridge score pad out of her purse and held it up like a shield. Maxine held her breath and sat stone still. After an eternity, Mrs. Babcock said something to Rupert and left the room.

Maxine exhaled and pressed her hands on the desk to stop them from shaking.

"She's gone to get help," Louise said.

"That's OK," Peter said. "I'll drop the session if she finds anyone. In the meantime, I've frozen the camera so that Rupert only has a blurry vision of Mimi's last smile." He turned from his command console to Maxine. "OK, Max. Take it away."

Maxine tried to swallow and couldn't. Her fingers were blocks of stone. Letters swam across the screen, but she was too dizzy to read them. She thought she might throw up. Then Louise punched her on the arm and everything came back into focus.

Rupert's first question popped up. "Have you ever worked with an aging population?"

Maxine snorted. She was an aging population. She began to type. Mimi, Peter, and the condo all evaporated as she focused on Rupert's questions. She answered them honestly and thoughtfully, finessing the traps as best she could.

Yes, she believed in economy on trips. Rupert would be happy. She neglected to mention what kind of trips she would arrange.

No, she did not think the elderly should be subjected to excessive stimulation. Of course, she didn't know anyone who qualified as elderly.

The questions themselves were unimaginative and, frankly, boring. Maxine tilted her head from side to side to relieve the tension. Out of the corner of her eye, she watched Louise doodle on her score pad. In *Octavia's* column, she drew smiley faces, stars, or flowers every time Maxine answered a question. In *Rupert's* column, she drew stick figures in dunce caps every time he asked another vapid question.

The glitch came at the very end.

Rupert was typing. Behind him, Mrs. Babcock burst into the room accompanied by a man wearing a *Computer Guru for You* uniform.

Maxine froze. How in the blazes had a computer repairman gotten to the Foothills so quickly?

Time stopped. Space expanded.

Miraculously, Celine appeared behind Rupert's shoulder carrying one of the large flower vases from the formal living room. Maxine watched in fascination as Celine tripped and dumped the flowers onto Rupert and the Guru. Oriental lilies, gladiolas, hydrangeas, and water

splashed everywhere. In the ensuing chaos, Celine grabbed the computer cable and gracefully, and ever so carefully, fell into Rupert's lap.

The screens went blank. The interview was over.

Maxine blinked.

Peter let out a giant whoop. He lifted Maxine out of her chair and
spun her in a circle. "We did it! You did it!" He enveloped Louise in a
bear hug. Then he vaulted over the coffee table and grabbed Mimi in yet
another bear hug. They all started laughing and talking at once.

"It worked!" Mimi said.

"I almost fainted when the Computer Guru appeared," Maxine said.

"What about Mrs. Babcock?" Louise asked. "I was sure she was looking straight at me."

"You ladies were awesome!" Peter performed a break-dance maneuver involving muscles that Maxine was pretty sure she'd never had.

Mimi fist-bumped Maxine, then gave her a warm hug. "You were
wonderful," she said, her blue eyes sparkling. "I hope you get the job.
Your answers were exactly the same ones I'd have given."

"I wouldn't go that far," Louise said, tucking her scorecards away.
"But she did all right."

Maxine leaned on the desk to steady herself. "You—and Celine and
Fermez—you've all been wonderful. How can I ever thank you?"

"What happened to brunch at The Summit?" Louise asked. "I
thought you were going to take us all there on Sunday."

"Well of course that's still on," Maxine said. "But it hardly begins to
repay you for all the trouble—"

"Maxine," Peter said. "It wasn't any trouble. It was fun."

"But I do have one question," Mimi said.

Maxine turned to the young woman who'd given up her lunch hour
to help a virtual stranger.

Mimi took both of Maxine's hands in hers. "How on earth did you
manage to get reservations at The Summit? I've been trying for a month
to book a table there. It's the hottest place in town right now."

Maxine attempted a mysterious, Mona-Lisa smile, but she was too
happy to hold it and burst into a grin. "One of my former students is the

manager of reservations. Fortunately, she did well in class, or we might be dining at the Road Kill Cafe."

All of their computers beeped. The Computer Guru's image filled the screens. "Hello?"

Peter lunged for his laptop and punched a button.

The computers went blank.

The room went silent.

"That was close." Peter began clicking like mad. "Let's shut these babies down."

"Wait." Maxine held up her hand. "Shouldn't Octavia send Rupert a thank you note?"

"Good idea." Peter clicked some more. "But we'll switch you to email first."

"Tell Rupert that you look forward to speaking with him in person," Louise said.

"Are you crazy?" Maxine asked. "We just went through all of these gyrations to avoid precisely that."

"I know, but you need to sound interested."

Mimi lightly touched Maxine's shoulder. "Ask Rupert when you might expect to hear from him again, and tell him that you'll be pulling for him at the Tour de Tucson competition."

"What Tour de Tucson competition?" Maxine asked.

"The one he registered for," Mimi said with a Mona-Lisa smile of her own. "It's half an Ironman."

"How do you know?"

"You forget. I'm with the Office of Tourism. That's what I do: coordinate events. We mailed the contestants their entry packages yesterday. There can't be more than one Rupert Brookstone in Tucson. Besides, he listed the Foothills as his business address."

Maxine looked at Louise, who shrugged.

"It makes sense," Maxine said. "He's always swimming or running or cycling. But would it be too . . . too forward to mention the Tour de Tucson?"

"Trust me," Peter said, pulling out his desk chair for her. "He'll love it."

"He'll be intrigued that you know," Mimi said.

Maxine sat. When she did, sunlight glinted off the photo over Peter's desk. The cactus wren appeared to wink at her. Maxine winked back and began to type.

15

ON THE WAY HOME from the interview, Maxine and Louise picked up some takeout at Dana's Deli. Back at the Foothills, Maxine pulled into a parking space in front of Louise's apartment. The car had barely come to a stop before Celine flew out of the building clacking two feather dusters together. In the ensuing cloud of dust, she rushed the car.

"Come inside. It's not safe out here." She fled back into the building.

Maxine raised an eyebrow at Louise who raised her shoulders and shook her head.

"Here," Maxine handed Louise the deli bag. "You take the sandwiches. I'll get Seabiscuit."

Inside, they found Celine crouched behind Louise's dieffenbachia, peering into the parking lot through its broad leaves.

"What on earth are you doing?" Maxine asked.

"I don't want her to see me."

"Who?"

"Mrs. Babcock. I saw her arguing with Mrs. Helmsley."

"The General? Arguing with Carlotta? About what?"

Celine stepped back from the window and into the shadows. "I don't know. Mrs. Helmsley had a big manila envelope she kept waving around, and Mrs. Babcock kept shaking her head and pointing toward the office. *That's* when they turned and saw me see them. That can't be good."

Maxine shivered. It didn't sound good to her either.

Celine hugged herself and rocked. "I don't want to get on Mrs. Babcock's bad side. She already mistrusts me just because I dumped a tiny vase of water on Rupert's computer."

Maxine could see the General's point. She turned to Louise for guidance.

Louise sprang into action. "You poor dear," she said. "Come have some lunch and tell us all about it." She held up the deli bag. "Two Gray Ladies: turkey, Havarti, and cranberry relish on sourdough. Maxine and I are splitting one."

Celine eyed the bag. "I shouldn't."

Louise shook the bag. "From Dana's Deli."

Celine's eyes grew wide. "Well, maybe just a bite."

Louise loaded the sandwiches and a month's supply of paper napkins onto Seabiscuit and headed toward the dining table. Maxine and Celine followed close behind.

Louise gave half a sandwich to Maxine, kept a half for herself, and passed the bag to Celine. "So, what happened after you pulled the computer cable and plopped into Rupert's lap?"

"Honestly," Celine said. "You'd think those folks had never seen flowers or water before."

Louise handed them each a fistful of napkins. "For a minute, I thought you were going to bean Rupert with the gladiolas."

"The vase was brilliant," Maxine said. "What made you think of it?"

"Well . . ." Celine studied her hands. "I wanted to call and warn you, but I *might* have gotten distracted for a minute and misplaced my cell phone. So when I saw that Computer Guru with Mrs. Babcock, I just grabbed the nearest thing and ran."

Maxine shook her head to keep from laughing. "What did they all do after you fell on Rupert?"

Celine blushed. "Rupert was kind of speechless. I'm guessing he wasn't used to having such a good-looking woman land in his lap." She smoothed her perfectly aligned kaftan.

Maxine suppressed a smile.

"Mainly he seemed glad his computer wasn't broken. Mr. Guru

stared at the computer, but he kept his opinions to himself. And Mrs. Babcock asked what I thought I was doing."

"What did you say?"

"I told her that Gladys Black thought she'd heard a mountain lion in Rupert's office, and I was coming to his rescue when I tripped on the computer cord and fell."

The laughter was spontaneous, universal, and joyous. Even Seabiscuit snorted.

"Brava!" Louise clapped her hands.

Maxine pumped her fist. "Poor Gladys. I bet they didn't even question the story."

"No one batted an eyelash. Not even Mrs. Babcock."

"Well done," Louise said, unwrapping her half sandwich. "Please eat. I'm starved."

Maxine reached for her half sandwich but was distracted by faint strains of the "Hallelujah Chorus." She looked around. She looked away. She looked at Louise and Celine. The noise seemed to be coming from Celine's bosom.

"I think we've located your misplaced cell phone," Maxine said.

Celine pulled the phone out of her bodice. "That's a relief! I put it in there for safekeeping while I was listening to Katie."

"Katie?" Maxine said. "Where did you see Katie?"

"In the formal living room. That's how come I almost missed Mr. Guru. I was listening to her play the piano."

"The piano? In the formal living room? Today?" With each question, Maxine's voice went up a notch. "Are you sure?"

Celine looked over her glasses at Maxine. "Well, unless you have some other woman's photo all over your condo, it was her. *And* she played, *and* she was *good*."

Maxine struggled to rearrange Celine's words into something that made sense.

"Tell us about Katie," Louise said.

"I was dusting behind the couch when I heard someone come in through the big French doors." Celine paused to unwrap her sandwich.

"You know, *some* people cut through the formal living room instead of walking around the building on the formal paths."

Maxine feigned surprise. She cut through the formal living room on a regular basis. It saved time and bypassed Carlotta's apartment.

"So I peeked over the sofa to see who it was, and this young woman breezed through. She started to go right past the piano, but then turned and studied it. Like she was reconsidering something. Then she kind of stroked the keys without actually playing them. The next thing you know, she sat on the bench. On the very edge. Like she might take off at any moment."

Without meaning to, Maxine crushed her napkins into a ball.

"I kept real quiet," Celine said. "Didn't want to disturb her. Then she kind of ran her fingertips over the keys, like she was rehearsing a piece but so softly I had to get close to hear it."

Celine looked at Maxine. "She was playing 'Amazing Grace.'"

The ball of napkins fell from Maxine's hands and rolled across the room.

"So I said, 'You need to play that piece,' and Katie snatched her hands back from the keyboard like she'd been burned. She swung around in a fury."

Celine mimed the action, then shrugged. "Guess she hadn't heard me come up behind her."

"What did she do?"

"She said, 'Sorry' in a voice that could have melted ice."

Maxine knew the voice. It was Katie's corporate voice. The one that didn't actually apologize.

"I told her again that she needed to play that piece. She said she didn't play and started to get up. But I didn't budge, so she couldn't move."

Maxine gasped.

"What did Katie do?" Louise almost whispered her question.

"Said she hadn't played in twenty-two years. Didn't remember how. So I told her she did too remember how to play. Then, I kind of put a loving hand on her shoulder and held her in place." Celine demonstrated on Louise.

"You didn't!"

"I told her to play the piece she'd just been practicing. She said she wasn't practicing anything. So I hummed it for her."

Celine hummed a few bars of "Amazing Grace" for them.

"Oh my." Maxine raised a trembling hand to her mouth.

Celine nodded. "Katie did seem kind of startled to learn what she'd been playing. Then she turned around, almost like it was against her will, and played it while I hummed. The music was kind of halting at first, but it smoothed out some. So when she finished, I told her to play it again."

Louise blotted her eyes with one of her napkins and handed another to Maxine.

"I told her she'd been blessed," Celine said. "Told her she still had music in her soul and it was time to let it out."

Maxine swallowed, unable to speak.

"What did she say?" Louise asked.

"Nothing," Celine said. "Didn't have a chance. That's when I heard the front door slam, and there was Mrs. Babcock dragging that Computer Guru down the hall towards Rupert's office. I couldn't find my cell phone, so I grabbed the vase of flowers from the fireplace and ran after them. And you know the rest."

Celine picked up her sandwich. "So tell me, how did the interview go from your end of things?"

Maxine's world spun out of focus. She reached for Louise's hand.

Louise squeezed it gently. "Go, find Katie," she said, shooing Maxine away.

Maxine blinked, stood, sat, then stood again. She handed Celine her untouched half-sandwich and a handful of Louise's unused napkins.

Celine nodded. "You're welcome."

16

MAXINE ENTERED HER CONDO quietly in case Katie was on the phone, but a quick check of the rooms and the patio revealed no daughter. Puzzled, Maxine walked back to her bedroom.

That's when she spotted it. A yellow sticky note had been added to her daily desk planner on today's page: "Gone to the pool."

Smiling, Maxine picked up the note. Katie had always loved to swim. The first thing Maxine and Tom had done when they moved to Tucson was build a backyard pool for Katie to use during her visits. These days, the Foothills' pool was the one place where Maxine wasn't hampered by arthritis. She felt young again in a pool.

She checked her watch. It was too late to join Katie in a swim, but she could at least watch.

She bent to re-paste the sticky onto her planner and froze.

There, in bold letters, she'd written: "INTERVIEW at 11:00. Be at Peter's by 10:30."

The room swirled. She grabbed the back of her desk chair and lowered her head, hoping the blood would flow back into her brain. She struggled for air.

The thudding slowed and the room stopped spinning. Her breath returned to normal.

She raised her head and studied her calendar. It was where the family had always left notes for each other.

She tried pasting and re-pasting the sticky note. She ran her index finger over the page. In the words of June's grandson, she was SOL.

THE POOL WAS EMPTY except for Katie doing laps. Maxine silently crossed to a lounge chair in the shade of a large umbrella. She watched as Katie's arms sliced through the water with soothing, rhythmical strokes. Maxine closed her eyes for a moment. The weather was nearly perfect: warm with the smallest hint of a breeze. The only sound was the slight splashing of Katie's turns.

"Earth to Maxine."

Maxine jolted upright.

Katie was leaning on the edge of the pool, her goggles pushed up on her forehead.

"Goodness," Maxine said. "I must have dozed off."

Katie smiled her crooked grin. "How was bridge? Did you win?"

Maxine blinked, momentarily confused. "You know, I'm not sure who won today. How was your day?" She tossed the question out casually and waited. The next move was Katie's.

Katie pulled herself up the pool's ladder and reached for her towel. "The massage was wonderful!"

"Oh good. Did you have Fermez or Alan?"

"Alan," Katie said toweling off. "I liked him. He was attentive without being intrusive. And I liked his massage room. The walls were the color of a good café au lait."

"Did he show you his water fountain? He made it out of sacred rocks from a small canyon in northern New Mexico. The healer who lives in the canyon blessed them and loaned them to him. If he ever loses his touch"—she rubbed her thumbs across her fingertips—"his massage touch, he has to give them back."

"I know." Katie sat on a chaise lounge next to Maxine and joined in the storytelling. "He's already given back a red rock. It was too powerful. Did he tell you that the rocks in the fountain are stacked, not glued?"

Maxine nodded. "Yes, and he rearranges them every new moon."

Katie laughed. "Alan says you and I are the only people who've ever asked."

"It's such a lovely story," Maxine said, relaxing into the narration.

"His stories and his massages are both great." Katie put on sunglasses and one of Maxine's broad-brimmed sun hats. "Thanks for arranging that for me while you . . . played bridge."

Maxine froze. She studied her daughter and tried to decide if the pause in her last sentence was pregnant. Katie's face remained impassive. She'd always had the best poker face in the family. Behind the dark glasses and big hat, it was impossible to guess her intent.

Maxine shifted uncomfortably.

The silence droned on.

Maxine decided the next move was hers. "I'm glad the massage went well," she said. "Did you do anything else today?"

There was a half beat of silence before Katie spoke. "Not much. Just relaxed. I've been in the pool for quite a while."

Maxine sat back. The air fairly crackled with tension. The tiny hairs on Maxine's arms stood at attention, and she shivered despite the heat. Were they at checkmate already?

In the dissonant silence, Maxine failed to mention her interview and Katie neglected to bring up the woman in a purple kaftan who'd forced her to play the piano.

Katie broke the deadlock. "Some young guy was here for a long time swimming laps. He had a stopwatch and marked his times on a clipboard."

"A blond?" Maxine said, relieved to be back to neutral territory.

"Yes."

"That was Rupert. He's the director. He's training for half an Ironman competition, but no one is supposed to know."

"How do you know?"

"A friend told me."

Katie pulled her sunglasses down to the tip of her nose and examined her mother. "I can tell you're plotting something."

Maxine stiffened. "What do you mean?"

Katie took off her hat. "Your brow is furrowed, and you're tapping your finger on the lounge chair."

"You sound like Louise," Maxine said, stalling for time, well aware that a voluntary confession *before* her interview would have been far preferable to one extorted now.

"That's because Louise was the one who told me to watch out for the brow and finger. So what is it? What are you planning for Rupert and his Ironman?"

"Rupert?"

"Yes, Rupert. The blond?"

Maxine fanned herself with Katie's hat and sent a silent prayer of gratitude to the gods of parental deception for sparing her this one time.

"I don't think Rupert has many friends outside the Foothills," she said. "Maybe Louise and I could go to the race and cheer for him. We could show support, even if he is fairly useless as a director. Talk about someone being caught in the wrong job."

Katie reclaimed the hat. "I bet he'd love it. You should get t-shirts made."

"Rupert's Groupies?"

Katie laughed. "More like Rupert's Rowdies."

"Oh, I do like the sound of that." Maxine's fingers tapped double-time.

Katie stood. "In the meantime, I'm starved. Is it too early to go to dinner?"

Maxine rocked herself out of the lounge chair. They'd weathered the storm. "No, it's not too early. In fact, I'd say now is the perfect time."

"Good." Katie plopped the hat onto Maxine's head. "I need to make it an early night tonight. I'll have to get up at four tomorrow morning to catch my flight."

Maxine's shoulders slumped even though she'd known Katie was leaving on the early flight.

"I need to get back, but I'll remember what you said about making time for my tattered hiking jeans." Katie wrapped the towel around herself like a sarong. "Thanks for listening this morning, Mom."

Maxine stumbled and nearly fell into the pool.

Katie grabbed her arm. "Are you all right?"

Maxine nodded. "Just clumsy," she said, dismissively, while her heart did cartwheels. *Mom.* She'd been promoted from *Mother* to *Mom.* They could talk about Katie's piano and Maxine's interview later—much later.

PART THREE

FINESSE:

THE OPPOSITION

17

MAXINE WOKE UP a minute before her alarm was set to go off. 3:59 AM.
She rocked herself out of bed. Down the hall, the light was already on in
Katie's room. Maxine knocked softly.

"It's OK, Mom," Katie said. "I'm up. Come on in."

Maxine opened the door. "Are you sure you don't want me to make
you a lunch? How about some granola bars? Or a bag of trail mix and a
box of raisins?"

Katie laughed. "No thanks. I'll be fine." She zipped her suitcase shut.
"You know they do have food in New York."

"Must be a new thing," Maxine said, still trying to think of something
more she could offer her daughter. She hated good-byes, especially good-
byes with Katie. There was never enough time, never adequate words.

Katie stuffed her laptop into her carry-on. "That's it, I think. I'll call
when I get to my apartment." She hesitated. "Thanks again."

They hugged and then, all too quickly, Katie was gone.

Maxine hugged Tom's robe closer and wandered into the kitchen.
Might as well make tea. She wouldn't be able to go back to sleep anyway,
and a pot of tea could keep her company until the breakfast buffet opened.

MAXINE LIFTED HER TOAST in a salute as Rosemarie slid into the chair
beside her at breakfast. Rosemarie was dressed in her version of weekend
casual: a long denim dress perfectly offset by traditional Navajo jewelry.

Today she wore Maxine's favorite pieces: a silver chain with a single turquoise pendant in brilliant Bisbee blue, matching earrings, and a squash blossom watch bracelet. The watch itself was the Mickey Mouse watch that Maxine had given Rosemarie last Christmas.

Maxine smiled. Rosemarie dressed for comfort and unknowingly achieved natural elegance.

Rosemarie transferred her coffee, toast, and scrambled eggs from the tray to their table. "How was your visit with Katie? Did she get off all right?"

"She left at a quarter past four this morning. Now I'm feeling empty and out of sorts." Maxine waved her hands about aimlessly, then crossed her arms to anchor herself.

"If I'd gotten up that early, I'd be feeling just plain out of it." Rosemarie stirred half a packet of raw sugar into her coffee. She paused, then uncharacteristically dumped the rest of the sugar into her mug.

Maxine raised an eyebrow.

Rosemarie looked up and rolled her eyes. "You aren't going to believe what happened yesterday." She buttered her toast so hard it broke.

Maxine raised both eyebrows and waited. The news must be juicy.

Rosemarie switched to jam, but the toast continued to crumble under her assault. "Mrs. Babcock finally gave our committee copies of the applications for the assistant director's position, along with a list of the interviews Rupert had scheduled so that we could sit in on them."

Maxine froze, her spoon suspended halfway to her mouth. She swallowed and tried to think of something to say.

Rosemarie lowered her knife. "Actually, Mrs. Babcock had the applications and interview schedule photocopied and *mailed* to us by Kevin's Copy Center way over on East Twenty-second Street. Carlotta didn't receive the package until Friday afternoon, *after* the last interview had ended."

Maxine exhaled slowly and gratefully.

"When Carlotta opened her mail she was so angry she chased the General down in the parking lot. They had a first-class shouting match.

Then Carlotta called for an emergency committee meeting last night. Guess whose granddaughter wants to be our assistant director?"

Maxine shook her head. "No telling."

Rosemarie tilted her chin toward the far table where Carlotta sat hunched in conversation with Fred.

Maxine inhaled. "No."

Rosemarie nodded. "Yes."

"Not that horrid little redhead, what's-her-name?"

Rosemarie nodded. "Evie Helmsley Hill. She's twenty-six, recently divorced, and looking for a job. Naturally, Carlotta thinks she'd be perfect."

Maxine struggled to keep her voice down. "That narcissistic, narrow-minded little twit who tried to get bridge banned from the Foothills?"

"That very twit."

"The one who stood on Louise's oxygen hose until she passed out? The one who gave Daisy beer instead of water when she was a puppy?" Maxine succeeded in keeping her voice low, but her body stiffened with each question.

"The very one," Rosemarie confirmed.

"That's outrageous," Maxine stirred her tea into foam. "And it's nepotism." She slammed her teaspoon on the table. "And it's unconscionable, and unbearable, and, and . . ."

Rosemarie leaned closer. "And it gets worse."

"How could it?"

"Evie's qualified."

"No!"

"She has a Master's in Public Administration."

"A degree can't compensate for a lack of basic human decency."

"She did her internship at a retirement community and wrote her thesis about the elderly."

"We are *not* elderly!" Maxine slammed her fist in protest.

At the next table, Paul and Peggy Stone looked up with concern.

Maxine lowered her voice. "Well, we're not catatonic anyway, but we will be if Carlotta has her way." She sipped her tea to mask her anger.

"You won't believe the title of her thesis." Rosemarie pulled a piece of paper from her pocket and adjusted her glasses. "'The Effects of Appropriate Activities in an Elderly Population: Moral Movement for the Majority.'"

Maxine choked on her tea.

Rosemarie pounded on Maxine's back, and Paul rushed over to help.

"I'm fine. I'm fine," Maxine spluttered when her breath returned.

Paul retreated to his table. Ministers knew when to tread lightly and when to avoid treading at all.

Maxine pointed archly to Evie's title. "*That* is pure poppycock! What is 'moral movement' anyway?"

"Beats me. All I know is that Carlotta found out about the assistant director's job the very morning that Rupert posted it. By lunchtime, Evie had applied, and by dinner Carlotta was lobbying for a two-person interview committee. Thank goodness the residents voted to increase the committee to five, or Carlotta and Fred would have already anointed Evie."

Maxine clenched her jaw so hard her teeth hurt.

"Remember when the committee asked all of the candidates to submit essays on their so-called 'philosophical approach to retirement communities'?" Rosemarie made air quotes.

"I certainly do."

"That was Carlotta's doing. She insisted that all graduate schools required similar essays. She forgot to tell us that her granddaughter had applied for our job, but she remembered to tell us that Evie had received an A++ on her essay."

Maxine bristled. The grade was preposterous.

At that moment, Carlotta and Fred stood up to leave. Maxine swore that Carlotta looked directly at them with a glint in her eye.

Rosemarie shoved aside her plate of crumbled toast. "I am *not* looking forward to interviewing Evie."

Maxine jerked.

"Interview? What are you talking about? Didn't you just say Rupert already did the interviews?" She could hear the sharp edge of hysteria creeping into her voice.

Rosemarie stared at her.

Maxine pretended not to notice and flicked an imaginary crumb off her blouse.

Rosemarie shrugged and leaned forward conspiratorially. "We were furious when we found out that Rupert had interviewed three candidates without us, but Carlotta was positively apoplectic when she found out that Evie was *not* one of Rupert's candidates."

"She wasn't? I can't imagine Rupert having the chutzpah to ignore Carlotta's granddaughter."

"Rupert claimed he never saw her application. Carlotta thinks Mrs. Babcock lost it."

"That's absurd. Mrs. Babcock has never lost anything in her life. She either files it or shreds it." Maxine stopped. Evie's application wasn't the important part. "What's the committee going to do about the people Rupert interviewed?"

Rosemarie shook her head. "What a mess. Evie gets to resubmit her application and our committee gets—" Rosemarie signaled more air quotes "—*gets* to screen all of the applications and interview any *additional* candidates."

Maxine placed her hands on the table to stop them from trembling. She studied her arthritic knuckles. "About the interviews, the thing is, I—"

"The thing is," Rosemarie said, "you know how Carlotta is. She won't stop scheming. She'll stack the deck, and we'll be stuck with Evie as our next assistant director. It will be disastrous." She raised her hands as if in surrender. Her shoulders sagged and her head drooped.

For the first time Maxine could remember, Rosemarie looked not elegant but discouraged, defeated, and, well, old.

Maxine's hackles rose. "We'll see about that," she said. "We'll just see about that."

18

MAXINE THREW HER KEYS on the kitchen counter, grabbed the telephone, and dialed Louise.

"Saddle up Seabiscuit; we're going for a trip."

"OK. I just need a few minutes to feed Seabiscuit."

"Do you remember Evie Helmsley Hill?"

"You mean the Cruella De Vil of Tucson?" Louise said. "Carlotta's sociopathic granddaughter?"

"The very one. She's applying to be our assistant director."

Louise's end went very, very silent.

"Louise? Are you there? Are you all right? Louise?"

"I'm here." Louise's voice was flat and measured. "I'm just censoring everything that occurs to me to say. You know: if you can't say anything nice . . ."

"I know exactly what you mean. Evie has a master's degree from the university. I want to check out her thesis."

"Let's take my car," Louise said. "We'll need the handicapped permit to park within a day's hike of the library. I'll pick you up in ten minutes."

THE SIGHT AND SOUND of students scattered throughout the library took Maxine back to her days as a professor. She loved the undercurrent of energy. She loved the sound of debate in the library lobby and the smell of smuggled coffee wafting from the carrels. She even loved the students who had fallen asleep on their books, cramming for exams.

Louise, on the other hand, seemed disoriented. "Where's the card catalogue?"

"Everything's online," Maxine said a tad ruefully. "The old wooden catalog drawers have been turned into recipe boxes all over America."

"How will we ever find Evie's thesis?"

"We'll ask that nice graduate student over there." Maxine pointed toward a cheerful-looking, pony-tailed brunette at the Reference desk.

"How do you know she's a grad student?"

"She's wearing jeans and a Grateful Dead t-shirt. Staff might wear jeans, but not t-shirts. The best student worker jobs in the library are at the Reference desk, and the grad students always claim them before undergrads can. Come on."

"Excuse me," Maxine said to the brunette. "Can you help us find a master's thesis in Public Administration?"

The young woman looked up and smiled at them. "Sure. That's even my area. Do you know the author or title?"

"'The Effects of Appropriate Activities in an Elderly Population: Moral Movement for the Majority,' by Evie Helmsley Hill."

The smile disappeared from the student's face. In fact, she looked as if she'd just tasted something very sour.

"Do you know her?" Maxine asked.

"She was in my Research Methods class," the student said in clipped tones. "I'll show you where the thesis is." She turned and walked away.

Maxine and Louise exchanged glances and followed obediently.

"I don't know very much about public administration." Maxine paused, then laughed at herself. "Actually, I don't know a blessed thing about public administration, but the title of the thesis seemed a bit non-sensical to us. We wanted to see what 'moral movement' was."

The student kept her lips tightly shut as if trying to force her opinions to stay silent. Maxine decided to give an extra shove. "We thought it sounded rather like an ad for a laxative."

The student burst into laughter but remained cautious. "Do you know Evie?"

"Yes, unfortunately," they said in unison.

The student nodded. "The work is closer to a laxative than to public admin." She pulled a dusty volume off the bottom shelf and handed it to Maxine. "Here it is, but if you want to read something good, you should read this." She handed a thin, battered volume to Louise.

"'Reversing Aging in a Retirement Community by Increasing Variety in Planned Activities.'" Louise straightened her glasses. "Well, the title's a mouthful, but at least it makes sense."

"Academic titles are always ungainly," Maxine said. "The longer the title, the more ponderous the work. Be wary of any work with more than one colon in its title."

The student choked back her laughter. "My adviser's latest book has two colons, one dash, and three commas in the title. I can't make sense out of a single thing he says in it."

Maxine smiled. "I'm Maxine and this is Louise and her trusty steed, Seabiscuit. Could we buy you lunch at the Park Street Grille? Maybe you could give us some pointers to help us get through these tomes—or at least their titles."

The student hesitated, checked her watch, then laughed again. "I'm Ashley. It's time for my brake, and I'm starved. I missed breakfast. Let's do it."

OVER LUNCH, ASHLEY REVEALED that she had been in Research Methods with both Evie and Michelle Lafayette, the author of the other thesis. "Michelle was super-smart and really nice. Every semester, she ran free yoga classes during exams. It helped with the stress. Evie, on the other hand, was a royal pain in the ass." Ashley caught herself and blushed. "Oh, I'm sorry."

Louise patted her arm, "Don't worry. We find Evie a bit hard on the derriere ourselves."

"Here's the deal. Evie had an internship at Mountain Estates Retirement Community, and she used the residents as her research pool. It was totally unethical and violated all kinds of research principles. She didn't even have them sign the required waivers. It was a big scandal."

Ashley had already finished her burger and fries, so Maxine slid her own untouched fries toward her.

Ashley attacked the fries and a vanilla milkshake. "The rumor was that Evie's data contradicted her thesis, so she simply faked the data."

Maxine slammed her fist on the table. "That's outrageous! How did she ever get a degree?"

"Now that's where the story gets really juicy." Ashley added more ketchup to the fries. "The word I heard was that she slept with her professors." Ashley devoured a pickle. "Of course, I don't know if there was any truth to the rumor, but I do know that the lecherous old goat in Research Methods couldn't keep his eyes off her in class. She wore tight tank tops and cut-offs and sat in the front row and sold it, if you catch my drift."

Maxine nodded. She had a general idea where that drift was going.

"At any rate." Ashley licked her fingers. "Evie passed the course, and the following semester, the old goat's wife divorced him."

Louise picked up the other thesis. "What about this one?"

"That was published in a good journal." Ashley absently wiped her fingers on her jeans. "I run into Michelle all the time at the grocery store. A couple of weeks ago she applied for her dream job but never heard anything back."

"The poor dear. Think how she must feel to hear nothing," Louise said.

Ashley placed her hand over her heart. "The eternal silence of these infinite spaces fills me with dread."

"Excuse me?"

Ashley blushed. "That was Pascal. I did an undergraduate honors thesis on him, but it's not easy to work his quotations into a conversation."

"I suppose not," Maxine agreed. "I did my work on Shakespeare. He's a bit easier to work in."

"You English types have all the luck." Ashley slurped the last of her milkshake. "Anyway, the library has a video of Michelle being interviewed. Everyone who's applying for a job watches it for pointers."

"*Now* you tell me!" Maxine buried her head in her hands.

"Tough interview?" Ashley asked.

Maxine nodded. "You might say it culminated in eternal silence and infinite dread. I hadn't done an interview since Pascal was polishing his *Pensees*. I certainly could have used a video with pointers."

Ashley laughed and sat back, a contented smile on her face.

"Would you like some dessert?" Maxine asked, aware that Ashley had cleaned all the plates.

"No thanks. I've got to get back to work, but that was great! Those fries saved my life."

Ashley stood up to leave, then sat back down. "Here's the deal," she said, lowering her voice even though no one was near them, "Evie was sneaky and mean. She had a way of getting her way. Be careful and don't trust her."

"Don't worry," Maxine and Louise said in unison. "We don't, and we won't."

19

MAXINE STARED AT the two master's theses lying on her desk. She'd spent all afternoon reading them. She'd even taken notes. This was one case where you could tell a book by its cover. The thin volume by Ashley's friend was battered and stained from evident use, while Evie's ponderous thesis was pristine from neglect. The spine had literally cracked when Maxine opened it. Clearly it was seldom, if ever, opened. And no wonder. Evie had padded her work with meaningless graphs, murky statistics, and irrelevant citations until it was all but impossible to read.

Maxine could feel her professional ire bubbling up to volcanic levels. After some thirty years of teaching, she was used to slogging through convoluted arguments and inflated rhetoric, but Evie had taken the art of obfuscation to a whole new level.

Maxine started to rise, then sank back to her chair.

The problem was that Evie's thesis was carefully crafted obfuscation. Obfuscation that would sell. Rupert would like her assertion that an assistant director's primary goal was to assist management in the cost-effective administration of a "facility for the aged."

Maxine crumpled her notes into a ball and hurled it at her wicker wastebasket. The ball bounced off the rim and rolled back to her feet. She gave it a kick that sent it careening off the wall and under her desk.

Facility for the aged! Evie might as well have called it a prison for the mentally deficient. Her thesis made it clear that was how she thought of the residents: mentally compromised objects that needed to be fed, exercised, and returned to their cells.

For all of his shortcomings, even Rupert didn't think of the Foothills as a prison—unless he thought of it as his own prison. All he wanted to do was train for his Ironman competition. He'd be happy to turn things over to Evie if that left him free to train. He'd be seduced by her focus on efficiency. The less money she spent on social programs, the blacker his bottom line. Although he'd barely glance at Evie's thesis, Rupert would like what he saw.

The Foothills' residents would like what they saw, too. They'd be impressed by the client satisfaction numbers. Evie claimed that 100 percent of the Mountain Estates residents were 100 percent satisfied with 100 percent of her programs 100 percent of the time. Maxine had analyzed enough surveys to know the numbers were never that good, but Carlotta and Fred would tout them like the second coming.

Maxine drummed her fingers on the desktop.

Evie's academic dishonesty was chilling. Even more chilling was her underlying assumption: to Evie, the residents of a retirement community were not individuals with dreams and desires, they were problems to be controlled and managed.

Maxine slammed her fist on the desk. "D.A.M.N."

She shoved Evie's thesis to the far side of the desk, next to the other thesis. It was everything that Evie's thesis was not. It argued that people who continued to learn—to explore new activities and meet new people—stayed young.

Maxine took off her glasses and rubbed her temples.

But . . .

She replaced her glasses and straightened her shoulders.

But Evie's plague had not been visited upon them yet.

She picked up the phone and dialed. "June? What are you doing?"

"I'm looking for Harry. It's almost time to go to the dining room for dinner, and he's disappeared. Honestly, I spend half my life looking for that man. I'm thinking about getting one of those invisible fences and a dog collar to keep him from wandering off. I bet he's over at Ralph Jordan's watching golf. How can anyone watch golf?"

"Well," Maxine said, "it's better than baseball."

"Or poker. Did you know they show poker on the sports channels? How is poker a sport?"

"It's all that training the poker players do: you know, heavy lifting of chips and cards."

"Right. I should be on ESPN for all the chasing around I do looking for Harry," June grumbled. "Anyway, what's up?"

"Did Rosemarie tell you about Evie?"

"Yes, and if she becomes our assistant director, I'm moving back to New York to become a bag lady."

"If she becomes our assistant director, I'll join you," Maxine said. "In the meantime, do your friends still live at Mountain Estates?"

"Lorraine and Mike Hampton? Yes. Why?"

"I've been reading Evie's thesis. It's based on her internship at Mountain Estates. I was wondering how the residents felt about Evie and her so-called research."

"I'll call them."

"Thanks." Maxine felt better already. It wasn't much, but it was a start.

She pushed herself out of her chair and waited for her knees to straighten and hold. She'd been sitting in one position far too long. Now her whole body ached. She placed her hands on the base of her spine and leaned backward. Her vertebrae snapped, crackled, and popped in protest.

Operational once more, she checked her watch: 6:10. She needed to hurry. By 6:15 everyone would be milling about in the hallway outside the dining room waiting for the doors to open at 6:30. Although most people sat in the same place every night, when the doors opened, there'd be a rush to lay claim to a favorite table. The rush for the tables was silly, but the fifteen minutes of mingling gave Maxine a chance to catch up with friends she might not otherwise see. And fifteen minutes was the perfect amount of time to gather the essentials of a story without getting trapped in a discussion about someone's latest ailment or entire medical history. Tonight she wanted to find Paul and Peggy Stone and make amends for her behavior at breakfast. She'd been so flustered by the specter of Evie's candidacy that she'd been inexcusably rude when Paul had tried to keep her from choking to death. She needed to apologize.

AS SOON AS MAXINE entered the hallway, a short, perky woman with brassy red hair, a tight top, and an artificial cheerleader smile bounced over, trailed by Carlotta. The brassy woman threw both of her arms around Maxine in an unwanted hug. "Oh, Maxine, you were always one of my fav-o-rite people."

"Evie, what a pleasant surprise," Maxine said, trying to sound as if she meant it. "What brings you to Tucson?"

Evie simpered and smirked. "I just missed my dear grandmother and her friends at the Foothills *so* much that I simply had to move back."

Evie and Carlotta looked at each other and giggled like adolescents.

"And you won't believe it," Evie said, "but I've *just* found out that you need a new assistant director, so I've applied. Won't that be fun?"

"Isn't that wonderful?" Carlotta asked and batted her eyes.

Maxine wondered if the weight of Carlotta's mascara could overpower her eyelids and cement them shut.

"The only problem," Evie said, "is that Mr. Brookstone can't find my application, so I need to give him another one before I can be hired."

Carlotta flapped her eyelashes some more. "Thank God I'm on the Residents' Advisory Committee, or we might not have realized Evie's application was missing. Isn't that incredible?"

"Yes." Maxine said. "It is."

Carlotta narrowed her eyes, but Evie burbled on.

"Oh Maxine, you are such a dear. Isn't it just so amazing? I might get to come play with my fav-o-rite people and get paid for it."

Maxine clenched her teeth to keep from gagging.

Evie, who was a good four inches shorter than Maxine, draped her arm over Maxine's shoulders. "Tell me," she said in a confidential tone, "how are your dear friends Lois and May? Are they . . ." Evie paused as if searching for the most delicate word. "Are they still here?"

Maxine straightened. "Their names are Louise and June, and where else would they be?"

"I was so worried about them, especially Lois. She seemed to be having such trouble with her oxygen."

"Oddly enough, she's had no trouble at all since you left," Maxine said, her eyes locked onto Evie's.

"Thank goodness," Evie gushed and dug her fingers into Maxine's shoulder while pretending to give her another hug.

"Mazel tov to that," June said. She and Harry had worked their way through the crowd to stand by Maxine's side. "How are you, Evie? Where is that good-looking husband of yours?"

"Yes," Harry said. "Where is Martin Hill? That's his name, isn't it?"

Maxine never ceased to be amazed at what Harry remembered or what June had the chutzpah to ask, knowing, as they all did, that Evie was now divorced.

Before Evie could respond, however, the doors to the dining room swung open. The crowd surged, propelling them forward and forcing Evie to release her grip on Maxine's shoulder.

"It was nice seeing you!" Harry called after Evie. "By the way, we still have Daisy."

Evie hesitated, then marched into the dining room without acknowledging Harry or his comment.

Maxine looked sharply at Harry, who gave her a sly wink. "That hussy once tried to inebriate our dog."

Maxine took Harry's arm in hers.

INSIDE THE DINING ROOM, Ralph Jordan approached them. "May I join your table this evening?" he asked in his formal manner. "I've been supplanted at my usual table by Carlotta's vivacious granddaughter."

"Of course," Maxine said. "You can join us anytime you like. You don't need to ask."

"Why do you sit over there anyway?" June asked.

Ralph looked down at his hands, like a shy boy caught in an embarrassing moment. "When I first moved here, it was the only spot open. Now, after so much time, it would be rude to move. I talk sports with Fred. And Gladys is quite sweet. Once a month, she bakes me cookies whether I need them or not."

Maxine bit her lip. Once a month, Gladys made cookies for every eligible male at the Foothills.

"And I enjoy talking with Mark and Catherine Dupree about their adventure travels. Did you know that they're going to go camping in Alaska to photograph wolves?"

"I thought they were going camel trekking in Morocco," June said.

"That was last year."

"Forget all that and come sit by me," Harry said. "These women couldn't tell a good golf story to save their lives."

While the men talked fairways and bunkers, Maxine and Louise told June and Rosemarie about their trip to the library and Evie's thesis.

"That reminds me." June reached for the coffee pot. "I called Lorraine and Mike Hampton. They'd just returned from a bicycle tour of Iceland. God knows why they call that a vacation. Give me a restaurant tour of Manhattan any day. Anyway, they said everyone at Mountain Estates hated everything Evie did. She treated them like children one day and indentured servants the next. By the end, no one would go to any of her activities."

They fell into an unhappy silence.

Maxine hugged herself and rubbed her arms for warmth.

Louise adjusted her air hose with trembling fingers.

Rosemarie pursed her lips and stared into space.

June poured herself another cup of coffee, then forgot to drink it. She turned to Rosemarie. "You're on that committee. Can't you do something to get rid of Evie?"

Rosemarie shook her head. "It's already too late. I'll get the committee to request her thesis from the university, but Carlotta has already begun her campaign to foist Evie upon us."

Maxine uncrossed her arms and planted her elbows firmly on the table. "What's she doing?"

"She's hosting a series of afternoon teas. Ostensibly they're to welcome Evie back to Tucson, but I think the whole point is to drum up support for Evie's candidacy."

"But Carlotta is head of the Residents' Advisory Committee," Louise said. "Isn't that a conflict of interest?"

"Of course it is," Rosemarie said. "That's why she's calling them 'Welcome Back Parties.' The first one will be tomorrow afternoon. She's reserved the recreation room."

Maxine slumped into her chair and stirred the peas and carrots aimlessly about her plate. She'd lost her appetite.

Loud laughter floated over from Carlotta's table, where Evie was holding court.

Maxine studied Evie and her over-bright smile. She had leaned forward to talk with Fred, who had a dazed look on his face. Maxine followed his gaze. Evie's tight top had a plunging neckline. When she leaned forward, she offered Fred a hint of paradise. She jiggled and bounced and he practically drooled.

Maxine stabbed her roast beef with a fork and sawed off a piece, but she couldn't eat.

"I don't get it," Ralph Jordan said quietly to Maxine. He nodded in Evie's direction. "She wants to be our assistant director, but she doesn't like old people."

Maxine looked at Ralph with renewed respect.

Ralph blushed and stammered. "I mean, have you ever noticed? When she's talking to any of us, her smile never makes it to her eyes."

20

EVIE THREW HER PURSE onto the striped burnt-orange and sienna couch. Her studio apartment sucked. No wonder the previous renters had broken their lease and migrated back to Minnesota ahead of the other snowbirds. This apartment had probably never had a repeat renter—not with its fake Spanish-settler décor, imitation adobe walls, machine-carved furniture, and wrought iron everything. The place was terminally tasteless. The only thing remotely authentic was the sheepskin throw rug, and it was dingy with age.

She kicked off her shoes and scuffed her way to the couch. She needed to get a real place to live, not some cast-off rental that her grandmother had found.

She sat cross-legged on the couch and flipped open her laptop. It was a royal pain in the butt to have to reapply for that stupid job at her grandmother's rest home. She didn't for one minute believe that pansy-assed Rupert had lost her application.

She'd take care of Ruuu-pert's tendency to lose things. This time she'd hand-deliver her application. Thank God she'd saved it. She'd hate to have to come up with that stuff all over again, especially the statement of her "philosophical approach." Her philosophy was that she needed a job and this one was available. But she couldn't say that. She needed to play the game, and once again, please her busybody grandmother.

All her life, Evie'd had to please her. When she'd gotten married to that piss-ass, now ex-husband of hers, Evie'd had to wear her grandmother's gown. Couldn't get one of her own, one that was in fashion or flattered her figure. Now even her grandmother could see how well that had turned out.

In school, she'd practically majored in geriatrics in order to get her grandmother to help with tuition. It had been extortion, plain and simple.

Even as a child, she'd had to do endless errands for Grandma. The worst was when she had to watch her grandfather. Even now, any mention of that old man brought it all back.

"EVIE, DARLING, I'M GOING to the grocery store," Grandma had said. "Please watch your grandfather for me."

Then the door banged shut, the lock clicked, and Evie was alone with Grandpa Karl. Grandpa Karl smelled bad, and he talked funny. He made no sense. One time he made her put on her grandmother's mink stole, and they spent the whole afternoon walking around the living room looking for an apartment to rent in New York—and he kept calling her Carlotta instead of Evie.

When she complained, her mother said Grandpa Karl was living life backward. He'd lived it all through forward, and now he was going back, like a clock winding the wrong direction. The older he got, the younger he'd get. Pretty soon he'd be just a baby boy younger than Evie, and she shouldn't worry a thing about it but just walk all over her grandmother's house pretending it was New York and wasn't that fun.

One time, Grandpa Karl walked right out of the house, even though they were supposed to stay there until Grandma came home. He took her hand and made her go with him and wouldn't even let her go to the bathroom first. And they walked and walked until her feet hurt and her legs ached and all the nice houses with big yards had turned into big brick buildings with broken windows and no yards and men who stood on the corner and stared or called after her with smoochy sounds she didn't like.

She started crying then, and Grandpa Karl got mad and yelled at her, calling her Carlotta. Then he slapped her so hard she bit her tongue. And then he just walked away, leaving her with those nasty men by the buildings with no yards. She ran after him crying, but he wouldn't stop for her.

After that, they put locks on both sides of her grandparents' doors. No one could get in, and Evie and her grandfather could not get out.

It was best when Grandpa Karl was asleep. Evie never wanted him to wake up. She wanted him to be quiet and still and not scary. Old people needed to be kept neat and in order. They needed to be locked up. When Grandpa Karl was asleep, Evie could take her doll and hide under the dining room table and play at beautiful things like weddings and ballroom dances. There everything was in order. There she was safe.

THE PRINTER WHIRRED and spat out the last page of her application. Evie opened her eyes. At least this time, she'd be in charge.

21

MAXINE'S MOTHER WOULD have disapproved. It was already Monday, and Maxine hadn't properly thanked her co-conspirators for their help with her interview. Oh sure, she'd taken them to brunch at The Summit, but that wasn't the same as writing individual notes. Time to get on with it.

She tossed a box of stationery onto her desk. It slid across the surface, smacked into her pen, and sent it flying. In turn, the ballpoint barrel-rolled onto the floor and taxied to a stop, just out of reach. Determined not to get out of the chair, Maxine sucked in her breath and lunged toward the pen. She snagged it and returned to vertical before vertigo set in.

Panting, she leaned back in her chair.

"D.A.M.N."

She was losing flexibility.

Maxine swatted the pen away, stood, and tried to touch her toes. Her fingertips dangled a distressing six inches above her slippers. She straightened and dialed June. "Would you take yoga if we had it?"

"I prefer ice cream, but yogurt is all right."

"Yo-GA. Not yogurt. Exercise, not food."

"Well, it's nowhere near as much fun, but sure. Where are you going to get a teacher?"

"Maybe Fermez knows someone," Maxine said. "She's a massage therapist. They play the same kind of music. Maybe they all hang out at music stores together."

It turned out that Fermez did know someone: Mimi. "She used to teach yoga to help pay all those nasty school bills."

Mimi, in turn, was delighted by the idea. "Let's start Saturday. Have people bring whatever authorization forms the Foothills requires."

And so it was settled in a matter of minutes.

FIFTEEN SECONDS LATER, the phone rang. The caller turned out to be a breathless, and therefore incomprehensible, Louise.

"Slow down," Maxine said. "Breathe first. Talk later."

"No time. Celine in trouble. Come to the library."

Minutes later, Maxine burst into the library and nearly knocked Louise off Seabiscuit. "What's wrong?"

Louise's eyes were wide, her lips blue, and her knuckles white from the death grip she had on Seabiscuit.

"Should you sit?" Maxine asked.

Louise shook her head, but her chest heaved.

Maxine shoved a Chippendale over.

Louise collapsed into the chair with a nod.

Maxine waited.

Seabiscuit snorted.

Louise's breathing slowed, but her eyes remained wild. "Carlotta and Mrs. Babcock want to fire Celine."

Maxine jerked as if hit by a cattle prod. "What!"

"I went by the front desk to sign up for the bridge tournament, and they were in Rupert's office arguing. The door was open, and they were loud. They want to fire Celine."

"But why?"

"Shh." Louise pointed at the open door. "Because they don't trust her."

"That's absurd!" Maxine began to pace like a caged mountain lion. "Celine is one of the most trustworthy people I know. Why don't they trust her?"

Louise ticked off reasons on her fingers. "Because she dumped a vase of water on Rupert's computer. Because they saw her talking with us after their big argument in the parking lot. Because they think she's spying for us."

"Spying!" Maxine grabbed a throw pillow and threw it. It thudded against the wall and fell to the floor. "That's idiotic. They can't fire Celine because *they're* paranoid." She grabbed another pillow and cocked her arm.

Louise motioned her to stop. "That's what Rupert told them."

"He did?"

"Not in those words, of course."

Maxine dropped the pillow back on the couch. "Then, is Celine's job safe?"

"No! The General claims Celine was late to work every day last week."

Maxine's knees buckled and she sank onto the couch. "I saw her working late, but I assumed she was on flex time."

"According to the General, it wasn't flex time if it wasn't approved in advance. If Celine's late again today, they're going to fire her."

"Where is she anyway? She's supposed to be at my place."

Louise shook her head. "They can't find her, and Carlotta's furious. She wants Celine to set up tables and chairs in the recreation room for one of her parties for Evie. She even threatened to call corporate headquarters if the room's not ready in time. Then she stormed out of Rupert's office so fast I barely had time to duck into the mailroom."

A commotion echoed in the hallway. Maxine stuck her head out the door just as Rupert and Mrs. Babcock marched into view. Rupert's shoulders drooped and his face was grim.

Maxine stepped into the hall and blocked their passage.

Mrs. Babcock scowled. Rupert tried to muster a smile, but failed.

"Good morning," Maxine said in a cheerful voice. "Um . . ." She turned to Louise, who was positioning Seabiscuit so that the cart blocked the hallway. "Um . . . I've been wanting to ask you both a question, but I just haven't had time to come over. I just don't know where the days go." Maxine turned to Louise. "Do you know where the days go?"

Louise was much better at small talk. Even Rupert and Mrs. Babcock seemed hesitant to interrupt her.

After several minutes, however, Louise ran out of breath and tossed the filibuster ball back to Maxine. She launched into a meandering monologue about computers and the need for a lab with ergonomic keyboards, wireless laptops, scanners, printers, and all kinds of equipment that she neither understood nor wanted. She knew enough of the jargon, however, to give the illusion of sense.

As if on cue, Rosemarie appeared. Maxine lobbed the ball into her court, knowing that the subject of technology would make the taciturn woman loquacious—but not for long. Fortunately, June arrived. June could talk for hours about nothing without even knowing she was supposed to.

Mrs. Babcock finally raised her hand like a cop directing traffic and signaled June to stop. "That's all very interesting," she said, "but your request needs to be filled out in triplicate and filed with the appropriate committee by the third of the month."

Rupert edged down the hall toward his office. "This is really a question for Resident Affairs."

The General blocked his retreat. "We are on our way to your place, Maxine, to speak with Celine."

Maxine blinked. "She's not there. I swapped days with June."

"No you didn't," June said, unaware of the game that was being played.

"I spoke with Harry at dinner yesterday." Maxine silently begged for Harry's forgiveness. His faulty memory seemed like the safest place to hide Celine.

"He never told me," June said. "Isn't that just like a man?"

"What's just like a man?" Fred clumped down the hallway toward them dressed in his red-and-green-plaid golf pants and a lemon-yellow Polo shirt. "What's going on?"

Maxine used the question as an opportunity to reopen the computer lab discussion. Soon there was an animated group gesturing and arguing about what had become known as Rupert's idea to create a computer room.

EVENTUALLY, MRS. BABCOCK MARCHED Rupert toward June's place; Fred went into the library to read the newspaper; and Maxine and Louise hurried back to Maxine's condo, where they found Celine whirling through the place like a tornado, vacuuming with one hand and swishing her feather duster about with the other.

Maxine and Louise fired off the questions in rapid succession.

"Are you all right?"

"Where have you been?"

"What's going on?"

"Can we help?"

Celine responded without missing a speck of dust. "Yes. Car trouble. Night school. Thanks, but I don't see how."

Celine grabbed her scrub bucket and headed toward the bathroom.

Maxine and Louise followed.

"What do you mean?"

"What kind of car trouble?"

"What's this about night school?"

"Of course we can help."

Maxine said this last with such assurance that everyone paused for a second before Celine flew back into her cleaning.

"Nope. No way. No time. I was due at Fred's condo thirty minutes ago."

"Perfect," Maxine said. "He's in the library. He won't know what time you arrived. Go."

"But I'm not done here yet."

"Just go. I'll call Rupert and tell him I had my weeks confused and you were here all along."

"What?"

"Don't worry." Maxine bustled Celine toward the door. "Just don't tell anyone you were late today."

Celine halted and crossed her arms. "I'm not telling anyone any stories."

"Wait." Maxine grabbed a plastic bottle of canola oil from the kitchen and dropped it at Celine's feet.

"What are you doing?" Celine grabbed the bottle before it could leak.

"Good." Maxine took back the bottle. "If anyone asks where you were today, you can tell them I dropped a bottle of cooking oil, and you cleaned it up." She shoved Celine out the door. "We'll talk later."

"I clean the library at three," Celine called over her shoulder.

AT THREE O'CLOCK, Maxine strolled into the library wearing her trench coat and Tom's old fedora. Louise looked up from the table where she was playing a complicated version of Solitaire. "Who on earth are you supposed to be?"

"Peter Sellers in *The Pink Panther*? Or Humphrey Bogart in *The Maltese Falcon*?"

"I think you're too tall for Bogart," Louise said. "Wasn't he really short?"

Celine barged into the room. "I'll tell you what's short. The General's temper is short. She's on a royal rampage. I had to set the recreation room up this morning for some party. In a minute, I have to go clean it again so the General can inspect it before she goes home. She thinks you would steal the folding chairs if we left them unguarded."

"Of course we would," Maxine said, "because they are so very attractive and comfortable."

"Forget all that." Louise waved her hands as if erasing their conversation. "Tell us about your car trouble."

Celine rolled her eyes. "Last Sunday I sold my canary-yellow Mustang convertible to pay for my tuition at Casas Adobes. I bought a used Escort. It's turning out to be the little engine that couldn't. Worst excuse for a car I've ever seen. Monday it had a flat. Tuesday it just sat there going *click click*. Wednesday the steering fluid leaked out. Thursday the headlights stopped working. Friday the fan belt broke. I let it rest over the weekend, but today it sat there silent as the tomb it ought to be in. Wouldn't even go *click click* anymore."

"That's not good," Louise said.

"No problem," Maxine said. "We'll call Peter. In the meantime, you can use my car."

Celine backed away. "No way. Your Buick's practically a collector's item. I wouldn't want to risk it."

Maxine narrowed her eyes. "At least it runs, unlike *some* people's cars."

Louise shoved Seabiscuit between them. "Take my car. It works and I don't."

"I can't do that. What if something went wrong with your oxygen machine? I wouldn't want you and Seabiscuit trying to thumb a ride to the doctor."

"Good: it's settled," Maxine said. "You'll use my car until Peter can help us with yours." Before Celine could protest, Maxine changed the subject. "What's this about school?"

Celine stuck out her chin and clenched her fists. "I'm getting my G.E.D. I'm getting a high school diploma so I can go to night school and get a degree in music so I can be a choir director and there's nothing you can say to stop me."

"Why on earth would we want to stop you?" Maxine asked. "I think that's wonderful."

Louise threw her arms around Celine. "It's better than wonderful. It's . . . well, I can't think of a word, but I'm so proud of you."

Celine scuffed her toe like an embarrassed child. "It's not that big a deal."

Maxine looked at her sternly, "But of course it's that big a deal! Don't you ever let anyone tell you it isn't. It's one of the biggest deals ever. It takes a lot of courage to go back to school after . . ." She paused to calculate the elapsed time, but when Celine narrowed her eyes, Maxine opted for discretion over accuracy. "To go back to school after a short absence. What are you taking?"

"I've just got one semester to make up, but they won't let me take more than two courses at once. So I'm taking Algebra II and English IV."

"Algebra II?" Louise made a face. "I hated math. How can you take Algebra II without Algebra I?"

"I already took Algebra I. Math doesn't bother me. I had all A's before

I quit. It's the English that's killing me. All those books and papers make me crazy."

"That's easy," Louise said with a breezy smile. "Maxine taught English at Middleburg College. She can help."

Celine spun toward Maxine. "You did? But I liked you!"

Maxine laughed. "Thank you, dear. I like you too. But I did teach English, and I'd be happy to help if I may."

Celine's face took on that proud and stubborn look that Katie's would get just before she refused any reasonable offer of assistance.

"Tell you what," Maxine said before Celine could object. "Let's meet for fifteen minutes after work. You can tell me what's going on in your English class: what you're reading, what you think about it, what your assignments are. And I'll listen and maybe ask a question or two."

Celine looked dubious. "And that's going to help?"

Maxine shrugged. "It might. It might not. Wouldn't cost much to try it."

Celine's proud look started to come back, and Maxine recognized her error. "We'll do it as barter. We can meet at my place, and you can help me reorganize my cabinets and closets while we talk."

Celine looked even more dubious.

"I can't find anything, but I can't make myself straighten things up. I get too bored. But if you were to tell me about your classes while I worked . . ." Maxine saw the frown on Celine's face. "I mean while *we* worked, I'm sure we could impose some order in no time. And it would be a huge relief to me."

Celine raised an eyebrow and stared at Maxine, who met her gaze.

"OK?" Maxine asked and held the gaze.

After a long moment, Celine gave the briefest of nods. "For fifteen minutes, and that's only because you saved me from the General this morning."

They shook hands, and Celine left.

Louise shot her hand up like a student with an urgent question.

Maxine examined Louise over the top of her glasses.

"Excuse me," Louise said. "But you have the neatest cabinets and closets of anyone I know."

"I know." Maxine tugged the fedora to a jaunty angle. "So let's go disorganize something."

"All right!" Louise wheeled Seabiscuit around and headed toward the door. "Let's start with your food pantry. No one should have her cereals arranged alphabetically."

22

UNABLE TO HEAR over the racket that Louise made as she disarranged the kitchen, Maxine called Peter from the phone in her bedroom. She returned to the kitchen, shaking her head. "Poor Celine."

"What's wrong?" Louise called from the back of the pantry. "Can't Peter come?"

"He's coming right over," Maxine said, automatically restoring alphabetical order to the cereals that Louise had left on the counter in disarray. "But he said total silence in a car is not a good sign. A *click click* sound would be better."

Louise emerged from the pantry and swatted Maxine's hand. "Stop it. I've already disorganized those."

Maxine moved away from the cereals and absently began re-ordering the soups that Louise had scattered across the countertops.

"Go away," Louise said. "You deal with Peter and Celine while I finish here."

MAXINE RESISTED THE URGE to pace. Peter had been poking and prodding under the hood of Celine's Escort for fifteen interminable minutes. Finally he stood and shook his head.

"Uh-oh," Celine said, "that doesn't look good."

Peter jammed his hands in his pockets. "It's not. The engine's blown and the body's full of rust. It would cost more to fix it than to buy a new one. I'm sorry."

Celine kicked the front tire of the Escort. "Damn!"

Celine never swore. Maxine wasn't sure which was more disconcerting, Celine's swearing or her subsequent silence.

"Where did you get it?" Maxine said. "Maybe we can get your money back."

Peter and Celine both looked at her as if she'd spoken in tongues.

Peter broke the silence. "Whoever sold this car knew what he was doing. The oil pump is new. I'm betting the previous owner never changed the oil. When the old pump froze, he replaced it, steam-cleaned the engine, paid for a cheap paint job to cover the rust, demanded cash, and moved out of town."

Celine nodded. "Double damn. There goes my tuition money."

"No," Maxine said. "Use my car. I can ride with Louise or June anywhere I need to go."

"Nu-huh. No way. No how."

"Peter, tell Celine how silly it is . . . Peter?"

Peter was not listening. He was sorting through his toolbox.

"Eureka!" He held aloft a key ring with two keys and a miniature set of fuzzy dice. "Here." He dropped the keys into Celine's purse.

"What's that?"

"Keys to Old Betsy," he said with obvious delight. "You take Old Betsy. She got me through school and now she can do the same for you."

Celine's jaw dropped. "You mean that beautiful '56 Bel Air?"

Peter beamed and nodded.

"I can't do that." Celine thrust her purse at Maxine to hold while she rummaged through it for the keys. "I can't." She fished out the keys. "I just can't."

Peter jammed his hands back into his pockets. "Of course you can. Old Betsy needs someone to love her and drive her."

"No. I can't." Celine placed the keys on Peter's toolbox.

Peter looked at Maxine.

"But Celine . . ." Maxine stopped when she saw the look in Celine's eyes. Celine had clearly reached her limit.

Maxine warned Peter off with a slight shake of her head. "We don't need to settle all that right now. We can figure it out tonight after . . ." She paused, uncertain if she should mention the tutoring session. "After Celine and I finish some personal business."

Celine started to protest, but Maxine shot her one of her schoolteacher stares, the kind that freezes boiling water at twenty paces. Maxine knew the look would not hold Celine for long, so, after thanking Peter, she simply turned and walked away, carrying Celine's purse with her.

BACK AT HER CONDO, Maxine tried to get Celine to sit at the table.

"No way," Celine said. "A deal's a deal. We're cleaning your cabinets as we do this, remember?"

"Oh right." Maxine tried to recall which cabinets Louise had been disorganizing. "Let's start with this cabinet." She pulled open the pantry. It looked as if a herd of teenagers had stampeded through it in a feeding frenzy. You wouldn't think mild-mannered Louise could wreak so much havoc in so little time.

Celine peered into the cabinet. "This place is a mess. You don't even have your cereals together. Me, I like to alphabetize them."

"So do I." Maxine recognized her slip. "I mean, I like that in theory. Let's try it."

"Do you want to pitch or catch?"

"Excuse me?"

"We need to empty this cabinet before we can straighten it," Celine said with exaggerated patience. "One of us should pull the things out and hand them to the other to put on your counter over there."

"Good idea. You pitch: I'll catch."

"OK," Celine said, burrowing into the cabinet. "You might want to group the stuff as you put it on the counter. It'll be easier to organize later."

Maxine was already alphabetizing the cereal. "So tell me about your English class."

"Nothing to tell." Celine dove further into the cabinet. "What are you doing putting pots in here? This here's a food cabinet."

Maxine stared at the large saucepan that appeared in Celine's hand. Just how much of her kitchen had Louse disrupted?

"Believe me; I have no idea what it's doing in there." Maxine reached for the cabinet next to the stove. "Maybe it will fit in here." She was relieved to see the rest of her pots were where she'd left them.

"And what about this?" Celine pulled out a potted plant.

"That's an oxalis. Looks like a shamrock. It's really hardy. Would you like a cutting? Just stick a piece in a glass of water and it will grow roots in no time."

Celine eyed the plant with suspicion.

Maxine grabbed the plant and shoved it into the utility closet where Celine couldn't see it. "What did you say your assignment was for English?"

"It was just plain dumb." Celine started banging canned soups and vegetables on the counter.

Maxine decided to let Celine play both pitcher and catcher until she'd finish banging the cans.

"We were supposed to read 'The General Prologue' to *The Canterbury Tales* by a guy named Chaucer who died about a million years ago. You ever heard of him?"

Maxine stifled a smile and nodded. "Yes, as a matter of fact, I have heard of him."

Celine spun around and put her hands on her hips. "So how come he's supposed to be so great? He's either simple-minded or flat-out stupid."

"Why do you say that?" Maxine had heard a lot of complaints from students who didn't want to grapple with a fourteenth-century work, but no one had called Chaucer simple-minded before.

"Well, the dude is going on a pilgrimage with twenty-nine other folks," Celine arranged the canned soups and vegetables in a line as if they were the pilgrims.

"Let's say Chaucer is this here can of tomato paste, and he's traveling with all these folks he doesn't know: monks and nuns and knights and millers and everyone. I mean he's got everybody there, including some good, decent folks and some downright nasty scoundrels."

Maxine nodded. Celine's analysis was right on target.

"But he thinks they're all good. He takes them at face value." Celine grabbed a can of kidney beans and a can of asparagus. "I mean, he can't tell the difference between a philandering, lying, hypocritical friar"— she brandished the kidney beans—"and a hard-working, honest, decent parson." She waved the asparagus. "Why should I read something by a man can't tell beans from asparagus?"

"How do you know some of the pilgrims are hypocrites?" Maxine pointed to the kidney beans. "And some are not?" She gestured toward the asparagus.

"Well, say this asparagus is the parson." Celine placed the can carefully at the head of her line of cans. "He's always doing good works and saving people and preaching good sermons. And he's not afraid to tell a sinner to straighten up and fly right—even if that sinner is a knight or a king. He even rides out in the rain to visit the sick."

Celine put the kidney beans at the end of her line of cans. "Now this here friar, he's out begging and bribing and even fathering children."

Maxine nodded. "You're absolutely right."

Celine pointed her finger at the tomato paste and spoke with some anger. "So this simpleton Chaucer thinks they're all good, thinks they're all who they say they are."

"I see your point."

Celine took a step back. Evidently she was not used to English teachers who granted her points.

Maxine picked up the small can of tomato paste and a large can of whole tomatoes. "Let's say Chaucer the pilgrim is this can of tomato paste. He's traveling with the other folks and, as you say, he somewhat naively takes them at face value."

Celine nodded.

"And the reason we know that some of the pilgrims are not what they pretend to be is because we have all those wonderful details you mentioned, like the friar fathering children, and the parson riding out to visit the sick."

"That's what I'm saying."

"And you're right," Maxine said. "But what about the large can of whole tomatoes?"

"Say huh?"

"Remember, this small can of tomato paste is Chaucer the pilgrim, a rather naive *character* who is going on this pilgrimage. But this big can of whole tomatoes is Chaucer the *author*, the man who wrote *The Canterbury Tales*, the guy who put in all the details you noticed. He has a very keen eye and sees what everyone is really like."

Celine looked dubious.

"It's only confusing because he gave this character," Maxine held up the small can of tomato paste again, "his own name. Maxine grabbed a tin of tuna. "If he'd named him something else, something like Ralph or Charlie, readers would see the difference between the author and the character right away."

Celine played with the cans for a minute. "OK. I get it, but why would Chaucer the author name one of the characters after himself? What's the point?"

"Good question," Maxine said. "What do you think the point might be? What difference does it make to the story that Chaucer inserted himself into it as a character?"

Celine stared at the cans a long time. "I think it makes the story seem more real because he's on the trip and he's real."

Maxine nodded.

"And it makes the story less harsh," Celine said.

Maxine raised both eyebrows. "What do you mean?"

"Chaucer the pilgrim doesn't make any judgments or point any fingers. So it kind of keeps us from doing it either. It's like we're all pilgrims on the same journey, so we just leave the judgment part to God."

Maxine smiled. "I think you are absolutely right."

"You do?" Celine seemed dumbfounded.

Maxine pretended to alphabetize the cereals. "Yes, I do. You understand literature a whole lot better than you think you do."

"I do?"

"Yes, but I like talking with you about books, so let's keep meeting." Maxine stopped sorting cereals and looked directly at Celine. "OK?"

Celine bit her lip and toyed with the cans, arranging and rearranging them. "OK. This is kind of fun."

Evidently embarrassed by the admission, Celine plunged back into the cabinet. In a second she reemerged. "You aren't going to believe what else is in here."

Maxine dared not think.

Celine brandished one of Louise's small, emergency oxygen tanks.

Maxine laughed until tears came to her eyes. "That Louise is a lot like that can of tomato paste: there's more to her than meets the eye."

Celine nodded. "Next time, tell her she doesn't have to do quite such an elaborate job disorganizing things."

Maxine nearly dropped the tomato paste. "You knew?"

"I was suspicious," Celine said. "After all, I clean this place; I know how organized you are. But I knew for sure when I found the potted plant. It goes on your coffee table. I watered it this morning. If you pull it out of the utility closet, you can still see the place where I stuck my finger in to see if it was wet enough."

Maxine bowed and tipped an imaginary cap to Celine. "I guess Chaucer's not the only clever one here. Things are never quite as simple as they first appear."

Celine nodded. And shrugged. "We're all just cans of food on this here pilgrimage."

23

"SPEAKING OF PILGRIMAGES," Maxine said as she and Celine tucked the last of the soups and cereals back into Maxine's cabinet. "It's time you started on your own."

Celine stopped shelving. "Say what?"

"Catch!" Maxine threw her car keys at Celine, who had to catch them in self-defense. "Use my car tonight," Maxine said. "I'm playing bridge at June's tomorrow, so I won't need it until Wednesday at the earliest."

Celine's protest was cut short by the ringing of the telephone. Maxine lunged for the receiver, grateful for an excuse to end the argument. Smiling in sweet victory, she waved Celine out the door.

"Hello?"

"Hey, Mother. It's me."

Maxine went on the alert. She'd been demoted back to *Mother*, and Katie sounded nervous. Katie, who'd made a million calls involving billions of dollars, sounded nervous. In response, Maxine tried to make her own voice sound casual. "Hey, you."

"I hope it's not too late to call."

"Heavens, no. I've just finished tutoring Celine."

"Who's Celine?"

"A new friend." Maxine paused, struck by the similarities between Celine and her daughter. "How are you?"

"I'm good. In fact, I'm great. I found my old hiking jeans, and they still fit!"

"I don't know which is more astonishing," Maxine said. "That you found them or that they still fit. I wish I could still wear my jeans from fifteen years ago."

"I bet you could. You never gain weight. In fact, I bet you do still wear the same jeans."

"Not really. The ones I liked I wore out. The others I gave to thrift stores."

"I have some other news too."

Maxine heard the excitement and uncertainty in Katie's voice. "Yes?"

"I've rented a piano—just to test-drive it, you know, see how it feels."

Maxine's heart skipped. "That's wonderful! How does it feel?"

"A bit strange." Katie paused. "Well, to be perfectly candid, it feels absolutely terrific."

In the background, Maxine heard Katie running a finger the length of the keyboard. The glissando was like the cracking of ice announcing the end of a long winter. "I'm so happy for you!"

"Thanks. I'm pretty rusty. I'm not even sure where middle C is."

"It shouldn't take you too long to find it." Maxine wiped her eyes with the back of her hand. "As I recall, there are only eighty-eight keys to choose from."

"And only fifty-two of them are white. I should have it narrowed down in no time."

Mother and daughter chatted about the piano for several more minutes before lapsing into silence. Maxine waited for Katie to take the lead. When she didn't, Maxine asked the obvious. "Have you thought any more about your job? Have you had a chance to sort through your options?"

Katie exhaled.

"Yes and no. I don't know." Katie's voice began to get high and thin—like a child's. "I mean, I have an extraordinary opportunity here. I could be the first female full partner. Or, I could run my own company." She stopped after restating what they both already knew.

Maxine spoke gently into the silence. "It sounds as if there is a *but* that follows each of those sentences."

"That's just it. There is a *but*, only I don't know what it is exactly. The jobs—both of them—are great opportunities."

"Katie, dear, are they great opportunities for *you*? I know you could do either of them, but do you *want* to?"

"In point of fact," Katie began in the aggressive voice she'd perfected for her high school debate club.

"Yes?" Maxine tried to sound encouraging, nonconfrontational.

"In point of fact," Katie said in a much softer tone, "I really don't know."

"Fair enough. So what are the pros and cons of each job? I'll write, you talk."

"Mo-om," Katie stretched the word into two syllables the way she had as a teenager.

"I'll start," Maxine said. "I'm putting money, fame, and power in the pro side of the list. That has to be part of the attraction. It would be for me. The pressure to be the first woman to make partner must be enormous."

"It is," Katie said. "I feel almost an obligation to shatter that glass ceiling."

"OK, but I'm putting obligation in its own column. It's neither pro nor con, or maybe it's both. Now what else do you like about the jobs? The adrenaline? The travel? The negotiations?"

"Not really." Katie sounded surprised. "There's an adrenaline rush all right, but there's no abiding pleasure. It's like the difference between riding a roller coaster and playing a sonata. The roller coaster is wild but passive. The sonata requires physical, emotional, and intellectual engagement. In a roller coaster, I'm just along for the ride. In a sonata, I'm part of the creation."

Maxine knew what Katie meant. For her, teaching was like playing a sonata, and being the head of the department was like riding a roller coaster.

Katie cleared her throat. "The thing is, I'm going back to Phoenix at the end of this week. Would it be all right if I stopped in Tucson on Friday night? I'd have to catch that early flight back to New York on Sunday."

"Of course it's all right!" Maxine pumped her fist in celebration. "It's too bad you have to go back on that early flight. We're going to Rupert's race on Sunday. I could still order you a t-shirt."

Katie laughed. "Wish I could." She sounded almost wistful. "Instead of that, maybe we could get Peter to join us Saturday for a hike along that riverbed near his place."

"Great idea. I'll call him."

"Perfect."

Maxine's fingers trembled slightly. "I want your opinion about something." She stopped, shocked by her own words. She'd blurted them out without thinking them through.

"Yes?" Katie said.

Maxine fumbled the receiver and nearly dropped it. She swallowed. "It's about last Friday."

"What about last Friday?" Katie's voice sounded tight and flat and formal, the way it did when she was hurt and angry.

Maxine prayed for the courage to confess. When it eluded her, she prayed for mercy instead. "But it will be easier to explain in person."

The line went silent. Maxine gripped the receiver until her fingers ached.

"Fine." Katie's voice was curt and clipped.

Maxine held her breath, fearful lest the slightest sound topple them back into an abyss from which they might never emerge.

As if aware of the danger, Katie shifted the conversation to safer ground. "While I'm there, let me take you and your bridge buddies out to dinner. Is there anyone else we should include?"

Maxine exhaled softly, grateful they'd toppled away from the brink. "Well, I'd like you to meet Celine. Maybe I could reserve the private dining room at the Foothills."

"Nope. Let's go out. Littlehouse, Ferris, and Jones can treat us all."

Maxine relaxed her grip on the receiver. "That would be wonderful."

"Good. See you on Friday."

"Bye, dear. Love you," Maxine said, but Katie had already disengaged.

PART FOUR

GRAND SLAM:
THE PRESENTATION

24

MAXINE SURREPTITIOUSLY CHECKED the clock on June's sunroom wall. It felt as if time had stopped and Friday, with Katie's visit, would never get here. Thank goodness for bridge.

If June's Italian tile table were a clock, Maxine sat at six and Louise at noon. Rosemarie and June occupied three and nine o'clock, respectively. Daisy lay stretched out under the table, snoring softly. Occasionally, she would yelp in her sleep and twitch her paws.

"I wonder what Daisy dreams about," Rosemarie said.

"Chasing jackrabbits," Maxine said. "Just look at those paws go."

June doted on Daisy. "If I know my Daisy," she said in a dismissive tone that did nothing to hide that love, "she's getting into the garbage to finish off Harry's pizza crusts."

At the mention of his name, Harry looked up from his chair in the living room where he was reading Carl Sandburg's *Abraham Lincoln: The War Years*. June shook her head, and he returned to his book.

"Amazing how he and Daisy both have developed selective hearing," June said and led with the ten of clubs. "They can hear a box of cookies being opened in another room, but neither of them can hear me call them to come."

"Chuck used to drive me crazy." Louise tossed out the king of clubs. "When I first got my walker, he'd come running every time I blinked. But let me try to find him for dinner and I could call him until the cows came home to roost, for all the good it would do."

"Men can't help it," Rosemarie said, slapping the ace of clubs on Louise's king. "They're genetically defective."

"I've never understood the 'cows coming home' thing." Maxine trumped Rosemarie's ace with the two of hearts. "I mean, don't cows come home quite regularly to be milked and fed?"

"You were void in clubs?" June stared at the lost trick. "The bridge gods are a contrary lot. Personally, I've never understood 'the whole nine yards' thing. I mean people say it as if they were getting the whole thing, you know what I mean?"

They nodded, concentrating on their cards.

June continued. "But nine yards doesn't buy you a first down. 'The whole nine yards' is still a yard short."

"It's from concrete, not football," Harry called from the living room, nose still buried in the Civil War.

The women raised their heads in confusion. June looked as if she wished he had not spoken.

"What's from concrete, Harry?" Maxine asked.

"The saying 'the whole nine yards.' That's how they measured concrete. If you got a whole truckload, you got the whole nine yards."

"Seriously?"

"How on earth do you know that?" Maxine asked.

Without looking up from his book, Harry tapped his forehead with his fingers and whispered, "Kidneys." It was the punch line from a retirement center joke so old that none of them actually remembered it.

"And you're so old that you eat dessert first," Rosemarie said, picking the cashews out of the mixed nuts.

"And don't buy green bananas," Louise added.

"Crows," June said. "The saying is 'until the *crows* come home to roost.' Not cows."

"Even so," Maxine said, "don't crows roost at predictable times?"

The women glanced at Harry to see if he knew any trivia about crows, but he shrugged and turned the page.

Rosemarie dealt the next hand. "Speaking of cement trucks, Carlotta's obtained the whole nine yards from Rupert."

They sorted their cards.

"One spade," Rosemarie said, reaching for the nut dish. "Rupert has agreed to our committee's request."

Maxine pretended to resort her cards. "What request?"

"Candidates for the assistant director's position will be asked to meet with all the residents."

"But they've already been interviewed." Maxine fanned herself with her cards. The room was suddenly much too hot.

"We've selected three finalists who will be asked to give a short talk and arrange a small event so that everyone can meet them. It should make the whole process more equitable, given that Rupert interviewed some candidates without the committee." Rosemarie turned to Maxine. "Your bid, dear."

Maxine passed despite her strong hand.

June jumped to game. "Four spades."

"Two hearts," Louise said.

Everything stopped. Louise never made bidding errors.

"Are you all right?" June asked and reached to adjust Louise's oxygen line.

"What? Why? I'm fine." Louise slapped June's hand away.

"The bid was four spades," Maxine said.

"Oh. Sorry." Louise blushed. "Pass."

"When are the candidates supposed to present?" Maxine asked. "And I pass."

"It's not your turn," Rosemarie said. "Oh never mind. I pass too." She began playing out the hand. "We're hoping one candidate will come on a Friday or Saturday night for each of the next three weekends."

Louise and Maxine stared at each other.

"Louise, are you sure you're feeling well?" June asked. "You just trumped your partner's ace."

AFTER LOSING DESPITE THEIR GOOD CARDS, Maxine and Louise rushed to the computer in the library.

Maxine brought up her email and groaned.

"What?" Louise said. "Didn't you get invited?"

"I did. They want me to give a twenty-minute talk followed by a sample event or activity. In just two and a half weeks—on Saturday."

Louise collapsed into a chair. "The cows have come home to roost."

"Girlfriend, you are in serious trouble," a deep voice said.

They spun around to face Celine.

"How do you do that?" Maxine asked.

"Do what?"

"How do you manage to sneak up on us every time we're on the computer?"

Celine leaned forward and whispered, "Technology."

Maxine straightened.

"My vacuum cleaner is really a wireless transporter and this here can of Pledge is the remote control."

Maxine sighed. She'd half hoped that Celine really did have some secret technological toy for transporting people elsewhere in a hurry. Right now she could use it.

"So what are we going to do?" Celine said. "Someone from the Foothills is bound to notice that you're you."

Louise bounced in her chair like a kid at Christmas. "No. Yes. That's it! It's perfect. Everyone will know it's you."

Maxine studied Louise to see if she had lost her mind. "I may be missing something here, but you aren't exactly making sense."

Louise took a couple of deep breaths. "This is what we wanted." She gulped for air.

"Wait." Maxine held up her hand. When Louise's chest stopped heaving, she lowered her hand. "OK. Now."

Louise nodded. "You've made it through the hoops. Now people can see it's you. They know you: they love you."

"Not all of them." Celine batted her eyes and waved an imaginary cigarette holder.

"No, not all," Louise said. "But most. You wouldn't want this job if they didn't want you. Now is the time to step forth."

Maxine made a face. "You make it sound like a debutante ball."

"Precisely. It is. It's your coming-out party. You're coming out as a legitimate candidate for assistant director."

"Besides," Celine said. "You don't have a choice."

Maxine narrowed her eyes at Celine.

Celine shrugged.

"But what am I going to do for an event?"

"I Iave music." Celine held her feather duster like a microphone. "Everybody loves music. Get a live band."

"You could do a sing-along," Louise said.

"Thank you, Mitch Miller," Maxine said slumping in her chair. "But it's called karaoke these days."

"That's what I'm saying." Celine flashed a double thumbs-up. "Have a band do a set then let the audience join in. Those old folks will go wild."

Maxine and Louise both narrowed their eyes at Celine.

"What? I'm talking about those *other* folks. They're not like you. *They're* old. They need some music rejuvenating them."

"Where am I going to get a band? They've given me a fifty-dollar budget."

"Fifty dollars?" Louise said. "Rupert is such a cheapskate."

"Get Mimi and me for free. We can—"

Louise interrupted. "June's grandson—what's his name—plays in a band."

Maxine looked over the top of her glasses at Louise. "He lives on Long Island and he plays in a heavy metal rock band."

"So?"

"The name of his group is Renegade Road Kill," Maxine said. "The band members all have stage names like Smashed Squirrel, Putrid Possum, and Crushed Cat's Guts."

Celine grimaced. "That's just adolescent boy nasty."

Louise tried to salvage her idea. "Maybe they know some songs we'd recognize and like."

"We probably wouldn't even recognize their playing as music," Maxine said. "I can't hire Renegade Road Kill."

Celine placed her hands on her hips. "In case anyone's forgotten, I've got lots of musical connections, and our stage names are a lot nicer."

"I can't impose on you like that," Maxine said. "It would be—"

"Nonsense," Louise said. "Of course you can. That's what friends are for."

"Besides," Celine said, "you don't have a choice."

"Wait," Maxine said. "Let me think a minute." She closed her eyes to consider her options. Nothing came to mind. Celine was right. She didn't have any choice. She opened her eyes.

"Well?" Celine said.

Maxine closed her eyes again. Still no alternatives presented themselves. She opened her eyes.

"OK," she said. "I'll accept your help with a band, if you accept Old Betsy from Peter."

"Nuh-uh." Celine glared. "No fair."

Louise shoved Seabiscuit between them. "It's a deal!"

Maxine and Celine both started to protest, but Louise waved their objections aside. "Too late. A deal's a deal. A card laid is a card played."

"Say what?"

"Never mind," Louise said. "Shake hands before either of you backs out."

Maxine and Celine stared at each other, deadlocked.

Louise glared at them. "Do you want Evie to become the assistant director?"

Maxine shuddered.

Celine squirmed.

They looked at each other. They looked away. They looked back again and shrugged.

Celine lifted her chin. "I'll borrow Old Betsy, but only if I get to be"—she placed one hand on her hip and fluttered the other in a pose worthy of Fermez—"the artistic director for your event."

"Oh, for Pete's sake." Maxine backhanded the air as if she were swatting away cobwebs. "All right, but from now on you do at least two drafts of all your papers."

"Perfect," Louise said. "Now shake."

Maxine and Celine faced off like cowboys in a shootout with fingers twitching, neither willing to make the first move.

"Shake." Louise ordered, and they obeyed.

"Honestly," Louise said. "The two of you are just alike. I'm going home to roost."

"And I'm going to go line up the talent for my gig." Celine swept out of the room like the diva she aspired to be.

Maxine watched them go, unable to suppress a niggling suspicion that she'd overlooked something important during their negotiations. The muscles in her neck tied themselves in a knot. She tipped her head—right ear to right shoulder, left ear to left—but the knot and the suspicion both remained.

25

MAXINE ROLLED HER SHOULDERS. Mimi's Saturday morning yoga class had worked wonders. For the first time in weeks, she felt relaxed. She tilted her head from side to side. Even the knot in her neck was gone. Tucking her mat into a canvas bag, she waved good-bye to Mimi and headed toward her condo to check on Katie just as Celine charged up the staircase, with her head down and her arms full of what looked like sheet music.

"Whoa." Maxine flattened herself against the wall as Celine stormed past.

"Goodness." Celine pressed her stack of papers to her chest. "You gave me a start. You shouldn't sneak up on people."

"Me?"

"Never mind," Celine said. "You probably can't help it. How was Mimi's class?"

"Excellent. I feel ten years younger and two inches taller." Maxine swung her arms and twisted her torso like a top. "Now I'm loose as a goose."

"Looks more like you've got a screw loose."

Maxine stopped swinging. "There was one tense moment at the very end when Evie and Carlotta came in."

Celine made a face. "What did they want?"

"They turned on the overhead lights in the middle of shavasana and demanded we get authorization forms."

"What happened?"

Maxine gloated and pulled a handful of fuchsia and orange forms out of her bag. "We'd already signed them."

Celine grinned. "Atta girl! That explains why they were in such a snit just now. They even tried to throw Katie and me out of the formal living room."

"What were you two doing in the formal living room?"

Celine shifted her stack of papers. "I was on my way upstairs to see Mimi when I heard Katie playing the piano. Thought she might need another lesson with me."

Maxine raised an eyebrow. "Does Katie know you're giving her lessons?"

"No. That's the beauty of *my* method." Celine puffed out her chest. "*I'm* subtle. I listen, and she plays. Works like a charm. Pretty soon she'll be ready to join a band."

"Speaking of bands." Maxine eyed Celine's stack of papers. "How are you and Mimi doing on our event?"

Celine hugged the papers closer. "Gotta go." She bolted past.

"But—"

"Mimi's waiting," Celine called over her shoulder and waved goodbye without turning around.

Maxine frowned and rubbed her neck. The knot was back.

MAXINE LINGERED IN THE DOORWAY. As usual, the formal living room was cool and peaceful. Sunlight filtered through half-closed blinds, making the space feel empty and expectant, like a sanctuary between services.

Maxine smiled at the image. If the room was a sanctuary, then the giant stone fireplace was its entirely unsatisfactory altar. Someone had replaced the vase Celine had broken with another huge vase filled with exotic-looking flowers. Even so, the real focal point of the room was the grand piano where Katie was playing some Bach.

Maxine leaned against the doorframe. Her daughter was beautiful—not in a simple, external way, but in some profound, organic way.

Maxine didn't quite know how to articulate it, but when Katie played the piano, she was transformed. She became an extension of the music, a moment of pure grace.

A discordant rendition of "Chopsticks" jarred Maxine back to the present.

"Earth to Maxine," Katie said. A smile tugged at the corners of her mouth.

"You caught me wool-gathering," Maxine said. "How's the piano? I think they just tuned it."

"It's very nice." Katie played snatches of popular songs. "It has a good tone, and I like the action in the keys. The pedals are a bit soft, but you retirees probably stomp on them pretty hard during rock concerts."

"At least they've sanded out the gouge marks from our tap dancing on the lid."

Katie stood and closed the piano. "How about buying me a second cup of tea, and we can talk about whatever it was you wanted to discuss."

Maxine stiffened. When Katie had called to say she was coming, Maxine had intended to tell her about the interview. But that was then, and this was now. She forced a smile. "I have a wonderful selection of teas, as long as you like Orange Pekoe." She tried to sound enthusiastic, but she was fairly certain her performance would win no awards.

AS IF BY UNSPOKEN AGREEMENT, Maxine and Katie headed to the patio to drink their tea.

Maxine sat down, stood up, walked to the patio wall, leaned on it, looked out, turned around, walked back, sat down, and stood up.

"Mom!" Katie's voice was sharp.

"What's wrong, dear?"

"That's what I was going to ask," Katie said. "As Dad used to say, you're jumpier than a jackrabbit."

"I'm sorry." Maxine sat back down. "It's just that, well, I have a confession to make: I wasn't entirely honest with you last week." Maxine's voice trailed off as the woman in front of her metamorphosed from her beautiful daughter into a powerful executive, angular and tensed for confrontation.

Maxine shivered despite the heat.

"Yes?" Katie's voice was neutral.

Maxine twisted her wedding band. If ever she needed Tom's guidance, now was the moment. Well, that wasn't really true. She always needed, or at least wanted, Tom's presence and guidance.

"Mom?"

"Sorry dear. I was thinking of your father. He was so much better at this than I am."

"So much better at what?" Katie was beginning to sound frustrated, or maybe bewildered.

Maxine stared into her tea mug. "Better at knowing the right words, or the right order to the words." She drew a deep breath. She needed to speak before she lost her courage. "I wasn't at a bridge tournament during your last visit. I was at a job interview—a rather elaborate webcam interview." She stopped and raised her eyes to meet Katie's gaze. "I'm sorry I lied to you."

Maxine braced her shoulders as if preparing herself for the scourge. Part of her brain observed that Katie's shoulders seemed similarly locked and rigid, as if preparing for battle.

"Why didn't you tell me? You told Peter." The accusation was flung like a punch.

Maxine didn't flinch. "Peter helped me with the webcam. I told him because I needed his help." She could see the anger building in Katie's eyes. "I didn't tell you because I thought it would distract you from your own job decisions. And because I thought you'd be opposed, and I didn't want you to be angry. And most of all, because I didn't want to lose you."

"Lose me?"

"Yes. Not now. Not when we're starting to . . ." Maxine's hand wavered in the air between them.

Katie looked at the mountains and then back to Maxine. Her shoulders softened. "Yes. I know." Her rancor was gone.

The tension eased from Maxine's own shoulders.

Katie leaned forward, elbows on knees. "Why are you interviewing for a job? You don't need the money."

Maxine exhaled softly, aware for the first time that she'd been holding her breath. Katie's question had shifted the conversation away from Maxine's betrayal back to a simpler world of financial exigencies. Facts and figures were not a comfortable part of Maxine's mental landscape, but they were a lot easier to traverse than the complicated dynamics of their mother-daughter relationship.

Katie pressed on. "Because, you know, your portfolio's in good shape." Her voice wavered. "And even if it weren't, I'd take care of you. You know that, don't you?"

Maxine heard the pleading in the question. "Yes, dear. I know that. But I don't ever want to be a burden to you."

"Mo-om." Katie raised her hands in supplication and frustration. "My job sucks, but they pay me buckets of money to do it. I can't possibly spend it all. How many Gucci bags can one woman use?"

Maxine smiled. "I don't know. You've evidently been using one pair of jeans for fifteen years."

Katie whooped with delight.

Maxine snorted.

They burst into laughter—wild, uncontrollable laughter. They laughed until tears ran down their faces. They laughed until they gasped for breath.

Maxine was not sure if they were tears of joy, or relief, or both.

Katie regained her breath first. "So what job did you apply for?" she said.

"Assistant director of the Foothills Retirement Community."

"Assistant director!" Katie's eyes were wide. "You applied to be assistant director here, at the Foothills?"

Maxine hushed her. "No one knows except Louise and Celine. We didn't even tell Rosemarie and June. And yes, I applied to be the assistant director." Maxine narrowed her eyes. "I suppose you think I'm too old."

"Of course not. You can do anything." Katie said it as if she were stating the obvious.

"But?"

"Well, let me ask you the same question you asked me. Do you really *want* to be assistant director?"

"Of course," Maxine responded automatically. "The Foothills needs me. You should see the silly application Rupert came up with. Anyone capable of breathing would be qualified. And now Evie Helmsley Hill has applied, and we can't let her become the assistant director. It would be suicide or genocide or something; she'd bore us to death. It would be the end of all intelligent life here."

Maxine paused for a breath and Katie looked at her appraisingly. "Yes, I can see why the Foothills needs you, but I still don't see why you need the Foothills—or at least the assistant director's job."

Maxine started to reply, but Katie cut her off. "I mean it seems to me the job contains all of the things you most dislike and none of the things you love. It's a roller coaster, not a sonata."

Maxine had the disturbing suspicion that Katie might be right.

"If you're going to work, why not do something you love? Teach or write or something?"

Maxine studied Katie. "That's a good question. I wish I had a good answer."

Katie flashed her crooked smile and shook her head. "Aren't we a pair? At least we're both getting better at asking the questions, even if neither of us has a glimmer of an answer."

"Who knew life could be so complicated?" Maxine said.

"My mother must have warned me, but I didn't listen to her."

"I don't blame you, dear. I wouldn't listen to her either."

They relaxed into comfortable silence.

Eventually Katie opened her laptop and Maxine picked up the newspaper.

An ad for yoga supplies caught Maxine's eye. "Do you think knee cushions would help my arthritis?" she asked, holding up the paper for Katie's inspection.

Katie shrugged. "No idea," she said. "Why not ask your instructor?"

"Good idea." Maxine got up to look for Mimi's phone number.

She hunted through her address book, desk, purse, and telephone book. "D.A.M.N."

"What's wrong?" Katie called from the patio.

"I've misplaced Mimi's phone number, and there's no La Fievre in the phonebook."

"Would Louise know?"

Louise's line was busy, so Maxine called Celine. "I've misplaced Mimi's phone number, and there aren't any La Fievres listed."

"That's because that's not her name."

"What do you mean that's not her name?"

"That's just a stage name that Fermez gave her. Her real name is Lafayette."

"Lafayette? That sounds familiar."

"It should if you took any history."

"No, I mean—oh well, it doesn't matter." Maxine jotted down the phone number Celine gave her. "Speaking of numbers," she said, trying to sound casual. "What numbers are you and Mimi singing for the event?"

"Girlfriend, you just leave everything to us and stop worrying."

"But . . ."

"But nothing. You made me artistic director, so butt out."

"But . . ."

"Tell you what," Celine said. "You can come up with a name for our group, and I'll handle the rest of it."

"OK. But—"

"Look, it's a surprise. Gotta go." The line went dead.

Maxine was pretty certain that Celine had made up the part about it being a surprise, but she didn't see an alternative. She dialed Mimi's number and got only her voicemail. She left a message, then wandered out to the patio.

Katie looked up from her laptop. "What's up, Mom? You have that furrowed-brow look."

"Celine is working on a surprise for me," Maxine said.

"That's nice. Isn't it?"

Maxine shook her head. "Lord only knows."

"Any luck with Mimi's phone number?"

"Well, that's another thing," Maxine said. "It turns out Mimi's real name is not La Fievre. That's just a stage name Fermez gave her."

"That's good. Can you imagine going through high school with a name that means *fever*?"

"Yes, but . . ."

"But what?"

"I can't quite put my finger on it."

"Don't worry. It'll come to you, probably at two in the morning." Katie turned back to her laptop.

"I'll call you when it does."

Katie responded without looking up. "Thanks, but Louise should probably be the first to know."

Maxine smiled and sat down to read the sports page. At this moment, she was totally and perfectly happy. She closed her eyes and saw Tom's face. He'd been right, of course. She had needed to tell Katie about the interview. She sent him a silent prayer of thanks and could almost feel his fingers caress her cheek as he responded in his best Humphrey Bogart voice, even though he never got the line right: "Looking at you, love."

26

WITHOUT BREAKING STRIDE, Rupert grabbed a cup of water from the table and poured it over his head.

Damn, it was hot. What moron had decided to route the running part of the Tour de Tucson through town, across campus, into the stadium, and around and around this blasted track?

The heat bounced off the track and struck him in the face. It was like being bludgeoned. It sucked all the air out of his lungs. Or maybe it was more like running with a wet pillow over his nose. He couldn't decide. Couldn't think.

He spotted one of the fluorescent orange t-shirts of the race volunteers. This volunteer was holding out more water. He grabbed it as he ran and poured the water over his head. It felt hot as it rolled down his neck. Despite his headband, sweat dripped into his eyes, blinding and burning him. The faces in the stands blurred.

Was he beginning to hallucinate? Every time he passed the shady corner of the stadium, he heard people chanting his name.

"Run, Rupert, run!"

"Go, Rupert!"

"Rupert, you're the man!"

Not people: women. He heard women. Angels maybe. Maybe he was near death. All he could see was the bright light bouncing off the stadium, off the track, off the fluorescent orange t-shirts. Weren't you supposed to see a bright light just before you died?

No one he knew was here. If he died, his dad would read about it in the newspapers. "Loser Son Dies in Triathlon Half." And wouldn't it be just like him to die in a half instead of a full Ironman?

Rupert stumbled and staggered, but did not fall.

"Run, Rupert. You can do it!"

He was glad he had not told anyone he was entering the race. He didn't need anyone. The race committee provided all the help he needed.

"Run, Rupert, run!"

Did the race committee provide cheerleaders? He wished they hadn't. His angels were annoying. They wanted him to run. If it weren't for them, he could stop, rest, breathe again.

He knew his brain was getting fuzzy. He hated running in circles. He lost track of time and place. Swimming and biking were easy for him, but running was hard. Running in circles was torture.

Maybe the race committee had sent a letter to his parents. He had to list next of kin on the entry form. Maybe the committee had invited his dad to watch his demise. Maybe the committee wanted his parents there to deal with the corpse. Save ambulance fees.

Rupert's head began to bob. He couldn't breathe and he couldn't see and he couldn't hold his head up. It was too heavy, too bright, too hot.

"Run, Rupert, run!"

"Go, Rupert!"

"We're proud of you, Rupert!"

Rupert's head snapped up. The voices weren't his family. No one in his family was proud of him. Rupert glanced to the stands as he ran. The fog cleared for a moment. The voices were coming from a group wearing matching t-shirts and waving pompoms.

No one had pompoms at an Ironman race. Especially not at a half. Rupert shook his head to clear it. He needed more water.

He grabbed another cup of water. This time he gulped a few swallows as he ran.

"Run, Rupert, run!"

As if of their own volition, his feet began to pound out the rhythm of the voices.

Run, Rupert, run. —Run, Rupert, run. — Run, Rupert, run.

Then his dad was on the track trying to stop him. Reaching, grabbing, blocking. He didn't want Rupert to run. Didn't want him to succeed.

Rupert lowered his head and ran harder. Run, Rupert, run.

"It's OK, son. You're done. You can stop running." It was not his father. It was a man in an orange t-shirt. He ran beside Rupert and tried to edge him off the track.

"You can stop running, son. You've finished the race. You've already run all your miles."

Rupert stumbled.

Someone poured water on his head. Someone put something cold on the back of his neck.

"Yay, Rupert! Yay!"

"Rupert, you're the man!"

"Way to go, Rupert!"

The man in the orange t-shirt chuckled. "You've got quite a cheering section there, son."

Rupert panted between each word. "Who . . . are . . . they?"

The man looked surprised. "Don't you know?"

Rupert shook his head. "No . . . one . . . knows . . . I'm . . . here."

"Well, someone knows," the man said, walking Rupert toward his fans in the stands. "They're wearing matching t-shirts that say 'Rupert's Rowdies.' Are you Rupert?"

Rupert nodded.

"Of course they do look a little bit old to be Rowdies," the man said. "But they've moved down to the rail to greet you. Here you are."

Bewildered, Rupert squinted toward the faces and directly into Maxine Olson's blue eyes.

How the hell had she known he was running the race? And where did they get those damn t-shirts? Rupert's anger flashed and evaporated. He was too tired to be mad.

"Rupert, you were wonderful! We're so proud of you."

He shook his head. Didn't they understand? He hadn't won—not even for his age group.

As if reading his mind, Maxine leaned over the railing. "You ran a good race, Rupert. And you finished it! We're proud of you."

Rupert blinked the sweat out of his eyes and shook his head again. "I . . . can't . . . believe . . . you . . . have . . . pompoms," he said.

Maxine shrugged. "We didn't know how to make banners."

Thank God, Rupert thought. When he bent over to catch his breath, he felt something drop lightly over his shoulders the way fans dropped flags over the winners in the Olympics. He pulled the fabric off his shoulders to see what it was. Another t-shirt. This one said "Rupert Rules."

Rupert looked to see who had given him the shirt. Leaning over the railing of the grandstand was a tall redheaded woman he'd never seen before.

The redhead winked and smiled. "We had this shirt made just for you, darling. I do hope it fits. I had no idea your shoulders would be so broad."

Maxine leaned over the railing. "Rupert, this is my friend Fermez La Bouche. Fermez, this is Rupert Brookstone, a tri-athlete."

Tri-athlete: the word sounded good to Rupert. Like a trophy he'd won.

"Thank . . . you." He panted again, but it was getting easier to breathe and talk. He could even stand upright for several seconds at a time.

"Honey, I'm a massage therapist at Shady Acres." The redhead had a deep, throaty voice. If the blood weren't still pounding in his ears, he'd probably find it sexy. "Come by tomorrow at noon and I'll give you a free massage. Believe me, you'll need it."

Rupert tried to decline, but it made him dizzy to shake his head.

The redhead leaned closer. "I won't take 'No' for an answer. I'll be there. No need to call. Just come by at noon."

Then Harry Silverman started pounding him on the back. "Good race, son. Good job." And Harry's wife, June, reached over and patted him on the head despite his sweat. "You were wonderful, Rupert."

Louise McMaster clapped and Rosemarie Dukakis squeezed his shoulder in her iron grip. "Excellent job, Rupert. We're so proud of you."

Before Rupert could think of a response, the man in the orange t-shirt was back. "OK, Rupert. You can talk to your fans later. Right now you better walk around a bit before you start to cramp up. We've set up a recovery tent over this way. Come with me."

As the man led him away, Rupert heard his fans chanting, "Rupert rules! Rupert rules!" When he looked over his shoulder, they swished their pompoms in a six-person version of a wave. Rupert raised his hand, then turned quickly away. The damn sunlight made his eyes water.

THE NEXT DAY Rupert felt as old as the residents at the Foothills. There was probably a spot on him that didn't ache, but he didn't know where it was.

Gingerly, he slipped his bare feet into loafers so he wouldn't have to bend over to put on socks or tie his shoes. He struggled into a short-sleeved buttoned shirt. A polo shirt would be more comfortable, but he couldn't raise his arms to put it on. He'd definitely go without a tie today.

He wondered if it was too late to change his mind about that free massage. The redhead had said she'd be there at noon. He didn't need to call.

MRS. BABCOCK WAS WAITING for him at work. She glanced pointedly at her watch when he entered. He knew he was late, but he hurt too much to care. Before the battle-ax could attack, he made a preemptive strike of his own.

"Good morning, Mrs. Babcock. I hope you had a pleasant weekend." Rupert gave her his most seductive soap-opera-star smile, the one that always caught Mrs. Babcock up short. She probably never watched the soaps and certainly never was the recipient of one of those smiles in the Army. Or anywhere else for that matter.

Before she could gather her forces for an assault, he struck again.

"I need to ask you for a favor this morning." He never asked her for favors. The word stopped Mrs. Babcock dead in her tracks.

"This morning I want to focus, without interruption, on our applications for the position of assistant director. Can you handle any problems that arise?"

The question was purely rhetorical. Mrs. Babcock could, and did, handle anything and everything. What's more, Rupert suspected that she saw through his feeble ruse, but he was counting on her years of military service. She wouldn't question the closest thing to a direct order that he'd ever given her.

"Yes, sir," Mrs. Babcock said.

Rupert nodded, entered his office, locked all of its doors, and lay down on the thick Oriental carpet to sleep until his massage.

FERMEZ HAD BEEN RIGHT: the massage did help. It was a good thing too, because Rupert decided to stay until dinner to thank the Rowdies. He'd never had his own fans before. He circulated through the dining room, stopping at each table to exchange pleasantries, saving for last the table where the Rowdies sat. They greeted him warmly.

"Pull up a chair, young man," Harry beamed.

Rupert suspected that Harry had forgotten his name and used the generic phrase to cover his memory loss.

"I wanted to, um, thank you," Rupert stammered. "For, um, coming yesterday." His heart thudded as if he were running sprints.

"It was our pleasure," Maxine said.

"Yes. It was great fun to watch your . . ." June hesitated just long enough to make Rosemarie elbow her in the ribs. ". . . race."

"You were wonderful," Louise said. "I was so excited I almost ran out of oxygen myself."

Rupert smiled. "Well, anyway," he took a deep breath and squared his shoulders. This was harder than he'd thought it would be. He'd raced for his self-respect. Now he had to confess for his integrity. "I never would have finished the race without you."

"Nonsense," Maxine said. "You were splendid all on your own. We just cheered."

"No," Rupert shook his head. This was difficult, but he wanted to be clear. "I wanted to collapse. I was dizzy. Hell, I was hallucinating."

He was so caught up in trying to articulate his point that he'd broken one of his cardinal management rules: never swear in front of the residents. Fortunately, this table did not seem to take offense.

"I wanted to quit, but I kept hearing you chant, 'Run, Rupert, run.' And I couldn't stop. It was like the chant took over my feet and made them keep going."

Maxine touched his arm. "You may have wanted to quit, Rupert, but you didn't. Our chant didn't keep you from collapsing. You did that. All we did was cheer on your determination."

Rupert looked at the kindly old lady. He owed her one. Not only had she led a cheering section that kept him going, but then she'd given him credit for the race. His father would have taken the credit for himself.

"Well, thanks," he mumbled. "Thanks for everything."

"No problem, my boy." Harry beamed. "Here comes dessert. Have a hot fudge sundae on me."

"No thanks." Rupert grinned. "I'm in training, you know. Besides, I'm too stiff and sore to lift a spoon."

27

MAXINE STIRRED HER COFFEE and chatted idly with Rosemarie and June while Louise tallied the scores from their afternoon of bridge at Rosemarie's apartment.

"It's too bad Katie had to leave before Rupert's race on Sunday," June said. "She could have helped us cheer for all those cute little buns in their Spandex shorts."

Rosemarie placed a platter of cookies in the center of the table. "I thought we were going to have to hook you up to Louise's oxygen."

"It's a good thing Mimi taught you how to do yoga breaths." Maxine eyed the platter longingly.

"Oh, honey." June reached for a cream-filled chocolate delicacy. "Those tight shorts called for lots of outright heavy breathing."

Rosemarie selected a paper-thin butter cookie and nudged the plate toward Maxine. "Try one. They're from Dana's Deli. They're incredible."

Maxine resisted even though the platter included a dark-chocolate thin mint.

Louise waved the bridge tally over her head and began to sing Nat King Cole's "Unforgettable."

"Does that mean you won again?" Maxine asked, feigning exasperation.

Louise shrugged with exaggerated modesty and announced the prizes. "Fifty cents goes to unforgettable me, thirty to incredible Maxine, fifteen to irresistible June, and—last and definitely least—a regrettable nickel for Rosemarie."

Rosemarie made a great show of pocketing her nickel. "As a gracious hostess, I happily claim the booby prize."

June turned to Rosemarie. "Speaking of booby prizes, how is the Residents' Advisory Committee doing? Are we going to have a new assistant director soon?"

Louise and Maxine busied themselves putting away the cards and tally sheets.

"I'm meeting-ed out," Rosemarie said. "Thank God, the committee is in pause mode right now while we wait for the finalists to give their presentations and stage their events."

"Are any of the finalists any good?" June asked.

"Two-thirds of them are wonderful." Rosemarie refilled their coffee cups. "But you know what Evie is. Honestly, you wouldn't believe what she wrote in her essay. Wait." She set the pot on her buffet table. "I'll get it. I can't possibly do it justice."

Rosemarie retrieved a stack of papers from her desk.

"Now promise me you won't tell anyone I read this to you." Rosemarie looked at each of them in turn. "I don't want to get kicked off this committee just when it's getting interesting."

"Who would we tell?" June asked. "Everyone I'd tell is sitting right here."

Rosemarie nodded. "I know. That's why I'm willing to read it, but swear anyway."

Maxine raised her hand. "I solemnly swear not to tell a soul that you read us literary proof that Evie is an idiot."

"Me too." Louise imitated Maxine's swearing gesture.

"Me either." June waved her right hand absently over her head.

"OK." Rosemarie assumed a superior attitude and pompous tone as befitted Evie's piece. "Here goes: 'There are four principles to being a good Assistant Director at a rest home.'"

"Already I hate her," June said, interrupting Rosemarie's dramatic reading. "There is a world of difference between a retirement *community* where people go to *live,* and a rest home where they wait to *die.*"

Maxine wanted to hug June. That was precisely how she felt. She just wished she had articulated it that well in her own essay.

"Uh-hem." Rosemarie cleared her throat and struck a histrionic pose. "'First of all, a good Assistant Director must be efficient. Her goal is to provide services that do not stress the budget.'"

"Rupert must love that." Louise made a sour face.

"'For example, a trip to a nearby mall provides the geriatric—'"

"Geriatric!" Maxine set her coffee cup down so hard the cookies bounced on the platter.

"'— a trip to a nearby mall provides the geriatric with stimulation for the cost of the gasoline alone. Similarly, crafts should be the simple kind that don't require extravagant tools like weaving looms or pottery kilns. In all cases, the elderly should purchase their own supplies from the rest home's craft center.'"

"What!" June fingered the buttons on her handmade sweater. "I bet her craft center charges a hefty mark-up on its supplies."

"'Second, a good Assistant Director must be a figure of authority. She must be able to command the compliance of the elderly under her care to ensure their own safety and protection.'"

Maxine slammed her fist on the table so hard that everyone's coffee cup bounced. "Do you think we will have to salute Her Authority?"

"Oh, I hope so," June said. "I was afraid we'd have to get on our knees and genuflect. With my arthritis, I'd much rather salute."

"'Third, the ideal Assistant Director is an integral member of the management team, enforcing policies and contributing her expertise into the decision making processes.'"

"Mrs. Babcock won't like that part," Rosemarie said. "She wants to pull Rupert's chain without anyone else's help."

June turned to Maxine. "If this paper had been written by one of your students, what grade would you give it?"

"F Minus. It's specious, wordy, and dull, Dull, DULL!"

"'Fourth, a good Assistant Director plans activities to enhance the ethical fiber of her patients. Studies have shown that such activities lead to moral movement in the elderly.'"

June spit out the coffee she had been in the process of swallowing. "Patients! She called us her patients."

"Well, after all." Maxine lifted her own cup with exaggerated delicacy, being careful to crook her pinky finger. "She is going to improve our movements by giving us fiber."

"That's crap," Rosemarie said.

"Precisely," Louise said, and the four of them laughed until tears ran down their cheeks and they wheezed for breath.

"Stop, stop. I can't breathe." Louise readjusted her oxygen level.

"Is there more?" June asked, wiping tears from her eyes with her napkin.

Rosemarie skimmed the papers. "Let's see." She mumbled key phrases: studies have shown, fiber, moral movement. "Oh yes, here it is."

"Wait." Louise held up her hand. "The studies she refers to, would they be *her* master's thesis?"

Rosemarie flipped through the pages. "She doesn't actually cite her sources, so I'm guessing it is. By the way, I reread her thesis last night. Even without the suspect data and sex with her professor, the study is flawed."

Three coffee cups clattered into their saucers as Maxine, Louise, and June all looked at Rosemarie with interest.

"Her statistical methods are . . ." Rosemarie paused, a slight smile playing at the corners of her mouth. "How shall I put it? Caca. Merde. Crap."

"Let's hear it for moral movement!"

This brought another round of laughter that took on a life of its own, escalating every time they looked at each other.

"Stop. I'll pee in my panties." June rocked herself out of her chair to rush to the bathroom.

While she was gone, Rosemarie tried to explain the mathematical flaws in the thesis. Maxine couldn't follow the explanation, but she trusted Rosemarie. If she said they were caca, they were. The problem was that no one else on the Residents' Advisory Committee would understand the implications.

June returned. "All I can say is that moral movement sure does work."

"Ladies." Rosemarie assumed a mock ministerial tone. "Let us continue. Uh-hem."

She resumed reading from Evie's essay. "'Examples of activities with demonstrated benefits include the following . . .'"

Rosemarie stopped reading. "Never mind. The rest of this is straight from her thesis. She drones on and on about examples and data that she made up from her internship at Mountain Estates Retirement Community. Naturally, Carlotta's using Evie's pretentious ten-page essay to undermine my favorite essay." She leafed through her pages. "Here it is. It's less than a page."

Maxine looked at Louise then scanned the room for an escape.

Rosemarie readjusted her glasses and began to read. "'As assistant director, my goal is to provide the tools and activities necessary for the residents to lead rich and rewarding lives. I will plan events that enable the residents to:

- Expand their physical capabilities
- Explore diverse ways of thinking about and interacting with the world
- Experiment with new activities
- Enhance existing friendships and develop new ones.

Residents want an environment where they can be actively engaged and grow as individuals. They want to face their fears with courage so that they may live their lives with joy and passion. They want to follow their dreams, no matter how improbable or impossible they may seem. As assistant director, my first responsibility is to be responsive to these needs and dreams.'"

June lifted her coffee cup in a toast. "Now that's my kind of assistant director."

Maxine and Louise squirmed in their seats.

Rosemarie stared at them thoughtfully.

"Whose essay is it?" June asked. "Does the committee like her?"

"Octavia Olson." Rosemarie looked at Maxine, who could not meet her eye.

"Octavia?" June said. "Nobody's named Octavia any more. Where is she from?"

Maxine shot Louise a look.

Louise looked at her watch. "Goodness, who knew it was so late. We better get going or we'll miss dinner."

Rosemarie checked her own watch. "It's only three-thirty."

Louise gave an artificial laugh. "Oh my! I guess I misread my watch. Maybe I need new glasses. I know I need a new eye doctor. Who do you go to?"

Rosemarie ignored the question and turned back to her papers. "Here it is. Octavia's from Tucson. She lives at 4468B Calle Ocotillo." Rosemarie squinted. "That seems familiar."

"Doesn't Peter live on Calle Ocotillo?" June asked.

Maxine reached for a cookie and blindly grabbed a coconut macaroon. She hated macaroons.

Louise cleared her throat.

Rosemarie stared.

"What's the phone number?" June asked with dogged persistence.

Rosemarie read the number. "I know that number."

Maxine massaged her temples. Rosemarie never forgot a number.

"Well, I really need to . . ." Louise stopped, evidently unable to think of anything she really needed to do.

Rosemarie picked up the phone and dialed.

"What are you doing?" June said. "You can't just call her."

"I'll hang up if she answers. But I swear that I've called this number before."

Maxine prayed that Peter's phone was out of order. She took off her blazer. It was beginning to be much too warm in here.

"Busy," Rosemarie said and hung up. She looked at Maxine again.

"What's her email?" June asked in a remarkably focused effort to solve the mystery.

Maxine closed her eyes. Her doom was complete.

Rosemarie scanned the application. "Here it is. ToThemAx."

"To the Max?" June said. "Isn't that your email, Maxine?"

"Don't be silly," Louise said. "Maxine's grammar is too good. She would never say *To them ak*s. She would say *Ask Them*. How about a hand of blackjack?"

Rosemarie, who already had on her poker face, waited. She reminded Maxine of her childhood minister the time he'd caught Maxine and three playmates using the church pews as balance beams. In that instance, having no alternative, they'd confessed immediately and had been forgiven. Maxine crossed her fingers and hoped that confession would lead to absolution this time too.

"Maxine?" In the space of two syllables, Rosemarie's voice went up an octave.

Maxine abandoned all efforts to bluff her way through it. "Don't be angry. I couldn't tell you because you were on the Residents' Advisory Committee."

Rosemarie closed her eyes in apparent disbelief.

June caught on surprisingly fast. "Well *I'm* not on the committee. Why didn't you tell me?"

"Because I couldn't tell Rosemarie. It wouldn't be fair to tell you and leave her out."

"But you told Louise," June said.

"Not exactly. She helped me do it."

They all turned to Louise, who was intently examining her oxygen tank.

"When Carlotta told us how silly the online application was, we couldn't believe it," Maxine said. "We thought she was just trying to stir things up. So we checked it out for ourselves. When we saw that it was even sillier than Carlotta had said, we just sort of applied." Her explanation sounded lame even to her. She kicked Louise.

Louise sighed and accepted the metaphoric baton. "It was after breakfast. June was in water aerobics and Rosemarie had gone to one of her high school accounting club meetings. So we just did it ourselves and then sort of forgot about it."

Maxine took the handoff. "Then Carlotta had her meeting, and Rosemarie was elected to the committee, and it was too late."

"But *you* nominated me," Rosemarie said.

"Yes. I knew you'd be great and that you'd protect us from Carlotta's schemes," Maxine said.

Louise grabbed the baton and turned up the speed. "It was only later that we remembered Maxine had applied."

Maxine headed for the finish line. "We thought if we didn't tell you, it wouldn't be a conflict."

"Besides," Louise said, breathing hard, "we wanted Maxine to win on her own merits."

"Not because we're friends."

Their relay over, Maxine and Louise waited to hear the race results.

Rosemarie gave an exasperated sigh.

"Holy shit!" June said.

Rosemarie shook her head and crossed to her desk. She came back with a calendar. "Evie's supposed to present this Saturday. Octavia is scheduled for next Saturday. And the following Friday we have the third candidate—the one whose name I can never remember."

Maxine swallowed and nodded.

Rosemarie waved her calendar over her head. "What on earth are you planning to do for your event?"

"Oh, that's a surprise." Maxine avoided Louise's gaze.

Louise narrowed her eyes. "You don't know what they're doing, do you?"

"What who's doing?" June asked.

"Celine and Mimi," Louise said.

"Doing about what?" Rosemarie asked.

"My event," Maxine said. "And no, I don't know. We made a deal."

"What kind of deal?" June said.

Maxine shifted uncomfortably. "Celine agreed to borrow Peter's car if I'd make her the artistic director for my event."

"And?" Louise had an annoying tendency to focus on the very details Maxine was trying to avoid.

"And I thought she just wanted a title." Maxine turned to Rosemarie and June for support.

"But?" Louise said with irritating persistence.

"But Celine really wanted to be the director. Now, whenever I ask about the event, she complains that I'm interfering with her artistic creativity."

Louise closed her eyes and groaned.

June nearly dropped the coffee pot.

Rosemarie collapsed onto the couch and fanned herself with her calendar.

Maxine became defensive. "What? Celine says it's a surprise."

All three women stared at Maxine over the tops of their glasses.

Maxine sagged. She recognized an indefensible position when she'd struck one.

Rosemarie cleared her throat. "Let me be sure I understand this. You put Celine in charge of your event?"

Maxine nodded in defeat.

Rosemarie rolled her eyes heavenward, apparently speechless.

"At the risk of repeating myself," June said, "holy shit."

28

MAXINE LEANED AGAINST the back wall of the elevator and crossed her arms. "I'm not going."

"Of course you are," Louise said as the elevator opened. "We have to go to Evie's event in order to scout out the competition." She and Seabiscuit trotted ahead without a backward glance.

At the entrance to the recreation room, however, Louise halted in her tracks. When Maxine caught up, she saw why. Evie had put life-size cutouts of palm trees on the walls and beach blankets across the tables. She'd even dumped a mound of sand in front of the podium and set up beach chairs and an umbrella. Tacky ukulele music blared from the sound system, making it impossible to think.

Maxine steadied herself on Seabiscuit. "Am I still alive, or have I died and gone to meeting hell?"

Louise patted Maxine's arm. "Don't worry, dear. We're not dead, but I'm pretty sure we're going to wish we were."

Dressed in sarongs and matching bikini tops, Carlotta and Evie guarded either side of the entrance like Scylla and Charybdis. It was impossible to steer between them without being festooned with party-store leis.

"Aloha!" Evie burbled. "Welcome to our Hawaiian Beach Party. Please help yourselves to drinks. Lemonade is in those cute pineapple-shaped glasses and iced tea is in the coconut-shaped ones." Evie flashed a plastic smile. "If you want something with a kick, try the glasses with chunks of fruit and little umbrellas."

Maxine tugged the lei away from her throat. "I'm sure tonight will be a real kick all by itself."

Before Evie could react, Louise steered Maxine toward the beverage table, where June was sniffing a glass and making faces.

"Never trust a drink with an umbrella in it," June said. "I'm not sure what drink this is supposed to be, but when I get home, I'm going to check to see if anyone has drained the gasoline out of my car."

"Have some lemonade instead." Maxine offered them each a plastic pineapple.

Rosemarie shook her head and picked up a coconut-shaped glass. "No thanks. I'm going for iced tea in the hope that there's enough caffeine in it to keep me awake."

"Are you sure you want to be awake?" June asked.

"I don't know about you, ladies." Harry winked and held up something that looked like a silver notebook. "But I know I'll enjoy the evening. Did you know you can watch basketball games on an EyeFad?"

"It's called an iPad," June said. "Just keep the volume down and wake me if anything interesting happens."

Harry saluted. "OK, Chief. I'll be right back."

"Where's he going?"

June smiled at Harry's back. "Probably to show off his new toy. In the meantime, do you see anywhere to sit? It looks as if all the tables are taken."

Louise surveyed the room. "They aren't full. Carlotta has planted one of her friends at each table."

Maxine's temper started to simmer. "Like spies?"

"More like prison guards." Rosemarie dumped her iced tea into a garbage can that had been disguised as a sand castle.

Harry rejoined them. "Quick. Ralph Jordan is saving his table for us. He wants to see the game. I just hope my EyeFad works over there."

As they took their seats, Rupert bounded onto the stage dressed in a Hawaiian shirt, white slacks, and sandals.

"Do you think Evie gave him the shirt, or just bribed him to wear it?" Maxine asked.

"Probably both." June sounded as cynical as Maxine felt.

"Aloha!" Rupert shouted into the microphone. "Good evening ladies and gentlemen, and welcome. Tonight we are delighted to have Evie Helmsley Hill here to share her vision for the Foothills. The presentation will be followed by a very special program. So, without further ado, let the beach party begin."

Carlotta's friends cheered and applauded. Maxine groaned silently, clapped politely, and resigned herself to the uncomfortable chair.

Evie bounced up to the podium and began a presentation that seemed to wander aimlessly and endlessly.

June tapped Maxine on the shoulder. "It's times like these that I envy the hearing impaired. They can turn off their hearing aids."

Maxine rolled her eyes. "I wish I'd brought a book to read."

"What's with Louise?" June asked.

Maxine turned. Louise had a rapt expression on her face, as if she were living and dying on Evie's every word.

"She's replaying bridge games in her head," Maxine said. "Look at her hands. Every now and then you can see her dealing the cards."

"Like Daisy running in her sleep," Harry said without looking up from his iPad.

"How's the game?"

"It's halftime. Wildcats are up by two."

After what seemed like hours of obfuscation, phony data, and irrelevant anecdotes, Evie concluded her presentation to unenthusiastic but polite applause.

"People, people. Listen up," Evie said. "Tonight I have a special treat for you." She stopped as if expecting applause. When none occurred, she gave a phony cheerleader smile, clap, and jump. "We're going to have a beach party!"

The men all seemed to like the jump, or at least the way Evie's breasts continued to jiggle long after the jump had ended. Perhaps Maxine had underestimated Evie and her bikini top. She seemed to be rejuvenating the male population, although it wasn't clear if their reactions counted as "moral movement."

"First, we're going to have a little contest based on theme-ing." Evie spoke to them as if they were preschoolers.

"Did she say *scheming*?" June asked.

"*Theme-ing*," Maxine said. "Whatever that is."

Evie shot them a dirty look. "Theme-ing is paying attention to the details; it's having palm trees and coconuts for a Hawaiian beach party. What I'm going to teach you tonight is how to use your crafts to make theme-ing a reality. And we'll do it as a contest."

Maxine hated contests even more than she hated plastic pineapple glasses and imitation luaus in the middle of the Sonoran Desert.

"We're going to use crepe paper to make hibiscus name tags for the ladies to wear in their hair. And the men will weave palm fronds into laurel crowns."

"That's botanically impossible," Rosemarie said.

"Aren't laurel wreaths Greek, not Hawaiian?" June asked.

"I'd rather have the hibiscus," Harry said, rubbing his bald head. "It would be less scratchy."

"People!" Evie called them to order. "You'll want to pay attention because we have some splendid prizes: sarongs for the ladies and Hawaiian shirts for the men."

Maxine gagged. Surely, no jury would find her guilty if she strangled Evie.

Evie gave some incomplete and contradictory instructions and then turned them loose on the crafts while she circulated among the tables providing unsolicited advice. Given that Fred hated to be schooled in any way, Maxine couldn't wait to see how he'd react to Evie's "advice."

But Evie knew her audience. When she leaned over Fred's shoulder to help him with his laurel wreath, her breasts swayed and bumped his ears until he turned bright red.

After the flowers and wreaths, Evie assigned another element of theme-ing to each table. Carlotta's table was assigned invitations, which explained the handcrafted invitation already poking out of Carlotta's purse. Evidently, she'd wanted a head start on the competition.

Peggy Stone's table was supposed to develop a menu. Maxine

thought that was the best task, since they didn't actually have to produce anything other than a list of food that they would have cooked in some alternate universe.

Maxine's own table was given the unenviable challenge of creating a centerpiece out of crepe paper and pipe cleaners. The assignment pushed Maxine to the edge. With sarcasm untempered by good manners, she suggested they substitute goldfish in bowls for centerpieces and was appalled when Evie clapped in delight and set her breasts to bouncing again.

Evie reclaimed the microphone and launched into a tedious explanation of the judging process and the winners of the awards.

Rosemarie rose. "I'm going to see if there's any tea left. Anyone else want anything?"

"No way." June rocked herself to her feet. "I already have to pee."

"Yes!" Harry pumped his fist.

Maxine raised an eyebrow.

"Wildcats won on a last-second shot," he said.

"All right." Maxine slapped a high-five with Harry.

"Speaking of winning," Louise said, "our table didn't, but at least we can leave now."

"Music to my ears," Maxine said and pushed out of her seat. She waited for her balance to return, then held Seabiscuit while Louise stood. "Come on. I'll walk you back to your apartment."

"THE GOOD THING," Louise said, tossing her hibiscus nametag onto her coffee table, "is that I don't think people were particularly enamored of Evie's event."

Maxine threw her hibiscus next to Louise's. "The good thing is that it's finally over. I thought I was going to have to stuff my lei in Evie's mouth if she sang 'The Hukilau Song' one more time."

"Who knew she could play the ukulele?"

"Who cared?" Maxine said. "If she knew how to play the bagpipes, she probably would have staged the Highland Games tonight."

"Who says she doesn't know how to play the bagpipes? She's probably already planned a Highland Festival as the first event in her reign of terror if she gets the job."

"It would be just like her to learn to play them out of spite," Maxine said a bit illogically. "I'm going home before I—"

Strains of "Rhapsody in Blue" floated from Louise's entryway.

Maxine raised an eyebrow.

"Celine installed a new doorbell for me," Louise said.

Maxine raised both eyebrows. "OK, but who would be ringing it at this hour?"

"Beats me." Louise wheeled Seabiscuit over to her peephole. "It's Celine and Fermez in sparkling evening wear." She unlocked the door.

"Tell us, tell us," Celine said before the door was even halfway open.

"We're simply dying of curiosity," Fermez said. "How was Evie's event?"

Louise waved them in.

"We barely escaped with our lives," Maxine said.

"Skip the part about the presentation," Celine said. "We can guess what that was like. We want to know what Evie did for her event."

With much grousing and groaning, and only minimal exaggeration, Maxine and Louise recounted the evening.

When they finished, Celine crossed her arms and stared at them over her glasses. "Let me get this straight. Evie had you make nametags out of crepe paper?"

Louise held up the evidence. "Hibiscus-shaped name tags."

"Mon Dieu." Fermez took the nametags from Louise and twirled them in her exquisitely manicured fingertips. Her nails were a chili pepper red that perfectly matched both her lipstick and her beaded earrings. "Je me sens désolée pour elle."

"You can't be serious," Maxine said. "How can anyone feel sorry for Evie?"

"Really, I do," Fermez insisted. "The poor dear is simply ob-sessed by fashion."

Celine rolled her eyes. "Talk about the kettle calling the pot hot."

Fermez thrust her already well-defined breasts out even further. "The difference, dear, is that I can pull it off."

To emphasize her point, Fermez did a fashion-show strut across Louise's living room. Maxine had to admit that Fermez knew more about fashion than the rest of them combined.

Fermez executed a flawless runway turn and strutted back. "Think about it," she said. "Evie has a passion for detail, but she has neither the figure to be a model nor the training to be a designer. So what's left?" Fermez flipped the nametags into the air and extended her empty hands. "Rien!"

Maxine caught the crepe paper flowers in mid-air.

"C'est tragique. Non?"

"Very tragic," Maxine said and absently tugged on the crumpled petals. "I can see the headlines when Evie becomes our social director: 'Fashion Diva Wannabe Becomes Prison Warden for the Aged.'"

Louise snatched the nametags away. "Shush. You'll hex us if you speak of her."

Fermez reclaimed the flowers and tucked them behind her ears. "Don't worry: Evie doesn't have the élan to pull off prison-guard gray."

Maxine thought Fermez had rather missed the salient point, but she let it go.

"The thing is . . ." Fermez fluttered her fingernails. "I know what Evie should be when she grows up."

They all turned toward Fermez.

"Evie should become . . ." Fermez paused for maximum dramatic affect. "A wedding planner!"

Even Louise gasped. "I do try to think the best of people," she said haltingly, as if choosing her words with extreme care. "But don't you think Evie might be just a tad heavy-handed to be a wedding planner? A wedding is supposed to be a time of joy."

Celine snorted. "She'd be the wedding planner from hell. She'd be bossing folks around, making them do this and that just 'cause she said so."

"Precisely!" Fermez said. "After all, what do people want from a wedding planner?"

"Beats me." Celine huffed. "I don't want anything from some opinionated woman with big bazoombas."

Fermez gave Celine a long and meaningful stare. "Talk about the pot questioning the kettle's mettle."

Celine looked blankly back.

Fermez rolled her eyes. "People go to a wedding planner because they want someone else to take control, make decisions, and manage a million annoying details."

The room fell silent.

"Details. Decisions. Control." Fermez fluttered her fingernails. "Evie would be perfect."

Maxine tried to find the flaw in Fermez's logic. The image of Evie as a wedding planner was simultaneously horrific and compelling. Evie would actually care about the myriad of miserable details that attached themselves to a wedding.

"She's right." Louise whispered, as if unwilling to say it aloud.

Celine sank into the couch, evidently stunned. "She could be her little dictator self and people would pay her for it. They'd actually *want* her opinion."

Maxine shook her head. "What a shame she wants to be our assistant director instead."

Fermez tucked the hibiscus nametags into her clutch bag. "We'll see," she said. "Comme ci, comme ça."

"Come whatever." Celine hoisted herself out of the couch. "We've got to go. You were due back at Benny's fifteen minutes ago."

"My fans await." Fermez lifted her chin, swept her arm toward the stars, and glided out the door and into the night.

Celine shook her head and followed Fermez.

Maxine turned to Louise. "Any idea what that was all about?"

"Beats me."

"Me too," Maxine said, aware that she was far too tired to worry or wonder. "See you tomorrow."

29

CELINE CHECKED THE TIME on her cell phone: 2:41. She had time to vacuum the library. Rupert and Mrs. Babcock were both leaving at three—Rupert to buy a fancy new bicycle, a kangaroo-something, and Mrs. Babcock to get her eyes tested. With them both gone, she could finally do some deep cleaning in their offices while staying off Mrs. Babcock's radar. Rupert might have cancelled the firing squad last week, but the General was still lobbying for a court martial.

She dragged the vacuum cleaner into the library and stomped on its power switch. The beast roared to life. She cranked up the volume on her cell phone and adjusted the earbuds. *Amazing grace, how sweet the sound.*

Celine pushed and pulled the old Hoover in time to the music, drawing patterns in the deep pile of the carpet—curls and swirls and fleurs-de-lis. She was just finishing a particularly intricate design when four tennis-shoed feet planted themselves in her path.

She snapped to attention.

Maxine and Louise smiled triumphantly.

"Mercy." Celine clapped a hand over her heart. "You frightened the bejesus out of me."

Maxine and Louise bumped fists, then tried to bump hips but missed.

Celine switched off the vacuum "What are you doing here anyway?"

"We're starting a vigilante group," Maxine said, crossing to the computer.

"We're going to vanquish evil-doers." Louise followed Maxine.

"Which evil-doers?" Celine tagged along, Hoover in tow.

"Sexual predators."

"Say what?" Celine stopped so fast the Hoover took a nose-dive.

Maxine settled into one of the computer chairs. "Did you see the news story about that poor teenager—the one who thought she'd made a friend on the internet and was nearly abducted? Thank goodness they found her."

Louise lowered herself into the chair next to Maxine. "Kids have no sense about what they put online."

Maxine powered up the computer. "So, how do we get to one of those social networking sites?"

"You aren't going to join one, are you?" Celine edged closer to the outlet. She knew a thing or two about pulling computer plugs.

"We just want to see how they work," Louise said.

"Uh-huh. But why?"

Louise blinked, then turned toward Maxine.

Maxine shrugged.

Celine crossed her arms. "Thought so. If you want to be sleuths, you should get a job with the F.B.I. Become one of those Grannies for Good."

"Become what?" Maxine asked, but her focus was on the computer.

"You know. Those old ladies in California who helped the police by pretending to be teenagers on the internet."

Maxine swung around so fast she nearly knocked Celine over. "What old ladies?"

"It was on the news last month," Celine said, moving a safer distance away. "A story about some folks in a retirement home who had time to chat on the internet."

"D.A.M.N."

"Say what?"

Maxine pointed at the screen where a pornographic ad had appeared. "I told Rupert he needs to put Pop-Tart security on here."

Celine stared at Maxine. "*You* told Rupert he needs better security?"

"Yes." Maxine repositioned the keyboard and began clicking. "He needs programs to kill Pam, Pop-Tarts, and Bacteria."

Celine appealed to Louise, but Louise only closed her eyes and shook her head.

Celine stepped directly behind Maxine's chair. "You sure do know a lot about computers for someone who pretends to know nothing."

Maxine leaned closer to the computer.

"Maxine?" Louise said.

Like a turtle hiding in its shell, Maxine hunched her shoulders and continued to click.

Celine tapped Maxine on the shoulder. "We can still see you."

Maxine sighed and swiveled her chair to face them. "I *might* have asked Peter to help me buy a computer and give me lessons. He told me about all those security gizmos."

Celine rocked back on her heels. "Whoa!"

Louise bounced on her chair. "Can I get one? Will he help me too?"

"Yes, of course. We can take lessons together."

"Well, I'll be." Celine fanned herself with her duster. "I can't believe you two have decided to join this century."

Maxine blushed. "It's about time, don't you think?"

"Time?" Celine jerked. "What time is it?"

"Three-twenty," Maxine said. "Why?"

"Rupert doesn't like to have his desk doodads moved. And Mrs. Babcock doesn't like anyone entering her office or Rupert's."

"Excuse me?"

"Here." Celine handed her feather duster to Maxine, then bent to retrieve the toppled vacuum. "They're both gone. If I hurry, I can get in, do some real cleaning, and get out before they return." She took a deep breath and hoisted the Hoover with a single snatch.

Maxine returned the duster. "Good luck. May you escape detection."

"Thanks." Celine twirled her duster and studied Maxine and Louise over the top of her glasses.

"Yes?" Maxine said.

"You know, you two might be really good at the Grannies for Good thing."

Maxine's eyes narrowed. "Because we're old and have lots of time?"

"Because you're smart, and you're pretty good on that." Celine pointed at the computer.

"Oh." Maxine pretended indifference.

Louise scuffed her feet like a little kid.

Celine twirled her feather duster and waited.

Maxine and Louise cocked their eyebrows at each other. Maxine drummed her fingers. Louise bit her lip.

Maxine shrugged. "Maybe I'll just gaggle 'Grannies for Good.'"

Celine pumped her fist. "Knew it." She was out the door before they could respond.

CELINE DRAGGED THE VACUUM into Rupert's office and shut the door. Thankfully, Rupert and Mrs. Babcock were still out. She turned on her music and dusted the window sills, chairs, and lamps before turning her attention to the polishing of Rupert's desk.

Rupert was out-of-control compulsive. She'd noticed it during her interview. She'd inadvertently bumped his gold pen and pencil set. Without missing a beat, he'd repositioned it before she could even take a breath. Ever since, whenever she talked to him, she couldn't resist the temptation to move something. Back when her tin-can excuse for a car kept breaking down and he was threatening to fire her, she'd moved everything. She'd even moved his coaster when Rupert took a sip of that fancy French coffee he liked. He'd been so busy replacing items that instead of firing her, he'd given her a raise.

But when she cleaned, she made a point of putting every little doo-dad back exactly where it had been. She knew Rupert's limits. And hers. She wanted this job: she needed this job.

She centered the pen and pencil set, spun the wheels on Rupert's little nuts-and-bolts bicycle, and stepped back to survey her work. The office was immaculate; the desk, pristine.

Satisfied, she checked the time: 3:48. She cranked up her music and began dusting the shelves in Rupert's closet. *Swing low, sweet chariot.*

Celine sang along as she straightened the clothes that Rupert kept in his closet for emergencies. The man had a spare outfit for every occasion, from funeral suits to padded-ass bicycle shorts and swimsuits, from wingtips to flip-flops. He even had a freshly pressed Hawaiian shirt still hanging in its plastic dry-cleaner bag. She slipped her fingers inside the bag and smoothed the shirt.

The touch unleashed a flood of memories, all of them of Alonso Makepeace in cool silk.

On his first day as choir director, Alonso had come to practice wearing a loose Hawaiian shirt and sunglasses. Under his arm, he'd carried a whole new batch of music. Music with a beat and a soul and a message. He'd brought jazz and blues and even rock. "If it's music," he'd say, "then the Lord is in it."

Celine shook off the memory and tugged the plastic bag back into place: 4:04.

Rupert stored boxes of office supplies in the back of his closet, but he never wanted her to take the time to vacuum behind them. Well today was the day.

She pushed the boxes out of her way. Just as she'd suspected: dust bunnies and dead bugs everywhere. Honestly, how could a compulsive man be so dense about dirt? It was gratifying to finally have a chance to clear out the landfill back there. She powered up the Hoover and adjusted the volume in her earbuds. *There's room enough in Paradise.*

Celine finished vacuuming and shoved the boxes back into the closet. She shoved too hard. One box hit the back of the closet and its lid went catty-wampus. Rupert would notice catty-wampus.

Grunting, she tugged the box out and lifted off the offending lid. Inside, instead of printer paper, the box contained file folders. Not just any file folders, but the *missing* application folders. Evie's blessed folder was right there on top.

Sweet Jesus. Mrs. Babcock had grilled her five ways to Sunday about those files, and there they were.

She flipped through two or three more folders. They were all applications—applications from some pretty qualified people.

To think, after all the hoopla, these folders had been under their noses all along. Rupert ought to give her a big reward for finding them. She could buy a new car, or redecorate her apartment, or buy herself a new sound system. Or she could fly to California . . . find Alonso . . .

Ignoring the tears, she stroked the tattoo inside her wrist and rocked. *There is a balm in Gilead to make the wounded whole.*

Celine stopped rocking. Her breath slowed. She swiped the tears with the back of her hand and stared blankly at the closet: wingtips to flip-flops, suits to shorts. Everything perfectly organized.

She straightened.

Rupert was way too compulsive not to know the contents of every one of the boxes in his closet. These folders weren't lost. And as far as she was concerned, she'd never seen them.

She jammed the lid on the box and shoved it into its corner. She struggled to her feet, turned, and smacked into Mrs. Babcock.

"Lord Almighty!"

Mrs. Babcock looked like vengeance itself. Her arms were crossed, and she wore a pair of wrap-around sunglasses from the eye doctor. Her mouth moved, but Celine couldn't hear anything over the pounding of her own heart.

Mrs. Babcock's mouth moved faster.

"Wait." Celine turned off her music. "What?"

"What are you doing!"

Celine flinched. Visions of unemployment flashed through her mind.

Mrs. Babcock yanked off the sunglasses. Her eyes were big and round and furious. Anger etched white lines onto her red face. "What are you doing?"

Celine pointed to the Hoover. "I vacuumed the dead bugs in the closet."

Mrs. Babcock's face went from red to purple. Her eyes darted back and forth as if searching for something.

Searching . . .

Celine exhaled.

Sweet baby Jesus. If the General had actually seen anything, she wouldn't still be searching. She'd be throwing her mean-spirited weight around and ordering Celine to pull out the box.

Celine opened her palms in a peace offering. "Would you like me to vacuum your closet?"

The General's arm swung like a bayonet. "Go."

Celine didn't wait for a second invitation. *In that great getting-up morning, Fare you well! Fare you well!*

30

MAXINE CHASED HER PEAS around the cranberry jelly and into the mashed potatoes. Her tablemates were eating and chatting as if everything were normal, as if the world were not going to end at seven-thirty when she gave her presentation to the residents of the Foothills and revealed herself as a liar, fraud, and fool.

She stabbed her roast chicken with a fork and sawed at it as if she were felling redwoods. Her fork slipped and chicken flew into the centerpiece while peas scampered across the tablecloth and cranberry somersaulted onto the front of her dress—the expensive powder blue silk dress that she'd bought for tonight's event.

"D.A.M.N." Maxine slapped the cranberry back onto the plate, dunked her napkin into Louise's nearly full water glass, and began dabbing at the crimson spot.

Louise grabbed Maxine's hand. "Stop! You'll only make it worse."

Maxine surveyed the damage. Louise was right, of course. She'd only succeeded in spreading the scarlet stain. She dropped the napkin onto the table. "Now I know how Hester Prynne must have felt."

"Don't be silly," Louise said with a chipper voice. "She was cast out by her society for being an adulterer, not for applying to be its assistant director." Louise squinted at Maxine. "Unless of course you're having an affair with Fred."

Maxine shuddered. She most definitely would not have an affair with Fred: not now, not ever, not if the fate of humanity depended on it. Nonetheless, she was about to be outcast by her own society. She might as well wear a scarlet *A* for *A*ged Imposter or *A*ddled Fool or *A*wful *A*pplicant or—

"Good evening, ladies and gentlemen."

Rupert had materialized at their table out of nowhere. He looked especially dapper in a well-tailored navy blazer and taupe dress slacks. But he was hiding behind his silly soap-opera-star smile, and he kept adjusting the knot of his elegant silk tie. *He* didn't have to make a fool of himself in an hour. What right did he have to be nervous?

"Please forgive me for interrupting," he said as if he were speaking to Emily Post. "I need a word with Rosemarie."

Maxine crossed her fingers. With any luck, Rupert was here to tell them that a category-four hurricane was about to sweep through Tucson and force the cancellation of this evening's program.

"I thought Octavia would be dining with you," he said. "I'd like to welcome her to the Foothills. You know I never got to meet her in person."

The table went as silent as the tomb Maxine wished she were in. Evidently her webcam interview with its cross-stitched servers had projected Mimi's image onto Rupert's computer and into his brain. No wonder he was dressed to the nines and nervous—his libido was in over-drive.

Rosemarie squirmed, stared wide-eyed at Maxine, then spoke to her mashed potatoes. "Um, Octavia called earlier, and, um, she got caught in traffic, but she'll be here by seven-thirty."

Rupert's smile disintegrated and his crest fell. "Would you bring her by my office when she arrives?"

"Of course." Rosemarie sounded nonchalant, but her eyes were wide.

Rupert left, and they all exhaled.

"What do I do now?" Rosemarie asked.

Maxine saw her opportunity. "Let's call the whole thing off. We can say Octavia's car was caught in a dirt devil and blown to Kansas."

"Don't be so melodramatic." Louise poured herself a fresh glass of water. "We just need something to distract Rupert, something that will keep him busy until seven-thirty."

"We need an emergency. A flood or snowstorm or . . ." Harry paused before adding rather lamely, "or something."

"How about a fire?" June asked. "A fire in the laundry room caused by that dryer that always overheats."

"We can't set the place on fire," Maxine said.

"No, but we could set off the sprinklers. They would cause a flood and Rupert would have to attend to it." June's enthusiasm grew with each preposterous idea.

"But we don't want to frighten people," Maxine said. "What if someone had a heart attack?"

"Good idea," Harry said, rather missing the point. "Get Gladys Black, the drama queen. Just the suggestion of a fire should set off a spectacular performance."

Maxine turned to the ever-logical, never-nonsensical Rosemarie to put a stop to the foolishness before someone got hurt. "Do something."

Rosemarie looked at Maxine and blinked. "Right." She sat up taller and assumed a posture of authority. "All right, people: focus. How can we get the sprinklers and alarms to go off?"

Maxine groaned.

"Simple," June said. "Carlotta's cigarettes used to set them off all the time until they made the laundry room a No Smoking area. Just light up and leave."

Harry waved an imaginary cigarette holder. "Better yet, get Carlotta to light up."

Rosemarie smoothed and folded her napkin. "We can't. She doesn't smoke anymore."

June's passion for mystery novels rose to the challenge. "Then steal her cigarette holder and leave it as evidence. Rupert will find the clue and all hell will break loose."

Maxine used her most austere, professorial voice. "Let's not get carried away."

Rosemarie nodded. "Maxine is right. That plan won't work."

Maxine sighed with relief.

"People might believe that Carlotta still sneaks a smoke, but no one is going to believe that she was doing laundry on a Saturday night." Rosemarie folded her hands and placed them on the table with an air of calm deliberation. "We're doomed."

Maxine groaned again and cradled her head.

"Don't worry dear." Louise spoke for the first time in a long time. "June and I know just what to do."

"We do?" June said.

Louise rose. "June, you come with me. Maxine, you go get ready and don't worry about a thing."

Maxine didn't know which was more terrifying: getting ready for her presentation or leaving Louise and June unchaperoned to carry out whatever plan Louise had concocted.

"I wish I had a migraine." Maxine rubbed her temples. "Because a migraine would eventually go away."

"Now, now. Don't be a party pooper, " Harry said. "Here, you can have my dessert."

He gallantly offered her a bowl of ice cream that was rapidly melting into soup. It looked about as miserable as Maxine felt.

"Thanks anyway, Harry, but I have to go change into someone else."

BACK AT HER CONDO, Maxine considered running away to join the circus but was distracted by the blinking light on her answering machine.

"Hey, Mom. Sorry I missed you. I'll be thinking of you tonight. You'll be great. Don't worry about the audience. Just enjoy the music."

Maxine smiled at the last part. She could almost hear herself telling Katie the same thing before each of her childhood recitals.

For the billionth time today, she dialed Katie's number in New York, but once again she reached only voicemail.

She tapped a finger on her answering machine, then pushed *Replay*. Katie's voice sounded positive, supportive, maybe even a little excited. That would have to do.

She checked her watch. She had to hurry. She still needed to change out of the cranberry-stained dress.

She jerked open her closet and plowed through her clothes, trying on outfits and throwing them with increasing panic onto a mounting pile of rejections.

She grabbed a big-name-designer dress from the back of her closet. June had talked her into buying the dress because "it made a statement." Maxine didn't know what kind of statement the dress made—perhaps that she had more money than sense the day she bought it. The dress was a fussy floral print that made her feel exactly as she had as an adolescent in ballroom dancing class: out of place, awkward, and a great deal like wallpaper.

Maxine yanked the dress on over her head and twisted, turned, and fumbled for the zipper. Widows should never buy dresses with zippers up the back.

She finally snagged the elusive zipper-pull and gave it a violent tug. The zipper caught on the fabric. She gave a more violent tug and the zipper-pull came off in her hand, making the dress both floral and backless.

"Oh, hell."

She squirmed out of the dress and threw it on the rejection pile. Even if she was going to play the fool tonight, she didn't have to dress like one. If she was going to self-destruct, she'd darn well do it in something comfortable.

She returned to her closet and pulled out her favorite dress: a black, streamlined silhouette. Ignoring the showcase of jewelry that she'd borrowed for this evening, Maxine selected the simple gold necklace, bracelet, and earrings that Tom had given her for their fiftieth anniversary. She loved the clean lines of these pieces.

She slipped the bracelet onto her wrist and draped the necklace over her head. The metal felt cool against her skin. She traced a finger across the smooth surface of the bracelet. Tom had given Katie a similar set of jewelry when she'd graduated from college. At Katie's graduation party, mother and daughter had unwittingly appeared as a matched set, each dressed in a chic black sheath adorned only by the gold jewelry.

Maxine stuffed the borrowed jewelry in her sock drawer. No more adornments. No more deceptions.

She glanced in the mirror without actually seeing herself and made a perfunctory adjustment. She was about to deliver the most difficult talk she'd ever given.

It was ironic, really. In more than thirty years of teaching, she must have given thousands of lectures, presented hundreds of reports, and given God knew how many presentations to faculty and literary critics, an audience whose sole mission in life was to find fault. But this twenty-minute "talk" with the residents of the Foothills had her flustered. In part because the residents were her friends and neighbors. In part because she was going to shock them all, perhaps to the disappointment of her friends and the delight of her opponents.

She checked her watch again. She could still withdraw. Claim that Octavia had changed her mind. Weasel out of the whole thing without anyone's being the wiser.

Anyone except her closest friends.

And herself.

She crossed to her desk and picked up the fossilized sand dollar she'd given Tom.

She could take the easy way out. Not show. Not be humiliated. But at her age, inertia was a greater danger than humiliation. A body at rest tends to stay at rest, and a body in motion tends to stay in motion. The trick was to stay in motion. To avoid stagnation.

She picked up Tom's carving of Don Quixote with her other hand and weighed the two objects. The sand dollar felt cool and smooth, hard and perfect. In contrast, the rough-hewn carving was angular, asymmetrical, its dark wood battered and scarred, like the Don himself.

Maxine's lips formed a tight line.

The choice was hers: tilt at windmills or become a relic.

She straightened and returned the objects to her desk. In their stead, she picked up Tom's photo.

"This is it," she said. "Wish me luck."

The photo smiled back. She could practically hear Tom do his faulty Bogart imitation: "Looking at you, love."

He'd be proud of her no matter what happened.

She took one last look in the mirror and actually saw herself this time. An eighty-two-year-old woman with good posture and—thanks to Louise—stylish eyeglasses stared back, a wry smile tugging at the corners of her mouth. The image in the mirror nodded. Maxine squared her shoulders and winked: "Looking at you."

31

MAXINE LEFT HER CONDO without a backward glance. She strode to the formal living room, where Louise waited beside the stone fireplace. Louise had been Sancho Panza to her Don Quixote for almost forever.

"Break a leg," Louise said.

"At our age, it's more likely to be a hip." Maxine surveyed the room. No sign of Rupert anywhere. "Did you and June successfully distract our fearless director?"

Louise's eyes sparkled. "I think you could say he was flooded with interests other than meeting Octavia."

"What did you do?"

Louise placed a hand to her breast in mock innocence. "Moi?"

"Vous."

"I don't know what you're talking about, but I did hear something about someone dumping a full jar of Metamucil down the kitchen sink. When the staff tried to do dishes, the drains backed up and the whole place flooded."

"No! That's brilliant! How did you do it?"

"*I* didn't, but I did *happen* to be in the kitchen for just a *few* minutes to compliment the chefs on tonight's dinner and to ask about monosodium glutamate levels. I suppose someone *could have* slipped in and dumped the Metamucil while I was talking with the cooks."

"There's no MSG in roast chicken."

"Yes, I learned that. Isn't it a comfort?" Louise turned toward the formal living room.

"Wait." Maxine scanned the area. "Where are Mimi and Celine?"

Louise put a hand on Maxine's arm. "Don't worry. Peter's with them. He'll make sure nothing goes wrong. Right now, they're meditating in the Green Room." Louise closed her eyes and placed her palms together, thumbs at her heart. "Om."

"They're what?"

Louise opened her eyes. "They're hiding in the library. They're fine. Let's go."

Maxine started toward the library, but Louise grabbed her arm and pulled her back. Louise was strong for someone so short.

"They said to tell you . . ." Louise released her grip and enumerated the messages on her fingertips. "One: don't worry. Two: everything's all right. Three: performers are like brides, no one is allowed to see them before the wedding."

"That's absurd," Maxine said.

Louise shrugged.

"Celine said that last part, didn't she?"

"You know how temperamental a star can be."

"I never should have agreed to let them surprise me." Maxine squinted at the library door and tried to determine if it was open a micro-millimeter. "There's no telling what they'll do. The only saving grace is that Fermez is not performing with them."

Seabiscuit snorted.

Maxine swung her attention back to Louise, who avoided eye contact.

"Don't worry," Louise said. "Mimi has good sense, and Peter is with them. I'm sure it might be OK." With that, Louise and Seabiscuit trotted into the formal living room.

Maxine stared at her friend's retreating back. She cast one last longing look toward the library. The door opened a crack, and a gloved hand shooed her away.

AT "OCTAVIA'S" REQUEST, the room had been set up cabaret style with chairs arranged in informal clusters around small tables rather than in the regimental rows Fred favored.

June and Rosemarie had saved seats at a table near the front. Rosemarie waved them over. June leaned forward to say something, but before she could, Rupert bounded up to the microphone. He looked rattled. His normally impeccable hair drooped over his forehead, giving him a little-boy look that was far more charming than his phony soap-opera-star smile.

"Good evening, ladies and gentlemen." He sounded a bit breathless. "We are here tonight to meet with our second candidate for the position of assistant director."

Maxine moistened her lips and swallowed. She wished she'd brought a bottle of water. Right on cue, Harry handed her a paper cup of cold water.

"I must apologize to our guest." Rupert adjusted his tie. "In the, um, flood of activities this evening"—this comment brought snickers from the residents who knew about the clogged kitchen drains—"I've not been able to meet and greet her. I believe I saw her briefly a moment ago, but I don't see her now. Is she here?"

"She's ready," Rosemarie said.

Maxine fussed with her outfit and twisted her wedding ring. In no way was she ready.

Rupert nodded. "Thank you to the Residents' Advisory Committee for taking care of our guest."

Fred and Carlotta glared at Rosemarie, clearly annoyed that they'd not been involved in whatever it was that was happening.

Rupert consulted a soggy piece of paper clutched in his left hand.

Louise elbowed Maxine. "Those are his notes for Octavia's introduction. They fell into the sink when he was trying to unstop it."

"Poor Rupert."

Rupert smoothed the paper and squinted at his notes. He held them at arm's length, readjusted the distance, and finally abandoned the effort altogether.

"So, um." He blushed. "Without further ado." He wadded his notes into a damp ball. "Let's welcome Miss M. Octavia Olson." Rupert bowed and swept his arm as if he were welcoming the Queen of England. Then he darted to his chair along the side wall.

The audience looked around, and the buzz of expectation grew to a steady hum. Maxine looked helplessly at her friends. Louise took Maxine's hand and patted it; Rosemarie crossed her fingers; June winked. Across the hallway, the library door cracked open another inch. Maxine imagined Celine and Mimi watching. She knew that Peter would have stationed himself behind the ficus tree with his handheld spotlight.

Maxine took a deep breath and stood. Her knees cracked and wobbled, but they held. She forced herself to walk to the front of the room. No one noticed her, or if they did they paid no attention. They were too busy looking for Octavia.

Maxine stood at the podium for a few moments and caught her breath. A bead of perspiration trickled down her back. Slowly, the hum in the room turned to a hush as residents realized she was at the microphone. Rupert stared, confusion etched on his face.

"Good evening." Maxine leaned too close to the microphone and got a loud burst of feedback. "Excuse me." She straightened and adjusted the height of the microphone. "How's this?" she asked, testing the volume.

"It's good," Rosemarie called.

Maxine clutched the edges of the podium for support. The wood felt warm and familiar.

"I know you are wondering why I'm up here," she began.

"That's for damn sure," Fred shouted. "We want to hear Octavia Olson."

"Well, as a matter of fact," Maxine said as sweetly as she could, "that's me."

The residents stared.

"Octavia is my middle name. I'm Maxine Octavia Olson."

The room fell into absolute silence. Since Louise seemed to be holding her breath, even Seabiscuit was quiet. The only sound was the jackhammering of Maxine's heart.

She plunged on before her knees gave out. "But as you can imagine, with initials like mine, I don't use my middle name often."

There was a half beat while the audience thought about Maxine's initials.

Ralph Jordan mooed, and everyone chuckled.

The tension eased out of Maxine's shoulders. The residents had laughed. She'd be OK if they were willing to laugh. Her hands relaxed their death grip on the podium.

"When I applied to be the assistant director," she said, "I wanted to be evaluated like all the other candidates, without any special advantage because you knew me."

She looked as many people in the eye as she could. Paul and Peggy Stone nodded encouragement. Gladys Black gaped like a fish out of water. Rupert had a pinched expression as if someone had sucker-punched the wind out of him.

"I apologize for deceiving you," she said. "I'm willing to wager there was a better way to ensure everyone received the same impartial consideration, but I couldn't think of it."

Carlotta turned purple. She couldn't actually object to Maxine's candidacy and accuse her of an unfair advantage, because her parties had given Evie a similar advantage. In fact, even tonight Carlotta and Fred were using subliminal advertising to promote Evie. They'd dressed in the same Hawaiian outfits they'd worn to Evie's event. The only difference was that Carlotta had substituted a blouse for her bikini top and a long, Italian silk scarf for her plastic lei.

The audience stirred.

Maxine took a deep breath and pressed on. This was it: time to deliver her version of the assistant director's position.

Because she meant what she said, the words came easily. Fear and uncertainty evaporated. She was the teacher once again, committed to her students and to the message they needed to hear. She abandoned her script and let passion be her guide as she shared her vision with them.

Aging was like a dance marathon. The trick was to keep moving and learning. If they stopped, they'd be eliminated. They'd turn into fossilized versions of themselves. They needed an assistant director who shared that vision, not someone who wanted to restrict their movement. They didn't need a guard or a babysitter or a paleontologist. They needed someone to encourage them to keep dancing. Help them grow. Challenge them to tilt at windmills, if that's what was needed for them to pursue their own excellence.

Maxine paused to catch her breath.

The residents nodded. Paul and Peggy Stone saluted her. Ralph Jordan double-pumped his fist. Gladys Black even started to clap until Carlotta elbowed her.

It was time to wrap up.

"In conclusion." Maxine paused just long enough to gain everyone's attention. "The assistant director's role is to encourage and enable each of us to pursue our own improbable, impossible dreams."

The audience burst into applause. Paul and Peggy Stone shouted, "Brava! Bravissima!" Ralph Jordan whistled loudly. Maxine took advantage of the applause to scan the room for Rupert. She'd spoken from her heart to her fellow residents, but her fate lay in Rupert's hands.

She spotted him leaning against the far wall. His arms were crossed and his head was tilted to one side as if he were assessing her. After a long moment, he acknowledged her with the smallest of nods. Maxine returned the nod and held his gaze. Almost involuntarily, Rupert's impassive face bent into a wry smile and he gave her a surreptitious thumbs-up.

"Thank you," Maxine said into the microphone. "Thank you very much. To help demonstrate what I mean, I've arranged for a performance by Tucson's own musical sensation, The Improbable Dreamers."

On cue, the lights dimmed.

Maxine retreated to her table and crossed her fingers. *Please, let Mimi and Celine be—*

Peter's spotlight flashed around the room and settled on the library door behind them. The audience turned in unison, just as the door burst open and Fermez entered wearing quite possibly the sexiest gown Maxine had ever seen. Entirely be-sequined in silver, it shimmered and sparkled with every breath Fermez took. Its plunging neckline and soaring slit left nothing—or rather everything—to the imagination.

"Oh my God," Maxine clasped her bosom. She turned to Harry. "Get ready to fake a heart attack if Fermez goes into her Mae West routine."

"I won't be faking it if she does that." Harry spoke without taking his eyes off Fermez.

Certain that her blood pressure was mounting, Maxine spun around to see if Rupert was about to pull the plug on the act. But Rupert was practically salivating. In fact, all the men seemed to be salivating as Fermez vamped her way across the room and up to the microphone.

"Please, don't let her speak." Maxine clasped her hands and held her breath.

Fermez gave the crowd a sultry wink. Then the spotlight swung back to the library door, where a figure dressed in a black sheath stood with her back to the room, one arm raised against the doorframe. A simple gold bracelet glittered in the spotlight. The pose was stunning. The figure was elegant.

But the figure was also a brunette. Mimi was a blonde. Maxine's blood pressure went up another notch.

"Who's that?" she demanded.

"Shh! It's the pianist," Louise whispered.

"What pianist?"

Before Louise could respond, the figure turned.

Katie.

Maxine gasped.

Louise chuckled.

"What's going on?"

Louise laughed.

Maxine turned to her. "Did you know?"

"She's been staying at Peter's. We thought you deserved a little surprise."

"Little?" Maxine swiped at her tears. "Little!"

The spotlight swung again. This time it revealed Celine, dressed to bedazzle in her red sequined gown. For the occasion, she'd pulled her hair into a magnificent jumble with glitter and sparkling combs. She'd stopped short of a tiara, but she didn't need one. She was regal without it. As Celine swept in, Maxine realized that most of the audience had not recognized her.

Finally, Mimi entered in a floor-length, white silk evening gown. She had piled her blonde hair into a loose French twist that emphasized her slender neck and fine features. She was positively ethereal.

Maxine's eyes brimmed. She loved these women.

Fermez picked up the microphone, and Maxine sucked in her breath.

"Après Fermez, le déluge," Rosemarie whispered.

Maxine's throat was too dry to respond.

"Good evening," Fermez said in her most seductive voice. She couldn't resist striking half a dozen poses. The postures stayed on the conservative side of overtly sexual, but the men still got the point. So did the women. Thankfully, they all seemed to be enjoying the show. In fact, the whole room vibrated with sexual energy. The women leaned forward. Men sat back. Feet twitched. Fingers tapped. Perspiration glowed on upper lips, bald heads, and exposed cleavage.

Louise poked Maxine. "Look at Carlotta's table."

Carlotta crossed and recrossed her legs. Her hand fluttered to her throat, her fingers played with her necklace. Fred had slipped his arm along the back of her chair and was toying with the folds of her scarf. The scarf slipped, and Fred's fingers strayed from silk to bare skin. Carlotta's mouth opened slightly.

"Pretty steamy for the formal living room," Louise whispered.

Fermez finished the introductions, and the music began with the deep, rhythmic pounding of bongos being played by Celine. Mimi began to sing. Katie's piano picked up the beat, and the Improbable Dreamers opened with "Night and Day."

At the end of the song, the audience showered the band with cheers and whistles and whoops. The atmosphere was electric. Mimi bowed. Celine dropped a deep curtsey. Fermez shimmered and swayed. Katie winked at Maxine, whose heart pounded a chorus of its own.

Maxine blew Katie a kiss.

Katie laughed and swayed as if blown off-balance by the force of the gesture.

Fermez introduced the songs and flirted with the residents until she had them eating out of her well-manicured hands. If she asked for audience participation, the residents clapped and sang. If she needed a percussion section, they vied with each other to be selected. Norman Tisdale tickled the triangle while Gladys Black strummed the washboard and Fred laid permanent claim to the bongos.

Maxine felt a sharp jab in her ribs.

"Why are you crying?" Louise whispered.

"Because I'm happy," Maxine said, not bothering to wipe her eyes.

The band played for thirty magical, musical minutes before Fermez cooed into the microphone. "Dahlings, was this as good for you as it was for me?" She did a coy Marilyn Monroe dip.

Maxine winced, but the boys in the audience yelled even louder.

"In that case . . ." Fermez did another dip and batted her eyelashes. "Won't you join me in a conga line for our final number?"

The other band members seemed startled by the suggestion, but they obligingly launched into a hot salsa number. Ralph Jordan, Gladys Black, and Paul and Peggy Stone jumped up and formed a line behind Fermez. The line twisted and snaked its way through chairs and around tables, picking up dancers along the way. When the line passed Maxine's table, Fermez tugged Maxine to her feet and made her head of the line. In turn, Maxine grabbed Louise and Seabiscuit and positioned them to lead the procession. By the end of the song, all the residents were up, clapping their hands and stomping their feet to the pulsing rhythms.

When the number ended, the residents remained on their feet, clapping and cheering.

"Encore! Encore!"

"More, more, more!"

Fred grabbed Fermez's microphone and shouted, "Hell no—please don't go."

While Fermez struggled with Fred for control of her microphone, the residents wandered back to their seats, and Katie took over as emcee.

"We want to thank you all for a lovely evening. Thank you especially for being so very 'Young at Heart.'"

With that, the band slid into one of Maxine's favorite songs. By the second verse, Maxine was humming along. By the last verse, everyone was singing and swaying in time to the music.

The song finished, and the residents leapt to their feet and broke into wild applause. Soon everyone had taken up Fred's chant, "Hell no— please don't go."

The band members tried to bow and escape, but the audience only chanted louder. Mimi, Katie, Celine, and Fermez exchanged glances.

Fermez reclaimed the microphone. "Well, dahlings, we haven't planned anything else, but if you call out your heart's desires . . ." She punctuated her sentence with another deep Marilyn Monroe dip. "We'll do our very best to satisfy you."

The audience roared and began calling out requests.

Fred grabbed the bongos and yelled, "'Too Darn Hot'! Play 'Too Darn Hot'!"

"Baby, I've got this one." Celine took possession of the microphone and proceeded to smoke even Ella with her rendition of the song.

The band played requests for another twenty minutes. Between them, Mimi and Celine seemed to know every song ever written. And, Maxine noted with pride, Katie could improvise her way through any-thing, including an upbeat jazz rendition of "The Impossible Dream," a song that Tom had always claimed was written with Maxine in mind.

While the crowd pleaded for more, Fermez sashayed to the center of the stage. "Thank you all for coming. You've been delicious, delightful, and deliriously sexy."

The audience purred its approval.

"We'd like to dedicate our final number to Maxine Olson, who is, in the words of the immortal Nat King Cole, 'Unforgettable.'"

FOR MAXINE, the moments after the concert were a blur of hearty con-gratulations, knowing nods, secretive winks, and whispered messages.

"You have our vote."

"Long live the Improbable Dreamers."

"Give us Fermez any day."

Maxine was high-fived, hugged, and hand-clasped until her fingers hurt.

Then the crowd shifted, and Maxine glimpsed Carlotta and Fred across the room, glaring at each other. Carlotta snatched the bongos out of his hands and leveled her cigarette holder at poor Fred's breast. His shoulders slumped. Carlotta tossed her head, spun on her spiked heels, and headed straight toward Maxine. At the last moment, she slithered to a stop and coiled inches away.

"'That was quite a performance." Carlotta's voice crackled with rage. "You were wise to get someone much younger to put on that spectacle for you. At your age, I'm sure you don't have the energy to lead a song, much less direct a retirement community."

"Frankly, I don't have the voice to lead a song," Maxine said.

Carlotta's lip curled up. "I'm surprised you consider yourself a candidate for Evie's job. Are you even eligible?"

Maxine braced herself for battle, but before she could reply, Katie linked an arm through hers and drew her away. "Come along, Mom. Your fans want to shower you with adoration."

An enthusiastic crowd quickly encircled Maxine, hugging, tugging, cheek-pecking, and elbow-rubbing. Carlotta was left to fester alone while the residents chattered and mingled. Exuberant groups recounted stories of concerts and dances from their youth. More than a few people sang snatches of their favorite songs. Others demonstrated dance steps from a bygone era. When Rupert finally flashed the lights, the party grudgingly broke up.

At the door, someone captured Maxine's elbow and pulled her to a stop. She turned to face Rupert.

"Rupert, I—"

He cut her off with a shake of his head. "You ran a good race, Maxine. You paced yourself for the long haul, and you saved a surprise kick for the end." He crossed his arms over his chest and examined her.

Maxine waited.

Rupert uncrossed his arms and gave a single nod. "You'd make a good marathoner," he said and disappeared into the crowd.

Stunned, Maxine bowed to Rupert's retreating back. A marathoner!

AT MAXINE'S CONDO, the post-party celebration continued.

"That Fred Grosskopf is something else," Fermez said, swishing her fanny. "He patted me on the derriere every time the conga line doubled past him."

"That's nothing, honey." Celine struck a pose worthy of any diva. "Carlotta told me I looked so familiar that she was sure she'd seen me in the movies or on TV."

"You're kidding," Maxine said. "She never recognized you?"

Celine waved her hand dismissively. "Somehow she got the idea that I'm a big-time gospel singer who agreed to help the band tonight."

"Well, you are," Maxine said. "I can't thank you enough. In fact, I can't thank all of you enough. I . . .you . . ." She'd written a longer speech, but words seemed inadequate.

Mimi touched Maxine's arm. "We should be thanking you. We had a great time being your band. Thank you for asking us."

Celine squeezed Maxine's hand. "Were you surprised?" she asked, her eyes wide with anticipation.

"I was dumbfounded and dumbstruck," Maxine said. "I had no idea the Improbable Dreamers would be so good." A warm flush climbed up her neck. She looked down at her hands. "I'm sorry I ever doubted you."

Celine raised her arms and broke into a victory dance that looked a bit like a wide receiver celebrating a touchdown. She spiked the imaginary football and turned back to Maxine. "What about Katie? Were you surprised to see her?"

For a moment, Maxine couldn't speak. She swallowed and nodded. "Very."

"Aw, Mom." Katie wrapped her arms around Maxine and hugged her hard.

The band cheered.

Louise cried.

Peter hoisted a bottle of Champagne in each hand. "Let's celebrate!"

"To the Improbable Dreamers."

"To the Dreamers!"

The toast led to more hugging and toasting and singing and even a short conga line.

Maxine wished the evening could go on forever. She nodded to Tom's photo on the mantle. He was the only thing missing.

Katie slipped her arm around Maxine's waist. "He would have been proud of you tonight," she said, tipping her head toward the photo.

"And of you. He loved to listen to you play the piano. He even thought your scales were beautiful."

Katie laughed and shook her head. "Sometimes I'd play in the wrong key or jumble pieces just to see if he'd object. He never did."

Maxine smiled. "I know."

"Sometimes he'd slip his own compositions into my music folder: bits of Beethoven mixed with strains of Sinatra or echoes of Armstrong."

Maxine straightened and cocked an eyebrow at Tom's photo. "I didn't know that."

"Oh, that was Dad all over." Katie took the photo off the mantle and stroked it with her fingertip. "One minute you thought you knew him like middle C, and the next he was a total mystery."

Maxine reached for the photo, but a male hand beat her to it.

"Isn't that the truth?" Peter held the photo up to the light. "The only person more mysterious was—is—Maxine."

"What? But—"

"But"—Peter returned the photo to the mantle—"it's time to call it a night. Your guests are turning into pumpkins."

As Peter drew them back to the party, Maxine glanced over her shoulder. Light glinted off Tom's enigmatic smile. What else had she missed?

"Here we are."

"Good night."

"Love you."

"Thank you."

"No, thank you."

"Here is the best part," Celine said, blocking the doorway.

Fermez cut in front of Celine and did one of her Marilyn Monroe dips.

Katie caught Fermez's gloved arm and gently pulled her aside.

Mimi stepped in and, raising her hands like a conductor, led everyone in one more chorus of "Young at Heart."

After more laughing, hugging, and humming, Maxine walked her guests out. She watched until the last taillight disappeared.

Alone, she lifted her face to the sky. Billions of brilliant stars splashed across vast space. Black holes were held in check by the harmony of the spheres. Bits of Beethoven blended with strains of Sinatra.

Maxine opened her arms and embraced the infinite.

A moment later, she shivered and lowered her arms. Her shoulders ached, and her feet hurt. It was time to call it a night.

PART FIVE

PLAY ON!

32

CARLOTTA FLUNG HERSELF on the bed and pummeled her mattress.

The phone rang and shattered the last of her frayed nerves.

"Not now, damn it."

She grabbed a pillow and hurled it at the phone. The pillow smacked into her neatly stacked pages of *The Foothills Retirement Community's Official Bylaws* and sent them spraying into the air as if shot from a geyser.

She fumed while the bylaws swirled about the room and the phone rang itself into silence.

Too late, she realized the caller could have been Evie. Carlotta had told her to come to dinner at the Foothills to do damage control after Maxine's event. Carlotta had seen the residents winking and nodding at Maxine, flashing her the thumbs-up and whispering in her ear.

Evie should have been at dinner in that lovely form-fitting dress with the plunging neckline. She needed to remind the men just exactly who they wanted to have directing their affairs.

But Evie had refused. After all that Carlotta had done for her: sent her to graduate school, paid for her apartment, found her a job. And Evie had refused! Claimed she had a business appointment. What appointment could she possibly have?

Carlotta shoved herself off the bed. She needed a cigarette. Surely there was a forgotten pack somewhere. She stomped around her condo opening drawers and slamming cabinets.

Carlotta slammed another drawer. She couldn't find a cigarette any-where. She'd have to settle for her cigarette holder. Clamping it between her teeth, she sucked hard. The memory of nicotine triggered a response in her brain and the tension in her shoulders eased.

Maybe Carlotta couldn't control Maxine, but she damn well could control Evie. Tomorrow they would *not* host a simple afternoon tea. Teas bought polite good wishes. Booze bought votes. Carlotta would launch a last-ditch series of cocktail parties.

Without bothering to turn on the lights, she stomped into her living room and paced in tight circles in front of her fireplace.

That sneak, Maxine, had bested her by having a gaggle of young floozies sing oldie goldies. The old fools at the Foothills had fallen for that schmaltz. Really, a conga line? At their age?

Thank God, Carlotta had been at the end of the line, behind Fred, so he couldn't see how clumsy she was. If she'd known in advance, she could have practiced, and she definitely would have worn a different outfit. Who could do a conga line in an Italian-silk scarf?

She grabbed a tissue off the mantle and blotted her eyes.

Frankly, given the circumstances, she'd done damn well at Maxine's event, but *that* was the point. With Maxine you never knew what the circumstances were going to be.

Carlotta shoved her accent pillows onto the floor and collapsed onto the couch.

Maxine and her bridge-playing, rule-bending friends would be a disaster. She'd treat absolutely everybody the same. Carlotta would have no control over anything. Maxine would oppose her every effort to improve the Foothills and modify its bylaws. She'd already thwarted Carlotta's motion to ban those damn walkers and wheelchairs. They were dangerous. Studies probably showed that it aged you just to be around them. Just last summer, Carlotta had tripped over Louise's con-traption and sprained her ankle. She'd been on crutches for a week. Fred had brought her meals from the dining room or she would have starved.

Thank God she had Fred. He was her rock. He'd seen her naked in broad daylight and still wanted her. He'd seen her speechless and still been persuaded by her eyes and caressed her breasts.

A wave of heat washed over Carlotta. She closed her eyes and lightly touched her own bosom. Fred wouldn't care if she mixed up her footing in the conga line.

Carlotta's eyes flew open.

But who knew where the conga line would have ended if she had not been holding onto Fred? It was bad enough that he'd spent the whole night banging on the bongos and ogling that floozy with the microphone.

She picked up an accent pillow and heaved it at the fireplace.

No. She couldn't risk having Maxine be in charge. She sat in her dark living room and stared into her unlit fireplace. There had to be a way to stop Maxine. There was always a way.

33

MAXINE HATED WAITING. She hated waiting rooms. She hated waiting for doctors. She even hated waiting for Louise while Louise went to the doctor.

This waiting room was like every other waiting room she'd ever been in: institutional, impersonal, and dark. It was filled with out-of-date magazines and those inevitable square chairs, which might have been comfortable if she were shaped like a box. Maxine shifted to relieve the pressure on her lower back. It didn't work.

She fidgeted with her watch. Not her good watch, but the cheap drugstore watch with extra-large numbers that she could read without her glasses. She checked the time. Louise had been with the doctor for an eternity.

Maxine worried.

First, she'd found Harry wandering around by the pool this morning. He hadn't been able to remember where he lived. Hadn't remembered Maxine's name. Hadn't remembered Maxine, for that matter.

She shivered and rubbed her arms. Waiting rooms were so damnably cold.

Alzheimer's ran in Harry's family. She knew it. They all knew it. They knew it and watched. And worried. The Foothills was not a continuous care facility. When the disease progressed too far, Harry would have to move.

She closed her eyes against the tears. She'd already cried once today. When she'd brought Harry home, she and June had held each other and sobbed.

Maxine opened her eyes and swiped at the tears on her cheeks. She would not cry again. Not in the waiting room. Not while Louise was being held captive by her doctor.

First Harry. Now Louise.

Louise had been having trouble breathing. She couldn't make it from her apartment to the dining room without stopping to rest. And she needed to change her oxygen canisters far more often than she used to. Not that Louise ever complained. But Maxine knew the rhythms of Louise's life as well as she knew her own. Better really. And Maxine was worried.

She opened a copy of the *Smithsonian* for the umpteenth time. The picture on the front was of some ancient ruin, a Mayan city or a Roman fort. She couldn't remember which. She didn't care. It was times like these that she most reminded herself of June's grandson, a teenager with the attention span of a gnat.

She forced herself to stare at the magazine. Whichever ruins they were, they were built in perfect concentric circles. Just like the Foothills, according to Harry.

She lowered the magazine.

Assuming Harry still remembered his theory about the harmony of the spheres. How long would it be before the shadow of Alzheimer's fell between them and obscured Harry's beautiful mind and eccentric wit?

Maxine forgot to breathe for a moment.

She dropped the magazine onto the table. She'd had enough of ruins.

She rummaged through her purse for her notebook and ruffled through it to a blank page. She began to list all the reasons Louise was not seriously ill.

She couldn't be.

Maxine loved her.

Everyone loved her.

She couldn't be.

Maxine slapped her notebook shut and drummed her fingers on the cover.

There was a water cooler in the far corner of the waiting room. The kind with the paper cones that leaked if you didn't pinch the bottom shut. She walked over and got herself a cup of water that she didn't want. Sure enough: it leaked. She checked the time.

Time was another issue. She did not have that much more time left on earth. She wanted to spend it wisely. Tutoring Celine and helping June with Harry. Those were valuable—essential—ways to spend her time. And being there for Katie. And getting Louise through whatever medical issues she was facing. All those things counted for something. She wanted to do them: she *needed* to do them.

What she did *not* need was to spend time planning events for residents of the Foothills. Not if it meant taking time away from the people she loved. She no longer had the energy to do both.

Maxine inhaled sharply.

She really *didn't* have the energy to do both.

A wave of heat flashed through her body and turned her knees to Jell-O. She steadied herself on the water cooler, then plopped into the nearest chair.

Katie had been right.

She'd have been damn good at the assistant director's job, had she but world enough and time. But she didn't have world enough and time.

She studied her hands with their gnarled fingers and arthritic joints. She traced the age spots with her index finger.

Her life had run almost its full course. Andrew Marvell had gotten it right: at her back she could hear time's winged chariot hurrying near.

She took several deep yoga breaths to slow the pounding in her chest.

She wasn't afraid of dying, but she was afraid of frittering away what was left of her life. She wanted to spend—extravagantly and expansively spend—her remaining time and energy on family and friends. On Louise. Louise had never been to the Giant Redwoods. Chuck had died before they could go. Maxine wanted Louise to see those trees before she died—

before either of them died. Maxine bit her lip to stop the trembling. Louise could not be ill. She simply could not.

Someone tapped her shoulder and Maxine jumped.

"What's the matter?" Louise asked. "Why are you crying? Do you need a hankie?"

Maxine jerked away. "Don't sneak up on me. You'll give me a heart attack."

"Why are you crying?"

"I am not crying." Maxine wiped her eyes with her fingers.

"Here. Use my handkerchief on those nonexistent tears."

Maxine took the handkerchief and dabbed her eyes. "Must be allergies."

Louise waited.

"I was thinking about mortality," Maxine said. "I guess I was thinking about my own funeral."

Louise studied her for a long moment. "I hope you're not going to have it very soon. I don't have a black dress that's right for this time of year. We're too in-between seasons, if you know what I mean."

Maxine nodded gratefully. She knew exactly what Louise meant. She pulled herself together and changed the subject. "What did your young Dr. Kildare say?" His real name was Dr. Ochoa, but he had such gentle, puppy-dog eyes that he reminded her of that actor who'd played Dr. Kildare on television eons ago.

"Well, he did a lot of tests and poked and prodded every which way and took my blood and ordered more tests for next week." Louise stopped to catch her breath. "But as far as he can tell, there's not a thing wrong with me, outside the obvious, of course." She gestured toward Seabiscuit.

This time Maxine didn't try to hide her tears. She enveloped Louise and Seabiscuit both in a gigantic hug. "That's wonderful! Did he know why you needed to change air tanks so often?"

"Yes, and you aren't going to believe it." Louise paused for dramatic effect. "My oxygen supplier switched me to a new brand. Although everything looks and costs the same, the tanks are actually smaller."

"That's outrageous!"

"I thought so too. So did our young Dr. Kildare. In fact, he was furious when he found out that no one had asked me about the switch or sent me any information about the tanks. So he called my supplier and raised hell. He told them to put me back on my former brand and not to put any more of his patients on the new tanks, ever."

"Mild-mannered Dr. Kildare did that?"

"I'm the third person he's seen this month for the same thing."

This time Maxine hugged Louise so hard she knocked her air hose out.

"Hey. I just got this fixed."

"Let's go celebrate," Maxine said. "Double decaf cappuccinos at Java Joe's, on me."

"Deal!" Louise said. "Afterward, can we stop at the mausoleum to tell Chuck and Tom the news?"

Maxine smiled and nodded. One of the first things she and Tom had done when they'd retired to Tucson was to make their funeral arrangements and reserve a double crypt at Forest Lawn Mausoleum and Cemetery. Louise and Chuck had purchased a neighboring crypt. Good friends for over half a century, the four of them would be positioned to watch over each other forever. And Maxine liked Forest Lawn well enough, with its cottonwood trees and garden walks. It was, however, the only place where she couldn't feel Tom's presence. She could hear him in a beautifully played piece of music, feel him in the polished wood of his old hiking stick, even smell him in the desert air after an afternoon thunderstorm. He was present to her in the things they'd loved together. But try as she might, she couldn't find him at the mausoleum.

Louise, on the other hand, enjoyed chatting with Chuck at Forest Lawn.

"Yes," Maxine said. "Let's definitely stop and tell them the good news."

Louise blushed. "Chuck may be a bit disappointed. I told him last night that I thought I might be joining him soon."

"Well, he can wait. He gets you for all eternity, but right now I need you."

34

MAXINE SQUIRMED IN HER CHAIR and toyed with her lasagna. It had been over twenty-four hours since her epiphany, and she still hadn't confessed to Louise, or anyone else, that she didn't want to be the assistant director. To make matters worse, Carlotta was clearly up to something and Maxine couldn't guess what. Carlotta's entire table was disturbingly festive. Carlotta repeatedly threw triumphant glances toward Maxine, while Gladys Black and Fred kept whispering and glancing Maxine's way. Eventually, people at other tables began to look at Maxine and wink. Whatever it was, word was spreading around the dining room like a wave around a football stadium

"What's going on?" June asked.

"I've no idea," Maxine said. "It's another one of life's inexplicable mysteries piling up around us. Many more, and we'll be totally buried."

"Speaking of the inexplicable," Rosemarie said in a low voice. "Here comes Gladys."

"Isn't the news about Evie wonderful?" Gladys cooed.

"What news?" Louise asked, as Gladys had so obviously hoped she would.

"Haven't you heard?"

"Heard what?" Maxine said, barely able to suppress her impatience.

"Evie's taken a job with Delbeck's Department store."

"What?"

"Doing what?"

"Who's Evie?" Harry asked.

"Why hasn't she informed the Residents' Advisory Committee?" Rosemarie said.

"I understand it's quite an opportunity." Gladys prattled on, enjoying her role as town crier. "She gets to create the department. It's a pilot program. Once she gets it running, Delbeck's will expand it throughout the Southwest."

"What department is she creating?" Maxine asked. Trying to pull a story out of Gladys was like pushing a wet string uphill.

Gladys feigned surprise. "Didn't I mention it? Evie's going to be the new wedding planner."

Maxine and Louise exchanged glances. Maxine put a hand over her mouth to muffle herself. Louise snorted.

They exchanged another helpless glance and burst out laughing. The more they tried to stop, the harder they laughed. Tears ran down Maxine's cheeks. Louise shook so hard she rattled the silverware.

"I don't see what's so funny," Gladys said and pouted. "I thought she was excellent the night she was here."

Maxine tried to stop laughing. "No. Not that. Yes. She was astounding. It's just that . . ." She didn't quite know what to say.

"It's just that we thought that would be an ideal job for her," Louise said into the awkward silence.

Carlotta barged into the conversation, shoving Gladys aside like an icebreaker ramming a floe. "Well, evidently Mr. Delbeck thought so too. In fact, *he* called *her*."

"Really?" Rosemarie said.

"Yes." Carlotta pointed her nose to its snootiest angle. "A very talented friend of Mr. Delbeck's saw a sample of Evie's work and recommended her. The friend is a French designer. Perhaps you've heard of her, Madame Fermez La Bouche?"

Rosemarie spit out the water she had been drinking, and June gave an odd little noise somewhere between a cough and a cackle.

Maxine tried to avoid making eye contact with anyone. The effort brought more tears to her eyes.

Carlotta glared.

"Excuse me." Maxine dabbed her eyes with a napkin. "It's just such a moving story."

"It brings tears to my eyes," June said with a straight face.

Louise snorted. When everyone turned toward her, she bent over and pretended to adjust her oxygen tank.

"Doesn't she want to be our assistant director?" Harry asked in what sounded like innocence.

Carlotta practically crowed. "Well, how could she possibly turn down a position this important? Mr. Delbeck as much as told her that his department chain would fall into ruin without her."

Carlotta raised her voice so that everyone in the dining room could hear. "And, of course, the Foothills simply can't touch the rewards of her new position: the salary, the benefits, and the travel. It simply *cannot* be believed."

Maxine suspected that Carlotta's version of the rewards *should not* be believed. "I think Evie will be a splendid wedding planner," she said.

Carlotta glared at Maxine.

"I truly do," Maxine said. "I'm happy for her. Congratulations!"

Carlotta leaned on the back of Maxine's chair. "Of course we're all hoping the *third* candidate will be wonderful."

Maxine wasn't just hoping the third candidate would be wonderful, she was praying for it. With Evie out of the running, the existence of a viable third candidate would spare Maxine the embarrassment of confessing to her friends that she didn't want to be assistant director. She could withdraw her application with impunity.

Carlotta hovered over Maxine like a bird of prey. "If the third candidate does not prove acceptable, however, we'll simply have to beg Evie to reconsider."

"I'd rather stab a stick in my eye," Harry said, reaching for a dessert.

Carlotta let go of Maxine's chair and spun toward him. "What did you say!"

Harry smiled cordially. "Let me grab some Boston cream pie. It's my favorite, you know." He offered her a slice. "Would you care to join us?"

They all stared at Harry, who smiled again and picked up his fork.

Carlotta smoothed her ruffled feathers and flew back to her table.

Maxine turned to Harry. "I thought your favorite dessert was a hot fudge sundae."

"It is." Harry winked.

Maxine winked back, then tossed her napkin onto the table. "Let's celebrate. I'll drive."

"Drive where?" Rosemarie asked.

Louise folded her napkin and tucked it under the edge of her plate. "To Benny's Bar and Grill. To congratulate Fermez on her coup."

"What exactly did Madame La Bouche do?" June asked.

Maxine and Louise looked at each other.

Maxine shrugged. "We're not exactly sure. All we know is that she took those silly hibiscus name tags Evie had us make."

"She thought Evie would make a perfect wedding planner," Louise said.

"More like Bridezilla," Rosemarie said.

Maxine nodded. "Exactly."

"No kidding!" June said. "That Fermez has balls."

"Exactly," Harry said, sending them all into another round of uncontrollable laughter.

HARRY OPENED THE DOOR at Benny's and peered in. "Are you ladies sure this is the right place? It looks a bit . . ." He faltered. "Well, a bit dark."

"Yes, dear." June sailed through the door. "Come along."

Harry hesitated.

"Don't worry." Maxine took his arm and guided him in. "Benny's is practically our second home. Mimi and Fermez work here."

"Speaking of the devil . . ." Fermez vamped over to greet them. "Here I am in all my glory." She turned in a slow circle, showing off a gold strapless, backless gown with a slit up the side that stopped just short of illegal.

"We've come to worship at your feet." Maxine raised her arms over her head and bowed in homage.

"We've come to thank you," Louise said.

"You can have my first-born child as offering," June said.

"But not the grandchildren," Harry said. "I've grown quite fond of them."

"Well, dahlings," Fermez said before switching to her faux French accent. "I adore zee adoration, but what zee devil are you talking about?"

"Evie's job!" Rosemarie said. "You've done it."

Louise pumped her fist. "She's withdrawn her application to be our assistant director."

"She's taken another job." June's voice rose with excitement.

"She's going to be the wedding planner for Delbeck's Department Store," Maxine said.

"Three cheers for Fermez the Fabulous!" Harry shouted.

Although the other patrons at Benny's had no idea what was going on, they enthusiastically joined in the cheers. "Hip, hip, hooray! Hip, hip, hooray! Hip, hip, hooray!"

Fermez favored her fans with an imitation of some movie star, Maxine was not quite sure which one, but the patrons at Benny's roared with delight, especially when Fermez concluded her performance by announcing a free round of drinks for everyone.

"You can't do that," Maxine said. "Here, let me pay for it."

Fermez put a gloved hand on Maxine's arm. "Don't worry. A free round always gets them going. They'll be treating each other to drinks all night long. Benny will make a killing off it."

"Then tell us," Maxine said as Fermez ushered them to the staff table. "How'd you do it?"

"Dahling, a lady never kisses and tells." Fermez blew a kiss to the room. "But since you ask . . ." She slid into the chair next to Maxine. "Del and I go way back. Twelve years ago, I introduced him to his partner and was bridesmaid at their wedding. He was happy to do me a favor. The hard part was dealing with Evie."

"You talked to her?" Rosemarie grimaced. "That's service above and beyond the call of duty."

"When? How'd you do it? What did you say?" June peppered her with questions without pausing for a breath, much less an answer.

"Well, if I do say so myself . . ." Fermez placed a hand to her breast. "I used my very considerable personal charm."

"What did you do?" Maxine asked.

"There's no telling *how* it happened." Fermez punctuated her comment with an airy wave of her hand. "But somehow Evie got the idea that I was a famous French designer who was visiting Tucson to consult with Mr. Delbeck."

"And how did this designer happen to get Evie's name?"

"I pulled out your hibiscus nametags. Told her that Katie had given them to me."

"Katie?"

"Yes, your daughter, the famous venture capitalist with whom I met in utter secrecy to discuss funding for a new line of designer jeans."

"You didn't tell her that," Maxine said.

"I did."

"And she believed you?"

"Dahling, I'm so good, *I* even believed me."

Harry raised his beer. "To Fermez the Fabulous!"

"Hip, hip, hooray! Hip, hip, hooray! Hip, hip, hooray!"

35

MAXINE PRACTICALLY DANCED in to breakfast, where she found Rosemarie and June staring sleepily into their half-eaten oatmeal.

"Good morning. What a glorious day!" Maxine said. In fact, it was overcast and unseasonably cold, but she didn't care. Evie had withdrawn her application. God was in heaven, and all was right with the world.

June grunted and reached for her coffee.

"You're certainly chipper," Rosemarie said.

Maxine was exceptionally chipper. With any luck, the third candidate would be wonderful, or at least acceptable, and Maxine would not have to become assistant director. She could step gracefully aside. She was saved. Life was very nearly perfect.

Maxine smiled and reached for the sugar. Today she was treating herself to a double cappuccino and two packets of raw sugar.

"One if by land. Two if by sea," Louise said as she trotted up with Seabiscuit.

Maxine raised an eyebrow.

"Carlotta is coming," Louise said.

"Thank you, Paul Revere." Maxine helped Louise transfer her tray to the table.

Rosemarie leaned forward. "Not only is Carlotta coming, but she's wielding that damn cigarette holder."

"Do you know how to tell when Carlotta's lying?" June asked and took a sip of her coffee.

Maxine's personal theory was that Carlotta batted her eyelashes when she was actively lying and waved her cigarette holder when she was silently scheming.

June set her coffee cup down. "You know Carlotta's lying . . . if her lips are moving."

Carlotta stormed their table, waving her cigarette holder and batting her eyelashes. "I'm so glad I found you, Maxine dearest," she said.

Maxine flinched.

Carlotta smiled a slow smile. "I wanted to say again how much I enjoyed your band's performance last Saturday."

June froze with her coffee cup halfway to her open mouth. Rosemarie choked. Louise stopped breathing. Maxine put a hand to her own chest to see if her heart was still beating.

Carlotta smirked. She drew a circle in the air with her cigarette holder. "If our third candidate decides not to be our assistant director, I'm sure you'll be adequate, dear, and I wanted you to know that."

Maxine could only blink.

Carlotta flapped her eyelashes. "Believe me when I say that I truly do hope the winner is you." She lowered her cigarette holder until it pointed directly at Maxine's chest. "In fact, I'm counting on it."

Maxine's heart spasmed. She felt a burning sensation so painful she couldn't speak.

Carlotta smiled at the silence, then turned and flapped away.

Maxine rubbed her chest. "What was that all about?"

"Who knows." June waved a dismissive hand and returned to her coffee.

"She obviously hasn't read her email yet," Rosemarie said.

Maxine reached for her long-anticipated cappuccino.

Rosemarie spoke in a low voice. "None of you can tell anyone, but Maxine may soon have another reason to celebrate."

Maxine raised an eyebrow as she stirred sugar into her cappuccino, being careful to disturb the foam as little as possible.

"The third candidate, what's-her-name, is withdrawing."

Maxine's spoon clattered to the floor. Her body went numb from her fingertips to her toes and everything in between, especially her brain.

Rosemarie continued as if the world had not just ended.

"She interviewed in Santa Fe, and they offered her a job on the spot. Instead of having her give a presentation tomorrow night, Rupert will name the new assistant director." Rosemarie smiled. "It has to be Maxine."

The room began to darken and swirl. Maxine clutched the edge of the table and waited for the black edges of her vision to clear. Evie had withdrawn. What's-her-name had withdrawn. No one was left. Maxine was doomed.

Her throat constricted and her stomach churned. She groaned and put her head in her hands.

"What's wrong?" Louise asked.

"She's swooning with the thrill of victory," Rosemarie said.

Louise stared at Maxine over her glasses. "Looks more like the agony of defeat."

"I was hoping for the thrill of defeat," Maxine said rather cryptically.

"Somebody kill me now," June said. "I haven't had enough caffeine to follow this conversation."

"Here." Maxine shoved her cappuccino over to June. She'd lost all interest in it.

"You are an angel of mercy." June cradled the cappuccino in both hands.

"To our angel of mercy and soon-to-be assistant director." Louise raised her tea.

"Shush!" Rosemarie pulled down Louise's hand. "No one is supposed to know."

"Oh. Right." Louise readjusted herself to a more serious posture. "In that case, who wants to come with me to use the computer? I want to look for bridge games. I've heard you can find some pretty sophisticated players."

June rocked to her feet. "Not me. I've got water aerobics."

Rosemarie stood. "Me either. High school accounting club. See you tonight."

Louise turned to Maxine. "Guess it's just you and me, kemosabe."

Maxine opened her mouth, but no words came out.

36

MAXINE WAS ROUSED FROM her funk by a persistent tugging on her arm.

"Look." Louise pointed to a long list of bridge sites that had popped up on the computer screen. "Nirvana!"

All Maxine wanted to do was find a black hole and dive into it.

"I'm signing us up," Louise said.

Before Maxine could respond, Celine burst into the room.

"What's wrong?" Louise said. "You look frantic."

"And guilty," Maxine said.

"We've got trouble!" Celine closed the door, opened it, checked the hallway, shut the door once more and leaned against it. "I knew you couldn't trust that sneaking, sniveling snake!"

"Which sneaking, sniveling snake?" Maxine asked.

"Carlotta, that's who."

"What's wrong?"

Celine pulled some legal-looking pages out of her kaftan.

"How *do* you keep things in there?" Louise asked. "Is there some kind of secret pocket?"

"Girl, I've got more secret pockets than you have time to hear about."

Maxine took Celine's papers. "What are these?"

"Bylaws for the Foothills," Celine said. "Read number twenty-two."

Maxine read aloud. "No resident may be in the employ of the Foothills Retirement Community." She looked up. "What's the problem? Although we'd love to have you, you're not currently a resident. "

"But you are."

Maxine looked at Celine blankly.

"If you become the assistant director, you'll have to move out."

Maxine stopped breathing. Louise gasped. Seabiscuit snorted.

"That's why Carlotta wished me well." Even to her own ear, Maxine's voice sounded weak and tremulous, the voice of an old woman. "She wants me to become the assistant director so that I'll have to move out."

Louise's eyes filled with tears. "Where would you go?"

Maxine reread the bylaws. "It isn't really clear what happens, is it? It just says, 'No resident may be in the employ of the Foothills Retirement Community.'"

"Are you sure those are our bylaws?" Louise asked.

"Uh-huh," Celine said. "I saw them on Mrs. Babcock's desk when I cleaned her office. I didn't think anything about it until I saw the same papers on Carlotta's desk, only she had a yellow sticky with the number 22 on it."

"That snake." Maxine's voice was ragged.

Louise's face turned ashen. Her entire torso heaved as she struggled for air.

Without asking, Maxine adjusted the oxygen flow and took Louise's hand. She motioned for Celine to pull up a chair beside them. They sat without speaking, the silence broken only by Louise's wheezing and the interminable ticking of the electric wall clock.

Slowly, the rhythm of Louise's breathing returned to normal. "So what do we do now?" she asked. Her voice was small and faint.

Maxine tried to rally for Louise's sake, but her body refused to cooperate. Her arms were leaden and her head ached. She'd run out of options. "If only the other applicants had been any good or even remotely qualified." She cradled her head in her hands.

"That's it. We'll find some new applicants." Louise said it brightly as if it were a real possibility.

Maxine responded without looking up. "That would be a great idea, except there aren't any other applicants. And even if they existed,

Carlotta would disqualify them for not having gone through her selection process."

The sound of the electric clock filled the room. Each tick fell like a hammer chiseling off another piece of Maxine's life at the Foothills. If she had the energy, she'd get up and break the damn thing. "Someone ought to stuff that clock in a box and bury it."

"Box? That's it!" Celine jumped up. "Girl, I've got you covered. At least on the applicant part."

Maxine refused to raise her head.

"What are you talking about?" Louise asked.

"There's a whole boxful of applications in Rupert's office."

"What do you mean?" Maxine raised her head a few inches.

"I mean I was cleaning his office last week and found a whole boxful of applications, even the missing one from Evie."

"That's odd." Maxine sat up.

"Why would Rupert have a boxful of applications in his office?" Louise asked.

"That's what I wanted to know," Celine said. "So I just happened to glance through some of them, and those folks were good. They had degrees and publications and experience and everything."

Maxine began to tap her finger on the desktop and tried to concentrate. Images, half-forgotten conversations, and bits of trivia swirled before her. But some critical element lay just out of reach, like misplaced pieces of a jigsaw puzzle.

"Those poor applicants," Louise said. "Think how they must feel. I wonder if they ever heard anything back about their applications. What was it Pascal said? Something about the silence filling one with dread."

Maxine stared at Louise. "What did you say?" She could almost feel the pieces of the puzzle falling into place.

"I said those poor applicants must wonder why they never heard anything."

Maxine straightened. The last piece clicked into place. "That's it! She never heard back."

"Say huh?" Celine turned to Louise. "What's she talking about?"

"I have no idea." Louise turned to Celine, "Does her brow look furrowed to you?"

"Uh-huh. Deep furrows. Could plant tobacco in them."

"Then she's up to something."

"I have to make a phone call." Maxine struggled to her feet. "Lafayette, we are here!"

37

BACK IN HER KITCHEN, Maxine flipped through the telephone book. Every year they made the print smaller and the paper thinner. It already felt like cheap tissue paper. Any thinner and it would be invisible. She moistened her fingertips and fumbled at the pages. In her haste, she ripped half a dozen. Fortunately, the page she needed was still legible.

She grabbed for the phone, but the receiver slipped out of her hand and dropped like an anchor onto her left foot.

"D.A.M.N."

Maxine removed her shoe and examined her foot. If they still made telephones out of that indestructible black material, she'd have a broken foot. As it was, she was going to have a nasty bruise.

She hopped over to the refrigerator, yanked out a bag of frozen peas, and laid it on her foot. The cold burned and then numbed. Good enough: she didn't have time for an injury. Balancing the bag of peas on her foot, she hobbled back to the phone and dialed.

A deep male voice answered on the first ring. "Good morning. You've reached the Reference Desk. How may I help you?"

Maxine hesitated. How could he help her? How could anyone help her? She should hang up and resign herself to becoming a bag lady. "I'm looking for Ashley," she said. "She works there. She has a brunette pony-tail and is working on a doctorate in Public Administration."

"Just a minute please." He sounded like an automated recording.

There was a loud bang. He'd evidently dropped the receiver on the counter. At least he hadn't switched her to that dreadful music they played in shopping malls and elevators.

"Hello? This is Ashley."

Maxine took a deep breath. Ashley was her best, last, and only hope.

"Ashley, this is Maxine Olson. A couple of weeks ago you helped me find two master's theses." Maxine prayed that Ashley remembered.

"And you bought me lunch and plied me with French fries. How are you?"

Maxine struggled to keep her tone light. "I'm just fine, dear, but I was rather wondering if you could help me again."

"I'll do my best. What do you need?"

Maxine squared her shoulders and stood as tall as she could on one foot. "One thesis was by Michelle Lafayette. Was she a good looking blonde, about five-foot-nine"?"

"Yes. Do you know her?"

Maxine could barely speak. "I think I might." She pressed the phone closer to her ear. "You mentioned that Michelle had applied for her dream job and was waiting to hear back. Do you know what happened?"

"As far as I know, she never heard back. Which is odd, because she has great credentials."

Maxine pumped her fist. "Bingo!"

"Excuse me?"

Maxine was too excited to explain. "Didn't you tell me the university has a video of her being interviewed?"

"Yes. It's a great video. The department uses it as a model."

Maxine's knees began to wobble. She leaned against the kitchen door to steady herself. "Could I borrow a copy? Just for a day or two?"

"Sure. The guys in Media Services can make a copy in no time. I could have it for you by noon."

Maxine's knees gave out entirely and she slid down the door and onto the cool tile of her kitchen floor. "I think you may have just saved my life."

"All in a day's work here at the Reference Desk," Ashley said in a Dragnet-like voice.

"Let me take you to lunch at the Park Street Grill to celebrate."

"Love to, but the fries are on me."

"No way, dear. I was once a starving graduate student myself. Besides, you're saving my life, remember?"

ON THE WAY TO MEET ASHLEY, Maxine watched Louise out of the corner of her eye. Her friend looked small and sad. Her honest blue eyes brimmed with unshed tears. Maxine tried to sound casual. "Is anything wrong?"

Louise gave a crooked smile. "I just feel so bad for you."

"For me?" Maxine swung her head around and stared at her friend in astonishment.

"Watch out!"

The car thumped onto the gravel shoulder of the highway and headed straight for a saguaro. Maxine jerked the steering wheel and bounced the car back onto the road with a bone-cracking bump. The car shimmied, swayed, and righted itself.

"Why do you feel bad for me?" Maxine asked as if nothing had happened, but her heart beat double-time.

Louise cut her eyes at Maxine and then made a show of checking her seatbelt before answering. "After all your hard work, just when it looked like you were going to become our assistant director, to have Carlotta dig up those old bylaws. It just doesn't seem fair." Louise took out a packet of tissues. She blotted her eyes with one and offered another to Maxine. "Here. Your hand is bleeding."

Maxine glanced down. The skin between her right thumb and fore-finger was indeed bleeding. She must have torn it on the leather seam of the steering wheel when she jerked the car back onto the road. "No one ever warns you that you become thin-skinned as you age."

"And thick-headed." Louise muttered loud enough for Maxine to hear.

"Don't feel sorry for me: I don't want to be the assistant director."

"You don't?" Louise turned sidewise in the seat and stared at Maxine. "Since when?"

Maxine hesitated. Louise wasn't going to be happy that she'd been kept out of the loop, and frankly Maxine didn't blame her. If their roles had been reversed, Maxine would have been furious. Fortunately, Louise was a much nicer person—more forgiving. At least Maxine hoped so.

"Well." Maxine crossed her fingers for luck. "I began to have my doubts when Katie asked me why I wanted the job, and I couldn't give her a good answer."

"I can see why you wouldn't want that job," Louise said. "You couldn't get me to take it at gunpoint. But why didn't you tell me *earlier*?"

Louise sounded a bit annoyed, but at least she hadn't erupted—not yet, anyway. Maxine ignored the question and tried to explain her logic instead. "I didn't realize that I didn't want the job until I was waiting for you at Dr. Kildare's office. But by then I felt obligated to keep Evie from taking it."

Louise ignored the explanation and homed in on the critical point.

"But why didn't you tell *me*?"

This time Louise sounded very annoyed. Maxine wiped her sweaty palms on her slacks. She was guilty and she knew it, so she went on the offensive. "I didn't tell you because your oxygen wasn't working and because you'd feel bad for me if I had to take the job."

"No I wouldn't," Louise huffed.

"What were you doing just now?"

"Nothing." Louise blew her nose and slipped the packet of tissues back into her purse.

They drove in silence for a several minutes.

Louise finally broke the silence. "I have some more bad news for you."

"What?" Maxine glanced over at Louise again.

"If we're meeting Ashley at the Park Street Grill, you just missed your turn."

"D.A.M.N."

As she circled the block, Maxine returned to her confession. "The thing is, I don't ever want to have to say to you or to Katie or Peter that I can't be there for you because I have to take a bunch of senior citizens to a baseball game."

"Maxine! You sound like Evie. When did the residents of the Foothills get demoted to senior citizens?"

"When I realized I'd have to prioritize them above my friends." Maxine pulled into the last parking spot in the lot. "That was really the problem: I was doing it to keep us from having someone like Evie. But now I've found someone better than Evie or me or the third candidate, What's-Her-Name." Maxine turned off the ignition. "Do you remember her name?"

"No. No one does." Louise shook her head. "Do you think we ever knew it?"

"She probably doesn't have a name." Maxine removed her seatbelt and picked up her purse. "Are you ready?"

"Wait," Louise protested. "Who did you find to be our new assistant director?"

"Mimi."

"Mimi?"

"Yes. She is Michelle Lafayette."

Louise stared, blinked, and caught on immediately. Maxine loved her for that.

"The one who wrote that lovely thesis?"

"Yes." Maxine walked around the car and helped Louise with Seabiscuit. "I'm sure of it."

"Even so, how are you going to make the switch? I'm pretty sure Rupert will notice that Mimi is not you."

"I haven't exactly figured that out yet," Maxine said as they walked toward the Park Street Grill.

"Besides, Mimi will never take the job."

Maxine stopped dead in her tracks. "Why not? If Mimi really is Michelle, the job is her dream job."

"But she thinks *you* want it."

Maxine looked at Louise for several seconds. "Good point. We probably need to tell Mimi she's going to get the job."

Louise sighed. "There's no point arguing with you when you're like this. I'm glad you've at least agreed to talk with Mimi."

"Right!" Maxine nodded as if conceding a point. "I'll pick you up at eight-thirty tonight."

"Where are we going at eight-thirty at night?"

"Back to Benny's Bar and Grill, of course." Maxine looked at her friend and shook her head. "Are you sure you have your oxygen adjusted correctly? Benny's was your idea."

Louise groaned.

"Come on," Maxine said, "Ashley is waiting for us with my ticket to freedom."

38

BACK AT THE FOOTHILLS, Maxine barely had time to turn off the ignition before Celine stormed their car.

"How did it go? What happened?" Celine asked.

Maxine waved the computer disk that Ashley had given them. "Help has arrived," she said triumphantly. "Now I just need to go to Benny's to talk to Mimi."

"I'll drive," Celine said as she helped unload Seabiscuit.

Maxine stared at Celine with her disapproving teacher-stare. "You can't come with us tonight. You have class."

"Nuh-uh," Celine said, shaking her head. "We get tonight off because exams start tomorrow."

"Don't you need to study for your exams?" Louise asked.

Celine waved her hand airily above her head. "Not me. I've got a tutor. Let her worry about the exams."

Maxine could feel her blood pressure rising.

"Besides," Celine added slyly. "I'm excused from the exam because my grades are so good."

"What?"

"Uh-huh. If you've got a 95 average, you don't have to take the exam, and I . . ." She pirouetted. "I . . ." She struck a diva pose. "I have a 96.2."

Maxine and Louise oohed and aahed and hugged and high-fived Celine.

"That's wonderful," Maxine said, brushing away tears. "I'm so proud of you."

"We're all so proud of you." Louise blew her nose.

Celine beamed, speechless for a moment—but only for a moment. "So what time should I pick you up?"

BENNY'S WAS CROWDED. So crowded that Celine had to circle the block twice before she found a parking spot.

Maxine leveraged herself out of the backseat and helped Louise saddle up Seabiscuit while Celine repositioned the Bel Air until its tires were precisely six inches from the curb.

"I don't want any scuff marks on my whitewalls," Celine said and double-checked her tire alignment.

Evidently satisfied, she swiveled through a complicated maneuver that made the sequins dance on her royal blue evening gown. "Let's boogie! Look at that crowd at Benny's. You'd think it was Super Bowl Sunday."

"Do you think we'll be able to get in?" Louise asked.

Two or three dozen burly men and women wearing black leather and chains were congregated in front of Benny's, smoking and blocking the entrance.

"Don't worry about a thing," Celine called over her shoulder. "Just follow me."

Her voice bounced off the buildings and echoed into the night. The gang stirred like some rough beast awakened by intruders. Celine stormed the crowd, armed only with her sequins and stilettos.

"Wait here," Maxine said to Louise. "I'll retrieve her." She hurried after Celine. But it was already too late, and Louise did not wait anyway.

"Ex-cuse me!" Celine barged into the gang.

The first two or three rows of hairy men and tattooed women gave way, but a three-hundred-pound giant lounged against Benny's front door and refused to budge. He wore tight leather pants and a chrome-studded leather vest over his bare and exotically tattooed chest. His auburn hair was pulled back in a frizzy ponytail.

"Ex-cuse me, pu-lease."

Celine's tone sounded insolent to Maxine. She thought of the rumble scene from *West Side Story* and wished she'd put pepper spray into her purse instead of lip gloss.

"What have we here?" The giant's lip curled, revealing a gold tooth in the center of his mouth.

The tooth reminded Maxine of something, something besides pirates.

"Looks to me like a little entertainment just arrived." The giant leered.

Aroused by the promise of entertainment, his gang closed ranks around them.

Prickles of sweat rolled between Maxine's breasts. Crowds made her claustrophobic, especially crowds dressed in chains and leather.

"That's because you are an ignorant, overgrown excuse of a boy." Celine tried to bluster her way past the giant, who laughed until tears came to his eyes.

"You're in luck, 'cause I like my women plucky." He wiped his eyes with the back of one tattooed hand. "But what's with the old biddies? Are they looking for a prince to kiss them and turn them back into toads?"

The gang roared. Maxine felt faint and reached over to steady herself on Seabiscuit, but Louise was no longer beside her. Instead, she was trying to ram the giant with Seabiscuit.

"Who are you calling old?" Louise swung her purse over her head as if it were a viable weapon.

The giant bent down and grabbed Seabiscuit with one hand and the purse with his other. He was close enough that Maxine could see a tiny tattoo of an alligator over his left breast. It looked just like the Izod logo.

"Izzy?" Maxine's voice startled even her.

"What!" The giant reared back, his nostrils flaring. "What did you say?"

"The tooth and the tattoo," Maxine said. "You're Izzy Goldman, aren't you?"

"Say huh?" said Celine.

"Do you know him?" Louise sounded more annoyed than surprised.

"Of course I do. He went to school with Katie." Maxine smiled at the memories.

The giant narrowed his eyes and clenched his fists. Perhaps his memories weren't as fond as Maxine's. He'd been a large and rather clumsy child with an unruly mop of curly red hair—the kind of child who was chosen last for every team. He'd probably been teased mercilessly.

Maxine's nurturing instincts kicked in. "He had the wittiest tattoo I'd ever seen," she said.

"Which one?" Louise asked.

Maxine pointed to the giant's chest. "Izzy, show them the alligator."

The giant seemed flustered and flattered to learn that his tattoo was witty. "Um. It's a crocodile," he said.

"Hey, that's cute." Celine pulled the vest away to expose thick pectoral muscles. "It looks just like the little lizard on those fancy knit polo shirts."

"Exactly," Maxine said. "I love this tattoo. It's so clever." She paused and looked at Izzy. Tattoos ran from his fingertips, up his arms, across his chest, and down to who knew where. "But in all honesty, it was a better joke before you added all those dragons and skulls and things."

"Poison ivy," Louise said.

"Excuse me?" Maxine asked. Louise was uncharacteristically off-point. Maxine hoped she hadn't damaged her oxygen supply when she tried to ram Izzy.

"The vine on his arms looks like poison ivy."

"You're right, it does," Maxine said, relieved that Louise was as sharp as ever.

"Do you mind?" The giant held his hands over his arms as if to protect his tattoos. "That's weed."

"Yes, I know poison ivy's a weed," Louise said. "I just don't know why you'd want it on your arms."

"No, not that kind of weed," he said. "You know: Mary Jane."

"No, I don't believe we've met," Louise said. "Who is Mary Jane?"

The giant looked helplessly to his motorcycle buddies, who collapsed in a fit of laughter. His face got that pinched, angry look that Katie's used to get just before a tantrum. He swung his attention back to Maxine with a ferocity that startled her.

"Who are you, lady? I'm Krusher with a *K*. Nobody calls me Izzy."

"That's too bad," Maxine said calmly. She was no longer frightened. Izzy had been a clumsy kid, but not a mean one. He just needed validation. "I always thought Izzy was an important name. The kind of name a man's man would have."

The giant straightened in surprise, then narrowed his eyes in suspicion. "Who are you?"

"I'm Katie Olson's mom." Maxine offered her hand.

The giant stared blankly.

"You took music lessons with Katie. She played the piano."

Maxine mimed playing a piano. Then she mimed someone playing the flute. "And you played—"

"The drums! I played the drums." He shot her a wide-eyed look, then twitched his head toward his gang.

Maxine caught on. "Oh yes, of course." Being a flautist was probably not high on the list of qualifications for gang leader. "You were the bad-ass drummer."

She transformed her flute-playing mime into a drum solo.

The giant gave her a barely perceptible nod.

"So what brings you ladies out here at this time of night?" He hooked his thumbs in his waistband and puffed out his chest.

"We need to speak with one of the performers."

"In Benny's?"

"Yes," Celine said, her bluster back. "So if you don't mind moving your big—"

Before Celine could finish, Louise bumped her with Seabiscuit.

"Ow! What'd you do that for?"

"Sorry. The brakes slipped." Louise repositioned Seabiscuit between Celine and the giant.

Fortunately, the giant chose to ignore Celine. "Benny's can be a rough place for ladies," he said. "I'll go with you to make sure no one gets any ideas. My friends will stay here and guard your car. Which one is it?"

It was Celine's turn to puff out her chest. "The second from the end."

"That's yours?" He was clearly shocked.

Maxine held her breath. If he insulted the car, there was no telling what Celine would do.

"If you mean that beautiful '56 Chevrolet Bel Air, it's a classic, and it's mine." Celine turned to the gang. "And if there's even one fingerprint on it when I return, I'm going to tan your fannies so bad you won't be able to ride those over-sized bicycles of yours for a month."

The gang looked to the giant for direction. For his part, the giant looked at Celine with respect.

"I've got a '64 Lincoln Continental Convertible," he said.

"No way! What color?"

"Regal turquoise with an alabaster top."

"Oh, sweet Jesus. That's the second most beautiful car ever made, right behind my Bel Air."

The giant beamed and stepped aside. "Right this way, ladies."

THEY ENTERED BENNY'S, and Fermez instantly floated up to them. "Well, dahlings! What a surprise; you're getting to be regulars. And look what a delightful door prize you've brought me." She swished her entire torso toward the giant, who stared back nervously.

"This is a friend of mine," Maxine gestured grandly. "He used to be called Izzy, but now he's called . . ." She wafted her hand in vague circles, trying to conjure the name out of the ether.

Fermez shifted impatiently.

Maxine gave up and rested her hand gently on Izzy's forearm. "I'm sorry, dear, but I've forgotten your new name."

The giant seemed flustered. "I'm Krusher with a *K*."

Fermez launched into her best Mae West imitation. "Glad to meet you, Krusher with a *K*. I'm Fermez with the most."

Krusher turned fire engine red and stopped breathing.

It was Celine's turn to be impatient. "We need to speak with Mimi. Can you let her know?"

Fermez shot Celine an annoyed look and flounced away.

Celine led them to their usual table. Although the women gladly sat, Krusher insisted on standing behind them with crossed arms. Like a member of the Royal Guard, he remained stone-still except for one tiny shrug that twitched open his vest and left his alligator tattoo clearly visible.

"WHO'S YOUR FRIEND?" Mimi asked when she joined them.

"He's our bodyguard," Celine said. "But I think we're going to have to do the protecting. Fermez can't seem to keep her eyes off him."

Maxine turned.

Fermez was flirting madly and offering Krusher free drinks, which he steadfastly refused. His eyes had a deer-in-the-headlights look about them.

Maxine knew exactly how he felt. She was beginning to wish they hadn't come.

It wasn't that she minded admitting her follies, as legion as they were. That was easy. She just wasn't sure she should ask Mimi to take a job that Maxine no longer wanted.

"Ouch!" Maxine's debate was cut short by a sharp jab in the ribs from Louise's elbow.

"It's *her* choice," Louise said, having clearly read Maxine's mind. "You have to tell her."

Louise was right, of course, but that didn't stop Maxine from elbowing her back.

"Tell me what?" Mimi asked. She took a long sip from her drink: water on the rocks.

"I've come to ask another favor." Maxine hoped that Mimi had not heard the catch in her voice.

"Your favors are fun." Mimi flashed an encouraging smile. "What's up?"

"I want you to be the assistant director at the Foothills."

"What?" Mimi's eyes widened and a blush raced up her neck and across her cheeks. She looked young and beautiful and astounded.

"I'm afraid I'm a bit slow," Maxine said. "Well, actually, I'm very slow. I've only just realized you are Michelle Lafayette, the woman who wrote the wonderful thesis on aging. You are, aren't you?"

"Yes, but—"

"No *but*'s, dear. I know that you applied for the job. In fact, I know it's your dream job. You applied, but you never heard back from Rupert—the dolt. I also know that you're the best person in the world for the job."

Mimi shook her head. "Don't be silly, Maxine. The job is meant for you. That's why I never told you that I'd applied. You'll be great at it."

"No, I won't," Maxine said.

"Yes, you will."

"No, I mean, I really don't want it."

Mimi's jaw dropped. "You don't? What happened?"

"Well . . ." Maxine tried to identify the precise moment when she'd known that the position wasn't right for her. "Well, I went to Louise's doctor with her, and in the waiting room I realized I didn't want to postpone our trip to the Redwoods while I organized bus trips to baseball games."

"What trip to the Redwoods?" Louise asked. "What are you talking about?"

Maxine hadn't actually planned a trip, but now that Louise had mentioned it, a trip sounded like a splendid idea.

"Hey, can I go?" Celine waved her hand to get Maxine's attention. "I've always wanted to see trees bigger than Krusher."

"Me too," said Fermez, who hovered within easy eavesdropping distance.

"Of course you can," Maxine said. "You're the drivers."

Fermez clapped her hands and Celine beamed. Maxine had a sinking suspicion that she might not have fully considered all the pertinent details of their proposed trip.

"I'm afraid I don't quite follow," Mimi said.

"I applied for the job as an act of protest against Rupert's insulting

288

online application. I was determined to prove that a woman in her eighties could be competitive."

The room grew much too warm. Maxine fanned herself with a beer coaster.

"But I overestimated my energy level," she admitted. "I mean, I could have done a good job, but I wouldn't have had any energy left for other things—things that are more important for me now, given the time I have left."

The others started to protest, but Maxine dismissed them with a wave of her hand. "I'm eighty-two. I want to enjoy my life, but I don't want it to stretch on interminably. Please don't wish that for me."

"Me either." Louise's agreement silenced their objections.

Maxine placed her age-spotted hands on the beer-stained table. She'd gotten to the hardest part. The unforgivable part. The part where she'd failed a friend.

"I'm afraid I got caught up in the competition. In the game. I should have paid more attention to the basic issue: we need a good assistant director." Maxine turned to Mimi. "And I should have paid more attention to you, dear. I should have realized much sooner who you are. I'm so sorry."

"Don't be silly," Mimi said. "You paid me the honor of accepting me for the person I claimed to be: Mimi La Fievre."

"That's right," Celine said. "You didn't judge her, just like that Chaucer dude."

Maxine shook her head. "There's a difference between not judging and not seeing." She felt a sharp pain in her chest. She swallowed and continued. "When you think about it, I was no better than Evie."

"No way." Celine shook her head.

"Bite your tongue," Fermez said, shaking her whole body.

"Never," Mimi said and gave Maxine's hand a squeeze.

"No effing way," Krusher added gallantly, even though he had no idea who Evie was.

"Utterly impossible!" Louise said it in a tone that brooked no contradiction.

Maxine felt tears welling up at their kindness, but she refused to let herself off the hook. "You deserved more from me. My actions—or inactions—were unforgivable." Her voice broke and the tears fell. She held up her hand to silence further protests. "The thing is: this job was meant for you. That is, if you still want it. We'll understand if you don't. Either way, I'm hoping you can forgive a foolish old lady."

Mimi jumped up and threw her arms around Maxine. "There's nothing to forgive."

Maxine didn't trust herself to speak. She looked at Louise, who came to her rescue.

"You'd be wonderful, dear," Louise said. "We'd be delighted and honored to have you be our assistant director. Won't you please say yes?"

"But . . ."

Krusher leaned in and tapped Mimi on the shoulder. "Excuse me, lady, but I can save you a lot of time. You may as well give in now. She's going to win anyway."

"Isn't that the truth?" Celine said, eliciting nods of agreement all around the table.

Louise didn't wait for Mimi to assent. "Good. So it's settled." She turned to Fermez. "I'd like to order a bottle of Champagne."

Fermez stared at Louise as if she had sprouted wings. "Champagne? At Benny's?"

"But what about Rupert and the selection process?" Mimi asked.

Maxine waved a hand airily. "Oh, I haven't figured that part out yet, but we have oodles of time."

The others looked at her. Even Louise's mouth fell open. Maxine shrugged and revised her assessment. "Well, we have nearly twenty-two hours."

39

FRIDAY MORNING, RUPERT ENTERED his office and was shocked to see the day's newspapers neatly arranged on his desk. Even more astonishing, he smelled fresh coffee brewing in the pot on his credenza. He inhaled, then closed his eyes and inhaled again. It was his favorite: Organic Dark Roasted French Premium from the gourmet coffee shop at the mall.

Something was wrong. Mrs. Babcock didn't believe in newspapers and she never, ever made coffee. She'd made that painfully clear on her first day when she declared that she would "not make coffee for anyone, for any reason, not even if ordered to do so by the president of the United States."

Rupert was pretty sure that Mrs. Babcock actually would make coffee if ordered to by the president, but she'd never make it for any other reason. Not even if she were being tortured by terrorists. Something was definitely up.

Before he could decide what to do about it, he heard shuffling and shouting in the hallway.

"Mrs. Babcock! Hurry, Mrs. Babcock."

He ran out of his office and nearly knocked over Louise McMaster and Seabiscuit, who were standing right outside his door. He grabbed Seabiscuit to steady both himself and the cart. "What's wrong? Where's Mrs. Babcock?"

"Here I am." The General marched out of her office. "What's all the ruckus about?" Her frown emphasized her displeasure at Rupert's disorderly conduct.

"But . . ." He stared at the two women, both of whom seemed perfectly safe and totally composed. He released his grip on Seabiscuit.

"I think I've solved the mystery," Louise said. "Come up to the laundry room, Mrs. Babcock."

"What mystery?" he asked.

"How many mysteries are there? I'm talking about the mystery of the smoke alarm that goes off all the time." Louise turned her attention back to Mrs. Babcock. "Hurry, Mrs. Babcock, before someone disturbs the evidence."

"What evidence?" he asked, even though Louise was clearly not talking to him.

"I've found the smoking gun, or in this case, the smoking cigarette holder." Louise turned Seabiscuit around and started back down the hall.

Neither Rupert nor Mrs. Babcock moved.

Without stopping, Louise called over her shoulder, "An ebony and silver cigarette holder."

The General scowled. "We'll just see about that," she said, shoving her way past him.

The two-woman detective squad trooped down the hall and out of sight, leaving Rupert behind and bewildered.

He shook his head to clear it, but nothing became any clearer. First, coffee and newspapers from Mrs. Babcock, and now this. He'd never understand women. He'd always considered Louise to be too kind to complain and too generous to tattle—especially to tattle on someone for smoking in the laundry room.

He retreated to his office.

Safely inside, he pulled a file folder out of his desk and began studying a spreadsheet of his training times. As if on cue, someone knocked on the door.

What now? How was he ever going to get anything done? At least the search for a new assistant director was almost over. If he'd known how much time he'd have to waste on that chore, he'd have . . .

Well, what else could he have done?

Married Sandra so she wouldn't quit in the first place? No.

Appointed the first person who walked in the door irrespective of her qualifications? No.

Refused to let the residents participate in the selection process? Like that was an option. Carlotta Helmsley would have gone straight to corporate headquarters with her complaints, and they'd have been looking to fill his position instead of the assistant director's.

Whoever it was knocked again, a little louder this time.

He shoved his training times back into his desk. "Come in."

Maxine Olson entered, carrying a canvas tote bag from the Desert Museum. "I know I'm interrupting," Maxine said, "but I need to speak with you before the meeting tonight."

He rose and smiled. He'd come to like the old lady. He offered her a seat on the couch, but she crossed to the extra desk chair instead.

"May I?" she asked. "The chair makes me feel taller and it's a lot easier to get out of."

"I know exactly what you mean." He poured them each a cup of coffee. "I'm glad you stopped by. I wanted to tell you again how much I enjoyed your event last Saturday. Your presentation was splendid, and your band brought down the house."

"People did enjoy the Improbable Dreamers, didn't they?"

"The Foothills loved *you*," he insisted gallantly. "Tonight I'll be announcing which candidate I've selected to be our new assistant director. I think you'll approve of my choice." He sipped his coffee, pleased with himself and his professional panache.

Maxine dismissed both his gallantry and his panache with an impatient wave of her hand. "I've come to tell you that I'm withdrawing my application."

Rupert choked on his coffee. "What?"

"Bylaw twenty-two," she said.

"What's bylaw twenty-two?" His voice cracked like an adolescent's. He adjusted his tie.

"Don't you know?"

"No. What are you talking about?" What the hell was wrong with her? First, she scammed him with her webcam interview so that she would be considered. Now that he was about to appoint her, she wanted to withdraw.

Maxine handed him a piece of paper.

"What's this?"

"It's from the Foothills bylaws. If I took the job, I'd have to move."

"Impossible."

"Nonetheless." She gestured toward the paper.

He read aloud: "No resident may be in the employ of the Foothills Retirement Community."

He loosened his collar and reread the bylaw. She was right. *Damn.* What was he going to do? Evie had already withdrawn—thank God— and so had the third candidate, what's-her-name. If Maxine withdrew, he'd have to start the search process all over. There'd be endless meetings with Carlotta's committee. His training times would be shot to hell.

He ran his hand through his hair. Holy crap.

He looked at Maxine, who seemed to be patiently waiting. "This is an absurd rule," he said. "I'll waive it for you."

He had no idea if he had the authority to waive a bylaw, but by the time anyone could file a protest, Maxine would be the assistant director and the residents would be happy. They'd been trying to bribe him all week to select her anyway: *Here's a cake I made for you. The recipe is Maxine's. She's so talented, don't you think? . . . I bet if Maxine were the assistant director, no one would ever steal the sign-up pens again.* They all loved Maxine. Well, almost all—there was always Carlotta. Still, it would be worth the risk to waive the rule and appoint Maxine.

"I'll waive it," he repeated.

"But I don't want you to waive it."

"You're kidding. You've got to be kidding." He reached for his coffee, but his hand shook and he sloshed coffee all over his desk. Too distracted to care, he blotted the spill with a section of his unread newspaper.

"No. I really do not want the job." She folded her arms.

"For Pete's sake, why not?" He dumped the wet newspaper into his wastebasket. "What am I supposed to do? We'd have to start all over." He stood up and began to pace like the cornered animal he was. "Good God, who knows what other hideous relatives Carlotta might have lying in wait. You owe it to your fellow residents to take the job."

Maxine looked away.

He'd hit a vulnerable spot. He quickly sat down and tried to press his advantage. "You have an obligation and a responsibility." He hammered on words her generation valued.

She looked down.

"Please, don't make us start all over again," he said.

Maxine looked up with what he hoped was a kindly look.

"You may not need to start all over," she said. "I think I've found a solution for you: a viable candidate. In fact, she's really the best candidate by far."

"Impossible. We've been through those application files a million times, and no one else is qualified."

Maxine pulled a computer disk out of her canvas bag. "Can you play this video?"

He tried to speak, but nothing came out. The woman was mad. The world was collapsing around them, and she wanted to watch videos.

"You'll see," she said.

He jammed the disk into his computer and stared as an image of a woman came on the screen. "Isn't that your lead singer?"

"Yes."

He stopped the video. An icy calm fell over him. "She's also the person I *thought* I was interviewing during our webcam interview."

Maxine retained her poker face and feigned innocence. "Really? How odd. As I recall, we did have technical difficulties with our audio and video connections."

He stared at Maxine for a long time. The old lady was good. Her sweet smile almost had him believing that he'd imagined the whole thing, except he had a very clear image of a beautiful blonde in his mind—and now on his computer.

"I never figured out how you did that," he said. "But I've decided not to think about it too much."

Maxine nodded. "Some mysteries are best left unsolved."

"Nonetheless." He leaned forward in an effort to gain control of the situation. "I can't just hire this woman."

"Her name is Michelle Lafayette: her nickname is Mimi."

"I can't just hire Mimi. We had a process. Who knows what her qualifications are. And she hasn't even applied."

"As a matter of fact, she did apply. Quite early, actually." Maxine fished a file folder out of her bag and slid it toward him. "Here is a copy of her application."

He opened the folder. The application looked vaguely familiar.

"The thing is," Maxine said, "she never heard back from the Foothills. I guess her application was misplaced about the same time Evie's disappeared."

Rupert narrowed his eyes. Despite himself, he glanced toward his closet.

When he turned back, she was smiling.

"Some people think Mrs. Babcock lost that file," he said, testing the waters.

"Yes, I know, dear, but that's preposterous. Mrs. Babcock never loses anything. It's far more likely the files were accidentally misplaced, say in a box of printer paper."

Rupert breathed heavily. He mopped his forehead. His career passed before his eyes.

"Or." Maxine smiled. "Perhaps Mimi's and Evie's applications were both inadvertently knocked into the space between your desk and your printer stand, and no one found them until—clumsy as I am—I knocked your pen into the same space, and when you went to retrieve it, voilà! There the applications were."

"What space?" he asked. "There's no space."

Maxine lifted the remaining newspapers off his desk and exposed a quarter-inch gap between his mahogany desk and his perfectly matched printer stand.

As if in slow motion, Rupert ran his finger over the gap. It had not been there yesterday. For that matter, it had never been there. A gap would have annoyed him. He would have corrected it. How had she gotten his furniture moved?

"Of course," Maxine said, "that's just one theory. Who knows how the applications might have been lost or found? This may be another one of those mysteries best left unsolved."

He sank back in his chair.

As if reading his mind, Maxine continued. "I give you my word, no matter what you decide, I won't say anything about the missing applications. I don't care about them. That's why I made a point of coming when Mrs. Babcock was out of the office. I didn't want her eavesdropping."

He exhaled. That explained Louise and the laundry room mystery.

He studied Maxine. The old lady had guts—brains and guts. But he was still responsible. As much as he disliked enforcing rules, he was the referee here. He crossed his arms. "You need to know: I won't hire Mimi unless she's qualified."

"I know you won't." Maxine said it as if there'd been no mention of the missing applications. "But Mimi is perfect. Not only is she gifted and well-liked, but you'll see from her application that she is well-qualified, with a master's degree, publications, experience, and a million glowing references."

"But . . ."

"And she's conducted not one but two events: not only was she the lead singer last Saturday night, but she also leads yoga every Saturday morning."

He sipped his coffee to mask his surprise. Carlotta had complained that a teenager was teaching the yoga classes.

"Nonetheless." He centered his coffee cup on a leather coaster. "We had a process. We interviewed candidates."

"Yes, I know," Maxine said. "I think you'll find that she answers all the same questions on that video that you asked me during my interview."

He ran his finger over the gap between his desk and his printer stand. Things were happening much too fast.

Maxine placed her own hand over the gap. "So you see, one could argue that Mimi has gone through our process. She applied. You have the interview. And she's performed at an event." Her eyes locked on his. "More importantly, she's qualified, talented, and interested."

"But . . ."

"And *most* importantly, she's not related to Carlotta."

Rupert groaned. "That's another thing," he said. "What about Carlotta?" He sounded plaintive, even to himself.

Maxine stood. "I'm sure you know best how to deal with her." She swung her canvas bag over her shoulder. "But I bet Carlotta wouldn't like it if she thought you were going to waive the bylaws so that I could live here and still be the assistant director. She'd much prefer Mimi to me."

Rupert weighed his options. He wasn't sure he wanted Mimi. No, that wasn't right. He might want Mimi in some ways; he just didn't know if he wanted to hire her. The only thing he knew for certain was that he damn well did not want to start all over again with Carlotta and her committee. He bit his lip and stared at his sculpture of a bicyclist. He spun the tires with his index finger. When the spinning stopped, he straightened his tie and rose.

"I'll review Mimi's application and watch the video," he said. "But on one condition only."

"What condition?"

"I reserve the right to appoint you to be the assistant director if Mimi is not everything you've promised. You can't withdraw."

Maxine stiffened and blanched.

He would have felt sorry for her if he weren't so desperate.

She closed her eyes, then opened them and met his gaze. "It's a deal."

They shook hands. Although her grip was firm, she suddenly looked older, more fragile, even frail. He walked her to the door. "You're one tough competitor, Maxine."

"It may not seem so right now, Rupert, but we're on the same team."

"Thank God," he said. "Because I'm no match for you."

She stopped. Her expression was serious, but the corners of her mouth twitched. "Actually, I think we're perfectly matched." With that, she was gone.

He closed the door and leaned against it. "Holy crap."

40

MAXINE WALKED THE PATH that encircled the Foothills feeling positively ... well ... ambivalent. It was splendid, of course, that Rupert had agreed to consider Mimi's application. He was bound to be impressed by her. Still, Maxine would feel much better if she were not on the hook to take the job herself should he decide that Mimi wasn't qualified. That was inconceivable, of course. Incomprehensible really. Nonetheless.

At the door of her condo, she shivered and rubbed her arms. Today even the weather was indeterminate, sliding from warm to cold and back again. Scattered gray clouds raced across the sky, caught on the mountaintops, and dissipated as if unable to decide whether to build to a storm or break to the sun. She studied the sky for omens and longed for clarity.

Inside, the phone began to ring. She scrambled to find her keys and unlock the door before the caller gave up.

"Hello?"

"Hi, Mom. It's me. How's it going?" Katie's voice sounded upbeat, even exuberant.

"Hey, you," Maxine said. "What's up?"

"I've decided what I want to be when I grow up."

"That's wonderful," Maxine said and, leaning against the cabinets, slid to a comfortable seat on the floor. "So tell me."

"I'm going to start my own company. We'll arrange microloans for musicians."

Maxine pumped her fist. "Way to go! You'll be splendid at that! Whatever that is."

Katie laughed. "It's venture capital on a minimalist level. Instead of arranging big deals between investors and innovators, we'll arrange smaller loans to help emerging musicians and composers."

"Who is *we?*" Maxine asked.

"My secretary and I are going into business together."

"Chamique?"

"Yes. When I told her what I was going to do, she asked if she could be my secretary. I told her I didn't need a secretary, but she could be my business partner."

"That's brilliant!" Maxine pumped her fist again.

"It's better than that. It turns out that Chamique and her family know half the jazz musicians in New York. Her dad used to play the drums with a dozen different groups, and her brother still plays the bass with a trio in the Village."

"I'm so happy for you." Maxine laughed and cried at the same time. "I have to admit, I was hoping you wouldn't stay at Littlehouse, Ferris, and Jones."

"No way," Katie said. "Far too much roller coaster and not nearly enough sonata. Speaking of which, how's your roller coaster of a job hunt going?"

Maxine groaned. "To tell you the truth, I could use some advice."

"To thine own self be true. Neither a borrower nor a lender be. Buy low, sell high, and leave everything to your daughter."

Maxine smiled. Katie sounded much as she had in high school the year she had filled in for a sick Polonius during the drama club's performance of *Hamlet*. She hadn't been able to remember all her lines, but she'd improvised admirably.

"So tell me," Katie said. "What's up?"

Maxine recounted the events of the last forty-eight hours, including her encounter with Izzy and her promise to Rupert.

There was a half-beat of silence . . . and then another, while Katie processed Maxine's account. "That's the most Byzantine thing I've ever heard, and I've made a living doing complicated deals. I can't decide whether I'm horrified or awestruck."

Maxine shifted the phone to her other ear. "The worst part is that there's nothing I can do now but patiently wait. And I'm really not good at patience or at waiting."

"Me either. It must be a genetic flaw. When I was little, my mother used to console me by quoting Milton. You know: 'They also serve who only stand and wait.'"

"What consolation is that? Your mother sounds like a real pain in the neck. And for that matter, so was Milton."

"You're telling me!"

The laughter in Katie's voice warmed Maxine. *Katherine* had been too prickly and humorless to tease.

"Mom, even if Rupert tries to appoint you, it's OK to refuse the job. Just because you *can* do it, doesn't mean you *have to* do it."

"Yes, but I gave Rupert my word that I wouldn't withdraw."

Katie sighed. "Yes, there's that. What you need is an agent. Next time you apply for a job, let me do the negotiating."

"I wish you would," Maxine said, surprised to realize that it was true.

"I wish I could be there with you," Katie said.

"Thank you, dear. Just hearing you say that gives me courage, but I'll be fine. I've enlisted an escort service for the evening."

"Not Izzy, I hope. Although it might be entertaining to watch Carlotta battle Izzy's bulk with her false eyelashes and a cigarette holder."

"Wouldn't that be delicious? Izzy and I could wear matching leathers."

"Please tell me you aren't going to do that."

Katie sounded as if she thought Maxine really might call Izzy. Well, maybe she would one day, but not today.

"No, dear. I didn't think to call Izzy, but Peter is coming over this afternoon to set up my new computer and all its high-tech attachments. He's promised to show me how to scan and fax and make videos and do all the fancy things people do in cyberspace. I expect to be computer literate and downright dangerous by dinnertime."

"You're already downright dangerous."

"Afterward, we're going to the Sunset Grill for dinner and then to the OK Corral for the big shoot-out."

"Make Carlotta and Fred check their guns at the door."

"I will," Maxine said. "Wish me well. Or maybe you should wish me poorly. It's a bit confusing."

"May the assistant director gods not smile on your application."

Maxine laughed. "That ought to cover it. Love you."

"Love you too."

Maxine pushed herself to her feet and replaced the phone. At loose ends, she wandered into her bedroom and paused in front of Tom's photograph.

"I wish you could be here to hear Katie laugh again."

She traced her finger around the cool metal of the picture frame.

"You know, the empty spaces you left behind will always be here— vast and cavernous." Her voice was husky, her breath ragged. "But I'm trying to be like you. I've anchored safety lines around the edges of that abyss, and I'm holding on. I want to be here for Katie and her new business; I want to help Louise with her oxygen, and June with Harry; I want to tutor Celine and take computer lessons from Peter." She shrugged a bit bashfully. "As Shakespeare should have said: 'If this be life, play on.'"

She looked out the window, across the desert to her mountains. The Ape's Head glowed in the afternoon sunlight, a beacon and a benediction.

She turned back to the photo. "So you see, I really don't have the time to be the assistant director."

Tom's eyes sparkled and she could almost feel the beating of his heart.

"I love you too," she whispered.

The doorbell rang.

"That's Peter with my new computer." She kissed her fingertips and touched them to Tom's lips. "Wish me luck. I'm about to become a geek."

AFTER DINNER, MAXINE WALKED INTO the formal living room on Peter's arm, glad for an escort. Although the room was nearly full, it loomed large and lonely. She'd never noticed that before. In the past, it had seemed warm and welcoming, but tonight it felt hollow and leaden. Down the hall, someone had left the dining room doors open and the odor of corned beef and cabbage hung heavy in the air, making Maxine glad that she and Peter had dined out.

June and Harry waved. They had saved seats up front. Maxine wished that just this once they'd found seats at the back. Who cared if they could see or hear? In fact, it might be better if she couldn't see or hear what Rupert had to say.

She trudged up the aisle to her seat as if she were walking the plank. Everyone's eyes were upon her: some hostile, some encouraging, but all prying. When she tried to smile, the faces blurred and swirled. She stumbled and clutched at Peter's arm.

"You OK?" he asked.

She nodded, but there was no way she was OK.

"So what do you think Rupert decided?" June asked by way of greeting.

Maxine shook her head. "I have no idea. I tried calling Mimi to see if he'd contacted her, but all I got was her voicemail."

"Me too," Louise said. "I tried Celine and Fermez as well. No one knows anything. Fermez has to work tonight, and Celine's gospel choir is rehearsing at a church across town, but we're supposed to call them both as soon as we know anything."

Rosemarie joined in. "No one on the Residents' Advisory Committee has heard a peep out of Rupert either—the little chicken. I just wish I knew if that was good news or bad."

"You and me both." Maxine's voice sounded small and tinny, like an old LP on the wrong speed.

"Here he comes," June said with a barely perceptible nod.

They watched as Rupert strode to the podium. He looked taller, more muscular than before, and his jaw had developed a hard edge. He marched past them without even glancing Maxine's way. If she were on trial and he the jury, her goose would be cooked no matter how mixed the metaphor.

Rupert leaned on the podium. "Good evening, ladies and gentlemen." He smiled his soap-opera-star smile.

Maxine hated that smile. It made him look like, well, a soap-opera star. One of the villains. The kind of person who would appoint her assistant director out of pure spite.

Maxine felt her chest constrict. The walls crowded in.

"I have a few announcements," Rupert said.

He seemed extraordinarily calm and deliberate. What had happened to that inarticulate young man Maxine had spoken with just this morning?

"First, our warm congratulations go out to Evie Helmsley Hill, who has withdrawn her application from the Foothills in order to head the new wedding planning department for Delbeck's department stores."

The applause was polite and brief.

Maxine scanned the room for Carlotta and her coterie. They weren't hard to spot. Carlotta was dressed in an emerald green sheath with a diaphanous gold wrap. The outfit made her shimmer in a vaguely electric way. Maxine stared. She felt certain that there was an extremely poisonous snake of precisely that color and shimmer.

"We also want to extend our best wishes to . . ." Rupert shuffled through his note cards. "To, um, our third candidate . . ." He rummaged through his cards some more. Evidently, he couldn't remember her name either. "To our third candidate, who has accepted a position in Santa Fe, where she can be closer to her parents."

Once again, everyone already knew Rupert's news.

"Our remaining candidate, as you know, is Maxine Octavia Olson, a resident of the Foothills."

The residents applauded Maxine warmly.

Maxine nodded and tried to smile, but it felt as if the muscles of her face had frozen.

"What you may not know," Rupert said when the applause had died down, "is that our bylaws prohibit a resident from working here at the Foothills."

Maxine forgot to breathe. The blood drained from her head, and she began to slide into a bottomless black hole. Louise grabbed her hand and pulled her back. Louise's dry skin and arthritic fingers felt solid and comforting despite their painful grip.

Most of the residents looked blankly at Rupert and politely waited. Apparently, they hadn't caught the significance of his announcement.

Carlotta exchanged gleeful glances with Fred.

Maxine swore Carlotta actually licked her lips.

"In other words," Rupert said, "Maxine has to move out of the Foothills in order to be its assistant director."

Carlotta looked like the cat that had eaten the canary—the canary, the parakeet, and the American bald eagle.

There was a moment of silence as people absorbed the news, and then protests rang out.

"No way."

"Don't move."

"Change the rules!"

"As a matter of fact," Rupert said smoothly, "I have looked into the process for granting a waiver to our bylaws."

Maxine tried to swallow but couldn't. She wiped her palms on her slacks. What was it Augustine had said? *Do not despair: one of the thieves was saved. Do not presume: one of the thieves was damned.* Which was it going to be?

"After much research and many telephone calls to our corporate headquarters," Rupert said and paused as if that were a complete thought.

Maxine shivered.

Louise squeezed Maxine's hand again, and Peter put his arm around her shoulder. Rosemarie crossed her fingers, and June, who was not Catholic, crossed herself anyway.

Rupert continued. "I've decided that the only fair and sensible thing to do . . ."

He paused again and looked, not at Maxine, but at Carlotta. "The only thing to do is to waive the bylaw and appoint Maxine."

The room gave a collective gasp. Then people began shouting and cheering or jeering.

Peggy Stone jumped up and down like a cheerleader at a national championship.

Fred stood on his chair, holding onto Carlotta's shoulder for balance. His face had turned purple with rage.

Gladys Black waved her arms over her head as if she were warding off bats. In the process, she bumped Norman Tisdale and knocked his toupee askew.

Maxine tried to stand, but someone grabbed her by the arm and yanked her down.

"What are you doing?" Louise's voice was insistent, her grip unrelenting.

Maxine struggled unsuccessfully to free her arm. "I'm going to withdraw."

"Maxine, you can't renege. You promised." Louise's light blue eyes had turned to a glacial blue—deep and frozen. "Besides, you're holding the dummy hand right now. Let your partner play his cards."

"But—"

"Wait!"

With every fiber of her being, Maxine wanted to withdraw, wanted to put an end to this charade, wanted to take some action, any action.

She glared at Louise—Louise, who had been her best friend for over sixty years. Louise, who was also the best card player anyone had ever known. Maxine took several deep breaths. If anyone knew about strategy, it was Louise. Maxine stopped struggling. If Louise said to wait, Maxine would wait.

"Order. Order, please." Rupert rapped his gavel on the lectern until everyone sat down.

"The floor recognizes Carlotta."

"We all recognize her for the snake she is," June muttered.

Carlotta jumped to her feet. Fred and most of her gaggle stood with her. Only Ralph Jordan remained seated. He folded his arms and stared at his feet.

"That takes courage." Maxine nodded toward Ralph. "He's risking Carlotta's wrath."

"And his place at the dining table," Louise said. "He's about to become an orphan."

"I like him," Harry said. "Let's adopt him."

"I protest," Carlotta shrilled. "We cannot and should not break our time-honored rules for petty grievances and temporal issues."

"Do you think she meant *transitory* issues?" Maxine asked, unable to suppress her pedantic side.

"Perhaps she means *temporary* issues?" Louise said.

"I think she's worried about time," Harry said and tapped his watch. "It's running out, you know."

"We must unite against this assault on all we hold most dear." Carlotta droned on.

Maxine groaned. Carlotta was spinning her wheels. It could take the rest of the night for her to get to her point. Maxine didn't think her heart could hold up that long.

"We are a social people bound by the laws of decency and common sense. To abandon our principles, even to serve a loyal friend, is to begin a quick descent to destruction."

"Who is she plagiarizing?" Rosemarie asked. "Lincoln? Jefferson?"

"Sounds more like late-night TV," June said. "The stuff that comes on after the Japanese-dubbed Italian-Westerns go off the air."

"I miss the old test patterns that used to be on TV when there wasn't any programming," Harry said. "Remember the Indian?"

"Or the target?"

"Target? I thought it was a quilt pattern."

While Carlotta's speech thundered on and Maxine's friends discussed late-night television and test patterns, Maxine replayed her conversation with Katie. Just because she could do the job, that didn't mean that she had to do it. At eighty-two, that was a novel concept for Maxine. She could refuse the responsibility and the position. She could pursue her own dreams instead.

Her spirits began to lift until she remembered her promise to Rupert.

She was caught between the proverbial rock and a hard place. It was her own fault, of course. Like a character in a Greek tragedy, she'd set everything in motion in the first place and acted out of foolish pride. All along, Mimi had been the best person for the job.

The tone of Carlotta's speech changed, and Maxine tuned back in to see if Carlotta had stumbled across her point.

"As much as I dearly love Maxine," Carlotta oozed, "and would wish for her to be our assistant director, for her good, for our own good, and for the good of those who shall follow in our footsteps, we should not, cannot, and must not grant her a waiver."

In the general pandemonium that followed Carlotta's speech, Maxine tried to recall Milton's first description of hell. Thwarted by the clamor around her, she raised her hand.

Once again, Louise jerked it down. "What are you doing now?" Louise said, the glacial glare back in her eyes.

"I'm going to agree with Carlotta and withdraw."

"You'll trump your partner's ace."

"What are you talking about?"

"Rupert's played this hand brilliantly. He's threatened to give you a waiver knowing that Carlotta was bound to protest."

"Yes. So?"

"So he's finessed her position."

Maxine tried, unsuccessfully, to jerk her hand free.

"Just sit still and watch," Louise said.

Maxine glowered, but she stopped struggling.

Rupert banged his gavel until the room had gone silent except for the muffled ringing of someone's forgotten cell phone.

"Carlotta's objection to the residency waiver makes it impossible for me to appoint Maxine. We'll have to start our search all over again."

Pandemonium erupted once more.

Residents surged out of their seats. Gesticulated wildly. Shouted and argued.

Carlotta captured the center of the room and brandished her cigarette holder as if it were an Amazonian sword.

Maxine sagged.

Someone touched Maxine's arm. She turned.

Harry smiled and offered her a bottle of water.

She nodded gratefully, realizing for the first time how inordinately thirsty she truly was. She took the bottle and drank long and deep. Water splashed down the front of her blouse, but she was beyond worrying about such trivialities.

Rupert banged the room into silence. "Given Carlotta's objection," he said, reminding them of Carlotta's responsibility for whatever he was about to say, "I do have an alternative suggestion."

"What is it?"

"Let's hear it."

"Anything's better than making us start the whole fricking process all over again."

The room fell into stunned silence at the language of the last outburst, especially since it seemed to come from Paul Stone, the retired minister.

Ralph Jordan broke the silence and came to Paul's rescue by slowly applauding the sentiment. Soon others joined in. No one wanted a do-over on this.

Rupert ignored both the comments and the clapping. "This morning, I discovered another extremely well-qualified individual who has followed our selection process quite precisely."

Maxine held her breath.

The room grew silent. Even the cell phone stopped ringing.

"I found her application, along with Evie's original application, lodged between my printer stand and my desk."

Maxine sent a prayer of thanks to all of the Greek muses.

"This candidate has applied; she has been interviewed; and she has completed not one, but two events for us."

Heads swiveled as the residents tried to determine how this was possible.

Maxine bent her head and saw that she was clenching her fists. Surprised, she opened her hands, rubbed her palms together, and waited for Rupert to play his cards.

"The candidate—who, by the way, has a master's degree, glowing references, experience, and brilliant publications—the candidate is Michelle Lafayette. Some of you know her as Mimi. She was the lead singer last weekend, and she teaches our Saturday morning yoga."

Carlotta collapsed in her chair, open-mouthed and glassy-eyed. She'd won the battle and lost the war.

"On the off-chance that you would be willing to consider Ms. Lafayette," Rupert said, "I've invited her here tonight. She has graciously agreed to share with us her vision for the Foothills and then to answer questions."

Mimi entered from the hallway in a turquoise and tourmaline dress. She looked stunning: professional and confident, relaxed and gorgeous.

Her yoga students stood and, placing their palms together, chanted "Om shanti, om shanti, om shanti, om."

She acknowledged them with a bow and a smile—a smile that radiated energy and joy. Then she bowed to Rupert and thanked him for the opportunity to describe her vision for the Foothills.

As Mimi spoke, the room became first quiet, then calm. Postures softened. Residents nodded their assent. For the first time in days, Maxine relaxed.

"I hope you're not too disappointed," Peter whispered.

"Disappointed? I'm delighted," Maxine said and squeezed his arm. "It was the right decision all along: I was just too caught up in the stratagems to see it."

When Mimi finished, most of the residents gave her a standing ovation.

Carlotta alone remained seated. Her impassive eyes swept the crowd. Then her lips parted in a slow, sly smile. She nodded as if in agreement with herself and rose to her full height. She shimmered green and gold and awesome.

"Mr. Chairman, Mr. Chairman." Carlotta called until she had everyone's attention.

"Yes, Carlotta." For the first time, Rupert sounded wary.

"I move we appoint Mimi our assistant director without further ado so that we can prevent any other, inferior candidate from causing trouble."

Peter leaned over. "Maxine, this is your chance. Second the motion."

Maxine shook her head and patted Peter's hand. "You must learn the value of inaction and the virtue of patience, my dear."

"But—"

Louise leaned over. "It will be better for Mimi if Carlotta thinks Maxine opposed her appointment."

Fred staggered to his feet and seconded the motion as if it were a call to arms, which, from his perspective, perhaps it was.

Chaos broke out again. The din reminded Maxine of the first, last, and only time she'd gone with June and June's grandson to a rock concert.

"What about Maxine?"

"Can you give her a waiver or not?"

"Make her move out."

"No, let's hire Mimi."

Rupert banged on his lectern until he had quieted the group.

Maxine turned to Louise and raised a questioning eyebrow.

Louise smiled and nodded.

Maxine calmly raised her hand.

"The floor recognizes Maxine," Rupert said, unable to hide a boyish grin of triumph.

"Carlotta is right," Maxine said to the room's astonishment. "The only way to preserve our process is to hire Mimi. She is clearly the best-qualified candidate. Let's vote."

The vote was unanimous. Afterward, the residents rushed to congratulate Mimi and welcome her as their new assistant director.

Peter turned to Maxine. "I'm not sure how you pulled this off, but you were amazing."

"Me? Don't be silly. It was all Rupert and Carlotta." Maxine bent to help Louise to her feet, then corrected herself. "That is to say, it was all Rupert and Carlotta and some excellent card sense."

Louise teetered, gained her balance, and threw her arms around Maxine in an uncharacteristic and bountiful hug. "Congratulations!" Her light blue eyes sparkled with laughter. "I'm so proud of you!"

"But I didn't do anything," Maxine said.

"I know, dear." Louise smiled and linked arms with her old friend. "And you did it brilliantly!"

41

SATURDAY THE FOOTHILLS buzzed with speculation about the assistant director's position, Mimi's last-minute emergence upon the scene, and Maxine's withdrawal. By Sunday, Carlotta was strutting and preening and pretending that Mimi had been her candidate all along. She even intimated that she had discovered the "lost" application and arranged for a private interview between Mimi and Rupert. Maxine and her cohort smiled mysteriously and allowed Carlotta her victory.

By Monday morning, everyone claimed that they had always been for Mimi, and talk turned from the assistant director's position to an analysis of the new oatmeal recipe.

"Frankly, I don't think it's a new recipe." Maxine stirred the excessively thin mix. "I think someone cleaned the pot for a change, and it's been so long since they made a fresh batch that no one could remember how much water to add."

June scowled as she stirred her bowl. "They should serve this with a straw. It's more like a milkshake than oatmeal."

"A tasteless milkshake." Rosemarie shoved her bowl as far away as possible. "It might be the right consistency for wallpaper paste."

"Or paper mache," Maxine said.

"I wonder if this would clog the drains as badly as a jar of Metamucil," June said.

"Did Rupert ever figure out how that happened?" Rosemarie asked.

"No," Maxine said. "But Celine told me that Mrs. Babcock tried to bribe her into pawing through people's garbage to look for empty Metamucil jars."

"That's absurd," June said. "The empty jar was right on the kitchen counter."

They all looked at her.

"Or so I've heard." She took a sip of her coffee.

"What did Celine do?" Louise asked.

"She refused, of course," Maxine said. "But for two weeks, Mrs. Babcock kept finding empty Metamucil jars in her office."

Louise laughed. "I wonder who was responsible for that."

Maxine smiled her Mona-Lisa smile. "I can't imagine, but did you know that you can get a very large discount if you buy Metamucil by the case?"

June looked at her watch. "Oops. I have to go. It's time for water aerobics."

Rosemarie stood. "I have to go too. At the high school accountant's club, we're discussing the accounting implications of the new tax laws."

Louise pretended to stifle a giant yawn.

"I saw that," Rosemarie said.

After June and Rosemarie had gone, Maxine turned to Louise. "Ready, partner?"

"Yes. How much time do we have?"

Maxine checked her watch. "D.A.M.N."

"What's wrong?" Louise asked.

"My watch stopped. So much for the illusion that we can control time."

"Maxine." Louise placed a light hand on Maxine's forearm. Anxiety lines joined the wrinkles around her eyes. "You *do* know that our fight against time is an unwinnable battle."

Maxine put her hand over Louise's. "Of course. That's why it's so damnably important."

Louise nodded. "OK then. Let's go."

"THANK GOODNESS NO ONE ELSE IS HERE." Maxine powered up the library's computer. "What shall we do while we wait?" she asked. "Want to ski the internet?"

"Surf," Louise said. "Go to that site with the maps and satellite photos of the earth. Let's see if they have a photo of the Foothills."

Maxine clicked her way to the information they wanted. "Here it is! Let's see how close we can zoom in."

Louise peered over Maxine's shoulder. "Look! Isn't that Carlotta's Cadillac parked in front of Fred's condo?"

"And there's Celine's car parked in Rupert's spot in the shade."

"You don't think I'm parking my Bel Air in the desert sun, do you?" Celine's voice boomed behind them. "Rupert can just park that boring white Toyota of his in those places he reserved for the staff. There's not one inch of shade there all day long."

Maxine and Celine looked at each other and smiled. They didn't turn around. Celine had arrived.

"What are you doing in here, anyway?" Celine asked. "Didn't Peter set up your new computer on Friday? Doesn't it work?"

Maxine turned. "He did, and it works fine." She paused for dramatic effect. "But we thought it would be more appropriate to do today's task in here."

"What task?" Celine asked.

"We wanted you to be here," Louise said. "After all, it was your idea."

"Nuh-uh. I don't remember having any ideas that involved having you two on a computer."

"Yes you did," Maxine said. "And it was brilliant."

"Well, of course, if it was brilliant, it was my idea." Celine drew herself up and preened a bit. "But just exactly which brilliant idea are we talking about?"

"Grannies for Good," Louise said.

"Say what? What about Grannies for Good?"

"We found the website." Maxine clicked and pointed to her screen. "And guess what?"

Celine's eyes narrowed. "What?"

Maxine clicked some more. "You can apply online to become one of their internet sleuths."

"Uh-oh." Celine took half a step back.

Louise motioned for Celine to step nearer the computer. "At your suggestion, we applied last week. Now we're going to check our email for their response."

"We wanted you to be here," Maxine said. "After all, it's been the three of us in here for quite some time."

Celine nodded at the computer. "More like the four of us. But you don't really want to deal with those nasty perverts, do you?"

"No," Maxine said. "But it turns out Grannies for Good also does tutoring."

"And electronic grandmothering." Louise was barely able to contain her excitement. "Kind of like big sisters, only older and online."

"Well then." Celine leaned closer to the screen. "Hurry up. Open your email."

Maxine clicked on the mailbox icon and held her breath while the list of new mail popped up. "Look." She pointed to the list. "They replied."

The three women looked at each other and then at the computer.

"Well go on," Celine said. "Open it."

Maxine tapped her fingers on the desk. "I'll open it, but someone else should read it."

Celine straightened. "No way, no how, not me."

"Let me!" Louise peered over Maxine's shoulder. "Wait." She adjusted her glasses. "OK. I'm ready. Open it."

Maxine clicked on the email and shut her eyes.

Louise was silent.

Maxine felt a hand on her shoulder. She opened her eyes and looked at Louise.

"I don't know how to tell you this," Louise said.

"But?" Maxine said.

"They want to interview us!"

Celine whooped, and they all burst into laughter. The laughter bubbled up and filled the room, drowning out even the ticking of the electric clock. They laughed until their eyes filled with tears and they gasped for breath.

Maxine was the first to recover. "Well ladies, if this be life, play on!"

ACKNOWLEDGMENTS

The writing of this novel has been a long and winding journey, made easier by the incredible generosity of family, friends, and total strangers to whom I owe my deepest gratitude. I am particularly indebted to a number of writers and researchers who unhesitatingly shared their time and talents. *Play On!* was improved enormously by their efforts; the faults that remain are my own stubborn doing. My heartfelt thanks to:

- Lynn York: For being my catalyst. The first assignment in your course on "Revising the Novel" was to interview one of my characters. I confessed that I had not yet begun to write and certainly didn't have any characters to interview. You responded, "You will." And I did.
- Georgann Eubanks: For workshops that opened the world of fiction writing and invited me in.
- Paul Mihas: For showing me how to say more by writing less.
- The Messengers: For being my first-ever writing group and for your unconditional love.
- The Salonistas: For sharing your wit, and wisdom, and devotion to the craft.
- The RCWMS Pelican House writers: For your honesty and bravery in listening and in sharing. For your silence during the day and your laughter at night.
- Rebecca Duncan: For being a trailblazer with boundless creativity and limitless energy.
- Linda Brooks: For your humor. For knowing how to write with a point, and how to quit when you've reached it.
- Arnetta Girardeau: For heroically stepping in and saving me from a copyright quagmire.

Very special thanks to the amazing people at RCWMS who made this novel a palpable reality. Thank you to:

- Jeanette Stokes: For your unflappable patience and indomitable spirit. For believing in *Play On!* from the start and for never letting go.
- Bonnie Campbell: For your brilliant, beautiful designs.
- Liz Dowling-Sendor: For finding the errors and challenging the assumptions.
- To Marcy Litle: For your great good humor and willingness to bend the rules.
- To Marya McNeish: For keeping us all on track.

Finally, my ever-lasting and profound thanks to:

- Debby Jakubs: For Sunday morning phone calls and late afternoon "whines" and wines. For your enduring friendship through this entire process, as through life.
- Mary Jane Rivers and Grace Pilafian: For lending me your home to use as my summer office. For including me in "Masks and Mirrors." And always, for your love.
- Frank McNair: For being the most generous and loyal of writing buddies. For your enduring support, abiding enthusiasm, and dogged insistence that I write and publish Maxine's story. Without you, there would have been no book. I am forever grateful!
- Laurel Ferejohn: For being the best-ever editor, friend, and guardian angel. For stepping into the fray whenever I was in a panic, and saving me—often from myself. Through more readings than either of us cares to remember, you were invariably kind, profoundly insightful, annoyingly meticulous, and—I have to admit it—always correct. Thank you for everything!
- Kokie and Brownstone: For taking me on walks when I needed distraction. I miss you still.
- My partner, Joan Peck, and my family and friends: For everything! For your astonishing patience, love, and support. For forgiving my absent-minded crankiness when the writing was not going well. For putting up with my euphoria when it was. For simply being there. For always being there. Thank you with all my heart! Always!

PRAISE FOR *PLAY ON!*

"No one should miss this romp, in which stalwart Maxine leads a posse of the most unlikely fellow travelers through an intricately plotted caper against an antagonist rivaling Cruella de Vil. *Play On!* is a rollicking modern fable of good and evil, a coming-of-age story in which 'age' is the real deal, and a morality tale whose ending will have you stand up and cheer, *play on!*"

—LAUREL FEREJOHN, winner of the Thomas Wolfe Fiction Prize

"Caution: Do not read this book while recovering from surgery! You'll laugh so hard your stitches will pop—but it is the best medicine!"

—DEBORAH TIPPETT, Professor Emeritus, Meredith College

"The drama is intense, replete with intrigue, cunning, and playful deception, all intermixed with moving scenes of personal awareness and enduring relationships. *Play On!* is a delightful read, filled with mystery, joy, and tenderness.

—NAPIER BAKER, President of Residents' Association, Carol Woods Retirement Community and retired Director of Pastoral Care, UNC Hospitals

"Witty and wise, *Play On!* leaves you chuckling and pondering. Set in a retirement community, the action follows residents bent on maintaining their independence while honoring their community. Managers, housekeepers, relatives and residents play parts in the dramas of daily life, each building relationships and gaining insights along the way.

—JEAN O'BARR, former Director, Women's Studies, Duke University

"What if Thelma and Louise had made different choices? Judy Dearlove's characters Maxine and Louise may be an ideal update. Older, obviously. Faced with age-related adversity, certainly. But creative spirits and resilient hearts prevail, and they *play on!*"

—SUSAN FISHER, Professor Emeritus, Meredith College